I0564374

My Dear Cousin:

A Novel in Letters

By

Celia Hayes

Copyright © 2021 Celia D. Hayes

ISBN-13 978-0-9897821-6-6
ISBN-10 0-89782106-6

All rights reserved. No part of this publication may be reproduced, stored in a retrieval system, or transmitted in any form or by any means, electronic, mechanical, recording or otherwise, without the prior written permission of the author.

Printed in the United States of America.

Original cover art by Covers Girl

Geron & Associates
A Division of Watercress Press.
2021

Thanks and Dedications

This book came about through an unusual inspiration. I dreamed the whole concept, very early one morning in July, 2020, and woke up in time to remember it all; the girl cousins, one in the Far East, the other in the European theater, writing letters to each other throughout the wartime years. I had nothing but time to write, as the Corona plague had demolished most marketing events for the rest of that year. I had a long and abiding interest in WWII, a range of good reference books on hand, and family recollections to draw upon.

Many thanks are due to experts, websites and FB pages who filled in those gaps in my knowledge of wartime Australia and Malaya, notably Peter Dunn's Ozatwar.com website. I had long been familiar with intimate details of the American and British WWII home fronts, but Australia was new territory. That website provided posts and links, a wealth of names. establishments, and titles of publications for further reference.

I would also acknowledge and thank the administrators of the Facebook page for the Malayan Volunteers Group, the MacArthur Museum in Brisbane, the historian's office of the Army Medical Museum at Fort Sam Houston, and Kate Paulk, who grew up in Brisbane and supplied much local-specific knowledge.

Celia Hayes
San Antonio, 2021

Contents

Celia Hayes

A Wedding Announcement
From *The San Antonio Light* – Sunday, May 22, 1938

Becker – Morehouse

Miss Margaret Susan Becker, of this city, was married on Sunday to Thomas St. John Morehouse, in a ceremony at St. Mark's Episcopal Church performed by the Rector, the Rev. A.R. McKinstry. The bride, 20, is the daughter of Charles and Evelyn Ingram Becker of this city. A reception following the ceremony was held for family, friends and guests at the home of the bride's paternal grandfather, the notable Western artist, Samuel H. Becker, and his wife, Mrs. Jane Becker. Mr. Morehouse, 28, is the son of the late Major Chadwick Morehouse and Edith Seaton, the present Mrs. Stanley Frobisher, of Brisbane, Australia. The groom is a graduate of Trinity College, Cambridge, and currently manages a rubber estate established by his family in Perak, Malaya. The happy couple will make their home in Ipoh and Singapore, following a honeymoon traveling in Hawaii and the Far East.

The bride was attended by her sister, Ivy, and cousins Venetia and Charlotte Stoneman, the daughters of Charles H. Stoneman of Deming, New Mexico. She wore a gown of ivory satin adorned with an overlay of Venise lace, and carried a bouquet of white roses, orange blossoms and pale pink carnations, while her attendants wore pale pink gowns with garlands of pink rosebuds in their hair.

Letter dated 2 April, 1938, Postmarked from Galveston, Texas

Dear Peg; I hope this letter catches up with you, before you and Tommy board the China Clipper for Hawaii. I enclose the cutting from the SA Light newspaper of the wedding. Your Granny Jane saved it out from their newspaper and sent it to me, because of the picture of us, all lined up on the church step outside, with the sun in our eyes and waiting for the photographer to do his duty. It was very impressive, since the editor put it at the very top of the weddings and society pages; your Granny Jane wrote in her note to me. Honestly, as newsprint goes, I think we all look very nice, although Ivy was complaining to me under her breath about how her feet hurt, and I know that Tommy was pinching your behind and saying that now he had the right to do so as a lawfully-married man! Well, really – Ivy is so vain about her tiny feet, so of course she will cram them into shoes a half-size too small. And yes, we both warned her about this.

I was so sorry that I could not see you off on your honeymoon journey, but I simply had to return to Galveston on the afternoon train, so as not to miss any more of my nursing classes than absolutely necessary. I had dispensation, at the pleading of all our kin, especially the Galveston branch to be your bridesmaid since I don't know when we will see each other again. I know that we vowed to each other that year when we were fifteen and summering at the Becker ranch that we would be bridesmaid to each other, but if I marry a handsome doctor-surgeon and you are away on Tommy's rubber plantation in

Malaya and cannot come Home, then I release you from that vow to reciprocate. I shall have to make an effort to make up for what I have missed in the two weeks that I was away from Galveston, but I should let you know that I do not regret this in the least.

It was such a nice time, seeing everyone again and spending time with Ivy, and Daddy, and Granny Jane and Granny Sophie and all, although I did endure the talk from Daddy about how serious I was regarding pursuing this training as a nurse, yet one more time! Well, as I haven't had a handsome and dashing Englishman like Tommy fall absolutely head-over-heels in love with me over one week and the next, I suppose I shall have to go ahead with this nursing qualification. One must do something, if the inclination or opportunity for marriage doesn't present itself at once, and I would rather not settle for waiting on tables. Did you know that Granny Sophie did, way back in the day before she met Grandpa Fred? Can you imagine, Granny Sophie, waiting tables? Honestly, the mind simply shudders in disbelief. I'd think this was one of Daddy's stories, but I asked Granny Sophie about it once, and she said that she had, and then changed the subject almost at once.

She is such a dear, worrying about me, studying in Galveston. Granny was there for the great hurricane in 1900 and was very much against me going to the nursing college there, telling me once and again how horrible it was to endure the hurricane, and most especially afterwards, when most of the city was wrecked. Well, I said, *'Granny – if it happens again, then I am a nurse and I can do good, and anyway, they raised up everything on the island to fifteen or twenty feet, so it's not as if we'll all be swept away and left knee-deep among bodies when the storm surge finishes.'* And she looked at me very sternly after I said this, and said, *'Vennie, don't be frivolous. I went among bodies in the morgue, afterwards, looking for a dear friend; can you imagine how sickening that was?'* and I replied, *'Well, I have had to help lay out the bodies of patients who died when I was on shift in the hospital, and no, I was not frivolous and didn't find it sickening at all.'* Just feeling a bit sad for their friends and loved ones, and if they had been in dreadful pain, knowing then they were relieved of it all. Our dean of nurses says that we should think of this as a kind of sacrament. I didn't say this last to Granny Sophie, I think she was shocked enough when she lamented that society is now so horribly changed from when she was a girl, and I said, *'Oh, thank heavens for that, Gran – it must have been positively medieval!'*

I really must begin the habit of biting my tongue when I feel a barbed retort coming on except that I have had to do so much of it while in training and on the ward that the excess comes foaming out like the fizz from an uncorked bottle of champagne. Anyway, enough about me. You must write to me about what you see on your way out east. It's so exciting that you and Tommy are traveling by airplane! The China Clipper to Hawaii, Manila, and points east! Tommy's mother and stepfather were so generous with that gift of a pair of tickets, all

4

the way from San Francisco to Manila. You must write down every detail that you can, although I fear that the mysterious and exotic east will be somewhat of a let-down after reading *Terry and the Pirates* in the comic pages! You simply must tell me, though, if you encounter any two-fisted ruffian adventurers, a blonde adventuress singing *St. Louis Blues*, a wicked pirate queen, or a pair of Chinese gentlemen – one a huge mute and the other a small, English-mangling shrimp.

All my love to you and Tommy,
Your devoted cuz,

Vennie

Chapter 1 – String of Pearls

At mid-morning, in a tropical lagoon, Peggy Becker – no, she was now Mrs. Thomas Morehouse – stepped carefully off the ramp from the magnificent flying boat which had brought her and her new husband a thousand miles and more across the Pacific Ocean and onto the floating dock, which rocked gently in a vivid blue ocean bay, only slightly less blue than the sky above, framed by the distant eminence of Diamond Head, slashing up into that horizon like a vast sleeping stone lion. A brilliant sea bird, the four-engine Pan-Am Clipper had settled into the crystal-blue waters, as if no more than slightly wearied after a day and a nighttime flight from San Francisco. The dock abutted a lush green lawn shaded by graceful coconut palm trees – a vision of tropical beauty only slightly marred by the view in the other direction; a grim and functional view of docks and mooring places for a crowding of grey-painted naval vessels, whose masts and gun muzzles gave to lie to a vision of a peaceful Pacific island paradise.

"Tommy," she exclaimed to her new husband, as he took her arm. "It's absolutely beautiful here – I love it already."

"Wait until you see Longcot," he replied. "It's a garden of Eden in comparison."

Peggy was tall and model-slender, an athletic girl with stick-straight hair the color of ripe wheat-straw, hair which defied every attempt to curl it in accordance with the current fashion. Her countenance was oval, pleasingly featured, accented with sky-colored blue eyes and shapely lips which owed little to brilliant red lipstick in accentuating their kissable attraction. Attraction to Tommy Morehouse most of all; Tommy was wiry and charming, as tall as his wife, but possessed of a personal magnetism which drew the attention of everyone in any room where he appeared.

Peggy had not quite figured it out – that attraction. Any room where Tommy appeared, he was instantly the star, for all that he wasn't tall for a man and didn't look anything like a movie star. Tommy was ... Tommy was Tommy; grey eyes and undistinguished brown hair – *dunduckety*, was how one of the Vining cousins had described him; lanky and angular, rather like an English version of a young Abraham Lincoln. Her cousin Vennie Stoneman had attempted an explanation. *'Tommy looks at you and talks to you as if you are the most singular and fascinating person in the room. He does this with <u>everyone</u>, and the thing is that he is completely sincere. Tommy loves people, he is interested in every single person he meets. And that is why most everyone loves him in response."*

Peggy had fallen for him almost from the moment of meeting, an encounter at a family dinner with her grandparents, in their big old house in the oldest part of Alamo Heights. A distant cousin of the family, her father had said vaguely, English and kin to Great-Aunt Lottie's husband in some degree, by way of explaining the presence of a stranger among the scattering of cousins, uncles, and aunts in Granny Jane's parlor on a rainy January Sunday.

"He's returning from home leave in England, the long way around," Daddy explained. "Quite pleasant when I spoke to him on the telephone; he had all kinds of questions. He works in Malaya, overseeing a rubber plantation."

"Boring! And yet another cousin," seventeen-year-old Ivy grumbled. "Don't we ever meet anyone who isn't a cousin?"

"He's not bad looking at all," Peggy murmured, and her heart had skipped a beat as hers and Tommy's eyes met. He had been leaning up against the upright parlor piano, talking to Grandpa Sam; something to do with the property up north in the Palo Duro country.

It was an instant connection, as if they had known each other always – or as Vennie observed humorously – as if they had known and loved each other in a previous life. Surely one couldn't in this modern day, fall in love at first glance? But Peg and Tommy had. The talks between them about the family ranch in the Hill Country where Peggy had spent most of the years growing up, and the property that he managed in the Malayan foothills were as meaningful and momentous as the companionable silences. Barely a week later he proposed; a month and a half later, married and boarding Pan American's luxurious China Clipper, resting now like a motorized water-lily leaf in San Francisco Bay. It was an unexpected luxury, this honeymoon journey; the tickets on the Clipper were a wedding present from Tommy's mother and stepfather.

8

"How long are we going to stay here, then," Peggy asked, as Tommy took her elbow. The morning breeze smelt a little of aviation fuel, with an overlay of salt water but teased a little now and again with the scent of flowers; ginger, plumeria, jasmine and gardenia. She inhaled, relishing the fresh air and the flowers, palm leaves rustling in an endless dance overhead.

"A week here, and a week or two again in Manila," Tommy replied, as half a dozen young women rushed forward, their arms filled with flower garlands, dark hair flowing unbound around their shoulders. They wore colorful bandeaus around their breasts, shell necklaces and more garlands of live flowers woven into their hair and around their necks, and shin-length skirts composed of some long fiber that looked like green raffia.

"Aloha!" the women chorused, flinging a garland around the neck of every departing passenger. "Aloha! Welcome to Hawai'i! Aloha!"

"I love this place, already!" Peg exclaimed again; the garland brought a richer scent of flowers to her than the erratic breeze. "I cannot imagine a place more different than Texas."

"Indeed," Tommy grinned. "Certainly, more different than Oxfordshire. A bit more like Malaya, though. Come on, Peggy – the hotel where we are staying is right on the beach. I believe, though," he confessed as he and the other passengers took their places in a handful of taxis and a small bus tricked out in the colors and emblem of PAA – Pacific Air Ways. "That this is a welcome laid on by the airline ... certainly very considerate of them to do so."

"I don't care – I love Hawaii anyway," Peg replied. "And I'm certain that I'll love Longcot Plantation even more. Tell me about the house again. I love to hear you talk about it."

"It's in the foothills above Ipoh," Tommy began with a wry smile, for this was a story told many times, like a fairy story to a child at bedtime. "Seventy hectares of mature rubber trees. My father and grandfather began planting them when the coffee crop failed, back before the War. The house is not a large one – two stories tall, and on tall pilings to catch the breezes. It has deep porches all around. Every room of it opens onto a porch, through tall French doors. The afternoon heat, y'know..."

"I know about heat," Peg replied, knowingly. "Summer in Texas means living in an oven, although it always seemed to be cooler in the Hills. I'm used to heat, Tommy."

"Mumma – my mother started a garden when she married Father," Tommy continued. "She has always said that the soil was so rich, it was a matter of planting a seed or a sprig, and then having to leap backwards as it grew so fast that it might hit you in the eye!"

"She lives in ... Australia now?" Peg wanted to refresh her memory of Tommy's family – none of whom were able to attend the ceremony, due to Tommy's impulsive haste and the long distance from Texas between his remaining family and friends; his side of the church had been practically deserted on their wedding day. His parents and half-sister were stiff figures in black and white photos, formal or caught on casual snaps on a small simple Brownie camera, pictures which he just happened to have carried with him on his 'home leave'. Neither of his parents really looked like Tommy. It was if he were a changeling child, deposited by the fae in the Morehouse family cradle, in faraway Malaya.

The taxi in which they were riding was skirting the harbor – a shining stretch of water on one side, and a precipitously-rising range of mountains on the other, mountains clad in lush greenery, attended by blue skies in which a range of clouds floated, like something arranged by a scenic painter. Peg spared a look outside the windows; now they were passing by the fringes of the naval base; nothing there but grim concrete and industrial metal, broken now and again by exuberant outcrops of palm trees and banks of lush plants. Yes, things grew in the tropics, as Tommy's mother said of her garden. *Stand back, or it will hit you in the eye.*

But always beyond that vista of cranes, docks and steel was the ocean, dark and brooding, even in the morning sunshine now slanting over those mountains, a deep blue ocean trimmed with the white of cresting waves.

"Yes," Tommy replied, and even though he spoke with typical English stoicism, Peg sensed the grief and loss which her husband must have felt. "Father was gassed in the War. Never entirely fit and well again afterwards. He died in 1921. I was at school then, of course. I was twelve; sent Home even before the War. It wasn't thought healthy for us English children to be kept in the East after about five or so. And Mumma married Stanley a few years later. Stanley's a good sort of chap. He was an agent for Guthries', in their office in Kuala Lumpur. They met at one of the Club do's; can't recall the occasion, since I wasn't there. Of course. Social life in Malaya revolves around the local club."

"He's not a wicked stepfather?" Peg smiled sideways at her husband, and he covered her hand with his and smiled in return. "No, he's not. Stanley's a jolly decent sort – the Army out in Mespot, during the war; doesn't talk about it much to this day. But he makes Mumma happy, and now he and Mumma and Mavis all live in Brisbane. They all write to me without fail, every week. Now, your turn. Tell me about your home."

"You never got to see it, in all the rush of the wedding," Peg replied, with regret. "I'm sorry for that because I loved the place so. Daddy managed it for Great-Uncle Dolph, and Ivy and I lived there on weekends and holidays. We boarded at St. Mary's Hall, during the week."

"Boarding school," Tommy had a particular wry grin on his face. "How very English of you all."

The taxi had now passed the outlaying establishments of the naval base, and now traveling along a good road; houses and small enterprises set in lush green plots and among thickets of tropical trees and vines. The green mountains rose up precipitously on the horizon to their left, and out to the right, between buildings, houses and stands of trees, the deep blue Pacific beckoned. Tommy had arranged for a week-long stay at the splendid pink hotel on the very beach, before continuing their journey.

"It was school, and we had to be there," Peg was indignant. "A very good school, I will have you know! Anyway, the Becker ranch was established by my ... I think, great-grandfather. Maybe another grand on top of that. I can't be certain, as it was simply ages ago. Anyway, he built a stone house for his wife, or the woman that he hoped would be his wife, and it was the first and oldest stone house anywhere in the neighborhood. That's the family story, anyway. There's a carving over the front door, of a bird in the nest of an apple tree and the date 1847."

"Practically modern, then," Tommy commented.

Peg was indignant all over again. "No, not at all! For Texas that is old, as old as the hills! The great-great-grand had land for his service as a soldier, and later Great-Uncle Dolph and his kin went into trailing cattle, all up the long trail to Kansas. Daddy says that this was how they made the original fortune after opening a general store after the War Between the States, and lucky we were to hold on to it, too." Peg settled against Tommy's shoulder with a sigh. "I loved the place. I wish I could have shown it to you. A lovely old house with gardens all around, and a walled apple-orchard supposed to have been planted by Great Uncle Dolphs' father. And Great Uncle Dolph planted an avenue of red-bud trees, all along the drive from the gate to the Home Ranch. His wife designed and set out the gardens. She was English, you know. It's a lovely place. When we have home leave once again, I can show it to you. We learned to ride there, Ivy and I, but she is better in the saddle than I am, and Cousin Vennie is better than either of us."

"Your cousin Venetia who was your chief bridesmaid," Tommy replied with a nod and a brief look of satisfaction at having recalled the names and the web of relations. "And quite an excellent dancer, too. I did several turns around the floor with her, at the reception dance. Did she also grow up on the family ranch with you?"

"Oh, no," Peg replied. "The Stonemans own a big place in New Mexico. They visited now and again, for family things. I can't recall the exact connection, it's terribly complicated, I think she is a second cousin, but I love her like a sister. Now, the funny thing, and the new thing that I have just remembered is that Stoneman isn't their real name. They changed it from Steinmetz about twenty years ago."

"To sound less Jewish?" Tommy ventured, and Peg giggled.

"No, silly – to sound less German. Because of the War! All the Beckers and the Stonemans came from Germany, about a hundred years ago! Vennie's father decided around 1915 or so that he didn't really want the grief of being considered foreigners and hostile foreigners at that. They were American, and that was an end to it, and if it took changing the name to something less tiresomely Germanic, then he could go to the courthouse and change it and solve all their problems."

"I understand that our very own dear royals had the same problem," Tommy chuckled – a rather cynical sound, and at

Peg's baffled expression, he enlarged. "Saxe-Coburg and Gotha was formerly the family name, since Prince Albert the Blessed, espoused of our own good Queen Victoria was of the old German nobility. They changed it to Windsor and vacated all their German titles after Kaiser Wilhelm and his filthy Huns dropped bombs on England during the War."

"You see? Problem solved," Peg replied, thinking privately that she had been so blessed in her impulsive choice of husband. She nestled into his shoulder and watched the passing landscape in blissful silence for the remainder of the journey into town from the Pacific Airways landing dock. The taxi was descending into the city now, a space of wide avenues, which now and again crossed over watery canals and ocean inlets. "Are we going to dance at the Royal Hawaiian? I expect they have a band..."

"For a certainty, they do," Tommy kissed her hand. "Every dance with me, Mrs. Morehouse?"

"Of course!" Peg promised. That was one of the silly things that she loved about her husband – that he was a good dancer. They fitted together, on the floor, the music binding them, every move, turn and gesture a magic thing, as if they sensed it without words. Now the taxi approached the grand hotel, a sprawling and eccentric edifice the color of pink cotton candy, set in groves of palm trees and gardens, with the dark blue pacific rolling in upon a sugar-white strand beyond. It was a palatial hotel, even the name reflected it. "What a lovely place for our honeymoon trip!" Peg sighed in absolute bliss.

Everything was perfect. Her wedding, her husband, and now their lives together could not fail to fall short of such a perfect beginning.

Half a world away, Venetia Stoneman, third-year student nurse sat, kicking her heels on the Galveston seawall, with her bicycle propped against the inland angle of the wall, looking out on the shifting gray-blue waves in the Gulf of Mexico and considering things. Things like what she would do with herself after graduating from the Sealy Nursing College as a qualified nurse.

Not go home to Deming, New Mexico: of that, she was certain. Not to hang around the home ranch, putting antiseptic dressings on her older brother's hired hands when they had done themselves a physical damage, and riding with them in the bumpy back of a farm truck to the hospital in Deming, or more settled points. It went without saying that at some point in all the work that ranch hands were heir to simply spectacular medical emergencies. Bloody and near-fatal injuries. That was a given and a situation with which Vennie did not want to deal. *Family obligations has limits*, Vennie told herself. *Besides, Fred can deal with it all. I want to live my own life, a life on my terms. I love my brothers and sisters – but I'm almost twenty-two years of age. Free and white, twenty-one and all that. Spread my wings ...*

Out over the blue-gray Gulf, the white gulls spread their almost-motionless wings, rising and falling on the thermal updrafts.

"I want ..." Vennie said aloud and left the sentence unfinished. Truly she did not know what she wanted, aside from a mildly envious wish left over from childhood to be tall and blond and pretty, like Peg. Vennie was not at all structured physically in the same glamorous mode as her cousin. Vennie had long ago come to terms with this; she was slight and small, with tightly curly light-blond hair, grey eyes, and fine features. Also, of an intellectual inclination, which had made the decision to attend nursing college a fairly easy one.

"What do you want, then," a familiar feminine voice spoke from the sidewalk at her back. Vennie turned and smiled at the interloper to her private thoughts; Helen Drinkwater – her roommate at the Sealy nursing college. "I'm not interrupting, am I, Vennie? Privacy is so rare a thing for us ..."

"Not at all," Vennie smiled. Helen was a welcome interlocutor. The other girl climbed onto the seawall, her trouser-clad legs hanging over the edge. Helen was in character as well as in name, as someone with a modicum of easy wit had remarked; a long, tall drink of water: lanky and dark-haired, and of a cynical turn of mind. Helen fished in her handbag for a crumpled packet of cigarettes and her lighter. "Smoke?"

"Sure," Vennie replied. "I was just looking at the sea, and wondering what I would do with myself, when we graduate the program."

"Get a job," Helen replied. She blew out a puff of cigarette smoke from her new-lit cigarette. "Things are picking up again. Jobs in plenty. Besides," she applied the lighter to the end of Vennie's cigarette. "You can always go back to your brother's ranch if everything falls through. Or work at the Sealy."

"Ugh," Vennie replied. "Three years is enough. I like the Island well enough, but not well enough to stay here. I want to go somewhere else. Anywhere else."

They kicked their heels against the sea wall, regarding the ceaseless churn of blue-grey Gulf water, dashing against the sandy strand below their feet. Vennie privately relished being in the open air, alone but for a quiet friend, after a full week of confinement within walls, obedient and required to be silent. Nursing school, she realized early on, had a certain element of hazing to it, of the kind which she had observed on the ranch, with new hands. An aspect of being tried and tested by the older hands and with luck, eventually found worthy. She had shared this insight early on with Helen; Helen, who was inclined to stand on dignity, and demand why ... why were the student nurses being required to do this and that humiliating task? Helen had nodded in acquiescence, upon seeing the sense of it all, and been accommodating, once Vennie had pointed out the real reason.

"I'm going to apply for a job with the Red Cross," Helen said, abruptly. "Because there'll be a war on, in a couple of years. The Red Cross is a reserve for military nurses. Have you considered that option, Vennie?"

"I have not," Vennie replied, rather startled. "What reason do you think that there will be a war?"

"My brother is in the Army," Helen replied. "Eugene. He works in … well, his specialty is in planning and strategy. He thinks that that this awful Hitler man in Germany is planning for a war in Europe. Eugene says that since Germany lost the last war, they are building up their military and spoiling for another round; one they think they have a fair chance of winning. He is quite serious about it. Haven't you seen the newsreels?"

"I don't see that it has anything to do with us in America," Vennie replied, stoutly. "Why should we care? We got pulled into the last War over a lot of hooey over atrocities, atrocities which got played up in the newspapers! Why should we want a lot of our boys killed in a new one? All for nothing and in a fight that really wasn't any of our business anyway?"

"A lot of people feel that way," Helen acknowledged, frankly. "I can't blame them in the least. Some bloody war in Europe ought not to be any of our affair, at all. Didn't your people come from Germany, back in the day?"

"They sure did," Vennie replied with heat. "A hundred years ago, to get away from being conscripted to fight in some stupid nobleman's stupid bloodthirsty war with his equally stupid and bloodthirsty neighbor. We're Americans now and I'm an American, too. I don't want to see us in America get caught up in another fight between who gets to be the big man in Europe."

"Noted," Helen sighed, and tossed the butt of her finished cigarette into the churning waves below. "Of course, no one really does. But Eugene says that there's kind of a toss-up between those who really want to try out their new martial toys and theories and those who thing that we might be pushed to it, reluctantly. Do you even pay attention to the news, Vennie?"

"No. I'm too tired from cleaning bathrooms and patient rooms and staying up late, trying to catch up reviewing my lecture notes. That brother of yours seems like he has war on the brain, since he is a soldier, after all."

"You ought to make a bit of an effort to keep up with current events," Helen chided her. She took out another cigarette from the battered packet in her handbag and lit it. "Another? No ... Well, I've never known Eugene to be wrong about this kind of thing. He has such a big brain; I'm surprised that bits of it aren't oozing out of his ears. There are patterns to things, he says. Look at events, and how they fit all together, and follow the breadcrumb clues with an open mind. Herr Hitler is a nasty piece of work. You did see how his hooligans went out and began beating up and arresting Jews and smashing their shop windows, while the police stood by and did nothing at all? It was in all the newspapers, a couple of weeks ago," Helen added with a touch of mild sarcasm. "Well, Eugene says that was just for practice. A warm-up exercise; preparatory to taking over the Sudetenland and annexing Austria. Who knows what the little maniac with the Charley Chaplain mustache will want next? Poland, Eugene says – on the excuse of claiming that the German elements there along the borders are being harassed and persecuted, or that those nasty Slavs are planning brutal war on the poor persecuted German minority, and that his noble master race must come riding to the rescue … and then Britain and France will have to do <u>something</u>, after having said 'this much and no more' so many times."

"I don't much care," Vennie replied. "Let Europe go hang – we have enough troubles of our own. My folks left Europe a hundred years ago, and why should we feel any obligation to Europeans, if they didn't have the nerve to get shed of a stupidly blinded ruling class and emigrate to America?"

"Your point is accepted," Helen dragged deeply on her new cigarette. They watched the seagulls, wheeling over the grey-blue waves, rattling the shingle and sand at their feet, relishing the long ocean vista and the relative silence. "The thing is," Helen observed after that long silence. "We might not be interested in war. But Eugene says – war might eventually be interested in us."

Chapter 2 – Begin the Beguine

Letter, dated 24 April 1938, Postmarked Ipoh, Perak – Federated Malay States

Dearest Vennie: We have finally arrived at Tommy's plantation, after hopscotching by railway, airplane, steamship, railway again, and automobile, until we reached the lovely little town of Ipoh on the River Kinta – all in very jungly and mountainous landscape, and not the least like the *'great grey green greasy Limpopo, all set about with fever trees!'* We stayed the night at the station hotel, as we arrived very late in the afternoon and we were both exhausted beyond words. I honestly would not have been the least surprised to complete this long journey in a rickshaw! *(We rode in one in Manila – a carriage pulled by a carabao – that is, a tame water-buffalo!)* Tommy's household apparently did not get the telegram sent from Singapore alerting them to our arrival. Well, never mind, said Tommy. I'll telephone in the morning and Chandeep Singh will send the auto for us. *(This Chandeep Singh is Tommy's butler/driver/right-hand manager.)*

I wrote to you from Hawaii, before we departed so I hope that you received my letter, sent via airmail! In case it has gone astray, I had a full account in it, about how Tommy met up with the famous champion Olympic swimmer, Mr. Duke

Kahanamoku, who was quite the resident celebrity where we stayed. During our week-long stay at the Royal Hawaiian, Mr. Kahanamoku made fast friends with Tommy and even favored him with a long session in the water, tutoring him on the technique of riding those long boards at the crest of the waves. Tommy said it was enormously good fun, rather like riding a horse in a steeplechase at full gallop, although he barely had gotten the hang of standing up on the board before we had to move on. My husband has the unerring ability to make friends with so many people, and especially relishes the companionship of those who are expert at so many things. Mr. Kahanamoku was fit as the athlete he was in previous decades, comely and dark brown. I would have thought him a Mexican, on seeing him at first glance, like one of the Becker ranch vaqueros.

Anyway, at the end of our week-long stay, we boarded the Clipper for the long flight to Manila ... oh, there were stops at a several miniscule islands scattered at convenient intervals across the Pacific, but we did not linger any significant length of time at them. We stayed a week at the completely luxurious and modern Manila Hotel on Rizal Park, recovering from the rigors (hah!) of the journey from Hawaii. While we were there, an old friend of Daddy's treated us to a splendid dinner at the Army & Navy Club. Do you remember Daddy mentioning his old friend and pal, Chester, who thought his best bet for a college education was to take an appointment at a military academy? Like Daddy, Chester was the grandson of one of the old original settlers in Fredericksburg. Indeed, Daddy insists that Chester's grandfather had once courted Great-Grandma Magda in the early days, but she decided to marry Great-Grandfather Becker instead. Still, according to all the family stories, they remained friends, and the Beckers and the Nimitzes were always on the best of terms thereafter. Anyway, Daddy's friend Chester had just finished a tour as the commander of a cruiser in the Asiatic Fleet. Are you impressed? I was, terribly. I expect Daddy sent him a telegram, which caught him as he was heading back to the United States to take over some fearfully responsible duty, something called "The Bureau of Navigation." Neither Tommy nor I could divine exactly what this meant. Apparently, Chester has spent the last couple of years with the Asiatic Fleet showing off the flag to the obstreperous Japs. Someone has to do it, although Tommy reposes enormous confidence in the Royal Navy when it comes to this tiresome obligation. Another thing which we must agree to disagree upon, the abilities of the British VS the American navies.

It was quite an enjoyable evening, though. I felt quite at home with Chester, almost as if Daddy had been with us – grave and blond and handsome. He reminisced to us about being a boy in his grandfather's house, and the doings of Fredericksburg – where his grandfather was simply the most awful man for pranks and tall-tale-telling *(or so said Daddy!)*, with the old Verein-Kirche in the middle of Main Street, his grandfather's hotel and ballroom all tricked out like a grounded steamboat, and the little Sunday houses for the families from the outlaying properties who came to do business on Saturday and church on Sunday, and marvelous barbeques for any celebration. I would have felt most homesick, hearing him talk about this all, and Tommy nodding with the deepest interest and asking him to tell us more. My husband has done it again, charming the most unlikely people by taking such an intense interest in their doings. We went to see many of the sights of Manila – the hotel had a view over the vast bay where the Navy has moorage and that was simply the most spectacular scene.

Then, on to Singapore, which was really more of the same, only with British accents. This was where we went by steamer. It was quite relaxing. Tommy presented me with a guide to the Malay language, which he says that I will simply have to learn as essential to my new life. I whiled away those days on the puttering passenger steamer, studying the pages of *Fraser & Neaves' Short Malay Handbook in Roman Characters*. Tommy says that I will absolutely have to be able to cope in Malay, with the servants and plantation employees. Well, I could swing it in Spanish when I was growing up on the Ranch! How hard could this be? Tommy was deeply impressed with how I got on in Spanish in so many places in Manila.

Depressingly hard, as it might be after a week or so wrestling with the vocabulary and pronunciation in that little, red-covered handbook, although Mr. Song the Chinese cook speaks very passible English. So much for the use of the cooking book that I was given as a wedding present from Ivy. I do not have any use for recipes at all, as Mr. Song does all the cooking and resents very much any interference with his methods and the organization of his kitchen.

Sigh. I am getting ahead of myself, aren't I? Longcot Plantation is named after some grim and moldy stately pile in England, which, if you ask me, would be embarrassed at sharing a name with a plain wooden cottage with a tin roof, even though it sprawls in every direction and boasts a splendid garden and a very green lawn, kept carefully mown by the syce. *(More about the resident servants later – Vennie, I now live in a veritable League of Nations when it comes to nationalities!)* Tommy's grandfather had some sentimental connection to the original Longcot House, I guess. But picture a simple wooden sprawl, with deep verandahs all the way around, and large stretches of windows covered sketchily by louvered shutters, if at all. It seems that the whole purpose of walls here is so that they may be as open to admit as much of the wandering and hopefully cooler air as is possible. Of course, mosquitoes and other flying insects are simply ubiquitous – we all sleep under clouds of mosquito netting. Nothing must be done to impede the fresh air, morning, noon, and night. It is hot here; which I admit I am accustomed to – and <u>humid</u>. You would simply not believe the amount of condensation sweated off a glass filled with plain water and ice, after five minutes! Picture that structure surrounded by tall trees of a jungly-nature, beds of fabulously flowering shrubs, and a sweep of green lawn ... it is so green, so lush, so burgeoning with tropical life ... honestly,

26

the Hill Country seems to be a barren desert by comparison. *(Save in spring, when the wildflowers overwhelm ...)*

At any rate, when we arrived, all the household staff and the local workers were lined up at the edge of the gravel drive to receive us, as if we were royalty on tour of some splendid pile or enterprise. Can you imagine anything more embarrassing, everyone bobbing curtseys and bows, and calling me 'Mem Peg' and greeting me as if they were swearing eternal devotion to us and our bloodline? Chandeep Singh practically did; it seems that he served with Tommy's father in some Indian regiment and followed him after the war to Malaya. Tommy has known Chandeep Singh for all of his own life and regards him as a kind of honorary uncle. Vennie ... this whole thing is more complicated than I thought, upon marriage to Tommy. And you are the only one whom I may confide in. I will write you again, in more detail about our dear little house and the conundrums that I find there.

Love, Peggy

PS – how might one be certain of being pregnant? Since you are a nurse, and you have knowledge of these awkward things. Let me know, soonest.

Letter, dated 1 June 1938, written at Longcot Plantation, and postmarked Ipoh, Perak, Federated Malayan States

Dearest Vennie:

   Tommy has happily taken up the routine from which he took Home leave for so many months, and I have just barely begun to set up my own, which jogs along comfortably in harness with his. I wrote to you last week regarding the house, and a little of the surroundings. We are not more than forty minutes' drive by the automobile from Ipoh itself, which is a pretty and lively town, the local seat, and full of every amusement and convenience what we could wish. Our nearest neighbors are another rubber plantation, owned by Reginald Dawlish, who is a great friend and rival of Tommy's – they play on a polo team sponsored by the local club, as it appears. Reginald is the same age as Tommy and married, with two children nearly of school age. It is riotously amusing to listen to Reg and Tommy banter with each other – almost like watching a play or something. Mrs. Dawlish came to call on me, the next day after our arrival. I am not entirely certain that I am, or will be, as fond of Ada Dawlish as I am of you and Ivy – but still. Proximity demands courtesy. She is one of those drawling and superior English roses, but she was raised on a similar rubber estate in Malaya and married into another one and appears congenial enough to me. She seemed genuinely fascinated by what I told her of the Becker home place, and the doings there, as well as the drama of our journey by China Clipper. She confessed that she has always loved the novels of Zane Grey and simply adores Gary Cooper when he appears in the infrequent cinema offerings in Ipoh. I have decided therefore that I might just as well take her on as my trusty native guide to a territory which is completely uncharted to me.

Anyway, an account of our days to follow, with the note that the hardship of our daily routine (hah!) is considerably eased by the labors of a perfect phalanx of servants, to whom Tommy is absolute lord. The most important of the household staff is Chandeep Singh, who is as imposing as a twice-natural-height statue, a Sikh from the Punjab in India, with his iron bangle, turban and kirpan – that is, a curved steel dagger which his tribal custom obliges him to carry at all times. He must be something near to sixty years of age, as his beard is almost entirely white. I realized a truth at once: Chandeep Singh performs the role of the austere autocrat, the relentless enforcer of custom and law, which allows Tommy to be the generous and kindly final judge, upon being appealed to. It is almost comic to me, to watch them go through this dance, as if a kind of authoritarian minuet. Daddy and Mr. Sibley did this at the Ranch for simply decades. Daddy was the sympathetic, understanding one and Mr. Sibley played the harsh dictator as the ranch manager. I know they did this deliberately, for when I was about twelve or so, I overheard them laughing about it in

Daddy's office. It was all part of management of an enterprise of any kind, Daddy explained. Now I know this to be true.

The next most important servant in the household is Mr. Song, the Chinese cook. He is also about the age of Chandeep Singh, although it may be difficult to tell with Orientals. He works in a small kitchen appended to the back of the house; a wood stove, and a couple of cupboards with pierced tin sides, and an ice box, and that is all that he has of modern convenience. You would not believe the exquisite meals which emerge from this crude little kitchen. We have meals of chicken or fish in infinite varieties most nights, for beef is quite expensive as it must be kept in cold storage, and the nearest such depot is some distance, and pork is quite out of the question. But of vegetables, and tropical fruit, and little cakes and pies, and puddings – Mr. Song is a master of all forms of cookery. I am supposed to consult with him every morning on the menus for the day's meals, but in truth at this point he is more given to suggestions which I then approve.

There are four housemaids, who see to practically everything; answering the door, serving meals, cleaning, and laundry: Rohaya is the senior, and I think a little older than I am. She is a widow; her husband was one of the rubber tappers. Faridah and Kubtiah are sisters, and Miri is younger, about sixteen, I think. They live with their families in the worker's little village of attap-thatched cabins, which is a little way from the main house, behind a thick hedge of casuarina trees, which look like a feathery version of a cedar tree.

As for the outside staff; there are five; a syce – Daud, who is sort of a groom and all-around errand boy, Arshad who keeps the gardens and grounds tended, and his assistant Farhan, Rahman who tends to the gasoline generator which supplies our electric and Samad, who sweeps the paths and sprinkles water on the drive to keep the dust down on dry days. I made a list of their names so I can remember them. Farhan and Samad are still quite young, boys really. Of the estate workers who manage the production of rubber under Tommy's direction, I cannot even begin to remember their names and relationships, although Tommy does. He is the absolute monarch of this place. Regardless, I am addressed as 'Mem Peg' by all.

As for our daily routine, Tommy is awake and at work before dawn, even before the wild roosters which live in the casuarina hedge begin crowing. The sap from the trees must be tapped early in the day, in the cool and shade of morning, and great care must be taken with the latex clean and uncontaminated. I sleep until about half-past seven or eight, and we have a light breakfast together on the verandah. Then Tommy returns to the plantation office, or to see to the business around the estate. I have my own occupations; to consult with Mr. Song about menus, especially if we are expecting guests, and to supervise housekeeping otherwise. Gosh, can you imagine me, keeping house? Or rather, looking on, while the maids sweep and dust, and straighten up the rooms? Tommy wants me to study Malay, so I have my book and lists of words to memorize. I have tried making conversation in Malay with

Rohaya and the other maids, and they indulge me with much giggling, which is a little discouraging. I try and take a walk in the garden, and through the nearer portion of the plantation before it becomes too hot. We have luncheon again on the verandah at about one in the afternoon – usually something cold and light, because then it is too hot to do anything else but lie down for a bit of a siesta. Then a light tea at about four o-clock, when the day begins to cool. Most often we take the car into Ipoh, to the club to meet Tommy's friends. That is the social time of day; to play a brisk tennis match, or bowls or croquet on a green lawn, manicured so carefully that it looks like velvet plush. We return home most evenings for supper at about eight – if not at our own house, then at the Dawlish bungalow, while twilight falls, and the moon and stars begin to shine. The palm and banana trees rustle in the evening breeze, and sometimes we see bats hunting insects under the lights. And then to bed – another day in my humdrum married life!

Love to you and all - Peg

PS: Ignore the PS on my last letter. Aunt Rose came to visit, as per usual

Letter dated September 4, 1938 postmarked from San Antonio, Texas.

Dearest Peg:

So happy to hear your wonderful news in your last letter? Is it a secret – and have you written to your father and the Grands yet? If you have not broken the news to them, and wish me to keep it in confidence, then I shall. But I will begin looking in the baby linen department at Joske's for suitable items for what my mother always jokingly called 'a little bungle' from heaven. I suppose it will not be too much expense to mail a gift from me to Malaya.

And I have happy news as well – I am employed as of two weeks ago as a private duty nurse! I had simply a mountain of good luck, upon graduating from Sealy, and qualifying as a registered nurse with the State. I was sadly packing my things and contemplating a return to Deming, since I was unable to find any kind of job in nursing when I received a letter from your grandfather. He and your grandmother are friends with a neighbor of theirs, a retired general whose wife is an invalid. Their last private nurse left to get married, and they were looking for someone to take her place. I should tell you that the list of applicants for any such advertised position quickly becomes at least one or two hundred long. The job situation for nurses (or anyone!) is still quite dire here and since the general and his wife are quite old, they were as desperate to hire someone qualified and immediately without having to interview an endless series of applicants. So your Grandpa Sam says to them, 'I just happen to know of a young relative who just qualified as a registered nurse' and he said some quite kindly things about me, and showed them pictures of your wedding party, and General Millefield asked, 'How soon can she come to take up work?' and Grandpa Sam replied, 'She may not be at loose ends for very long, as she is considering other serious offers,' so they dickered a bit, and Grandpa Sam said he would send a letter and I came up on the next available train, and met General Millefield and Mrs. Adele at their house.

The long and short of it all, we suited each other, all the way around, and so now I have a nice little room of my own in their big house among the oak trees, and Mrs. Adele is my one daily and nightly care, for the munificent wage of 15.75 a week. I have a half-day to myself on Saturday afternoons, but I do not mind. They are both very dear, sweet people. The General came into the Army as a cadet and came out West to serve as a cavalry officer shortly after the end of the War Between the States. He tells the most astonishing stories about fighting against the wild Comanche and Apache tribes. There are no children, and I am treated by them rather as a daughter or grandchild might have been. The General is ninety-two and still quite hearty, but Mrs. Adele, although she is twenty years younger, is terribly frail and requires constant medical attention. She still manages to be very brave and cheerful about it all. She is in an invalid chair most days, or in bed, if feeling particularly unwell. I must see to most of her physical needs – and I will not go into details over what that involves, save that you will discover most of them when you have an infant. I discovered them all when I began as a nurse-trainee. She reminds me very much of Granny Sophie, who was just the same sort of lady.

I will not tire you with an account of my days, save that I am on call for most of the night, should Mrs. Adele have any needs. They have a cook and a general housekeeper, who have been with them for decades, and a manservant/chauffeur who has been with them since the General retired in 1902! Everyone in this house has half a century on me! I suppose that the highlight of theirs – and my day – is in the late afternoon. The General and Mrs. Adele sit in their parlor, overlooking the garden, and we all have a glass of sherry, and they tell me yarns about the old days. I suspect that they relish the opportunity to tell them to someone who has not heard them twenty or thirty times before. Nonetheless, I find their stories fascinating.

For example, General Millefield recalls Grandpa Fred's twin brother, John, back in the day! They served together in some Army outpost, around 1880, when Great-uncle John was an Army surgeon. An expert hand when it came to surgically extracting Indian arrowheads, or so the General insisted. They made them from scrap metal bits, so the General avers and they would bend awfully, upon striking a bone, and extracting them without further trauma was considerable of a surgical challenge. It seems that Grandpa Fred was the shiftless willow-the-wisp, and Great-uncle John the respectable and serious one in comparison. I find that amusing, as I hope that you will.

Love, Vennie

PS – tell me if I am sworn to secrecy regarding your prospective bungle from heaven!

Letter, dated April 10, 1939, postmarked San Antonio, Texas

Dear Peg:

Just a brief note, to say how incredibly pleased we are with your happy news! Tommy must be over the moon with happiness. Send pictures as soon as you can of our new little sprout on this most distant branch of the family tree! I shared this splendid news with the General and Mrs. Adele as soon as I got your letter and they were so happy for me that the General went down to the cool room in the cellar and brought out a very dusty bottle of fine French brandy, to toast little Thomas with.

Your letters are about the only real excitement in my life, Mrs. Adele and the General live so quietly. They hardly ever go out, and most of their friends are similarly situated. Still, I do not mind terribly, for I feel most sincerely that I am of use in this world. I am not (well not very much!) envious of your mad social whirl. It must be exhausting to be so busy, when all you really want to do is rest, admire your baby boy, put up your feet and read a good book! Speaking of good books – I have read in the newspapers that they have finally begun filming *Gone With the Wind!* Can you imagine what a splendid movie it will be? Mrs. Adele and I can hardly wait. She has promised me that we will all go to a matinee as soon as the movie comes to a theater in San Antonio.

I received a letter from my friend Helen Drinkwater last week – she went and joined the Army's nursing service. She is convinced that there will be a war, eventually, and it would be her duty to care for the wounded in it. She says that I should volunteer as well, but I am agnostic on the possibility. Didn't the British Prime Minister, whose name I always forget because he reminds me so much of an undertaker's dummy – come back from Germany with a promise from Mr. Hitler pledging peace in our time? The General harrumphed and promised a dire future, and quoted someone or other, saying that 'Peace is the dream of the wise, but war is the history of men.' But honestly, he is an old man and always sees things in such terms. It's just too depressing to think about and I don't want to be depressed. I want to contemplate the flowers that are blooming everywhere, I want to go out dancing to fast music, and to see Clark Gable on the movie screen as Rhett Butler! Besides, I am quite fond of Mrs. Adele now, and it would break her heart if I left, just when she and the General need me the most.

With love to you and Little Tommy,
Vennie

Chapter 3 – We'll Meet Again

The errant breeze rustled the leaves of the stand of banana trees nearest the sitting room veranda; very loud in the silence after Tommy snapped off the radio, a silence broken only by the distant hum of the household generator. It would have been another leisurely Sunday afternoon, but for the tension which had been building for a week and cranked to the snapping-point in the last three days.

"Well, then, that's it," he said, in resignation. "Another bloody war. That bloody little man has got his wish, damn him."

"And half of Poland," Peggy replied, her heart aching, more for her husband and his friends than any peril for herself. She still thought of herself as an American, a welcome guest in a foreign but well-loved land.

Tommy laughed, a short and grim laugh. "On top of the Sudetenland, and poor bloody Czechoslovakia, Austria, the Rhineland ... everything he claimed was his last demand, absolutely, and no one had the balls to object and make it stick. Well, I guess Neville and his Conservatives has finally rediscovered his backbone after an exhaustive search, and not a moment too soon. I'll have a drink now, Peg, before Ada and Reg arrive."

There was a sideboard cabinet set up in the sitting room to serve as a small bar, with a covered basin of ice, and an array of various glasses. Reg and Ada Dawlish were expected for dinner that evening, but not until later. Peg silently mixed a stiff gin and tonic, adding a section of cut lime from the bowl which Mira had brought from Mr. Song's kitchen.

"Don't drink it too fast, love," she advised him. "Tomorrow morning comes early enough for you."

"I know," he replied, and leaned against the tall back of the tall bamboo-woven peacock-chair as if exhausted. "I'm tired already. It's too bloody much for one lifetime, Peg. And I wouldn't say any of this to anyone but you. Too bloody much. The last war was a meat-grinder. In the end, the whole thing appeared to be a means of turning men into acres of coffins and white crosses. The thing I recall most vividly – I was eleven at school in England in the year of the Armistice – was seeing women in black, everywhere. Couldn't throw a rock without hitting a score of widows, anywhere you went. Widows, or women mourning brothers, or men whom they might have married. My father was the oldest of five brothers. They were all gone by 1918 and he was hanging on by his fingernails after being gassed. And then the influenza epidemic, and after that ... all the crippled ex-soldiers. Couldn't go anywhere without seeing some poor blighter with no arm, or leg, or a frightfully disfigured face. I swear to you, Peg – I couldn't wait to return East, just to prove to myself that the whole world wasn't haunted by women in black, men crippled and disfigured, and more names engraved on marble memorials at every turn. Black crepe hanging everywhere, and women selling paper red poppies ... Oh, god, yes – I was happy to come back to Malaya. Now, it's about to start all over again."

"We're far away from it here, my darling," Peg said, as she handed him the tall clear and ice-frosted glass. "And you are in ... what is it they call it – a reserved occupation?"

"Yes." Tommy took a deep gulp from his drink. "Essential industry, so they tell us. Half a dozen bright young sparks, including Reg Dawlish's junior manager took it in their heads to return to England last month when it started looking dicey, to volunteer for the services. Not on your nelly, they told them. Run along back to Malaya and continue growing rubber; thank you all very much; that's just what Britain requires from you noble chaps. They had paid their own way, too – and now have to pay again to return."

"We're safe enough here," Peg replied. She mixed her own drink, more to keep Tommy company and because she wanted something cool – just a bare splash of gin, a twist of lime and fill up the rest of the tall glass with ice and tonic water. She settled onto the padded chaise lounge and looked out over the garden, fragrant and colorful with flowers. Overhead in the bright tropic sky, the edges of wandering clouds were touched with fiery golden edges ... it seemed incredible that war should be happening anywhere. Not when everything she looked upon reflected nothing but the sweet tranquility of peace and domestic order. There were footsteps in the hallway, and a low voice murmuring reassurance to a small and fussy baby. "Miss Hui has brought little Tommy – Do I have time for his late afternoon feed before the Dawlishes arrive?"

"Of course," Tommy replied, and Peg was secretly cheered by how his expression relaxed, as the baby amah, Miss Hui put his son into Peg's arms and stood back, beaming approval. Miss Hui, inherited from the Dawlishes when the Dawlish children returned to England, was an exemplary nanny. She was an ageless daughter of China, almost nun-like in plain black trousers and a white overtunic, an expert with babies and small children. Peg had felt inexpressible relief upon employing her, a month or so before small Tommy was born, after Ada Dawlish had taken her two children back to England for their schooling and had no more need of a baby amah. Peg herself knew nothing about caring for babies – so small, so frail! But Miss Hui knew everything about babies and small children, their behavior, their small illnesses, their noisy bouts of crying over mysterious discomforts, and the horrible messes in their diapers.

"Mem Peg," Miss Hui beamed as Peg unfastened the front of her dress. "Your son has done very well today! He turned over, all by himself – and he smiled at me ... look – he is smiling at you, Mem!"

"Of course," Peg replied, and settled her son in a comfortable position. "He knows where his supper is coming from!"

It was one of those atavistic things; Peg insisted on breast-feeding her child, against the vague disapproval of those in the Club set, and friends like Ada Dawlish who held that her bust would be ruined and made saggy by the practice. 'But what are breasts for, then anyway,' Peg had argued. Ada made no more comment, and Peg was certain that her insistence on this was written off to being an eccentric American. But never mind – if Miss Hui had the care of her son for the rest of his hours and days, Peg had this, with his tiny pink face pressed against the pillow of her breast. He was a sturdy morsel, with eyes which Peg were certain would remain blue, and a head of hair so pale that it was all but invisible; the look of the Becker kin still holding true. Little Tommy looked like every single baby picture in the Becker family photo albums, back to the last century. Now Miss Hui looked between Peg and Tommy, and with swift perception of the mood in the sitting room, she ventured a tentative question.

"Mem Peg, is there something wrong?"

"There is," Peg replied. "Britain has just declared war. There've been air raid alarms sounded in London already."

"Against the Japanese?" Miss Hui's expression brightened. "May they be driven from China soon, then?"

"Not against the Japs," Tommy chuckled without amusement. Miss Hui looked vaguely disappointed. "Against the Germans."

Miss Hui clicked her tongue, in disapproval. "Better to make war on the Japanese," she said. "Very bad people! Very bad people – their soldiers do wicked things in China for many years now, very many wicked things. Better to stop them now, before they do worse things here!"

"Duty before pleasure, Miss Hui," Tommy replied. "I think I will put some music on the gramophone, Peg. Something cheerful. God, I need cheering up!" He set his drink aside, and Peg noted that he had already drunk nearly half. He shuffled through the stack of heavy vinyl discs. "Ah – Glen Miller! *Wishing – Wishing Will Make It So!* Perfect! Will you dance with me, Mrs. Morehouse?

"The minute I finish feeding your son," Peg retorted, "And can I ask for more Glen Miller – *Stairway To the Stars*, maybe?" Miss Hui excused herself from the room as the scratchy sound of the gramophone gave way to pure music and outside, the noisy flocks of birds began their return to their normal night roosts in the trees around the plantation. Peg found this rather comforting. Soon the bats would be out, brief fleeting shadows, flittering about the open clearing around the bungalow. Tommy changed out the record and came to sit next to her on the chaise, admiring both his son and Peg's exposed breast. They sat together in perfect contentment, although Tommy got up several times to put on another record. Peg leaned her head against his shoulder between those intervals. No, it would all be all right, once everyone had a chance to absorb the intelligence that a war had been declared, a war far, far away from Malaya.

"We'll have a little dance party tonight," Tommy replied, his normally jaunty mood returning, as if his brief depression was banished between gin and tonic, and music. "May as well cheer each other up, Peg! Tomorrow is another day!"

"That's what Scarlett O'Hara said," Peg replied.

Tommy grinned. "She's a never-say-die type of gel, just like all you American gels – and I largely approve," he added, just as the sound of a distant motorcar coming up the long gravel drive alerted them that the Dawlishes were on their way. Little Tommy was satiated and content, although from a certain odor emanating from the direction of his diaper, his infant bowels had made way for the fresh intake.

Letter dated June 10, 1940, postmarked San Antonio, Texas

Dear Peg:

Mrs. Adele was buried yesterday in the cemetery at Fort Sam Houston. She passed very quietly on Sunday, at 2:35 in the morning. Her condition declined swiftly over the last few weeks. The General is devastated by her death, although it had been anticipated for months by us all. The General and Adele had been married almost sixty years; I don't know what he will do without her, just as I do not know what she would have done without him. We were never able to go see *Gone With the Wind* in the theater, which is the one thing I most regret. Mrs. Adele would have so loved that experience, even if it would have cost twice as much as a regular movie! I stayed several more days at the Millefields, just to make certain of the General's state of health, but now I am staying with your grandparents, for the next week or so, while I work out my own prospects.

I have not said anything to anyone of this, but I made up my mind to volunteer for the Army nursing service, as Helen has been urging me to do for months. I need work, Peg. I need to feel useful now that everything in the world seems to be bound for hell in a handbasket! This would suit me, I think. Helen has been awaiting orders transferring her to an assignment at the Army hospital in Manila. When I told the General and Mrs. Adele of this, sometime last month, they were quite entertained, and said that she would have the most marvelous social time and to be certain to pack enough evening gowns. You had a wonderful time when you stayed over in Manila during your honeymoon, didn't you? Ah, me – that seems so long ago now, in view of current events.

The news just now is terribly discouraging now that the British have retreated from France. I went to a movie matinee and watched the newsreel of the survivors coming back from Dunkirk; battered and bloody and exhausted, but making a brave face of it all, knowing that their country stands alone. Poor France! Poor Poland defeated and ground under a tyrant's heel. Now that I see that Helen and the General were right, different experiences, but the same conclusion. We might not be interested in war, but war is interested in us, sooner or later.

I suppose that the war feels very far from you, safe in Malaya and half a world away from bombs and air raid alerts. With Tommy in a reserved occupation – is that what they call it? That it is more important to the war effort for him to go on producing rubber than enlisting in the military. I suppose you are pleased that he cannot do anything more reckless than joining the local volunteers, which I think must be more like being in the part-time militia than a full-time soldier. At least he can stay at home with you and little Tommy. Meanwhile, your grandparents have made me very welcome, and say that I may stay with them as long as I need to…

(later)
Well, dear Peg – I went for an interview today, with a pair of senior nurses, to be considered for the Army Nursing Service; one very lean and grim senior nurse, and another who looked quite comfortably motherly. They asked simply a million questions or more, to assess my fitness, I presume, although I think that all those relevant facts about my training at Sealy, and my registered nurse status were in the stacks of papers on the table before them. Perhaps General Millefield may have called in a favor or two among his old military chums, and he is a total sweetheart if he did on my behalf, but they must have wanted to be absolutely certain of my fitness. Finally, the grim-looking senior nurse frowned severely and said, 'Miss Stoneman, you do realize that your patients will almost exclusively be male. You will be asked to deal with certain male ailments and bodily parts which most sensitive women will find disgusting and outrageous. Is that something to which you are agreeable? The military nursing service has no need of nervous nellies, and nurses without strong stomachs." I looked at her, straight in the eye and replied, "Ma'am, I was raised on a cattle

ranch in New Mexico – I have six brothers and three uncles. Nothing about the male sex would astound or shock me in the least ... and anyway, I have helped at round-up time with castrating bull-calves and cooked up a dish of calf-fries afterwards!"

At that, the grim senior nurse looked as if she had swallowed a live bee, and the motherly-appearing one looked as if she wanted to laugh but made herself not to, just in time. "You'll do, Miss Stoneman," she said. "I think you'll do, indeed. We will be recommended you to be commissioned. Welcome to the US Army, Miss Stoneman. Your orders will follow."

And so there I am, Peg.
With all my love, the soon to be,
Lieutenant Venetia Stoneman, US Army Nurse Corps.

Chapter 4 – This is the Army, Mr. Jones

Peg awakened to hushed voices, a tenor of emergency in them. She had been napping in the long hot afternoon, feeling particularly wearied by the weight of the new baby. Tommy stood with a with an empty small suitcase in his hand, Miss Hui a bare shadow behind him, both veiled like ghosts beyond the white mosquito netting around her bed. Tommy was in the dust-colored khaki tunic and trousers of the volunteer company of the local Malaya Volunteers. During her first years in Malaya, Peg had indulgently considered her husband's membership in the volunteers as a chance for them to play soldiers and go out drinking after their regular sessions of training and drill.

"Peg, get up and get dressed," Tommy commanded, and the urgency in his voice frightened Peg even more than the drowsy voice of her son in Miss Hui's arms, complaining. "Now, this very minute. Pack some things, a single suitcase – you and Ada must get to KL. Reg and I think you should go on to Singapore immediately. Safer there, anyway, especially in your condition. The Japanese Army has taken Penang; word was just confirmed. All British women and children in Ipoh have been ordered to get out to KL until the situation is sorted. Our volunteer company is ordered to be attached to the Regulars! I'm paying off the workers and the household staff, as I don't know when we'll be back. Ada Dawlish is here with her car. You have to go with her now."

"I have prepared what is necessary for Baba Tommy," At Tommy's elbow, Miss Hui sounded calm. "Mem Peg, what do you wish to take with you?"

"Shoes," Peg gasped, as she threw back the light coverings on hers' and Tommy's bed. This was so sudden, horrible and nightmarish. Her clothing for the afternoon had been laid out by Miri; a light cotton skirt and a smock, suitable for lazing around the bungalow and garden in her current condition – but not for travel, certainly not all the way to KL and then on to Singapore. There was no time, no time! She fumbled at the buttons of her nightgown, made clumsy by sleep, the burden of six months pregnancy and terror. The Japanese in Penang, barely a hundred miles away! They could be here in hours.

"Hurry, Peg, there's no time!" Tommy exclaimed, even as Peg fumbled with shoes and stockings. "The chaps and I have to leave, too. I was allowed time for a stop here, as we were going in that direction anyway." He flung an opened suitcase on the bed and began emptying Peg's underwear and stocking drawer into it, following that with a second drawer full of blouses and housedresses, all clean and neatly pressed.

"My jewelry-box!" Peg protested. "Don't forget that ... and my address-book and our wedding album! Tommy! Where's my watch – that was a present from Daddy on my 21st."

"Three minutes and no more," Tommy commanded. "If you can't find it in three minutes, then you must leave it behind!" Peg snatched up the silver-framed picture of Tommy and which sat on her dresser and thrust it into her largest handbag. She had her shoes on at last. Shrugging her light coat over her shoulders, she went to the sitting room. The bound photo album: a packet of letter paper, left on the small desk, where she had begun a letter to Daddy that afternoon. The little engraved silver prize cup she had won at the Club tennis match. On an impulse, the book of recipes – a book of recipes that she had never been able to cook from, a wedding present from her sister. She looked helplessly around the sitting room, barely lit by the afternoon sun, slipping in narrow bars between the chik shades. No time, and a single suitcase, but there was so much here which she treasured. Peg was too rattled and still half asleep in that moment to mourn all that must be left behind – everything that had made her life in Malaya with Tommy so comfortable. That would come in later weeks and months.

She emptied the random assortment into the suitcase, and Tommy pressed it closed and snapped the catches. *A scarf for her hair – where was her good hat? No time, no time!* Tommy took her elbow in one hand, the suitcase in the other, and hurried her through the house, and down the steps to the gravel drive. The Dawlish's automobile sat there, a comfortable Austin Sherborne sedan, engine purring. Beyond, the small truck which belonged to Longcot and used to ship cured rubber sheets to the central warehouse. The truck was at the center of a small cluster of khaki-clad Volunteers. She recognized a few from drill days; The young Malay policeman, Mr. Song's younger cousin who kept a little grocery store on the outskirts of Ipoh, two young Englishmen employed by a tin mine farther up into the hills, and Chandeep Singh. Mr. Song, Miri and Rohaya stood by, looking frightened and uncertain, along with a handful of estate rubber tappers from the kampong. The Volunteers were busy with the petrol cans, taken from the generator shed around in back of the house, pouring the contents of them into the Austin and the truck through a funnel and short hose.

"Tommy, I don't want to leave you!" Peg protested.

Her husband shook his head. "We have our orders from the Army! And I can't countenance leaving you here alone. God knows what those yellow devils will get up to when they get here, after all the horrid stories of what they did in Nanking."

"Where's Reg?" Peg demanded, now that she had caught her breath and began to think. Everything she had heard on the radio or read in the daily *Straits Times* had seemed as if the Malay states were pluckily holding fast, under air raids and invasion on both sides from the Japanese ... but now Tommy had rousted her out of bed in the middle of the afternoon, to pack a suitcase in five minutes ... all to catch a train. To evacuate the British women and children to Singapore.

"Reg is organizing transport for the Company to join a division of Regular Army, no doubt to assist in their orderly retreat to pre-prepared positions," Tommy replied grimly.

"So, the well-organized defense of Malaya against the invading hordes is not going all that well?" Peg replied, after an instant of consideration. Tommy grinned, a wry grin, devoid of mirth.

"According to the official bulletins, all is going as if planned," Tommy replied, and Peg realized in that moment how much she loved her husband, for his wry wit and grasp of essentials. He could, as Daddy had often said of an employee of whom he approved, take it as well as dish it out. There were no fleas on Tommy Morehouse.

There was an electric feeling to the air on this afternoon, as if a storm brewed, edging the distant clouds with brief lightening-flashes and distant rumbles of thunder. Only Peg didn't think it a natural storm. That would have been ordinary, expected, endurable. The Japanese were dropping bombs on Penang. What was coming was war, brute and cruel and raw. Peg folded her arms over her bulging belly and considered some of the awful stories she had heard of the war in China, of atrocities committed in Nanking; babies ripped from their mothers' arms, or even cut out of their stomachs. Now, Peg wished that she had not read all that, although Miss Hui must have known every horrific detail. There was also an old and ugly family story, related in whispers among the oldest relatives, of a pregnant woman killed in just that way by the Comanche, decades before. Until she was pregnant herself, Peg had not completely comprehended the horror of that experience.

"Peg, give me a moment," Tommy begged, while Ada Dawlish exclaimed,

"Hurry, Tommy – or we'll miss the train!"

Chandeep Singh opened the passenger door for Peg with his usual courtly flourish. Two pale faces regarded Peg from the back seat; Miss Hui and Little Tommy who was already almost asleep again. Ada Dawlish sat behind the wheel.

"Mem Peg," he rumbled, "A safe journey..."

"Wait a minute!" Peg exclaimed. "Tommy, what of Rohaya and Mr. Song and the rubber tappers and their families? Aren't they going to be evacuated as well? Surely ..."

"No, Mem," Chandeep Singh replied, austerely.

Tommy, a taller figure in his khaki shorts and tunic, was moving among the rubber tappers and household staff, dispensing bills from a sheaf of Straits notes in his hand. Mr. Song bowed deeply upon receiving his pay and shook Tommy's hand. Without further protest, Peg settled herself in the front passenger seat. She heard the gurgle of petrol filling the tank, then felt the car boot close with a slight bump.

Then Tommy, leaning in through the opened window, bestowing a hasty kiss on her cheek, and reaching across her to tousle Little Tommy's small head, "G'bye for now, Peg – take care. Tommy, chappy-my-lad, be good and promise to obey Amah, and do what she and your mum say. Ada, they're done with the petrol; you'll have an extra can in the boot, if you need it. Goodbye, my dearest Peggy."

"We'll soon be in Singapore together," Peg insisted, resolute as the wife of a plantation owner of no mean property. She was struck by a sudden realization. She opened her purse; there was a comb in it, and down at the very bottom, her powder compact and a single lipstick. "Tommy – you didn't pack my toothbrush!"

"Buy another one in Singapore," her husband replied, as he handed her his billfold. "Here; take all the rest of the notes, and the bank book. Sorry, only Straits dollars. We have an account at Barings, if you need more for expenses."

He blew her a kiss, as he stepped back from the Dawlish's Austin, and that was that. Ada turned the key in the ignition, and as they bumped down the long gravel drive, Peg cast one long look back, before a bend in the drive took her out of sight of all but the roof of Longcot Plantation. She had one final glimpse of Tommy, bare-headed, among the other khaki-clad Volunteers, standing a little apart from the cluster around the truck.

The road south to Kuala Lumpur was crowded, automobiles full of English families crawling slowly along in the afternoon heat. When they passed through a kampong, the pungent smell of garbage on the heavy air; of wood smoke and stagnant water in the ditches, privies and ponds surrounding the attap houses on stilts made Peg want to vomit. Ada Dawlish drove expertly, her hands clamped onto the wheel of the Dawlish's Austin sedan, her eyes fixed on the road, and the dusty bumper of the car just ahead, while the sun burned in a pitiless blue sky.

"Where are we to stay, once we get to KL?" Now that Peg was fully awake, she could think of practical things.

From the front seat, Ada Dawlish answered steely and determined, "I think we should go on to Singapore, as Reg and

Tommy said. We can go to my brother's place. He's certain to have room enough. Arthur has a house in the Lady Hill Road, near to the Tanglin Club. If he can't put us up, he'll know of a place. When Tommy and Reg get to Singapore, they'll know where to find us." The steely resolve cracked, just a bit. "Thank god the girls are in England! Safe enough from all this. I'd have stayed with them there, if we had the slightest hint that something like this would happen! Why can't we stop those yellow bastards! Isn't the British Army and Navy good for anything?"

In Miss Hui's arms, little Tommy stirred from sleep, and murmured something – good heavens, was it in Chinese? Whatever it was, Miss Hui produced a bottle of water from her own bundle of possessions. Little Tommy drank from it, thirstily, and Miss Hui met Peg's gaze.

"He thirsty, Mem," was all that she said, and Peg thought guiltily that she should have thought of all that. At the very least, considered that they all should have brought along something cool to drink for the long slow drive to KL. It was a nerve-wracking journey and seemed to take two or three times as long as normal, this slow, dust-clogged journey. More than once, Peg was horrified at the sight of airplanes swooping low over the road, the blood-red ball clear and plain on their wings. She remembered the newsreels, of refugee-clogged roads in France, machine-gunned by German Stuka dive-bombers. The very first time that it happened, Ada saw them coming, a line like the dark wings of gulls in the cloudless sky to the south.

Fortune had it that they were at a point in the winding road towards KL where Ada had space to pull the Austin off on the side of the road, a roadside thickly grown with tall trees and rustling stands of cane. Ada set the brake and snapped,

"Everyone out!" Ada flung herself out of the driver side door, and Peg, half-asleep from the heat, tumbled out from the passenger door, Miss Hui and little Tommy on her heels. They crouched among the stands of cane, as the roar of engines overhead blotted out all sound. There for a brief, heart-stopping moment, and in another gone, lifting up into the hot blue afternoon sky to the north. Peg picked herself up, comforted her son, who was fractious and frightened. They resumed their seats in the Dawlish's Austin, seats now hot and sticky from the enervating heat, and continued on down the road to KL.

Sometime in early evening, well after sunset and black-out time *(which would have made the roads nearly as perilous as an overt air raid)*, they finally arrived in the forecourt of the splendors of KL's enormous and sprawling main station, with the Mughal-style pavilions perched atop the grand staircase columns. Ada Dawlish parked the Austin as close as she could and looked at the keys in her hand.

"I don't know what I am supposed to do with the car," she said. "I wish that I could blow it up, to keep the Japs from using it. From what Tommy said, they might be here in a couple of days, maybe as much as a week."

"Those bastards," Peg replied, with feeling. "How could this all be happening so fast, Ada? Barely two weeks ago, everything was peaceful ... well, not everywhere, but here in Malaya. Everything was calm, ordinary. We had meals on the veranda, went for walks in the garden, played tennis and had stengahs with our friends at the Club. Then between one week and the next ..."

"I'll carry your suitcase," Ada replied, grimly, as if she had not heard a single word. "You shouldn't be lifting anything heavy in your condition, and I'm damned if I can see any porters around." She took out the two suitcases, already having her handbag slung like a satchel over her shoulder. "We're on the run, and running thin, as little as we like facing that reality, Peg. Ever since they sank the *Repulse* and the *Prince of Wales...* we've been at a disadvantage. Hate to say admit it but we are, and nothing broadcast over the wireless or published in the *Straits Times* will convince me otherwise. And nothing good will come from giving up Penang and running like cowards. We underestimated the Japs, and now we're paying the price for arrogance. But Singapore will hold out. It's a fortress, like Gibraltar, you know. Our chaps will be able to hold. We're being reinforced from India and Australia. And I wouldn't count out the Volunteers, no, not by any chalk."

Peg took Little Tommy's small hand; Miss Hui had his other, with her shapeless rucksack slung over her shoulder. Peg found Ada's comment rather bracing; brutal but realistic. At a time like this, brutally realistic had it all over unrealistic hopes, and soothing announcements on the radio. Ada put the keys to the Austin under the driver seat, and left the door unlocked, saying, "If Reg comes for it, he'll know where to find them. And if he doesn't, it means nothing. Let's go get our tickets, Peg – or if not, a room at the station hotel or at the Majestic until morning." She sent a searching look over her shoulder at Peg. "You look exhausted. You ought to get a good rest, if there isn't a train tonight. If you lose the sprog to a miscarriage, Tommy will never forgive us."

"I'm fine," Peg insisted, for she didn't feel nearly as frail as everyone insisted that a visibly pregnant woman ought to be. She had bursts of energy, where she honestly felt that she could climb mountains – albeit rather small mountains. They walked into the station together, into the chaos in the main hall. The main hall was filled with women and children, mostly British with a scattering of Australians, all loudly querulous. The few station staff present looked baffled and defensive. The roar of voices in the railway hall, amplified by the space, was nearly as overwhelming as the racket from the Japanese airplanes, buzzing the road from Ipoh.

"Dear God," Ada breathed. "It's been the usual cock-up on all sides, Peg. It looks like no one in KL had the faintest clue about an organized evacuation. About typical for this bloody war, I'd say."

"Shouldn't we do something?" Peg suggested, hesitantly, but Ada shook her head, and since her hands were full of suitcases, merely jerked her chin in the direction of a cluster of women. Two of them at the center of it seemed to be making lists and directing the rest here and there.

"I'd say that lot have got it sorted, but I'll check and see if they need anything else," Ada set down the suitcases close to the nearest bench, and went to speak to the other women, all of whom appeared as rattled and exhausted as Peg felt. Only Miss Hui seemed impervious to the enervating heat, the sense of subdued panic in the air, and the sheer unpredictability of it all. For this, Peg was grateful; Miss Hui's calm kept little Tommy on an even keel. She couldn't think how she would have managed a frightened, tantrum-prone toddler on this horrific day. Now Miss Hui made a seat for herself on the suitcases, with little Tommy half-asleep in her lap. Peg sank onto the bench, her handbag in her lap, a handbag bulging with all the unaccustomed items crammed into it at the last minute.

So many things, all left behind in that frantic few minutes. Nearly three years of her life – her married life with Tommy, all the little bits and pieces of a settled, happy existence, the easy routine of things in the sprawling bungalow – all swept away, but for a few bits in her suitcase. She had been half-asleep, and harried; she would have made a better and more sensible choice of things to take with her, had she been fully awake and thinking more rationally.

The baby turned over and kicked within her. Peg gasped, at once startled and relieved. No hurt taken to what Ada called 'the sprog' on this awful, draining day. Now it was Ada returning, with a somewhat lightened expression on her perfect English rose of a face.

"Not to worry, Peg. They are all mining people, from up-country. Their husbands work for Anglo-Oriental, and they're being taken care of; parceled out to the houses of Anglo-Oriental employees here in KL for the term of evacuation. I think we should get a room; I could murder a stengah or two, and you and the sprog ought to have something to eat, and a good long rest afterwards. Then," and Ada's expression hardened. "I believe we should go on to Singapore in the morning. As soon as we can."

Letter, from Peg to Vennie, dated December 27, 1941, postmarked Singapore, Federated Malay States.

Dear Peg:

As you can see from the postmark, Little Tommy and I are safe in Singapore, staying with Ada Dawlish's older brother Arthur Nicholl, who keeps a very comfortable home in a pleasant garden suburb of Singapore in the Lady Hill Road. All British women and children in Penang and Perak were evacuated at mid-month, by order of the L.D.C., because of the threat from the invading Japanese. Ada and I traveled together by car to K.L. – a hideously uncomfortable journey. When we parted, at a bare twenty-minutes notice, he gave me all the money that he had left after paying all the estate and household workers as well as his bank book so that I could draw on his account when we reached safety in KL or Singapore. Both Tommy and Ada's husband Reg had commanded that we should go to Singapore as soon as we could, for safety sake, which is what we did – a journey almost as nerve-wracking as the drive to there from the estate. The train was very slow, often interrupted for no reason that anyone could tell us, other that troop trains had the priority right of way. The war front is somewhere around Jitra, where there is supposed to be a great battle being fought by Indian and Gurkha troops.

I have had no word of my husband since his Volunteer company was detached to serve with the regular Army, and he kissed me and our son, said 'goodbye' and sent us off with Ada in her husband's car. He went in the other direction with his fellows in the Company, including Chandeep Singh, who is an old soldier, a veteran of many big and little wars. I hope that if anything, Chandeep Singh's good sense and advice will keep my husband safe. There is nothing but distressing rumors, yet the radio and the *Straits Times* maintain an air of cheerful assurance about it all. There was intense fighting up-country. Singapore is full to bursting, with evacuees like myself, and military troops from India, Britain, and Australia. There have been air raid alarms most nights, although with very little result that we can see. A range of shops along Raffles Place was hit by Jap bombs overnight. It's awful to see, in person, even after seeing years of this in newsreels. A place that I knew, where Ada and I had been, the very day before ... and the next morning, all blown up, burnt, and wrecked. We were both more deeply shocked than we confessed to upon our return to Arthur's house.

Vennie, it's all quite surreal. On the surface, everything seems most desperately normal. The tenor of our days, a leisurely breakfast on the shady verandah of Arthurs's house, looking into the lush green garden, a round of shopping, playing with little Tommy, a rest in the afternoon and the usual social round – all very much the life that I have enjoyed since coming to Malaya. Arthur has been the most considerate host. He was employed for many years by the Shell Oil company. He is very much older than Ada, and his villa is almost a museum of Oriental *objects d' arte.* He is quite the collector in his semi-retirement, so his house is full of beautiful things, as well as having been constructed on the most pleasing and comfortable lines. Quite honestly, I wish that our house on the plantation had been so sensibly designed, instead of built out in every haphazard direction as necessity commanded.

Ada and I occupy ourselves with much of the same amusements as we always have but there is a desperate shadow hanging over us, more marked because no one admits it. There is almost a feverish intensity in the air, a wish to behave as if everything were absolutely normal. Ada meets with old friends and goes dancing at the Raffles and playing tennis at the Tanglin. We went there all together for a grand Christmas Day buffet. *(She says that everyone went out dancing during evenings in the London Blitz in defiance of Mr. Hitler's bombs and who am I to argue about that?)* Arthur has old friends for tiffin in the late afternoon, and I join them, and then rest, and try and pretend for little Tommy that this is all either an exciting adventure – when the air raid siren sounds, and the guns go 'boom' – or otherwise a perfectly normal visit to friends in Singapore. The amah, Miss Hui, is wonderful in behaving as if all is perfectly normal. It reassures little Tommy, but I wonder for how much longer. Little Tommy is such a willful little boy, I don't know quite how I would manage him, if it were not for Miss Hui.

One of Arthur's young Shell Oil employee friends is American and from Houston! Peter Gregory. He says that he spent summers now and again with friends in Galveston. I wonder if you and he ever met there. I do assure you that I am not flirting with him, but how comforting to hear an American accent again, and to speak with someone dearly familiar with Texas, while I wait word from Tommy!

Dearest Vennie, how are you getting along, now that war has begun and we both are a part of it, willy-nilly? Your nurse friend Helen who joined the Army Nurse Corps and was sent to Manila – is there any word of her? I hope for your sake that she is safe, although from the news reports, I fear not; Manila is as much under siege from the beastly Japs as Malaya is. I saw a bevy of Australian Army nurses today and was reminded of you and your friend, who must go where you are needed the most, no matter what the danger.

Singapore is packed full of soldiers, anti-aircraft guns, naval ships and simply awesome land artillery. Everyone says that we can endure a siege, if the worst comes to worst. I wish I could be assured of my husband's safety. Then I could sleep peacefully at night. I have had no word from him since departing from Ipoh. If it were not my own determination to remain close to where he might be, I would be on the next boat to return to Texas and the Becker ranch.

Please write to me soon.

Love, Peg (and Little Tommy.)

Letter from Vennie to Peg, dated 6 January 1942 (Returned as undeliverable as of February 13, 1942)

Dear Peg: so glad to receive your last and know that you and the 'sprog' and 'sprog-to-be' are safe in Singapore. Naturally you want to be near to where Tommy is. You adore him utterly, and as far as I can see, he is your dearest of soulmates. If ever I envy you anything – aside from being tall and devastatingly beautiful, I envy you for having the everlasting devotion of a man like Tommy. I suppose that I shall eventually attract a love of my own of that sort, although I am also envious of the literary Elizabeth Bennet for attracting a man like the prickly but ultimately worthy Mr. Darcy with hardly any effort on her part! I hope that I might eventually encounter someone of that high degree, of intellect if not of income! But you see that my main obstacle is that I simply cannot stop myself from speaking my mind, and that mind of mine is almost always leaps and bounds ahead of the usual intellect encountered among the male of our lamentably warlike species. So, there I am – I did not join the Army Nursing Corps to find a husband; I did it because I wished to serve, to participate in a time of deep need, to care for those injured in the service of our country and this immense crusade against fascists of every color and persuasion. I will go eagerly to wherever I am sent in this great cause, and if I perish in it ... well, that will be counted against the bill for freedom.

Anyway, enough of my own Deep Thoughts. You ask about my friend Helen who was sent to Manila to serve in the Sternburg General hospital. I have heard from her. There were surprise Jap air raids on Manila, which were almost as devastating as that on the Pacific Fleet – just as there were on Singapore, and indeed, all over the Far East. She sent me a brief letter, saying that she was well and safe and that she had been sent to help reopen a new hospital at Ft. John Hay but now I see that the American forces have withdrawn to Bataan. I have had no word from her since then.

It is so strange, how suddenly all this came on it, and from the direction where hardly anyone had expected! And we were supposed to be in the middle of peace talks with the Japs, too – which adds insult to the injury. I think that we would have been at war against those awful Nazis eventually, as much as we Americans were reluctant to get involved in yet another ghastly European war, but this just came out of the clear blue sky, without any warning at all – a sneak attack when we were all supposed to be at peace.

Everything has changed at once. On one day, hardly anyone was interested in news of the war, except to be grateful that we were safe from it all and then the next! Dad wrote to me last week, saying that on the Monday after Pearl Harbor was attacked, nearly all of the wranglers and ranch hands went into Deming in a body to the post office to volunteer for the services – and nearly three out of four have either given notice or are awaiting call-up. Poor Dad is left with no one to help save two or three of the oldest hands, who being unfit for military service, are of little help at the strenuous work at the ranch. Dad says that come round-up and branding in the spring that he will have to hire young boys to do that work. On the bright side of the ledger, he says the market for beef will be most profitable. Mom is still worried about me, being in the Army – she has absolutely forbidden me to volunteer to go overseas. I hate to tell her that I have already told them that of course I will go wherever I am needed, and if to a war front, then that is where I will be. Write to me as soon as you can, Cuz. I say prayers every night, asking that you and Tommy and Little Tommy and your friends are kept safe.

All my love to you and yours,
Vennie

Chapter 5 – Wish Me Luck as You Wave Me Goodbye

Letter, from Peg to Vennie, dated February 2, 1942, left unfinished and never mailed.

Dear Vennie:

I fear that things have become perilous here in Singapore, although no one quite dares to say so out loud. No one wants to be thought to be an abject defeatist but the Japs now hold all of Malaya. I think in the nights sometimes; what are they doing with Longcot? Is there some camp follower wearing my clothes, my wedding trousseau that I had to leave behind? Is a Jap war-profiteer living in our bungalow, ordering around the folk in the kampong or have they burned the lot down? I almost wish that were the case. I'd rather think of it in ruins, rather than picturing those treacherous yellow bastards having the advantage of all the work that Tommy and his father and grandfather did on the plantation.

The Army retreated from Johor to the north three days ago and blew up the causeway connecting Singapore to the mainland. We hardly noticed the sound of that, among all the racket! So now we are truly besieged, and our only outlet is through the harbor and out to sea, if our ships can avoid Jap bombers! Arthur says that what we can hear now are not bombs, but their artillery firing across the Johore Strait. The newspapers are full of stiff-upper-lip cheer, insisting that 'Singapore can take it!'

I want to go home. If not to Longcot, then to the home ranch in the Hill Country. I want to wake up in my old bedroom in the stone house overlooking the apple orchard and the river beyond and know that we are all safe.

I have had no word of Tommy, nor Ada of her husband, or any of their comrades in the Volunteers. Their company was supposed to be attached to the Argyll and Sutherlands, and there was a bitter fight at the Slim River, but ... *(Letter ends here)*

"You should go soon, both of you and the boy," Arthur Nicholl said heavily, at tiffin, on the afternoon of February 11, in the verandah of his house in Lady Hill Road. "The beastly Japs landed on the north-east side of the island three days ago, and I don't think the fighting is going very well at all for us. The chaps in the Colonial Secretary's office have already begun burning important papers."

Arthur, some two decades older than his sister Ada, had deep shadows under his eyes, having spent a sleepless night as a volunteer air raid warden, patrolling the Lady Hill Road. He looked like a man of twice his years through the sheer stress and strain of the last few weeks. Still, he was arrayed in a pristine white linen suit, a knotted tie carefully arranged. Appearances and the stiff upper lip must be maintained, and Arthur's Chinese butler, Ang, likewise arrayed in pristine linen, arranged the plates of sandwiches and cakes on the small table. Ang murmured a few words in Chinese, as Peg didn't recognize them as Malay, and withdrew, the silver salver under his arm. In the distance something that wasn't thunder grumbled almost constantly; Japanese artillery pounding the north- western shores of Singapore island. Now and again a whiff of smoke came to them on the errant breeze, and clouds of smoke stood on the horizon over the harbor, where godowns, warehouses and oil storage tanks burned sullenly.

"I don't want to go, Art," Ada replied, stubborn as always. She also looked worn, but still impeccably dressed in a cotton dress, stockings and elegant shoes for a proper tiffin. "I can't possibly leave Singapore until I hear from Reg."

"You have the girls to think of," Arthur continued, implacable. It was the first time that Peg had noted anything of adamantine determination in Ada's older brother, who otherwise gave the impression of a languid and slightly effeminate aristocrat. "Safe and away in England. I am certain Mrs. Morehouse ought to go, also. She has the boy to consider and the unborn child as well. For your safety and hers – especially hers, since ..." Arthur Nicholl hesitated. "If Singapore is taken by the beastly Japs, it will not be a good place for a pregnant woman." He looked directly at Peg, who blushed furiously in the next moment, shocked at the uncharacteristic crudity of his next words. "A pregnant woman with her skirt around her waist can't possibly outrun a Jap soldier with his trousers around his ankles. Fact of life, my dears."

"Arthur, really!" Ada protested in great indignation, but her brother only sighed, and added a few more drops of milk – everyone presumed it to be goat milk, procured with ingenuity by Arthur's main household factotum. "You must consider leaving now, Ada sweeting, and you too, Mrs. Morehouse. The city will be under siege here for months at best. At worst, they will come in and take the place, after reducing it all to rubble. In any case, there will be the direst of hardships. If you and Reg both are interned here by the Japs for however many years until the war is over, what will become of your girls, Ada? I know they are in the custody of our sister and brother-in-law, and their boarding school, but eventually, they will need you. Your little boy, Mrs. Morehouse? Get out with him while you still can. That's my advice, considered in absolute sobriety. Three less mouths to feed during a prolonged siege," Arthur cleared his throat. "Get away while you can, and there is still a chance."

"I want to go home," Peg said, heartfelt, as the image of her childhood home, the Becker acres on the upper Guadalupe, the old stone house standing like a castle above the foaming white waves of the apple orchard in bloom below on the hillside came to her memory. "I want to go home. I can't stand another minute of this, Ada. Whether Tommy is safe or not, he will want Little Tommy and me to be safe. I'll go, Mr. Nicholl. How are we supposed to do it, then?"

Ada looked at her, over the tea table, and at first Peg thought Ada was going to be censorious, to condemn her for being a defeatist, a coward. Instead, the other woman sighed.

"I'll pack my suitcase, Art. You're right, and so is Peg. We should leave." In the shade of the verandah, and in the lush greenery of Arthur's small garden, her face looked particularly pale. "Reg would want me to be safe, and with the girls. How is this ignominious retreat to be managed?"

"Already taken care of," It didn't escape either woman that Arthur immediately appeared immensely relieved. "I've made the arrangements for you to have a passenger cabin on the *Empire Star*. She's a speedy refrigerated meat-hauling ship, fairly new. Probably not terribly comfortable under the present circumstances, but they're going to make a run for it before sunrise tomorrow morning, to Batavia and then on to Australia. Mr. Gregory will drive you to the dock and see you on board; I'll be on duty, you see. He'll be around with his car as soon as it's dark. A couple of hours. That should give you enough time to pack and have a bit of a rest before the raids begin, of course."

"Tonight?" Ada stared at her brother in absolute shock. "I didn't think ... as soon as all that?"

"There's not much time." Arthur replied, sedate as if he were relaying the schedule for a tennis tournament at the Tanglin Club. "Have your tea, then pack and say our farewells. And I regret that I must tell you, Mrs. Morehouse. It's only the two of you and the boy who will be allowed on board. Your amah must stay behind; No Chinese or Malay – only British and military personnel permitted on the evacuation ship. They're taking out as many of the military nurses and signal staff as they can."

"Leave ... Miss Hui?" Peg replied, shocked to the core. She couldn't leave without Miss Hui, Tommy adored her unstintingly, obeyed her without protest, and Miss Hui knew all about babies. She had been counting on Miss Hui – she was in all but blood part of the family, just as those Mexicans who had worked for the Beckers for three generations and more were. "I can't possibly; I need her!"

"I'm sorry, my dear," Arthur's regret was wholly genuine – of course, since he had been in the East for many years, he was fully cognizant of how fond the amahs could be of their charges, and how much their employers depended upon them. "I don't imagine that she has a passport or the proper exit permissions anyway. Miss Hui may stay on here; she was so good with your girls, Ada. Quite the family retainer. She'll be all right as long as she keeps her head down; our Singapore Chinese may not get half get the bad treatment that we English will get from the Nips, even if they have been at war with the bastards for three times as long as we have been. I'll do what I can for her, as long as I can. One of those religious sworn virgins, isn't she? There's one of their houses she can go to, if it all goes pear-shaped. Have a bite of Genoa cake, Ada. Ang will be so disappointed if you don't eat it, as he went through all kinds of trouble to secure the ingredients and bake it for our special tiffin. I will not see the dear old chap disappointed; you see."

Under that urging, Peg obediently took a bite of the luscious cake; preserved cherries and currents in a plain vanilla poundcake, and it was indeed lovely. How Ang had managed under the dire circumstances of war; likely he was as devoted to Arthur as Miss Hui was to little Tommy.

The cake instantly tasted like ashes and sawdust in her mouth, but she chewed and swallowed obediently, just as Ada did. *Keep the flag flying; don't disappoint the old servants who watch your every move and attend to every need.* This tiffin was the last gesture of defiance against the fate, which was curling in on them all, just like one of those magnificent ocean waves off that marvelous beach in Hawaii, where she and Tommy had spent a sun-kissed honeymoon. The wave would curl and crash, and only the fortunate and adept could ride it out, as Tommy had, on a long wooden board. *Where was Tommy? How would she explain all this to him, when – if ever – she saw him again?*

Peg took one last bite of the cake, a sip of the plain tea, and pushed the plate aside.

"Thank you, Arthur. I suppose that I should go break the news to Miss Hui. And pack. I haven't got very much more than what I brought from Longcot, so that shall make it easier."

"Australia," Ada mused. "Well, it should be easy enough to get a cabin Home from there. Will you stay with Tommy's people in Brisbane?"

"I suppose that I will," Peg replied. "His mother offered to put us up several times, when the war began, but I didn't want to leave Tommy. I guess I will stay in Australia, until we get word from him. I will not go any farther, until I know ... something. For certain."

She got up from the table, briefly unbalanced because the baby kicked inside of her. The baby: she must protect the baby and Little Tommy now that the nearest safety for herself and the children lay in Australia. That was a primal impulse, overriding all other desires.

She went to the rooms that had been given to her and Ada, and Little Tommy, in Arthurs' lovely and luxurious villa, where every room gave onto a shady verandah and a view of his meticulously groomed garden. Late afternoon, the time when she was accustomed, through war and disruption, to have a time to play with her son, to read him a story, while Miss Hui hovered attentively. Little Tommy was riding energetically on a carved and painted nursery horse, an aged item procured from somewhere in Arthur's household which Ada claimed that her own daughters had played with. Ada said it had been called "'*Arry, the 'Airless 'Orse*" by her daughters when small. It pleased Peg no end to see the energy with which Little Tommy rode the rocking horse, thinking that someday, God willing, she would see him ride on a real live horse. At home, at the Becker ranch in the far distant Hill Country.

Miss Hui supervised, as usual, crouched in attendance, not far from "'Arry the 'Airless 'Orse." She straightened and stood as Peg entered the room.

"The Oldest Son is doing very well today, Mem, as you might see. Mem Peg ..." Miss Hui hesitated and looked at Peg with a curious expression on her face. "Is there something wrong?"

"I am sorry," Peg felt tears start in her eyes. "Mr. Arthur has said that Mem Ada and I must go tonight on the evacuation ship. We have only two hours before the car comes for us. All us mems and our children must be gotten away before ..."

"The Japanese dwarves come," Miss Hui finished, solemnly, with calm acceptance. "The war goes badly for the *tuans*. Of course, you and Mem Ada should go. There are bad things which might happen."

"I'm so sorry," Peg said again, overwhelmed by a sense of despairing failure. "We've let you down; everyone who trusted in us. In the British. Everyone said that Singapore would stand a siege, that we could hold out like Malta did, but the Japs took all of Malaya in two months when they should have taken years, and Arthur says that they landed three days ago on the north shore! If they had been driven back, it would be all over the radio and in the *Times* but they obviously haven't and I don't even know of my husband is alive, or not ..." and suddenly she was sobbing unashamedly, crumpled on the floor. Everyone always said that pregnancy brought on these sudden tearful moods, but Peg had always thought that she was proof against all that, but not now, not here, where the grumble of distant artillery carried on the fitful afternoon breeze, and *where was she going to sleep tonight, or was she to even live for certain beyond the next few hours*?

Peg was aware of Miss Hui's firm hands on her shoulders, as she sobbed against Miss Hui's pristine white high-collared blouse, and then of Little Tommy at her side, asking something in Chinese? Chinese? Little Tommy was supposed to be spoken to in English, as his father had insisted. Miss Hui produced a clean white handkerchief – a man's handkerchief, broad and soft and devoid of any useless frippery trimming, and Peg wiped her eyes and blew her nose into it.

She must be strong now, strong for her son and the new little one. Else they would grow up without having any sure and certain confidence in the adults around them and that would be disastrous. It was the first duty of parents, to seem unshaken, confident, in control. Like Miss Hui. No matter what happened, nothing in her voice and conduct must fail after today, nothing must be allowed to damage her children's well-being.

Time to be a grown-up, Peggy, she seemed to hear Vennie say, acerbically. Vennie had said when Vennie and Ivy were dressing her for the wedding, in the sunlit bedroom of Grandpa Sam and Granny Jane's house in San Antonio. Vennie, so small and capable – she said that, as she settled the bridal tiara and veil on Peg's blond head and secured it with a handful of hairpins. Peg had suffered a sudden attack of bride's nerves; doubt and dismay at what she was about to do, in marrying a man she had only known for a month. *'Don't be such a baby, Peg,'* Vennie replied. *'You love him, and you said yes when he popped the question. Besides, if you change your mind now, your father will never be able to get your money back from Joske's for these ghastly dresses. They've already been altered to fit Ivy and me. Time to be a grown-up, Peggy.'*

Time. The memory of that brief exchange steadied her; nearly a miracle, considering the frantic fears and tears of before. Now – the time to be an adult.

"It's all right, Tommy," Peg said, and handed the soaked handkerchief back to Miss Hui. It calmed her, how even and bluntly practical her own voice sounded to her own ears. "It's just that we must go on the ship tonight and leave Amah. I'm sorry, but Amah doesn't have the right papers, just now. You and I will go to stay with your granny in Brisbane. She's been longing to see you."

Crumpled on the floor of the guest bedroom, Peg watched her son's face, as Miss Hui murmured to him in Chinese. She had no idea of what Miss Hui actually said – only that it was confident, and those words reassured her son. She watched his infant features go from tearful and confused, to an expression mirroring Miss Hui's own resolve. But he flung herself into Miss Hui's embrace, before Miss Hui kissed him on his forehead and set him on his feet.

"I will pack some things for Tommy-Baba," Miss Hui announced firmly. "And your own, Mem – have you considered those?"

"I don't care about anything that can be easily replaced," Peg replied, which meant the wedding album, to which had been added a collection of pictures taken on her own little Kodak of Longcot, and the silver-framed portrait of Tommy. A single suitcase with the necessities of underwear, and a change of clothes for her son. Once again, she and Ada were leaving with all that could possibly be carried in a small travel case.

"I can take Teddy-Pooh, can't I?" Little Tommy asked, tremulously.

"Of course, you can, darling," Peg made herself reply cheerfully. "We can't possibly leave Teddy-Pooh behind. You can't go to sleep without your silly old stuffed bear."

"I'll carry him myself, Mummy," Little Tommy promised, his small face quite solemn. "Amah told me I must be a help to you and Dada. Will it be a long way to Australia?"

"No, not as long as it would be to England, or to America," Peg promised, with assurance that she did not feel very deeply, but this contented Little Tommy.

At the appointed hour Ada and Peg waited impatiently in Arthur's sitting room. Their suitcases were already outside under the port cochère. It was just before twilight, a twilight darkened by a pall of black oil smoke spewing from the refinery at Pulau Bukom. Rumor in the Lady Hill Road had it that the Shell tanks and refinery had been deliberately set ablaze. Little Tommy sat on the steps to the house, engaged in a lively but imaginary debate with Teddy-Pooh, while Ang and Miss Hui lingered there, keeping watch and speaking quietly to each other. Peg didn't understand a word of Chinese, but they sounded worried. Arthur, already clad in his ARP overall, was reading the *Straits Times*, by the light of a single light in the room.

There was little to say that hadn't already been said; the two women waited in silence. It was quiet at the moment, only the distant grumble of airplane engines from the direction of the harbor. Almost certainly Japanese; they had not seen an RAF aircraft in weeks. There was an amusing and slightly incredible story on the front page, about an Australian sniper 'counting coup' by having a fellow soldier ventriloquist distract attention by throwing his voice. Peg was not sure if she believed it or not. It had the ring of a 'tall tale' such as the old ranch hands at the Becker place had often told.

Finally, Arthur set aside the *Times*. "I hear a car coming up the road. Must be Gregory. Are you ready, my dears?"

"We are," Ada replied, settling her hat on her head, and pulling on her light coat. "Thank you for everything, Art. I don't know..." her voice caught, and then she recovered. "If Reg or Tommy comes here, looking for us – tell him that we have gone. You really ought to think about getting away, yourself."

"Why should I?" Arthur replied, calmly. "Not the done thing to turn coward, Ada my dear. Women and children first."

"Birkenhead drill," Ada sounded as if she were caught between laughing and crying. "Silly old Art. Take care of yourself, old thing. I'll send a wire when we get to Australia."

"You do that," Arthur replied comfortably, although Peg was thinking that such a message would be unlikely to be sent, if and when the Japanese took Singapore. Arthur kissed his younger sister casually, as if she were departing for an afternoon at the Club. Silently, Peg donned her own hat and followed. The auto engine sounded louder, as it crept hesitantly along the road. To Peg and Ada's mutual relief, the vehicle turned in, driving between the gateposts before Arthur's bungalow; a small and battered Ford van with the Royal Dutch Shell company logo emblazoned on the doors.

Peter Gregory emerged from behind the driver's side door.

"Your carriage awaits, milady, and milady and young lord," he said, a reckless grin illuminating his face. He was lanky and angular, like Tommy, which was why Peg had noticed him among Arthur's friends at the Tanglin, and unmistakably a Texan, which made them kindred spirits in a relatively alien world.

"We were getting worried," Ada confessed with a laugh. "But you are the hero of the hour."

"Always happy to come to the aid of ladies in distress, ma'am," Peter Gregory drawled, so thick and country-Texan that one could slice it with a knife. "I'll throw your traps in the back. Hey, young fella, you an' that ferocious critter of yours want to come for a ride?"

"We're going to visit Granny in Brisbane," Little Tommy announced. He came and stood between Ada and Peg, Teddy-Pooh clutched firmly in one hand. "Are you the syce, then?"

Peg dissolved in an agony of embarrassment. "No, he isn't," she reproved her son. "He's a friend who is going to take is to the dock, to the ship we have to go on, to see Granny Morehouse. Now, come along. We'll all have to sit on the one seat together, since there isn't any room in the back."

"I'll take him on my lap," Ada said, as Peter Gregory opened the passenger door; and that was how they piled into the van; Peg in the middle, next to Peter Gregory, and Ada by the door, Little Tommy in her lap, with Teddy-Pooh clutched firmly to him.

"I had to avoid traffic on the Alexandra Road," Peter Gregory announced, as he put the van in gear, and they set off, wedged thigh to thigh on the van's narrow front seat. Overhead, the black cloud of smoke was edged with blood-red and fiery gold. "And I shall have to take side streets, now. To be safe, you see. Slower – but you should be in time for the *Empire Star*. They're waiting on other parties, who must come from farther away."

"Are you making plans for your own escape?" That was Ada, blunt as ever. "I don't think that Singapore will last very much longer."

"I sure am, ma'am," Peter Gregory smiled, as cheery as if he were on a peacetime drive in the country. "Me and some other fellows have our eyes on a fine little thirty-footer, moored at an out-of-the-way anchorage. Tomorrow, we'll wrap up our business and be on our way. Don't worry none about us, ma'am. We'll be fine."

"If you have a chance to convince my brother to leave," Ada said, "Can you take him with you?"

"I'll see what I can do, ma'am," Peter Gregory replied, his eyes on the road ahead, as the little van bumped along. "But I can't make any promises. We might have to leave in a hurry."

"I understand," Ada replied, and then she was silent, looking out of the van's windows at the darkening streets. There were few people about, and even fewer lights, because of the air raids. The smoke-darkened skies were almost entirely black by the time they reached the harbor area, and there were many more vehicles of all sorts, as well as pedestrians along the sidewalks, many of them carrying suitcases, rucksacks, and unwieldy bundles, moving along like silent and aimless automatons, returning to their houses at night, after taking shelter in fields and gardens from the constant Japanese air raids on the inhabited parts of the city. Eventually they were crowding into the road – many of them soldiers from their packs and flat helmets, straggling along. The little van slowed to a bare crawl.

"I'll take you as far as I can," Peter Gregory finally said. "They're setting up sentry posts and road-blocks close in. You might have to walk after that."

"We'll be all right," Ada assured him.

Peter, with one hand on the steering wheel, put his head out the window, shouting irritably, "Make a space all right? Two women and a kid here for the *Empire Star* tonight, do you mind?"

Out of the darkness several irritated male voices – Australian by their accents – replied with unprintably obscene suggestions and Peter laid on the horn and continued shouting impatiently from the window. That at least got space in the road for the little van to move ahead, edging closer, and closer to the docks. Against the dark, shielded lamps shed a little light. Out to the west, sunset left a malign red glow against the horizon. Peter Gregory's little van finally came to a halt at a barricade, where an armed sentry waved him to a halt, and an officer, the muted light reflecting on his gold pips, shone a shielded battery torch into the van from the passenger side.

"Sorry, sir. Further access in't allowed," the soldier said apologetically. "Passengers for the evacuation ships have to walk from here."

"How far, then?" Peg was exhausted, at least as much from tension from the short drive from the Tanglin neighborhood as from the burden of being heavily pregnant.

"Not far," the officer replied, as he helped Ada and Little Tommy down from their seat. Peg slid out, feeling awkward and clumsy. "Sorry, ma'am; I can't let your driver go any farther. Do you have your exit papers and passport ready? Oh, jolly good. You'll need them ready. Will you need help with the baggage, ma'am? I'm certain that I can..."

"I would hate to put you to any further trouble," Ada retorted grandly. "As you have already been so much help!" She had their pair of suitcases, which Peter Gregory handed to her from the back of the van, one in either hand. It didn't escape Peg that Peter grinned broadly at that sally, even as Ada thanked him for his care for them on the tension-ridden journey from Arthur's house.

"I'll see you soon!" He ruffled Little Tommy's hair, nodded to Ada and shook Peg's hand. "Safe journey, OK! See you in Australia."

"I'm sure we will," Peg replied. She was altogether positive that she would never see Peter Gregory or Arthur Nicholl again, not this side of the grave. "Take care, Peter."

He waved jauntily and got into the van – turning it with much care, among the fresh crowd, pressing against the guarded barrier. In a moment, the van was out of sight. Peg took Little Tommy's hand, and she and Ada walked along the crowded docks, following a crowd of other women, most of them trailing children and lugging suitcases just as they were, although there was a bevy of Australian nurses ahead of them in the straggling column.

There was an air raid alarm wailing near at hand. Hardly anyone paid attention, so hardened and accustomed had everyone came to these eventualities, and so urgent was everyone's need to board the *Empire Star*, whose black hull now blocked the view of the harbor. She was a well-traveled and well-known steamship at Singapore and KL, new-built for the express purpose of transporting cold-storage beef from Australia, in which enterprise she made frequent stops at ports all the length of the South China seas. An array of derricks and hoists sprouted from her top deck, all the better to shift cargo with. Not a particularly luxurious transport, but an accommodating one, which offered two-score of private cabins on the first deck for the convenience of travelers in no need of luxurious accommodations.

Exhausted beyond all but the most basic feelings, Peg took little notice of their cabin, which they were told would be shared with several other woman evacuees and their children. The deck of the *Empire Star* was packed thick with military trucks, and piles of gear covered in tarpaulins, while the *Star's* crew directed the evacuees below, or to the first deck cabins; Peg saw them as shadows in the dark, with hooded battery torches casting small puddles of light at their feet. Their voices were heavy with weariness and just-barely contained anxiety.

"I don't care," Peg said, crawling into the lowest of the four bunks. She was fully clothed, sweating from the humid heat in the confines of the tiny cabin. "I just need to lie down. I'm spent, Ada. I need to rest." Without a word, Little Tommy joined her.

"There, there, Mummy," her son said, with all seriousness. "Teddy-Pooh is here, now. Will you sleep well with Teddy-Pooh? I always do. Amah said that I am big and brave now, and Oldest Son. Do you need Teddy-Pooh, Mummy?"

"Not so much," Peg answered. She hugged Little Tommy and his precious bear to her, lying comfortably at her side on the narrow bunk. "I have you now, sweetheart."

Peg's exhaustion was so complete that she slept without waking until dawn. She was only roused at dawn by a change in the underfoot movement of the *Empire Star,* briefly roused as the great ship cast off and then she drifted off to sleep again, for some time. From a conversation overheard the night before, she and Ada gathered that it was too dangerous to attempt the passage out of the harbor in the dark. Unmarked minefields in the dark, or Japanese bombs and torpedoes in daylight – a fine choice for the captain of the *Empire Star* to have! Light gleamed around the blackout curtains secured over the cabin windows. She was alone in the bunk. The other women, with Ada and Little Tommy must have gone out to watch the last of Singapore diminish in the distance. Although Teddy-Pooh lay in the bunk, a sight which made Peg smile to see. She straightened the blanket and single pillow, and propped Teddy-Pooh on the pillow.

She was ravenously hungry and thirsty as well. *What provision had there been made for meals?* She opened the door to the cabin and realized with a slight sinking feeling that probably none at all. There were simply too many people on the ship. The deck was even more jammed with vehicles and gear than she could have seen in the dark the previous night. A sea of flat soup-plate shaped helmets met her gaze, interspersed with the occasional solar toupee, civilian hats – mostly female – and the flat-brimmed boaters worn by the Australian Army nurses, of which there were a scattering.

Singapore was veiled by smoke, under which the morning sun painted fingers of light against those buildings still standing along the waterfront and jumbled along the lush green hills behind. A vivid chiaroscuro, in which it was still barely possible to pick out those landmarks which had become familiar to Peg during the achingly-long two months in Singapore; the marine parade along the coast to the east of the harbor, punctuated by the spires of the various churches, the shouldering roofs and grand facades of those great buildings along Raffles Place. She looked for where she thought Arthur's garden and house might be, on the hills beyond, but all slowly dimished as the *Empire Star* crept cautiously out towards the Malacca Straits.

Several grey ships accompanying her at a distance, Peg noted, but then she spied Ada's hat, and the back of her pale teal-blue coat, among those crowding the rail, looking back at the place which had been home, and a touchstone for so many. Peg went to join her friend, noting with increasing alarm that Little Tommy was nowhere to be seen.

"I'm awake now," Peg announced, as she shouldered into a place at Ada's side. "And where is my son? What have you done with him?"

"That little monkey?" Ada's gaze didn't waver, from where it was fixed on the vista of Singapore, as the *Empire Star's* powerful engines churned towards the west, in the direction of the Malacca Straits. "Don't worry; I haven't dropped him overboard and anyway; he has a life jacket on. He's made friends with some Australian soldiers. He's quite their darling little pet now, since he told them all, solo and chorus, that he is going to Brisbane to see his Granny and that he is the brave first son of a very brave soldier. They're not quite upright chaps, though," and Ada turned to fix her gaze unswervingly on Peg. "There is a rumor that they've deserted their posts, the most of them, just to get on this ship."

"You can hardly blame them, Ada," Peg replied. "You've been saying for weeks what a cock-up the conduct of this whole bloody campaign is. I can't hold it against them for wanting to get out, by the fastest way possible. Can you?"

Ada fixed her gaze on the distant vista. "Perhaps not," she replied, a note of despair in her voice. "It is in my mind now, Peg, and I can't put it aside. Reg is dead, and this is the last that I will see of Malaya, ever. I'll go home to England with my girls and wait for the war to be over." There was nothing to say to that, and Peg kept a considerate silence. The sea breeze now turned fresh and salt, diminishing the heavy scent of smoke and burning oil, even as the harbor and shoreline diminished in the foamy wake of the steam ship. The steamer seemed to shudder under a new burst of speed from her mighty engines. "We're well out into the Straits. There's Mount Fabor." Ada continued, as if her momentary despair was set aside, once voiced. "I believe that they usually drop the pilot about now. You know, the harbor pilot who knows how to negotiate passage in and out? Singapore is especially tricky, so I've been told. You don't see the pilot boat anywhere, do you?'

"No," Peg answered. "It could be that he – whoever he might be – is evacuating as well. He'd be a valuable prisoner for the Japs." Unbidden, Peg's stomach rumbled from hunger. "I don't suppose there's a chance of a cup of tea, or a bite to eat?"

"With all these people on board? Not likely, but we'll try the salon. Maybe a cup of tea, but I don't think much more. With the warehouses all bombed out, I don't think they were able to find much." she lowered her voice and added, "Ang made up a little picnic bundle, a thermos of coffee and some biscuits and tinned meat, and the rest of that lovely Genoa cake. He was afraid that we might starve, you see – without him to cook for us. Miss Hui put in a bottle of cold ginger tea and some sweets for your son just in case you both feel the motion and get sick from it. Miss Hui swears by ginger tea."

"I feel like such a louse, leaving them behind," Peg confessed.

"At least you gave her the rest of your Straits dollars and told her to buy food with it, while they were still worth anything," Ada added, in an approving tone. "Honestly, I would never have thought of that."

"Family story," Peg answered. "From my grandfather - he remembered his mother telling someone at the end of the War Between the States that they ought to spend the Confederate money on food, as long as the bills had any value at all ... Ada, do you hear airplanes?"

"There," Ada pointed, off to the north and west. "See them? Japs, of course. Would there be any other in the sky today?"

"Find Tommy," Peg felt her heart turn cold within her. A ship at sea, and the Japanese overhead, cold, murderous and remorseless. And she was all alone with Little Tommy.

Chapter 6 – When The Lights Go On Again

"Where's Tommy!" Peg demanded of Ada, as the half a dozen dark gull-shaped objects in the distant sky dropped lower, becoming clearer and more menacing by the second. A Klaxon alarm somewhere on an upper deck began to blare, to the accompaniment of shrieks of dismay from the women around them at the ship's rail. "Oh, my god – I have to find him, now!"

"He was just here a moment ago!" Ada replied, completely rattled. "I only looked away for a moment!"

"That's all it takes!" Peg replied, in rising panic. "You take your eyes off him for a second, and he's running down to the kampong, or making friends with a stray dog, or half a block away because he has seen something interesting …"

"He's over there, with those soldiers," Ada slumped in relief. "See him?"

"I am so angry that we had to leave Miss Hui," Peg replied, through gritted teeth, and began pushing her way through the crowd, most of whom were scattering in the other direction, towards safety in cabins or below decks. She herself was headed towards where her son was perched on the shoulders of a husky Australian soldier, who was evidently hoisting him higher so that he could admire a pair of Lewis machine gun mounted on some prominent bit of the deck, a portion of which must once have supported a crane or derrick of some kind. "She knew him well enough not to take her eye off him for a single, solitary instant! Tommy!" Peg shrieked, trying to be heard over the panicking exclamations of other women, the blare of the ship's Klaxon alarm, and increasingly, the roar of airplane engines. She pelted along the deck, as rapidly as her condition allowed, Ada at her heels. Tommy's bright blond head stood out like a beacon, hoisted as he was above the crowd of soldiers in their dust-colored shirts. She saw her son's head turn in her direction and that he waved, childishly excited. This was a nightmare beyond any imagining. "Tommy, get down!" she cried again, over the deafening roar of aircraft engines, the answering Klaxon, and the thought-obliterating concussion as those guns mounted on the *Empire Star* began to fire.

She simply could not hear for a moment, as she reached the cluster of Australians with her son at the middle. The soldier holding him swung him easily down to the deck, and his lips moved as if he were talking...

"...below!" he said, as the soldier next to him looked around – a quick assessing glance. That one had several cloth stripes sewn on his shirtsleeve and displayed an air of competent authority.

"No time," the soldier with stripes shouted – at least Peg could hear those words. "Ma'am, take cover, now!" and without any ceremony at all, she and Ada were bundled and crammed into the narrow gap between two of those military trucks lined up on the *Empire Star's* crowded deck, and Little Tommy was shoved into her arms. "Keep low!' the soldier with the stripes shouted, and whatever else he said was lost in the awful cacophony. Peg shrank into the smallest space that she could imagine occupying, crouched protectively over her son, in between the two trucks. In a tiny corner of her mind, she was aware of smells; the odor of … something – cordite perhaps, overlaid with salt-water and fire, and pungent male sweat. Something else, a particularly sharp odor.

Fear. The odor of fear.

Over their heads – hers, Tommy's and Ada's and the soldiers; the heavy machine gun began to fire. Peg pressed her hands on her ears, but the very sound seemed to drive out all coherent thought from her brain. She could see over Tommy's head and Ada's shoulder to a thin strip of blue sky and sea beyond the *Empire Star's* rail and the Japanese aircraft plummeting down, down, larger and darker. Just so an attacking hawk must look to a small animal or a defenseless chicken, cowering on the ground.

Something hot fell from above and lodged in the collar of her blouse. With one hand, she brushed it away, and a brass shell fell to the deck. It would have clattered, but for the sound being lost in the cacophony.

Amazing; she could almost see streaks of white-hot fire from the muzzle of the heavy machine gun, arching into the sky towards the Japanese dive bombers. *Oh, that was called 'tracer'.* She dimly recalled Tommy talking about that to her, after a drill with the Volunteers. Every couple of rounds fired from a machine gun was a fiery tracing round, so the gunners could see where their bullets were going and adjust aim accordingly.

The soldiers around them were standing up and firing their own weapons. A useless gesture at best, but she thought, dizzily, that it was at least something. One of the soldiers standing above her stooped down and put his flat, soup-bowl shaped helmet on her head. He must have seen the hot brass falling, falling like a peculiar metal rain shower. Ada had another on her head as well. Peg felt a brief surge of pride in them; the best that soldiering had to offer at that moment, gallantly protecting women and small children to the best of their ability. Those Australians were Tommy's sort, the best and bravest that the male of the human species could offer.

She looked out through that narrow gap between the vehicles stowed on deck; obviously essential to the war effort, as they wouldn't have been taken off from Keppel Harbor otherwise. To her savage satisfaction, she saw that one of the torpedo bombers was wavering in flight, like a dove fatally winged in flight in a shoot over the fields below the Becker ranch in hunting season. It went down into the sea, in a brief sparkle of red flame, a plume of white-water spray and a cloud of black smoke just short of the *Empire Star*. A second torpedo bomber broke off from a steep attack dive, trailing more smoke pouring out of the tail section as it limped away just above the level of the *Empire Star's* masts.

She didn't see where the other dive bombers went, only the hideous roar of their engines somewhere out of her sight beyond the truck. A line of rapidly splintering gashes scarred the deck as they strafed the ship. She heard the crash of bombs landing on the *Empire Star*, felt the deck shudder, and the ship rocking violently. For a long moment Peg was certain that the ship was fatally struck and on the point of foundering; *where was her life jacket, then*? Although she was a strong swimmer, how would she manage to keep Little Tommy afloat! In the next second, the noise from the Japanese bombers diminished, even as the Klaxon alarm continued clanging. Someone somewhere cried out in pain. Incongruously, the sound of female voices singing floated up from somewhere below decks.

"Is the ship hit?" A dazed Peg clambered to her feet by leaning against the hood of the truck which had sheltered them all. Her ears still rang from all the racket. "Is it going to sink?"

"No bloody fear," replied the Australian sergeant. "She's hit, but not with anything that matters. The bloody Nip bastards 'ull be back again, though, bet London to a brick on it. You two better get below with that little nipper before they do."

"Thank you, Sergeant," Ada replied, as cool as if they had casually encountered on a city sidewalk. "I do believe we will take that advice. Thank you for the loan of your helmet, as well."

"No fear, ma'am" he replied, grinning, as the other soldiers also grinned. One of them ruffled Little Tommy's fair hair, and the other retrieved the helmet which Peg handed him with a murmur of thanks. "You take care; you and that little nipper!"

"Mummy, are you frightened?" That was Tommy, perfectly composed.

"No, not really," Peg lied, although her knees still trembled, and her heart felt like it would pound its' way out of her chest entirely.

Tommy scooped up three or four spent brass, which had been rolling around at their feet, exclaiming, "Treasure!"

"Save them for the next scrap metal drive," Ada advised, and added in a low voice. "I think that we had better put on our life vests, Peg. And have a bit of breakfast. One should always abandon ship with a full stomach, don't you think?"

"Not in front of the child!" Peg hissed, although it didn't appear that Little Tommy had heard that last. He was too busy showing off his spent shells to his soldier friends, juggling them from hand to hand, as they were still quite hot.

"It's all right, Peg – I was just teasing," Ada replied. She squinted into the sky, shading her eyes with one hand. "Whatever happens … We'll be all right. I think. I hope."

Letter from Peg to Vennie, dated March 4, postmarked 54 Heath Street, E. Brisbane, Queensland Australia

Dear Vennie:

I started a letter to you before we left Singapore, and never mailed it, so I do confess that I owe you one extremely long missive, containing an account of how Little Tommy and I came to depart from Singapore on the morning of the 12th, with

Ada Dawlish at the insistence of her brother Arthur, who had very kindly made us guests in his home in the Tanglin neighborhood – how dependent I am on the kindness of my friends, and my husband's kin! Arthur Dawlish made it possible for us all to depart on a fast steam transport ship, the *Empire Star*, which had a barely a dozen cabins to shelter more than 2,000 evacuees. I think that the larger part of them were military personnel, mostly RAF support technicians, Australian soldiers, and a great number of military nurses. Poor things; there was no place for many of them on deck or in cabins, so that they were down in the cargo holds, which were supposed to be used for shipping refrigerated beef! The decks were crowded with vehicles, and piles of essential gear, all covered over with tarpaulins.

We heard the nurses singing, quite bravely all throughout this ordeal. The ship was attacked in the mid-morning of the day that we left Keppel Harbor. It was quite nerve-wracking and ghastly, as you might well imagine. For about four hours, the *Empire Star* was under intermittent attack from the air, as we passed through the Durian Straits. Three bombs did land, but did only a little damage, apart from destroying one of the four lifeboats on board, and setting fires which were swiftly extinguished by the heroic efforts of the crew and some volunteers. Considering all those on board, there were only fifteen dead, and as many wounded. The dead were buried at sea a day later, just before we reached Batavia. Which was most fortunate, considering all the high explosives bestowed upon us by the Nips! Some of those were so close that they almost seemed to launch the ship out of the water entirely.

Ada and I and Little Tommy, with several other civilian evacuees took refuge in our cabin, although Ada declared now and again that she simply could not hide from this during the moments when the Jap attacks left off; she ventured onto the deck and brought back reports to us as we were huddling in the cabin, telling stories to amuse and distract our children! She says that we were attacked by nearly sixty bombers at once, and that falling bombs fell within ten or twenty feet of the ship – into the water and exploding on either side with only the result of sending up fountains of water! The crew of the ship managed to steer between those volleys launched against it! It was a miracle that the ship survived all this, relatively unscathed! The captain and crew performed with admirable courage and assurance. I cannot think how they managed it all; it makes me regret how useless and weak I am myself in these trying circumstances and respect you all the more for responding to a call to duty!

We reached Batavia safely on the 13th, spent two days there waiting on repairs, and continued to Freemantle, Western Australia on the 23rd. There were no more attacks by the Japs after that day in the Durian Strait – how fortunate we were! From news reports, many other ships were not so lucky as the *Empire Star*! Our compliment of evacuees in Freemantle were met first by the local chapter of the Red Cross, which was quite curiously comforting. They came with simply bags and bags of clean fresh clothing, to offer to us evacuees who had come away from Malaya with only a single small suitcase permitted. Honestly, I had nothing more than a couple of changes of underwear and a spare smock, and one change of clothing for little Tommy. You can imagine how unspeakable those garments had become, after a fortnight-long voyage in the tropics! Singapore surrendered to the bloody Japs several days after our departure.

Ada Dawlish parted from us in Freemantle. She is resolute in her determination to return to England, by any means necessary. She was able to secure passage on a liner to England, departing from there within weeks. She said goodbye to us with some regret. She still knows nothing about her husband's whereabouts. I think she has taken a mental refuge in assuming that he is already dead and beyond all aid and consideration. I am convinced otherwise of my own husband – I am certain in my heart that he lives, although he might be – almost certainly is in horrible peril. Surely, I would know, somehow, if Tommy were dead since our connection is so close!

Little Tommy and I were put on the train at Freemantle, and after many a days' journeying across the wide and desolate bulk of Australia *(seriously, a good portion of that journey does remind me of the bit between the Hill Country and El Paso, all bleak and featureless desert)* and several inconvenient and lengthy waits to change trains, we eventually arrived in Brisbane. I am staying now and for the foreseeable future with Tommy's mother, Edith, and her husband Stanley Frobisher at their absolute insistence. Of course, they both adore Tommy, and hope for his safe return. Little Tommy is also adored, and I can feel that at least for the time being I am arrived in a safe harbor.

Stanley is retired from employment with Guthrie's the rubber magnates and has an independent income. They live in a beautiful, airy house on the outskirts of Brisbane, not far from a pleasant park by the river, which is a short walk from their house. Picture a large bungalow set on tall pilings with a shallow corrugated tin hip-roof, and a deep veranda all the way around. The 'lectric' hasn't reached out from the city yet, so the house is lit by gaslight and kerosene lamps – quite old-fashioned. There is a well with a water-tank – just as there was at the ranch.

I love Edith and Stanley's house. Imagine all kinds of ornamental wood lace and ferns and flowers in baskets hanging from the eaves of that verandah. And – it's quite like where we both lived growing up: an outhouse in back *(they call it the 'dunny' here – a man with a cart comes once a week to collect the box full of once-used food.)* The little house behind the house is overgrown with jasmine vines. I must look out for redback spiders, a particular plague in this part of Queensland, whose preferred lurking ground is under the dunny seat. Ugh. *(It's not true that everything in Australia wants to kill humans. I believe the sheep are perfectly amiable.)* The garden surrounding Edith and Stanley's house is a perfect miracle. Every kind of tropical plant one might imagine, including several huge and shady mango trees. I would adore this, save the mangos go from 'not ripe' to 'disgustingly overripe' with the speed of light, and the odor of the 'disgustingly overripe' moldering on the ground is something to which I must become accustomed. Sigh. I loved our mangos at Longcot, always perfect, juicy, and full of flavor.

Tommy's mother Edith *(she wants me to call her Edith, not Mother or Mrs. Frobisher, or anything formal like that)* is fifty-something, and quite devastatingly masterful. Stanley is amused by her, it appears. He lets her have her head in most things, and now and again says something calm and mediating. Little Tommy has become quite his pet, as he has nothing but time to spend with our little boy. Stanley is teaching him how to whittle, and to bait a hook and go fishing in Norman Creek, a short way from the house!

Stanley and Edith appear to have quite a contented marriage. Since I am the espoused of Edith's cherished son, and the mother of her dearly beloved grandson as well as soon to be additional grandchild – anyway, it is all most refreshing, so far from home, to be considered all but blood their dearly beloved daughter. Since I only knew Edith through her letters and from what Tommy said of her, I feared that she would be the awful mother-in-law. I am relieved on that front; Edith and Stanley both insist, without reservation, that I must indeed stay with them, until something – anything! –for certain is known about Tommy, no matter how many years that might be. Tommy's income from the estate is all but drained. Until the war is over, there will be no support from that direction. But since his volunteer company was called to active duty, he is considered a soldier in the British Army, so there is a small stipend for us as his family on that account. I am terribly grateful for this allowance. Our baby is due in another month, so of course, I may laze about until then. But I do not wish in the least to be a burden on Edith and Stanley, and eventually I think that I must do something, even if only for a distraction from thinking and worrying about Tommy, night and day.

Mavis is Tommy's half-sister. She is almost 17 – I am not certain what to make of her. She is brash and forward, which may be to her advantage, since she doesn't have much in the way of conventional good looks. She looks like a female version of Tommy ... yikes! But she does have the promise of eventually being a handsome, elegant woman, rather than pretty. She is all but finished with school; I suppose in normal times she would have come to visit us in Malaya and perhaps found a husband there. She talks of getting a job in a war industry, or perhaps joining one of the women's services. I don't quite know how to talk to her. I feel as if I am ages older and can barely recall being her age at all.

(later) March 15

Vennie, I promised you a long letter, and a long letter you shall have. I have just felt so dreadfully tired these last few weeks. A delayed reaction to all that we have endured over the last few months, or so said the doctor who examined me. Edith absolutely forbade me to do anything at all, save sleep and rest, and then sleep some more, lest any further exertion harm the baby – which if the doctor is correct, will be born later this month, with all its' little fingers and toes. I received a brief visit from Peter Gregory, who had seen that Ada and I were safely embarked on the *Empire Star*! I had shared this address with him, hoping that he would make a safe escape from Singapore. He and twenty of his fellow Shell employees commandeered a motor launch and enough supplies and fuel, upon being told that the city would surrender to the Japs the following day. They made their way across the Malacca Straits and worked their way down to Batavia, by means of only traveling at night, and concealing themselves in river inlets and hugging close to islands during the day. He says they were spotted several times by Jap AC, but they had taken the precaution of wearing Malay clothing and suitable hats, so appeared entirely innocent from the air. At Batavia, they managed to take passage on a British warship which delivered them to Brisbane. Such were the frantic and disorganized conditions in those last days that he was not able to find Ada's brother, Arthur Nicholl, and convince him to escape as well. I do not think that Arthur would have come with them even if they had done so. It was a very difficult journey, and Arthur was an older man and not in the most robust condition to endure such hardships in an open boat in the tropics. The newspapers are full of accounts of other fortunate escapes from Malaya, and I hold onto the hope that my husband might be among them.

Love from your dear Cuz,

Peg, Little Tommy, and 'the bungle from heaven'

PS – added 26 April – Baby Bungle delivered safely last night – a little girl, to be named Olivia. Edith, Stanley and all very well pleased, and Little Tommy is over the moon with his new little sib, although disappointed that she is not a ready-made playmate -- Peg

Letter, dated 20 May 1942, postmarked Fort Slocum, New Rochelle, NY

Dear Peg:

So happy to hear your wonderful news! Does the Baby Bungle Olivia look like a Becker or a Morehouse! I can hardly wait to see pictures of her, and I suppose that her grandmother and step-grandfather are spoiling her every much as she (and you deserve!) Their house sounds so pleasant, in the word-picture that you draw for me. It is all for the very best that you have such a lovely home for now with Stanley and Edith.

It is so very reassuring in these times to have normal things like babies to take pleasure in, even at a distance of a wide ocean and most of a continent. As for myself, I am engaged in the pleasant occupation of sewing. The powers-that-be have finally conceded that we military nurses simply cannot be expected to wear our traditional white outfits when we are operating in a field hospital. Are you pleasantly surprised at their grasp of the painfully obvious? Alas, they have not been able to agree on anything the least bit official and practical in this regard. In the meantime, the interim solution is to issue us all several sets of Army overalls, which would be practical, except that these garments are sized for men; very large, very tall men! I tried on one of mine at first, to general hilarity.

My friend and roommate, Ruth N. said, "Vennie, don't you dare sneeze, or you'll lose everything!"

Honestly, one might have put two of me in these overalls or made them to serve as a shelter with the addition of a couple of tent-poles! We are busily employed in tailoring them to fit, or at the very least, to present a not so ridiculous appearance. We have also been issued helmets for use in the field. In overalls and helmet, I look like nothing so much as a large mushroom. I cannot even begin to find a pair of boots small enough to fit my feet, not without wearing several layers of heavy woolen socks. I am a martyr to blisters.

You asked in one of your letters, if I had heard anything more from my friend Helen Drinkwater, who trained with me at Sealy. She is a prisoner of war, I am afraid, as were all the Army and Navy nurses remaining on Corregidor. I had a brief note from her last month, carried by one of those who were sent out from there at the last minute before the Japs overwhelmed the fortress and tunnel complex. She said that she was well and hoped to continue being able to care for her patients, and that she would not have done anything the least bit different.

Has there been any word of Tommy? You would think, had the Japs any decency, that they would make a list of prisoners available to the Red Cross.

Love,
Vennie

Letter, dated 15 August 1942, postmarked APO, New York

Dear Peg:

Well, are you surprised at receiving this letter? I am in England now at regular garrison camp in a location which the censor likely will not allow me to name, with {unit redacted by censor}. There is a certain large prehistorical stone monument usually attributed to the Druids some miles distant from where I am now, which might give you a clue to the general area. I think this is not far from where your Granny Jane was born.

We could not say anything to anyone – loose lips sink ships, as it says on all the posters – nor can I say anything about the trip 'across the pond' except that it was refreshingly dull, against all of our worst fears. It was still a relief to be lightered off the ship, to look back and see how <u>big</u> it was at anchor, and then to set foot on solid ground again. We came by train from the port of arrival. I cannot say exactly how long the journey was. Again, loose lips, et cetera.

What did I think of England, though? Oh, dear Peg – everything is small, terribly quaint, and I must confess, comparatively made sad, grey, and dreary by three years of war and rationing of every blessed thing you can imagine, even though it is late summer. There are boarded-up windows everywhere, and even those which still have glass in them are covered with 'X' of tape in every pane. There are sandbag barriers in front of important buildings, and not a road-sign to be seen, anywhere out in the country. At night, the blackout is almost complete. You could see the stars ... that is, if it weren't for rain. Rain in late summer – what a bizarre thing!

We were at leisure for a number of days, and Ruth N., Muriel P. and I took the train to London to see the sights, such as they are. We got to look at the Tower of London from a distance, and admire Parliament, the tower of Big Ben, and Westminster Abbey. But you cannot imagine the hopelessness of seeing row after row of bombed-out buildings, and not a sign of rebuilding. Those streets of houses on the outskirts of London and other towns seemed inexpressibly dreary, for the sameness of dark red brick all grimed over with black coal soot. The people we met all along the way were most splendid, and the conductor on the train took the time to explain the money to us; a dear little man with an artificial leg and a country accent that we could hardly make sense of sometimes. *(Neither could we make sense of the money, either – and not for lack of him trying!)* He was a soldier on the Somme in the last war, you see, and couldn't do enough for us when he found out that we were Army nurses. Most people that we met were thrilled to bits and treated us almost as if we were Hollywood stars, although there was that one gentleman in the café who grumbled, *"Well, it was about time that Americans got into it!"* but the waitress apologized for him, and upon finding out that I was raised on a ranch and knew all about roundups and cattle drives and all that, she asked bashfully if I knew Mr. Gary Cooper personally.

Well, such was our brief holiday. I have bought some English picture-books at Foyle's the bookshop for little Tommy as a Christmas present from your devoted Cuz, and a tiny coral necklace for Olivia to begin her collection of jewels. I saw the necklace in a little antiquarian shop in Knightsbridge, and the owner said that it used to be traditional for babies to have coral necklaces. I will try to mail them to you when I can – and hope that they arrive in time. I like to think that they will have a shorter journey, going from England to Australia now!

Love,
Vennie

Chapter 7 – G.I. Jive

2nd Lt. Venetia Stoneman silently poured herself another cup of coffee in the near silence in the officers' wardroom of the *HMS Orbita*, an old and lumbering British ocean liner, now converted to a troop transport ship. The *Orbita* lay two miles off the shore of Algiers in the pre-dawn darkness. The wardroom was crowded with men and women officers, a good few of the men and all the women part of her unit, the 48th Surgical Hospital. The concussion of an artillery round landing close to the waiting invasion fleet sent the *Orbita* shuddering. Proud that her hand didn't tremble in the least, Venetia looked across the table at her friend, Ruth Norris.

"Welcoming committee," Vennie observed and Ruth grinned. She was a big, rawboned woman in her mid-thirties, a divorcee with a school-aged boy, now sent to live with Ruth's parents in Vermont. Polar opposites: the sturdy and stoic New Englander, and the short and outspoken Westerner, yet they were best friends. Nothing much shocked Ruth; ten years in nursing and a disastrous marriage had rendered her proof against any shocks which the Army could show her. Until now.

The Americans were about to land on an enemy shore. Vennie, Ruth and the rest of their medical team would be landing with the second wave, intending to aid the wounded on the spot. Vennie and Ruth were both fully clad in their field utility overalls, boots, and helmets, with packed musette bags at the ready; a last hot meal before ... before who knew what conditions would they meet? Vennie honestly wished they could get it over with – the butterflies in her stomach fluttered madly.

"I wish that I had more appetite for this," Ruth observed with distaste, pushing her plate away, as the sounds of the artillery barrage from shore intensified. "You know, everyone was hoping that we'd land unopposed, that the French would give in at first opportunity. But from the sound of it, we'll have work to do as soon as we land."

"A lot of work," Captain David Marcus nodded; he was a thin and highly-strung New Yorker, a married man with three children back in Brooklyn, a surgeon, and head of Vennie and Ruth's operating team. Vennie sometimes marveled at his hands. Captain Marcus possessed the most beautiful hands that she had ever seen on a man; as beautiful as they were skilled. He was a city boy, through and through, and insisted all through their outdoor training marches at Tidworth Barracks, in deepest Wiltshire, that there was something deeply unsound and unhealthy about so much untrammeled nature. He insisted that he preferred the sounds of car horns and tires on pavement to birds singing and crickets chirping. As for cows and horses, he affected to shudder in horror whenever Vennie told them stories of life on the ranch. They had all become quite good friends, since becoming part of the team, more like sisters and brother, without the least shred of romantic interest.

Now the senior nurse, 1st Lt. Margie Worth threaded her way between the wardroom tables. It appeared as if most of the others at breakfast had as little appetite as Ruth and Captain

Marcus. Lt. Worth was a former airline stewardess and had as much experience in Army medicine as the other three put together; a southern belle from Virginia, soft-spoken and model-slender, she made the roughly tailored Army overalls somehow look elegant.

"If you are all packed and ready, Colonel Mellish says that we can go up to A Deck starboard and watch the soldiers loading from B Deck, as long as we stay out of the way," Lt. Worth told them. "It'll be a good bit until the landing barges come back for us – at least a couple of hours."

"I'm for that," Ruth nodded. "I'd like to see what's going on."

"You'll not be able to see much," Lt. Worth warned them. "They've put down a smoke screen to hide as much as possible once the sun comes well up."

"Still, at least we can cheer them on," Vennie replied, but Lt. Worth was right; they couldn't see much, in the thin directionless light of what would have been a mid-morning. A thick cloud of smoke lay against the water, veiling the shore, occasionally punctuated with a brief yellow flash. Instead, she and Ruth could lean out over the A Deck rail and watch as two landing barges moored against the heaving metal flank of the *Orbita*. A fixed metal ladder gave access downward from B Deck to one, and a rope cargo net to the other. The barges resembled nothing so much as a shoe box with a blunt prow and a large engine attached.

"Dear God, I hope that we get to use the ladder!" Ruth commented.

"It'll be a bit of a drop, either way," Vennie observed, as the two barges heaved up and down in the gentle swell – which looked gentle from above, but at the bottom of each swell, the barge was at least a man's height below the end of the ladder. Left unsaid was the possibility of missing the barge and going straight down into the cold grey-green water.

They watched as each barge filled with men, anonymous in their field gear, packs and rifles and the tops of helmets all packed tight. As each laden barge pulled away, the men in it looked back and up at the *Orbita's* packed decks, waving a farewell. Then they faced front, as each barge vanished into the smoke barrier, lost to sight while another empty barge glided out of it, moored alongside, and began to fill in turn.

Around midday, Lt. Worth appeared on A Deck.

"All right, ladies, we're next. Colonel Mellish and his HQ company have already gone. Five nurses, two surgeons and twenty corpsmen to a barge, just as we were briefed. And – before you start down; unlace your boots, undo your pack and helmet straps. That way, if you wind up in the drink, you can wiggle out of them before they pull you down. When you get to the bottom of the net or the ladder, wait to drop off when the barge rises to the top of the wave. You won't fall as far."

"It wouldn't do to injure ourselves before we even get to shore, would it, ma'am?" Vennie observed, and Lt. Worth grinned.

"The Army wouldn't get the good out of having generously brought you all this way on this luxury cruise, would it, Lieutenant Stoneman?"

"Heavens to Betsy, we wouldn't want to scant the Army now, would we?" Ruth added.

"Off you go then," Lt. Worth bid them, for the crowd on the A Deck was already thinning out. *Time for the second wave. Now.*

Obedient to instructions, Vennie loosened her bootlaces and unfastened the strap across her chest that secured the small pack. Her steel pot helmet strap already hung loose. Drat – she had drawn the rope net and not the metal ladder.

She experienced a brief moment of vertigo upon climbing over the rail, clinging to the rope cargo net, and looking down. A wave of sheer terror swept over her, and she clung to the net, fighting a desperate urge to vomit. *No, not in front of everyone.* The barge was nearly full – she could not possibly be a coward and hold up the team. She forced her fingers to open their death-grip on the rope, felt with the toe of her right foot for the next step down. Then the left. Right, left, right left. One hand for the next grip on the rope. Down, and down, careful, and deliberate, the twenty-six pounds of essential gear in her pack tugging at her shoulders. *New handhold, down and down again* ... she looked across and saw Captain Marcus also moving deliberately down the net. He nodded in silent approval, and Vennie was reassured. No, this only looked awful from the top. They were nearly down to the barge, bobbing on the regular, rhythmical tide. On the next upward rise …

"Now!" Captain Marcus called, and he and Vennie let go of the net and fell into the bottom of the landing barge. She felt a brief bolt of pain shoot up her shin. Three more nurses, including Ruth, and Captain Romanesco, the medical company's dental officer were coming down the rope net with the same care. It didn't look nearly as far, from the bottom as it had from the top. The massive metal hull of the *Orbita*, studded with bolt-heads and scars of painted-over rust, rose and fell.

The landing barge offered a much rougher ride; if this went on for very long, Vennie was afraid that she would be vilely seasick. She found Ruth's hand, steady and warm, as the barge cast off and began circling away. The other barge, containing the rest of the medical party had already loaded up and moved away, bobbing like a cork on the ocean swell. They stood shoulder to shoulder, packed closely; as the men would say when they thought no woman was listening – nuts to butts. There was nothing to sit on, and no room to do so anyway. At their feet, water washed back and forth on the barges' deck, the racket from the engine tore away any words that anyone might say in anything other than a shout. The barge plunged into the smoke screen; for many long minutes nothing could be seen beyond the barge's sides, and nothing but the occasional rumble of artillery heard over the thunder of the barges' engine as it plunged through the water.

The smoke lifted. Vennie, by dint of standing on tiptoes could see a bit ahead; a long, low-lying shore, with a line of dark green hills in the far distance. She thought they must be less than half a mile from that shore. Captain Marcus cupped his hands around his mouth. It looked as if he were the senior officer in the barge.

"When we get close, crouch down as much as you can!" he shouted. "The minute the bow ramp goes down, get off, move as fast as you can to shore, and find any shelter you can! Got it?"

There wasn't much room to take shelter, below the level of the barge's sides. Being short, Vennie didn't have to crouch as low as some of the taller corpsmen, or the lanky Captain Marcus. She saw nothing more of the shore until twenty long minutes later while the barge wallowed forward, until the moment where the engine ceased to howl like a mad thing, and the bow-ramp clanged down.

There was North Africa, framed in the barge sides, tan and dark sullen green in the distance. A scattering of sheds, shacks and small buildings fringed the beach above the high-tide mark.

"Go!" shouted Captain Marcus into the silence, and the front rank of men stepped forward and off the ramp end.

"We're not close to shore at all!" Vennie cried, utterly appalled to see that the first men into the water immediately sank in it up to their shoulders. Something zipped like a wasp over her shoulder and struck the engine housing with a pinging sound.

"Move it or lose it, ma'am!" someone among the corpsmen shouted, and she was carried forward in the rush, stepping off the ramp into water up to her mouth. But only for a moment; Captain Marcus had her by one shoulder, one of the enlisted corpsmen had her by the other, and she was rushed forward between them through the cold grey-green water until her feet found purchase on the sand, and the water was only up to her waist.

"That place would be the best cover!" Captain Marcus gasped. 'That place' was a rickety shack on pilings fifty feet from the high-tide line. Soaked to the skin, Vennie and Ruth pelted toward that slender cover. On that hurried way, Vennie observed small spurts of sand leaping up, and wondered what kind of strange North African animal created that odd effect.

"Sniper!" gasped Ruth.

"*Mamzers!*" snarled Captain Marcus, as they hurtled at a dead run across the shore, and underneath the brief shelter offered by the shack on pilings. "Don't they see that we are medical personnel?! We have red crosses clearly displayed! What is wrong with them!"

"They don't care two licks, the Nazi-loving bastards!" Vennie replied, furious beyond all measure. She couldn't decide whether this was because of being soaked to the skin or shot at by snipers. In a few moments, they were joined by the other nurses from their barge, Lt. Worth, and a handful of corpsmen – all soaked to the skin. Vennie shivered; the wind bit through her wet clothes. *Who would have thought that North Africa would be cold, even in winter?*

"Did you see what happened to the other barge?" Lt. Worth asked, urgently. Vennie, Ruth and Captain Marcus all shook their heads.

"I didn't see them, after we came out of the smoke," Captain Marcus replied.

Captain Romanesco ventured, "I saw a barge off to our right as we came into the clear. I suppose it could have been them. If it was, they could have landed farther down the beach. If they've stopped sniping at us, I'll go and look for them."

"Good," Captain Marcus agreed. He looked around at the party huddled underneath the beach shack. "Right then. Lt. Worth, your girls best stay here for now. Ro, see if you can find the others. The rest of us will scout around and start assessing the walking wounded. I don't think we're anywhere near where we were supposed to be landed."

"We expected anything to go to plan, sir?" ventured the most senior of the corpsmen.

"I have my optimistic moments, Corporal Gregg," Captain Marcus replied, "In this case, I was absolutely convinced that we would wind up in Timbuktu. Successfully delivering us to North Africa is a most promising development. The sniper fire is diminishing from a heavy shower to merely a light drizzle. Off we go, then."

The two officers and the corpsmen scrambled from underneath the shack, vanishing in several directions. The five women huddled in the sand under the shack, listening to the rumble of artillery and the distant crackle of rifle fire. It did seem to be diminishing as the afternoon wore on.

"I think the firing is letting up," Lt. Worth ventured, after some minutes. She squinted at her watch. "Damn. I think the water ruined it. What time do you think it is?"

Vennie crawled on hands and knees to the seaward edge and squinted up at the sun, now sliding down in the western sky. "I'd guess it's about four o'clock."

"Oh, for a waterproof watch," Lt. Worth shook her wrist and lamented. "I've had this watch forever..."

"Maybe you can get it fixed someplace," Vennie replied. "Look – I think I see the others!"

Along the beach, a knot of people in drab green Army fatigues appeared – too far distant to make out individuals. But as they came closer, Vennie could see that the shortest among them were women, and that was Captain Romanesco leading.

"Oh, my, Muriel," she said, when the handful of other women joined them underneath the shack. "Don't you all look like a lot of drowned rats! What happened?"

"Our barge got off-course, and overturned," replied Muriel Prendergast. "And we all got dunked in deep water." Muriel's dark hair hung in strands down her back and shoulders. She crossed her legs to sit, Indian fashion on the sand, and began wringing out salt-water from her hair. Meanwhile, Captain Romanesco had been consulting with Lt. Worth.

"All right, ladies," Lt. Worth raised her voice. "Colonel Mellish has established his HQ in that big place farther up the beach. They've found a place for us to bunk up in for the night, since the fighting has moved back from the beach – that cottage over there." She pointed at a small house, another fifty or so yards in-land, sitting on the higher ground beyond the sandy beach." It's hardly the Ritz, since it was used as a strong point by the French, but Colonel Mellish and Captain Ro say that it's cleared, and a bit sturdier than this place, which the Big Bad Wolf could blow down in three puffs. We'll break out the C-rations for supper and spend the night there."

The sounds of battle had faded to a mere distant rattle, like someone making popcorn. The ten women abandoned the rickety shack and hurried over the short distance to the bigger, more substantial building. More solidly built than the shack, with plastered stone walls and a gaily colored tile floor in two rooms, the seaward facing windows had all of the glass in them broken out. There was not a stick of furniture in the place, and the tile floor was filthy with dried blood and excrement. Spent brass, broken glass and unidentifiable shreds of rotting garbage littered the floor.

"You are certainly right; it isn't the Ritz," Vennie observed philosophically. "I'm certain guests there are potty-trained."

"Be it ever so humble, there's no dump like home," Ruth agreed. The women hunkered down against the seaward-facing wall, a wall which had been warmed somewhat by sunshine, slipping off their packs with sighs of relief. Each of them had been supplied with three days' worth of C-rations. Vennie had 'stew with beans', and Ruth a can of 'stew with vegetables.'

"Honestly, I'm not hungry enough to eat a whole can," Vennie suggested. "Let's share."

"Wish we could make a fire and heat it up," Ruth said. "Make it a little less disgusting. Anyone got crackers?"

"I do," Muriel replied, and the three of them huddled together, scooping out the congealed stew and beans on slips of cracker, and watching the landing unfold.

Now that the heavy fighting had moved inland, more barges began arriving. The concealing bank of smoke had been allowed to disperse, and the stretch of ocean below was as busy as a disturbed anthill. Now the heavier landing craft arrived, carrying bulldozers, trucks, and tanks in an endless rotation. Bulldozers clanked along the shore, busily compacting sand to make a harder surface. For a time at dusk, several enormous floodlights made pools of light in the cavernous hulls of the landing craft, but after sunset, blackout was observed. Darkness fell, broken only by cold starlight and the distant greenish reflections of muzzle flash from artillery, reflecting off clouds in the fight for Oran, some twenty miles distant. With pieces of wood as brooms, the nurses succeeded in cleaning off enough filth off the floor inside, but the smells still lingered. Vennie pillowed her head on her pack – and did her best to sleep, aided by exhaustion, and only somewhat hindered by her damp clothes and the hard tile floor.

"Vennie, wake up. We're needed at battalion aid," That was Ruth, shaking Vennie's shoulder. "Colonel Mellish sent for us, to meet him at the HQ. We're to bring all of our gear."

"I'd love to get a cup of coffee first," Vennie uncoiled from the disgusting floor. "Maybe they have some at HQ. Doesn't a full bird have enough authority to lay in a coffee supply?"

"I wouldn't know, ma'am," replied the soldier who loomed beyond Ruth, a dark shadow against the stars outside of the broken window. "He just sent me to get Lieutenants Stoneman, Prendergast and Norris. That's y'all, isn't it?"

"It is, much as I am pained to admit it, Private," Ruth replied, as she gathered up her small musette bag and wriggled into the pack harness that set it onto her back. She took up her helmet, and said, "Take us to our leader, then. Any idea how the fight for Oran is going?"

"No idea, ma'am, not my pay grade, not my worry," the soldier replied. They followed him silently, the path faintly illuminated by starlight to an even bigger and more battered building where Colonel Mellish had set up medical HQ. Half the roof had fallen in. Their escort led them to a door in the wall of that half which hadn't collapsed in a shower of broken terra-cotta tiles and swept aside the Army waterproof shelter-half that sealed the small room inside against light escaping – light that could give a target for a sniper. Colonel Mellish, Lt. Worth, Captain Marcus and Captain Romanesco were inside, with another officer whom Vennie didn't recognize.

Vennie rather liked Colonel Mellish, who reminded her of old General Millefield, although two generations younger. They had shared a breakfast table now and again at Tidworth Barracks, and Colonel Mellish was absolutely tickled to discover that Vennie knew all the rude verses to the tune of *Garryowen*. Colonel Mellish was another of those old soldiers, now on his second or third war, and quite relieved to know that the nurses were sturdy and determined enough to go where duty led them, unflinching. "You modern gels," Colonel Mellish was given to observe now and again. "Did a good thing, allowing women the vote and all. The tougher sex, you know, even when most would claim otherwise. I've seen women walk away from the most appalling circumstances ..." He was given now and again to enlarge on those of the medical variety. At this moment, in the harsh white glow from a butane lantern hanging from the low ceiling, he looked every year of his age.

"Ladies, we hate to rouse you out in the middle of the night," Colonel Mellish said, as the door curtain fell to. "But there's been all hell to pay today, and the boys at the battalion aid in Arzew can't keep up with the casualties arriving so fast. I've got to send the three of you forward to help."

"Of course," Vennie said.

At her back, Muriel Prendergast murmured, *"Then I heard the voice of the Lord saying "Whom shall I send? And who will go for us?" And I said, "Here am I. Send me!"*

"Goodness knows what you will find there," Lt. Worth nodded her approval, "But I have every confidence you'll do as good a job as you can. At least, these will help those God-blessed boys if they are in too much pain." She handed each of them a substantial box of morphine syrettes. Be careful," she added. "We're running low on supplies, as well. Most of our stuff is still stranded out in the harbor, or God knows where. Are your water canteens full? Good; you'll need to save as much water for yourselves, until our supply lines get sorted."

"We'll be creative, ma'am," Vennie promised. She sketched a hasty salute, grateful that General Millefield had also taught her that. The other nurses had otherwise very little by way of instruction in the military courtesies.

A pair of enlisted soldiers waited outside for their party.

"There's a jeep for you all, over there," the nearest said, a dark shadow in an even darker night, after the light inside; a shadow who cursed inventively as a bullet whined overhead.

The jeep was a bigger, boxy black shape in the darkness. Vennie had her night vision working again. Captain Marcus climbed in next to the driver, and Captain Romanesco boosted Vennie, Ruth and Muriel into the back, before squeezing into the front. A soldier with a Thompson machine gun perched on the front fender – another in the back with the three nurses, and they set off toward Arzew in a clash of gears. Vennie thought that they had found a road after jolting over a series of ruts and craters. Every mile or so, a sentry with a shrouded flashlight emerged from out of the night, and their driver slowed, to exchange passwords and countersigns. To Vennie's unvoiced amusement, the password of that night seemed to be

"Hi-ho, Silver!" and the countersign was "Away!" Half an hour brought them to the edge of a city – narrow streets between tall, blank fronts of buildings, interspersed with the up-ended feather-duster shapes of palm trees. The faint staccato popping of gunfire intensified, as they came closer to the center of Arzew, which seemed to be a city of some size, as things in North Africa were considered.

Vennie racked her memory for anything that should recall reading which might afford some enlightenment; perhaps in the *National Geographic*, before the war began, or in the newspapers afterwards about the British Army campaigns in Libya and Egypt. Her bucket into the well of knowledge came up mostly empty: There was a lot of desert, and a handful of harbor towns scattered the length of the North African coast, with nothing much in between. It seemed that the American landings were supposed to be in aid of the British, or so had everyone agreed when the topic came up on board the *Orbita*, once everyone was briefed on exactly where they were to be going. Now the jeep rocked to a halt, in front of a tall gate in a high wall – plastered white, to judge from the faint starlight reflecting against it, and the ever-present and vigilant sentry. Once again, the password and countersign.

"In here," their driver gestured with his thumb. "There's a door across the courtyard – they'll let you in. This is the town hospital, and a real dump once the Frogs and the Ay-rabs got done with it. Good luck, Sir – and ma'am."

"Thank you for getting us here, in one single piece," Vennie replied, still sore from having slept briefly on a hard tile floor and then a comfortless journey in the back of a jeep. They fumbled their way across the roughly paved courtyard. There was a darker rectangle against the far wall, which hinted at a doorway. Another shadow moved – still another soldier sentry. The darker rectangle was a blanket, and behind it, a door, into even deeper darkness.

The sentry opened the door following on a brief head-count, saying, "OK – they sent for more doctors, you're them, all right? Follow me. Mind your feet ... Capn' Warren, the relief surgeons and the nurses are here."

Oh, my god, Vennie thought, as she went through the doorway. *The awful smell*. Dirt and blood and wafts of ether, pungent as anything from a cornered skunk. Almost as horrifying were the half-stifled moans in the darkness. Then the sentry at the door let the blackout curtain fall too and flicked on a flashlight. Vennie gasped in sheer horror.

Litters of wounded men covered almost every inch of the floor, with barely enough room between for one to step through and around – and puddles and seeps of dark blood oozed from beneath many of those litters, where dressings applied perhaps hours ago could no longer stop the bleeding of their wounds.

Captain Warren looked up from where he stooped over a litter, unshaven and cadaverous with exhaustion.

"Thank god," he said. "Ro and Marco – operating room is on the second floor. Scrub up and get started. Ladies ... you'll be assisting eventually, but we need you to start assessing the patients we have. We've been swamped since sundown, and they're still coming in. Sort out who needs surgery right now and send them upstairs. The rest can ... the rest can wait."

Vennie nodded. This was so much worse than she had expected. This was like that ghastly scene in *Gone With the Wind*; Scarlett O'Hara looking for a doctor at the Atlanta rail yard, and discovering the wounded laid out as far as the eye could see.

"They all look the age of my boy!" Ruth whispered, in momentary anguish, until she recovered control. Muriel's face was already set to endure, but Vennie thought that her lips were moving in a silent litany.

"Follow me, ma'am," urged the corpsman assigned to guide Vennie. "There's two more rooms on this floor." He also didn't look any older than Ruth's son, far away in Vermont. Vennie followed him into the farthest room, stepping carefully over and between litters. The last room on the ground floor was stygian dark, only relieved by the pool of light from the corpsman's flashlight. She stepped carefully between and bent over the first patient she came to. Another very young soldier, barely of an age to shave regularly.

"Where are you hurt, soldier?" she asked, gently, and he blinked up at her, dazed.

"C'n I have a drink of water?" he whispered.

"Sure, soldier," Vennie replied, already observing the cracked lips and sunken eyes of dehydration.

"Ma'am, there's no water in the city," the corpsman lurking at her elbow advised. "The Frogs cut off the mains – all there is here in this building is from a tank on the roof."

"I have an almost-full canteen," Vennie replied. She pulled the canteen from her belt, raised the young soldier's head. "Look – no more than a mouthful, just to wet your lips. We don't want you getting sick if we have to put you under."

A stronger voice came from several stretchers over. "Holy cow – it's an American woman! Where in the world did you come from!"

"Well, soldier, my mother always said I came from heaven," Vennie replied. "But I'm Vennie Stoneman, Lieutenant Stoneman, from Deming New Mexico, USA. And I'm a nurse and there are fifty of us over here, just to take care of you all. So, don't you fuss any, do what we and the doctors tell you, and we'll get around to fixing you all up soon enough."

"Yes, ma'am," the voice replied, already sounding stronger. Vennie bent over the wadded dressing on the first soldier's thigh and hip. This was one which had begun to ooze more blood.

"Take him upstairs," Vennie directed the corpsmen. "Tell the doctor – looks like something clipped the femoral artery. If it breaks open ..." she left the rest of that unsaid, knowing that the corpsman and Doctor Marcus would know how dangerous that wound might be without surgery, but the patient didn't need to hear anything of that.

Chapter 8 – When They Sound the Last All-Clear

In the early hours of the day after landing on the beach, Vennie completed her portion of the task of assessing the flood of wounded into the Arzew town hospital. The flood of new patients from the fighting to take Oran from the Vichy French had mercifully slowed to a trickle, although conditions in the hospital itself had not improved in any noticeable way. She joined Ruth and Muriel at the top of the stairs to the second floor, feeling as though she ought to be completely exhausted – but somehow curiously energized. This was what she had volunteered to do; why she had sworn into the Army, put on a set of baggy Army overalls, climbed down a rope net slung over the side of a troopship, all for the purpose of caring for American soldiers at the moment of their direst need. She had traveled to Arzew, down a long and winding road, to do exactly this. Ruth and Muriel looked as if they mirrored those feelings of exhausted triumph.

"Done for now," Ruth said. "Although – my god. I've seen the results of awful accidents come in by ambulance, but never anything as thick and fast and as many as this. Good Lord, in ten years of work in a big-city hospital, I've never seen as many bullet wounds as I did in half an hour in this last morning."

"And knife-wounds," Vennie added. "Dear god, I thought I had seen the worst that men could do to each other late on a

Friday night or a Saturday morning on the wards at Sealy. But there was a story that I heard ..." Her voice trailed off, and Muriel asked,

"What, Vennie?"

"About after a battle," Vennie answered. "From my grandmother. Granny Sophie had a great-aunt or something, who was a battlefield nurse during the War Between the States. She only talked about it once, to Granny Sophie, ages and ages ago. Now I know why."

They all started, as Captain Romanesco emerged from the room on the second floor which had been selected to serve as the operating room, mostly because it had boasted a twenty-watt bulb on a long length of flex and a sink with a faucet which provided a thin dribble of water from the cistern on the roof, until the electricity failed entirely, and the water tank ran dry. Captain Romanesco was haggard, and his bare arms were bloodied up to the shoulder. Proper antiseptic procedures had also gone by the board, in these dire circumstances. They were swabbing down the bare minimum in the operating theater with pure alcohol – for as long as that would last. It had turned out that all that the battalion operating station had to work with, was what had been in the various surgeon's kit when they departed the *Orbita*, twenty hours previous; a couple of pairs of surgical scissors, some clamps, and single scalpel and a tiny sterilizer fueled by alcohol. The one-time hospital had been looted bare after the Vichy French troops evacuated the city; no beds, no operating room table, nothing that wasn't nailed down.

Their operating table was a door laid across a pair of crates, and a third crate served as a seat for the anesthesiologist. Captain Ro's eyes looked like nothing so much as a pair of blood-shot fried eggs.

"Ladies, how long is your hair?" he asked, abruptly.

"What?" All three nurses stared back at him, utterly baffled.

Vennie was the first to make sense of the question. "To my collar-bone," she replied, and Muriel added.

"Mine's to the middle of my back. I haven't had a perm in months."

"Good," Captain Romanesco replied. "I'd trouble you all for a lock or so. We're out of surgical silk, you see."

"In the old days," Ruth enlarged to her baffled fellow nurses. "I had heard that they would use horse-hair for stitches. I guess there aren't any handy horses around here. It's for our boys. We can give up some of our hair if it saves a life."

"We're catching up," Captain Romanesco acknowledged, "For now. Stoneman, can you administer ether?"

"It's been a while," Vennie admitted, cautiously. It had been some time since she had assisted in the operating room.

"Same here," Ruth replied, and Muriel nodded.

"Beggars can't be choosers, then," Captain Romanesco said. "Come with me. I've got a maxilla-facial casualty up next, and I need an anesthetist."

As she followed him into the darker cavern that was the makeshift operating room, a stray puff of chill morning breeze blew the blanket covering the single window aside, and Vennie ducked as a bullet pinged off the stone wall at her back. Captain Marcus, standing over a patient on the makeshift table began to swear, in two languages. The corpsman with a flashlight trained on the surgical field snapped off the light and sprang to cover the window again, where a faint rosy flush had begun to lighten the eastern sky beyond the building opposite. Everyone else in the room either ducked low or flattened themselves against the wall on either side of the window, likewise swearing.

Nerves on edge from the brutal night of caring for the endless rows of wounded – this was just the final straw. There came the sound of shouting outside in the street, several more shots and then the sound of something heavy falling from a great height and impacting the street below with an unpleasantly liquid sound. There were no more shots.

"Got him," announced the corpsman nearest the window, listening to the voices outside in the hospital.

"Good," Captain Marcus answered. "More light on the patient now, please. I find that I am curiously pleased with that outcome. Funny – before today, I couldn't have imagined myself being satisfied over the death of an enemy. Such is life on the front lines ..."

Sometime that interminable morning Captain Marcus and Captain Romanesco finished and closed up the last surgical patient. Vennie, who had alternated with Captain Ro as anesthesiologist, leaned her head against the edge of the makeshift operating table and fell asleep, sitting up for nearly half an hour. She woke when Ruth touched her shoulder. Light was already seeping around the edges of the blanket hung over the single window in the room. Vennie looked at the watch, looped through a buttonhole on the front of her overalls, to keep her hands and wrists relatively sanitary. It was nearly noon.

"Vennie, we're doing rounds of patients – making certain that everyone that Marco and Ro operated on is doing OK or can wait until we're relieved."

"Or resupplied," Vennie straightened and stood, barely stifling a groan. She was so tired that her head felt as if it were stuffed with cotton wool, and her shoulders and hands ached, from the long hours of administering ether, and holding patients' jaws firmly, to ensure an open airway while they were under the effects. "Oh, Ruth – if fighting is over here in the city, surely the rest of the 48th can get to us?"

"I don't know," Ruth replied, with a yawn. There was a distant rattle of gunfire giving the lie to Vennie's hopes. The fighting was most definitely not over.

Again, the three women began on the first floor, every room packed tight with stretchers upon which the wounded lay, still clad in the filthy, blood and vomit-saturated uniforms which they had worn coming in from the fighting. There was nothing clean to replace the dreadfully soiled garments and blankets, and Vennie's heart ached for them, knowing that they risked dreadful infections, especially for those with abdominal wounds. But the blankets and uniforms, stiff with mud and dried blood, were all that they had against the cold and post-surgical shock. Vennie was relieved beyond words to see that most all surgical patients were doing well, or as best as could be expected, given conditions. The enlisted corpsmen had the situation on the ground floor well in hand.

"How are you doing with the morphine that Lt. Worth gave us," Ruth asked Vennie as they stumbled up the stairs to the rooms on the second floor. Outside in the street she heard several auto engines, but they only idled for a few minutes, and then the sound of them diminished in the distance.

"I had half the box left when Captain Ro asked me to assist, so I gave the rest to Muriel," she replied. "Muriel; how much is left?"

"Twenty syrettes," Muriel replied, despondently. "They have to relieve us soon. I've drained my canteen. And what are we to do about food?"

"I have no idea," Ruth answered.

Vennie looked at the stairs. "Are there any patients on the third floor, then?"

"No," Ruth steadied herself on the bannister. She looked positively ill. "I checked already. Nothing but rats the size of raccoons ... and the morgue. Which is full of corpses. I found a soldier in the hallway on a litter, but he was pretty bad-off. He died as they were bringing him downstairs for surgery."

"I'm sorry," Vennie comforted her friend, for she looked truly distraught. Ruth swiped at her eyes with the back of one hand.

"'s all right, Vennie. It's just that he looked so much like my little boy ... and we could do so little for him."

At that moment, the outer door opened, admitting Lt. Worth and Captain Warren, along with a gust of cold, dusty air from outside, as the blackout curtain blew aside. To Vennie's intense relief, other nurses, and corpsmen from the 48th followed after.

"Here they are," Captain Warren said. "Your relief."

Vennie was so tired that she sat down on the steps right then and there. She leaned against the wall and thought for a moment that she had dozed off, just as she had in the operating room. When she opened her eyes again, Lt. Worth sat on the stairs next to her.

"I was afraid that you all had forgotten about us," she said, and Lt. Worth laughed.

"Not to worry, Lieutenant. We had our own worries. The Italians came over and blitzed the shack on the beach and the cottage where we spent the night not twenty minutes after we walked away. We were all morning getting here." Lt. Worth put a comforting arm around Vennie's shoulder. "They found us billets in the French officer's quarters just down the road. Captain Warren is going to show you, but you'll have to walk, I'm afraid."

"I could use the fresh air," Vennie replied, and Lt. Worth laughed.

"That's the spirit, Lieutenant. Well, once you get there, get some sleep. We'll have plenty of work to do, once you're rested."

Letter from Vennie to Peg, dated 15 December 1942, Postmarked APO NY, headed Arzew, Algiers

Dear Cuz:

Well, here I am, at last with time enough to write you an awfully long letter! The French in North Africa surrendered a month ago, and the fighting front is over, more or less, having moved on from here to Tunisia. We continue here at Arzew, caring for our patients, but at not such a frantic rate as at first! Matters have calmed down, now that we are supplied and supported, and the hospital here has been fitted out with all that is proper and needful for care of our patients. We nurses are billeted half a mile away in old French barracks, which were so filthy and flea-ridden that they finally put up tents for us, on the former parade ground. We are escorted "home" at the end of every shift, and back again in the morning by an escort of Rangers from the First Battalion, and then by soldiers from the engineers, whose unit is repairing the harbor facilities. My friend Ruth, who is tall and sturdy of build – has been courted by a Ranger who calls her 'his little girl!' He is as tall as Paul Bunyan, without his ax and ox! A head taller than Ruth, who is amused no end. It is the first time in her life that she has been called 'a little girl!' At least, since got her full growth at fourteen or so. As for me, I've always been 'a little girl.' I'm done with the charm of that. Why can't I be as tall as a Becker? Enough of my lamentations regarding my personal shortcomings. Several of us had the opportunity to visit Oran late in November – sightseeing! Can you imagine? It was so very nice, to be driven in the back of a truck, rather than in a jeep in the dark, with my legs hanging over the back.

Oran is one of the leading cities in Algiers. I have to say that it looks very neat, beautiful, and clean from a distance – all whitewashed walls and red tile roofs, in terraces climbing up and down the hills from the harbor, punctuated by tall steeples, minarets, and stands of palm trees. The outskirts of the city were adorned with groves of orange and olive trees, and there were so many native Algerians in colorful robes and turbans – all so very exotic and romantic ... but that was at a distance. Up close, the walls are dingy and peeling, and the robes are faded, ragged, and the people wearing them have not washed themselves or their clothing for years, to judge by the smell. We visited the old headquarters of the French Foreign Legion in Sidi-bes-Abbes, where three of the French officers showed us around. There was a little museum in the Legion HQ, with examples of all the uniforms the Legion has worn, back to the days of one of their moldy old princes who established the Legion. They showed us through town as well but explained the reason for so many dark looks cast in our direction, as many of the locals were very pro-Nazi and not at all happy to have the

Allies in occupation now. We did not linger there for long. When we came back that evening to Arzew, we had a delivery of mail from home, and I had your latest letter.

What happy news for you, that Tommy is alive and a prisoner of war! Are you able to write to him, and send him comforts, and to tell him that he is the father of a daughter as well as a son? I do hope so. I have had no word from my friend Helen, who was reported to be interned among civilian women in Santo Tomas. It is hard to believe that just a year has passed since the attacks on Pearl Harbor, Manila and Singapore. How so many things have changed for us both in just a single year! If you can write to him, send him my love and best wishes. I was also happy to hear that the books and the coral bead necklace that I posted to you in England for Olivia and Little Tommy's Christmas presents have arrived in good time.

They should have a lovely Christmas in Australia! We at the hospital in Arzew are planning to have the same here in Africa! Lt. Worth, our senior nurse, has said that we should make it a most memorable Christmas for our patients here. Among things found by the Rangers in a warehouse near the harbor, which hadn't been looted and burned by the locals, were several bolts of red serge fabric. It is Lt. Worth's idea that we should sew Christmas stockings of red serge, trimmed with white from hospital sheets, for every patient in this place. We are sewing like mad elves, every moment that we can get – for we will need almost seven hundred. That is – when we are not working in a candy factory! Our supply officer and his sergeant assistants just happened to come by quantities of peanuts, milk, sugar and chocolate! (*We call him Ali Baba and his 40 Thieves, for no one closely inquires by what miracle they were able to come up with all this because it probably wasn't strictly regulation!*) We turn too, when off-duty and not otherwise occupied with sewing stockings – and make candy! Peanut brittle, fudge, and taffy – a lot of work, but such fun! It almost feels like normal, getting ready for Christmas. Not like last year, when everyone was so worked up over Japan attacking, and everyone looking over their shoulder and wondering what awful defeat would happen next. Now we have the Nazis on the run, and soon the Japs as well.

Got to go do candy duty in the kitchen – I'll write again when I can.

Your fond Cuz and auntie to your babies,
Vennie

Letter from Vennie to Peg, dated 26 December 1942, Postmarked APO NY, headed Arzew, Algiers

My dear Cuz:

We had our Christmas here in Algeria at the hospital and it was more beautiful and moving than I can describe. I should set the scene of it for you; the main hospital building has a central entrance hall across a small courtyard, with a wide staircase which goes halfway up the back wall with a dozen wide steps – there is a generous landing, from which two flights of narrower stairs go up along the wall to the second level. When I first arrived at this place, riding in the back of a jeep, crammed in with seven others, our legs hanging out every which way – I did not see this. It was as dark as a pit, and every inch of the floor of this hall was covered with stretchers of wounded. But as we took control of the city and calm and order returned. With hard work and dedication, our people have turned this back into a place of order and healing.

The wards are clean and airy, and the operating theater once again fully equipped with all the proper gear, brought up from the Army transports in the harbor. Our patients have clean linens and white sheets – blankets too, against the cold. You would not believe how cold North Africa is at night, during the winter!

We had such fun planning and creating a wonderful Christmas. It means so much to the men, and to us, so far away from home, and in a foreign and unfamiliar land. The comfortable rituals seem so much more meaningful. I believe that for the rest of my life I will remember this particular Christmas with much more clarity than those of my childhood, which seemed to all blend into one pleasant holiday blur, with not much to make any one of them stand out, not even the Christmases when I journeyed home to the ranch from Galveston.

Besides the candy that we made in the hospital kitchen – at least four hundred pounds of it! – the Red Cross director in Oran produced quantities of more hard candy, packets of cigarettes and small gifts for this enterprise, enough to fill every single stocking; all seven hundred of them! Our enlisted corpsmen at Arzew came up with tinsel slivered from the foil that X-ray plates come wrapped in, and many ornaments for the Christmas tree cut from empty tin plasma containers. A party among the Army engineers organizing the harbor went out into the country and cut a tall fir tree for us, which we put in the hospital foyer in a bucket of gravel and sand, just as we used to do at home. A sergeant among our patients *(recovering nicely from an abdominal wound)* was an art teacher in his previous life. He was busy cutting and folding heavy paper, and painting them with brushes and paint procured through the Red Cross *(again, all honors to the director in Oran who found these items for us)* to appear like lighted candles, pinecones, branches of evergreens, holly berries and leaves, and ornate bows and placards of Christmas greetings, to make garlands to adorn the lobby.

On the landing – which you must picture as being twelve steps up from the lobby floor – we had a small table, draped in white sheets, with more white sheets hung against the walls above, and a large cardboard cross, four feet tall, onto which we had hand-sewn purple bougainvillea blossoms was hung above it. *(Purple was the proper color for the Christmas rites, so Muriel tells me. She would know, as she is quite devout.)* The corpsmen had contrived a pair of elaborate candelabras, and filled them with wax tapers, and brought in some small palm trees planted in pots on either side of the altar, as well as two large vases filled with flowers behind the candelabras.

It was magnificent. Our Catholic chaplain, Father Powers began saying a solemn Christmas mass at midnight, at the foot of the altar. Any who wanted to attend were welcome. We had litter patients at the front, and ambulatory patients crowded in with the nurses and surgeons behind them. The choir of men – and they were all Catholic, Protestant and Jew together – began singing *"Silent Night"*. It was all so beautiful and deeply moving, Peg! I simply cannot describe to you how lovely it was. Although I am not Catholic and only indifferently Christian.

We had a small party afterwards, hosted by we nurses – with cookies and cocoa and then to our various beds. But in the morning, on Christmas morning, Captain Ro *(Romanesco, our unit dentist)* dressed in the Santa costume which we had made for him, of the same fabric that all of the Christmas stockings were sewn, and went around to all the wards, distributing Christmas stockings stuffed full of gifts: the candy, cigarettes and etc. I can't even begin to express how happy the men were to receive these simple presents, or how thrilled we were, to observe their happiness. In the larger sense, we can really do so little for them, for those who have received crippling wounds, wounds which I fear may shorten many lives, or at least make life a challenge for them. But they were all so happy with their presents – as if they were all small boys, receiving the one thing that they most desired in all the world.

This simple holiday in a foreign land, in time of war, Peg –
it all made it worthwhile to me.

All my love, to you and yours.

Vennie

Chapter 9 – Long Ago and Far Away

Peg Morehouse paused on her bicycle at the top of Park Avenue, on her way back from a fruitless errand to McWhirter's, the monumental department store in Fortitude Valley. She had left her bicycle at the Mowbray Ferry, and gone into the city proper. Once on the far side, she took the tram, searching for a pair of shoes for her son, who had been growing like a weed, lacking any respect at all for the limitations of wartime clothing rationing. Little Tommy was now nearly 4 and looking at least a year and a half older. Edith and Stanley's neighbors had begun to wonder why he was not starting school already. He was turning out to be tall and sturdy, like Peg's male cousins, with their fair straw-blond hair but his father's face and hazel eyes. Sometimes this broke Peg's heart a little, looking at her son and seeing the likeness to his father. On those occasions, she had to make an excuse to go away to her bedroom and cry quietly.

It was late in the autumn, but for Australia, it was a mild spring day. Peg lingered a few moments, wheeling her bicycle past Mowbray Park, thinking how curious it was, a springtime in the southern hemisphere; at a time when her own calendar said that it should be autumn, with oak leaves turning yellow and red, carving pumpkins for Halloween, and looking forward to Thanksgiving. The jacaranda tree out in front of the Frobisher house was decked in ruffled purple blossoms, and Ediths' spring bulbs were out in flamboyant swaths of yellow, red and blue. Earlier in the year, Stanley had hired a man to come and plough up a patch of lawn around in back for planting vegetables. Food rationing had begun; not as strict in Australia as it was reported to be in England, but still, something of a chore when it came to planning meals and clothing for the children. Edith was already planning to keep a flock of chickens and several skeps of bees, and Peg had to talk her out of trying to keep a cow for milk and butter.

"I was raised on a ranch with cows," she explained, "There's not enough in your yard to properly pasture a cow."

Edith protested, "But darling, just a small cow, a very small one!"

"The smell and the flies will drive you mad on a hot day, even worse than the dunny, and you'll be put the expense of buying fodder, or else it will help itself to your garden."

That had been the winning argument. Edith cherished her garden. Peg smiled, thinking fond thoughts of Edith and Stanley – her mother-in-law, and stepfather-in-law. Edith was tall and distinguished-looking rather than beautiful, with a slightly beaky nose and a wildly unruly cloud of hair which had had already gone quite white. She had the same hazel eyes as Tommy and little Tommy, and quite eccentrically preferred to wear men's trousers for every-day and a wide shady straw hat when she worked in the garden. This excited disapproval among the more traditionally minded neighbors along Heath Road, Peg knew, although most of the ladies wrote it off to Edith being eccentric and English anyway.

Stanley was a little shorter than his wife, with red hair which had gone in patches to grey where he hadn't gone bald entirely. His mustache was in red and grey patches as well. Genial and soft-spoken, he was the most erudite and widely read man that Peg had ever met. He worked crossword puzzles with an ink pen, rather than in pencil; Peg had never seen him to have to cross out anything and start all over. Stanley had already taught Little Tommy to read.

The two of them were magnificent as grandparents, but Peg was wearied by their frequent discussions over where small Tommy would attend school. Edith was all for Charterhouse, back in England, because Tommy had boarded there, but Peg firmly drew the line at that. No boarding school, half the world away for her small son, even if she and Olivia could afford, procure, or risk passage in time of war. Fortunately, no one else in the household at Heath Street thought that option was viable. Not with the war going on and all, as Stanley agreed comfortably. *Why not the Church of England Grammar School, just around the corner?* It was a most excellent school and Little Tommy could be a day boy at Churchie when he was a bit older. Even better, Stanley suggested in a spirit of optimism; when the war was over and the family returned to Malaya, Little Tommy could carry on as a boarder. Peg cringed at that thought. It was bad enough being parted from his father for God knows how long, but never from her children. Peg was already resolved on that. At this very moment, she wanted nothing more than to live in the present. Tommy was confirmed by the Army as a prisoner of war, somewhere in Singapore, Peg had been told. The Japanese had published a list of names on some radio broadcast or other. There was still no word of Reg Dawlish. Peg was afraid to write to Ada, now in England, for fear of hearing that he was still missing, or had been killed sometime in the six long months since she and Ada had driven away from Ipoh.

As long as I don't know for certain, she told herself. She mounted the bicycle again and pedaled off down Heath Street until she passed by another range of open parkland. On the far side, she waved to Judy Brooke, who was hanging out laundry from the clothesline at the side of the house. Judy was the daughter of a neighbor of Stan and Edith's, a courtly gentleman who was a verger at St. Paul's in East Brisbane. Judy was a pretty but sometimes flighty girl the same age as Mavis. They had been to the same girl's school together. Now both Mavis and Judy were done with school. Judy helped her mother with the household and volunteered at St. George's in Ann Street, the all-ranks, all services club organized by the Church of England parishes in Brisbane.

Edith and Stanley's house sat in the middle of next block, a rambling Queensland-style bungalow on tall pillars above a splendid garden and cropped green lawn, the tin roof like a square of tarnished silver in a jade-green frame. She walked the bicycle around the side of the house and leaned it against the shed where Stanley kept the lawnmower and his little Ford sedan, for which he had been allotted a perfectly stingy quantity of petrol coupons. Baby Olivia's massive black pram, inherited from Mavis, also was stored inside the shed.

Edith and Mavis sat on the verandah, which served as a comfortable extension of the dining room, with a pitcher of iced lemonade between them, and several tall glasses. Both were in the rough old trousers and loose shirts which served them for working in the garden. Both looked as if they had a satisfactory, albeit sweaty morning in that diversion.

Across another road and a row of houses was Norman Creek, which fed into the Brisbane River, upon whose bends and bows the town and outlaying suburbs had been built over the last hundred years, with plenty of trees and expansive parks and gardens. On the whole, Peg rather liked Brisbane, which appeared to date from the same era when most of San Antonio, and the little towns in the Hill Country had been built up; stately late Victorian and Belle Epoque structures, public parks and old neighborhoods of comfortable houses with large gardens. The neighborhood where the Frobishers lived was one of those; across the river from the main town, in a neighborhood which once had been open pasture or farmland.

"I hope that you like courgettes, dear," Edith said, as Peg came along the verandah. "There are already half a dozen as large as my hand."

"We can leave bags of the excess with the neighbors," Peg replied, "And ring the doorbell before we run away. Or ..." she sat down with a gasp of relief on the padded wicker chaise.

"Make pickles of them. Pickles are a good way to make the most of summer squash."

"We're just cooling off, before we tuck into lunch, in half an hour. Any luck with new shoes for Tommy?" Mavis asked, as she poured glass of lemonade for Peg, and Peg shook her head.

"I need a good pair of shoes myself and all the boy's shoes at Mcwhirters, and TC Beirne, or Overells asked too many points for them. What's the sense in spending all those ration points when I'll just have to do it again in four or five months when he grows out of them?"

"I'll ask around among my friends," Edith said, deeply practical. "Those who have children and grandchildren a little older than he is. Perhaps we can organize a rota among the children, to pass around shoes, once outgrown but still good. One can't have children go barefoot – just too common."

"And the nasty things one can pick up not wearing shoes," Mavis added. "Honestly, Peg, it's not as if everything in Australia is conspiring to kill us ... it's just that sometimes it seems like it."

Mavis was an undeveloped and younger version of her mother. She had finished school, and impatiently awaited her 18th birthday in five months, so that she could enlist in the Australian Women's Army Service, unlike Judy Brooke who seemed to have no other ambition at all but to flirt, and dance. Mavis was earnest and patriotic; she helped her mother and Peg manage the household and the bountifully burgeoning garden.

"Why take chances?" Edith added, comfortably. "I should go through my old wardrobe trunks. I had dozens of pairs of pretty shoes, and some of them I never wore more than once or twice. They shouldn't have gotten moldy or gone entirely out of fashion. We can get the best of them repaired or re-souled, anyway. It should be a badge of honor in times like these."

"Repair, reuse, wear it out, or do without," Peg repeated something that her grandmother had often said. Granny Jane had been practically mental about never throwing away anything the remotely bit useful.

"Exactly, dear." Edith beamed approval. "And such a good fortune that we all wear the same size!"

Mavis groaned and stuck out her own foot from underneath the table. "Thanks, Mum – reminding me that I inherited your bloody enormous gunboats."

"A tall building needs a solid foundation, dear," Edith replied, with equanimity.

"I still do need heavy shoes," Peg said again. "If we can find shoes for Tommy from among your friends, I can use my coupons to get a new pair for myself."

"Do, before all that is available is austerity stuff," Edith advised. "I remember what happened in the last war. Honestly, I'm as patriotic as anyone else, but I cannot countenance cheap and shoddily made, while everyone moans at you that it's your solemn duty to put up with it. Go and get your shoes tomorrow morning, and I'll turn out my old trunks. We're all on the roster tomorrow afternoon at the St. George Club."

"What lovely fun," Mavis sighed. "Washing dishes, serving up tea, and setting out games for the soldiers."

"We all must do our part for the war effort," Edith reminded them, and Peg sighed. Edith was very keen on the St. George Club and other service clubs and tirelessly active in organizing comforts and entertainment. The club was dedicated to providing a home away from home for military personnel on day pass or leave; tables for games, a canteen, a place to write letters and meet friends, to play records and otherwise remind the soldiers and sailors of what they were fighting for.

Peg could count on a coterie of men, Australian and American alike haunting her every footstep during the shifts she spent at the club, both for being an American, *"Hey, honey-lamb, how did a girl like you wind up in Aussie-land?"* and for being the wife of a prisoner of the Japanese. *"Go easy, mate – 'er husband was took in Malaya, an' she an' the nipper barely got away from Singapore."* In either case, the military men of three or four nations dogged her every move at the Club. Most all of them were nice boys, respectful and sympathetic and sometimes so overwhelmingly helpful that she had to beg for mercy and remind them that the purpose of the Club was to be there for them, not the other way around.

"Ahoy the house!" Stanley called from the garden below. "Lemonade! We are perishing of thirst," he added, as he and little Tommy climbed the stairs. "Tom – show your mum the magnificent fish that you caught!" Stanley and little Tommy had gone down to Norman Creek at mid-morning, armed with a pair of light fishing poles and a creel.

"Mumma!" her son exclaimed, as he ran towards her. "I caught a fish! A real fish!"

"Oh, my," Peg replied, as Stanley opened the creel and showed her the single gleaming fingerling fish which reposed there, in lonely silver splendor. "Your first fish, darling! Your Daddy would be so proud. I don't suppose that we can have it bronzed, or something..."

"We're supposed to eat it," Little Tommy insisted, and over his tousled small head, Stanley smiled at her in a conspirational fashion.

"It's too small to make a meal of," Peg explained, as Edith and Mavis loudly admired the fish. "Granny Edie has already luncheon arranged for today."

"Indeed, I have," Edith nodded. "Sausage roll and gravy, with boiled carrots and potatoes. Are you hungry, Tom? Do you know what I think you should do? We should bury your fish in the garden. It would make lovely fertilizer, you see. Wasn't there a legend of colonial days, Peg; about the Indians burying a fish with four grains of maize?"

"Anywhere but under the courgettes," Mavis said, "They don't need any more encouragement!"

Tommy agreed, although mildly disappointed. His fish was only about the size of a sardine.

"When you catch an enormous, big fish," Peg promised him, "We shall have it for supper! With bread stuffing and a garnish of lemon from Granny Edie's lemon tree."

"All right, Mumma," Little Tommy favored her with a particularly exuberant hug.

"I have to go nurse Olivia," Peg promised him, as she returned the hug. "After lunch we'll go to Mowbray Park. Take your fishing pole and see have better luck fishing in the river!"

"Yes, Mumma!" Little Tommy agreed with enthusiasm. "I want to say hullo to Daddy!" He loved Mowbray Park; the wooded paths, the gargantuan many-trunked Moreton Bay fig trees, and the waterfront walk along the riverbank, and to watch the river ferry bustling across from the city. He was also convinced, against all evidence and persuasion that the statue of the Light Horseman in the War Memorial was really a statue of his father.

"Then you will say hullo to your father, first thing," Peg promised, with a twist of pain in her heart. The face of the statue did look a little like the picture of Tommy that she had brought away from Singapore in her single suitcase. As the months passed, Little Tommy's memories of his father were dimmed; the largest part of what he knew of his father was through pictures. Sometimes Edith and Stanley shared memories of him, mostly as a boy, but Peg wondered how that could ever make him as real, as concrete in Little Tommy's mind as her own father was a part of hers. Inside the house, Olivia cried, cross and hungry.

"I'll just be a moment," Peg said, hastily. Her breasts ached – yes, definitely time to nurse Olivia.

"Take your time dear," Edith beamed at her. "Don't give Baby the colic by worrying so."

"She's a good baby," Peg answered, taking a last drink from her lemonade; sweetened with honey, by the taste of it. Lord knows where Edith had gotten the honey from, since sugar was so strictly rationed; likely arranged a trade with a friend in exchange for vegetables. Even with the extra ration allowance for nursing mothers, babies, and small children, it was hard to keep a table in the Frobisher household in the style to which it had become accustomed in pre-war years. Edith and Mavis worked like dogs in the garden and at various volunteer efforts; Mavis ate like a starving refugee and Stanley had a delicate digestion and simply could not eat certain things without upsetting it.

The smallest bedroom, with a broad window onto the verandah and overlooking the vegetable plot had been dubbed 'the Nursery'. Edith had seen to having it papered in a cheerful flowered William Morris pattern of green leaves, birds, and pomegranates when Mavis was a baby. The pattern had worn extraordinarily well and now the bedroom was where baby Olivia slept in the crib that had once been Mavis' and a small cot which Edith had procured from somewhere, just before Peg and Little Tommy had shown up at the Central Railway station in Brisbane.

Peg would never forget how she had emerged from the train on the day they had arrived under the tin roof of South Brisbane Station on the train from Sidney, a single suitcase packed with charity clothing in her one hand, and Little Tommy's small hand in the other; sick with worry, fear, and exhaustion.

Everyone they had met along that long torturous journey through Australia had been kind; almost overwhelming kind, sharing their billies of tea and damper bread, upon hearing *(not necessarily from Peg, since she was a proud woman and wife)* that she and her little boy had escaped from Singapore on almost the last boat to make it safely from there to Australia. Ever since the *Empire Star* made safe harbor in Freemantle, Peg and Little Tommy had been made welcome, helped along; really, almost overwhelmed with consideration and charity all along that long journey.

But on arrival in Brisbane, she would be met with Tommy's mother, stepsister, and stepfather. If they were awful, Peg feared – what would she do then? She had supposed that she might appeal by telegram with the last money in her purse to her father, for money to pay for a passage to come home to the United States, but how would she manage that, heavily pregnant and with a small boy in her charge? That was the fear that kept her awake at night, all during that interminable train journey through Australia, a fear that dissolved at once, when Edith and Stanley appeared on the platform, on that bleak morning when she and little Tommy arrived.

"Dear girl," Edith had said, after embracing her, straightaway. "You look exhausted. Come home and rest. You'll stay with us, for as long as needed. The house is simply enormous, and I wouldn't hear of Tommy's wife going anywhere else. You need not answer any questions from us about Tommy and what happened in Singapore until you are good and ready. I'll take that suitcase, dear." Edith then looked closely again at Peg that morning in South Brisbane Station. "I will call his surgery and ask if Doctor Moran can come to the house. You were in no fit condition for a journey such as what you have endured."

Stanley had swept up little Tommy into his arms. "Hullo, young fellow; how would you like to come fishing with me, after you have had a good rest? Oh, good. I'll teach you how to cast ... oh, and you know Chinese? Most excellent. Your amah was from Canton? How splendid. I know a bit of the lingo, don't ask me how I know it. Bit of a secret among us men, eh?"

As good as his word, Stanley took Little Tommy down to the marshy creek which traced a tangled way through the neighborhood that very afternoon – a neighborhood which was still quite rural in parts.

"Stan always wanted a son," Edith had commented, just a few days after that first meeting. "He adores Mavis, of course ... but it's different with boys. When I first met Stan in Ipoh, after the last war, he was such a Dutch uncle to all the single young men in the district. Honestly, I think that he might have been a better father to those who needed a steadying hand than those who had real fathers. It's a gift. He should have been a schoolmaster, like Mr. Chips, except that he loved Malaya and the tropics too much to have vegetated away at a minor public school."

Peg, nearly fainting with exhaustion and relief, allowed herself to be put to bed as if she were the same age as Little Tommy. For a few days, Edith had the visiting nurse sister come the house every morning, to take her temperature and listen to the baby's heartbeat. It was weeks before she felt entirely well, and then Olivia was born … and somehow it was accepted all the way around that she and little Tommy and the baby would live there, in Brisbane in the Frobisher house until the war was over, no matter how many years that might take. They even had ration books issued for them, with the address of the Frobisher residence.

Now Peg took up her daughter from the crib; Olivia immediately ceased fussing and smiled at her mother. Edith said it was merely gas, but Peg knew better.

"Luncheon is served, Livvie," she said to the baby, and Olivia grinned even more broadly, the corners of her eyes squinching almost closed. At six months old Olivia was plump and fair, so fair that her hair was practically white; a pink-cheeked and sunny-tempered baby, who only cried when she was hungry or had a touch of gas. It distressed Peg so very much that she couldn't share Olivia's developing character with Tommy. She couldn't even write to Tommy, or send him snapshots of the baby, couldn't even tell him that she and the children were safe in Brisbane. There was just a void in the world, where her husband should have been, as if he had winked out of existence the moment that Ada Dawlish's car went around the bend from Longcot, and Tommy and the other Volunteers lost to sight.

After Olivia was fed, Peg changed her diaper and her baby dress, and carried her into the dining room, where Stanley and Little Tommy waited. There was a tall infant chair set next to Peg's accustomed place, although Olivia was still too young to be fed anything more than rice, cooked and mashed. Mavis emerged from the kitchen, carrying a platter with the sausage roll and a small pitcher of brown gravy. Edith followed her, with a bowl of boiled carrots and potatoes, sprinkled with slivers of parsley and ground pepper.

"Custard and sliced mango for a sweet," Edith said, cheerfully. "And for tea, beetroot or cucumber sandwiches with a lovely cheese spread substitute for butter that Mrs. Burton told me about."

"We'll never starve, as long as Mrs. Burton reads all of those recipe pamphlets," Stanley observed. He couldn't eat whole meal bread since it gave him painful gas. Mrs. Burton was a younger neighbor, across Heath Street and two doors down, a mother of four hungry young sons, an inveterate reader of household arts magazines, collector of recipes and herbal remedies for all ills.

"Or as long as the garden yields," Edith added. "Stan, may I ask a favor? Could you build me a proper chicken coop? Mrs.

Burton has a brother-in-law who can provide us with laying pullets, as long as I have a coop for them ..."

"You'll want to keep them out of the vegetable garden," Peg added. "They tend to go after and root up anything green and edible."

"I suppose that I'll have to make a little yard for them as well," Edith sighed, momentarily taken back. "But think of it – eggs, to supplement the rations!"

"Heaven, my dear, sheer heaven." Stanley looked thoughtful. Eggs were one of the nourishing things which didn't wreak havoc with his tender digestion. "I shall see what I can contrive."

"Within a week, love, if you can manage," Edith began capably dishing out equal fifths of the small sausage roll, which was nothing more than a sort of steamed savory pudding featuring a small portion of sausage mince and a greater of chopped onion, seasoning and whole meal breadcrumbs. Nonetheless, it smelled wholly appetizing, and tasted even better, especially when doused with a little bit of brown gravy. Although Peg suspected that the gravy was made from Bisto with a leavening of flour and a meagre portion of the family's butter ration.

Stanley passed the larger portion of his sausage roll to little Tommy, which Edith heroically pretended not to see. It was good, in one respect, that Little Tommy had a grandfather to indulge and spoil him. But another reason for Peg's heart to ache anew. *Tommy should have been there, to indulge his little son, to spoil him and take him to fish on the creek. Tommy should have been with them. But for the war, this bloody awful war. He should have been there to take his son fishing, and to dandle his baby daughter and admire her for having a tooth coming in. It was all so bloody unfair!*

"We'll spend the afternoon in Mowbray Park, when we're done," Peg promised. "We'll be back in time for tea," she added, to reassure Edith.

"Stan will drive us into town then," Edith added. "And fetch us when our shift is done. We can spare the petrol, I think." She frowned, adding. "There's been a spot of difficulty between our Aussies and the American soldiers. They are so very well paid, you see. Your American lads…"

"Their uniforms are so much nicer!" Mavis added. "Tom, if you don't want the rest of that sausage roll, I'll take it." She scooped the rest of the sausage roll onto her plate from little Tommy's, upon his agreement.

"Waste not, want not," Peg said, as Mavis cut up the last, and swallowed it with the efficiency of an anaconda dining upon a small rodent.

"Mum! I'm still hungry!" Mavis wailed, upon intercepting Edith's disapproving look.

"I'd rather keep you for a week than a fortnight," Edith replied, and went into the kitchen to bring out the sweet.

After luncheon, Peg changed Olivia's diaper – just to be on the safe side – and carried the baby out to the pram.

"We'll be back for tiffin!" Peg called to Edith, clearing away the luncheon dishes. Edith nodded and waved. Mavis was already back in the garden, where she and Stanley seemed to be looking over the best place to build a henhouse and a sheltered pen for the chickens. Little Tommy trailed behind her, lugging Stanley's creel, and the smallest fishing rod over his small shoulder.

"Mumma," he ventured, before they had gotten very far. He was very pink, with the exertion of carrying the creel. He had already refused Peg's offer to hang it from the back of the pram. "Could I ask a favor?"

"Of course, darling," Peg replied, secretly amused at how Little Tommy was trying to sound so adult. He had already learned to read very well, through Stanley's tutelage.

"Mumma," her son sounded so earnest and mature, older than his four years. "I'd like to be called 'Tom.' Calling me 'Tommy' is a baby name. Grandpa Stan an' Granny Edith call me 'Tom'. I'm not a baby. I'm Tom. When I go to school, the other boys will laugh at me for being a baby."

"Of course, sugar," Peg replied, feeling as if her heart would now break into microscopic pieces. "You'll be Tom, if you want it. But your father is Tommy, to me and all his friends."

"That is Daddy," Little Tommy replied. "That's his name to friends and he's a soldier an' brave. I want to be Tom. That's me, Mumma. Me to all my friends. To Grammy Edie an' Grampa Stan. I'm Tom."

"Yes, you are, darling," Peg replied, around the choking feeling in her throat. "Who told you to be such a grown-up boy, then?"

"Amah did," Little Tommy – no, Tom – replied. Peg looked down at his earnest small countenance, as he walked beside her.

"What did Amah tell you?" Peg asked. "Was this when she said goodbye to us in Singapore?"

Tom screwed up his face, apparently trying to recall every word, and to put it into the right language. "She said I was the oldest son of a very brave and honorable soldier, and from that moment on I must always behave in a way that would make my father proud. That I should now put aside babyish ways because things were now going to be awfully hard, and it wouldn't be fitting for me to act like a baby, not when you would be depending on me. She said that my new brother or sister would be looking up to me as a good example. Then Amah asked me to remember her always. Sometimes," Tom confided, with touching gravity, "When I see a lady from China, I think for a moment that it is Amah, but it never is. I miss Amah dreadfully, Mumma but then I think of how she said that I should be the Oldest Son and it's not like I am a baby and need Amah. But," he added, with an expression of conspicuous virtue. "If Amah were here for Olivia ... well, then I wouldn't miss her so much. Mumma, do you think that Amah is safe?"

"I don't know, dearest," Peg replied. "I don't know that anyone is safe, in the hands of the Japanese."

Letter from Peg to Vennie, dated 12 December 1942, Postmarked Brisbane, Queensland

Dear Cuz:

I am almost certain that you were in a picture published recently in the *Courier Mail*, of American Army nurses in North Africa! At least, it looked most like you, and was supposed to have been snapped by a news photographer sometime after the landings in Algiers, so I suppose it must have been you. Tom – my little man insists on being called plain Tom now, as he thinks Tommy is just too babyish – was most impressed. He says that you are terribly brave, and can he marry you when he is quite grown-up? He is quite certain that the picture in the *Courier Mail* was of you, after a careful comparison under Stanley's magnifying glass of the wedding party, that picture of us all on the church steps after the ceremony when Tommy and I married.

Truly, that seems as if it were an age ago. Where did that comfortable, peaceful world go, Vennie? I think of summers on the ranch, and at Longcot, and it all seems so unreal, as if it happened to another person, someone with the same name as me. Edith says that sometimes she feels the same way, especially when she recalls her own life, back before the first war. Things change, she says, comfortably. She says with a laugh; did she ever really wear a long stiff-boned corset and skirts down to her toes, and a hat the size of a cartwheel, to stroll along a London avenue and take tea with her mothers' friends? There is pictorial evidence in her own albums of all this. She buries her worries over Tommy, and over Mavis *(who will enlist in the Australian forces in January upon her 18th birthday)* in volunteering at the St. George Club in Ann Street, which is a sort of Australian Hollywood Canteen for the military. Better than some comfortless barrack, or a sleazy grogshop; it's a big, comfortable place with a stage at one end, filled with tables for games. We have a kitchen which offers meals and teas for a small price, a library with books, places to write letters, and all that. Every few days we hold a dance, and now and again a fair, an amateur show or a masquerade party.

There are always a good many visitors to the Club, no matter the day or hour. There are so many American Army and Navy represented, you would think that half the young men of our country are here. The great General MacA has his HQ in Brisbane, in a fancy office block built by AMP, the mutual aid society and makes a royal progress twice daily from his residence in Lennon's Hotel to the office, back to Lennon's at midday for lunch, and then again at the end of the day. He is supposed to be a great man, but I honestly do not think very much of him. He is very stagey, as if playing the part of a flamboyant general and striking a pose for the applause of the audience.

There is an American officer, a colonel in the Air Corps whom Stanley made a friend of, through means I am not entirely certain. They have a common interest in all things mechanical. Colonel G. has been to tiffin with us several times, after which he and Stanley retreated to Stanley's mechanical workshop, not to emerge from that sanctuary for a good many hours. Colonel G. was a retired naval party, and had taken his family to the Philippines, where he had been instrumental in setting up a national airline there. He was activated into service again, when the war began and assisted in the evacuation of many senior officers from Manila by air, but his family was inadvertently left behind on the last of those missions. Colonel G. is not happy about how his sense of duty was manipulated by his commanders at the expense of his family, who are now all imprisoned by the Japs in the Philippines under the most trying conditions. He has been most sympathetic to me, upon being informed that Tommy was also a prisoner of war in Malaya. Colonel G.'s animus for the much-heralded General MacA is ... well, he is an officer, and can't say much, even in private, but it is obvious to us that Colonel G. bears rightful resentment. He has heard no more of his wife and three children in Manila than I have heard from Tommy, Reg, and Arthur in Singapore.

What if we hear nothing from our loved ones until the war is over? I suppose that is all the better reason for fighting it and winning. The battles in New Guinea and Guadalcanal are a first step in all this. It says so in the newspapers. But what isn't in the newspapers? Why should we read them again and believe the words printed on the pages, I wonder? *The Straits Times* was chock-full of cheerful news about the front, until the defenses of Singapore collapsed, and General Percival surrendered to the Japs.

A thing that won't get into the newspapers, I am certain; a riot between American and Australian troops in the streets of Brisbane, a week or three ago. It's all been hushed up officially of course and everyone is now very sorry that it all happened. But it did happen; everyone in Brisbane is certain of the cause.

As much as "we Yanks" are popular, not least among the unattached young ladies *(and not so-much-ladies)* and little boys, there is also great resentment among Australian troops. Even the lowliest enlisted Americans are paid three times as much as their equivalent in the Australian and British militaries. Their best dress uniforms are so much snappier and more attractive! Honestly, standing next to the Australian soldiers, the Americans look like Fred Astaire next to Gabby Hayes. The American PX also offers for a minimal price so many goodies that are strictly rationed or just plain unavailable otherwise to everyone else. Chocolate, coffee, ice cream, alcohol, cigarettes; things like that. They are terribly generous about sharing, but still... Bad form in making it so blatant, as Tommy would say.

Dear Cuz, I would absolutely murder for a decent bar of Hershey's chocolate! It's been ages since I had a taste, but pride and loyalty to Tommy prevent me from even considering chatting up an American soldier just for some chocolate and a pair of nylon stockings! Other women have and do, which makes the Australian soldiery absolutely simmer with jealousy.

Finally, the American MPs go about under arms and frequently resort to administering "hickory shampoos" on all and sundry with their batons, which excites disgust among civilians and other military. At any rate, these hard feelings all boiled over last week in a massive brawl lasting several nights: the American Army PX was ransacked on one night and on the next, the American Red Cross offices were threatened by a mob, a mob of Australian soldiers and civilians, which continued down to General MacA's offices, shouting abuse all the way and beating the stuffing out of any American GI's they caught. There are rumors that several were beaten to death, and that the Americans machine-gunned at least a dozen Australian soldiers *(piling the bodies on the steps of the post office!)* but Stanley says no – just horrid rumors. Edith and I passed the post office the very next day, on our way to the St George Club, and saw nothing of that sort or any evidence of such an awful event. I mean, there would be blood, etc., wouldn't there? But it has been very tense for the last few days. Naturally, and in the best interests of the war effort, barely a whisper of this has appeared in the newspapers. Mustn't spread alarm and despondency. The stiff upper lip simply must be maintained to the proper degree of stiffness.

Hoping that this letter will reach you uncensored. I remain,

Your Devoted Cuz,

Peg

Chapter 10 – I'll Be Seeing You

"How much longer?" Vennie gasped, coming down from the back of the Army deuce and a half truck. The hands of her watch gave the time as fifteen past three in the morning, the stars in the velvet-black sky overhead hung like white diamonds and hinted at the northern hemisphere. The desolation on every side gave no hint at all. There were no other signs of life, save for a faint flicker of light in the far eastern horizon and a distant and almost soundless rumble that might have been thunder – but likely was not.

"Jeeze, ma'am, I don't know!" Corporal Barker replied. He was the driver, a gangly youth who admitted in a moment of candor to his Army drill sergeant to having driven a taxicab in New York. Sensibly, the Army had detailed him to serve in the transport corps as a truck driver, instead of a clerk, a rifleman or some other military specialty with no respect for his previous civilian experience. This was a miracle of sorts, Vennie had come to realize. Corporal Barker had halted the truck at this place for no better reason than for everyone to relieve themselves, and to consult urgently with Vennie and the two corpsmen.

"Exactly how lost are we?" Vennie inquired, with a slight edge to her voice. She had been utterly appalled to discover that she was the senior officer in the very last vehicle evacuating the field hospital, and that somehow, they had also become separated from the rest of the convoy when the road west from

Tebessa had been briefly obscured by a dust storm. There <u>was</u> a captain among her litter patients in the back of that last truck, but he was unconscious with a fractured skull, and hardly fit to take command of the small party.

"We're not lost," Corporal Barker insisted. "This is the road ... <u>this</u> road. We've come twenty-three and a half miles along it since we collected you guys. And lady." Corporal Barker gestured at the map which he held up before the narrow slit of headlight.

"Couldn't prove it by me," replied Private Myers, the corpsman who had been riding shotgun.

"Or me either," Vennie added. "It <u>all</u> looks like desert, only slightly leveler ahead and behind than on either side. So, we've come twenty-three and a half miles. Good to know. And we're going in the right direction, which is also good to know. Let me see that compass again. You do know how to read a compass and find the North Star? The Little Dipper? See – there?" She pointed off to the right, where the constellation hung, just over the edge of a horizon chopped with steep, rocky hills. "You do know about cardinal directions, then?"

"The avenues go north-south, the streets go east-west, and they're all numbered in order," Corporal Barker replied, somewhat abashed.

"Fat lot of help here," Private Myers muttered. "If there is an avenue or a street anywhere within miles of this place ... where is it that we were supposed to head towards, Ell-Tee?"

"Youks-les-Bains," Vennie replied. "It's supposed to be west of here. It's on the map, here."

Colonel Mellish had briefed the volunteers before the main part of the hospital had evacuated in midafternoon the day before. To the best of her knowledge the American forces attacking Rommel's Afrika Corps from the west had been sent reeling when the Germans came boiling over the Kasserine Pass. Not just Americans were tumbling back, and back again, but the Bedouins as well. That afternoon she had been alarmed to see herds of camels at an ungainly run, over the broken ground a little north of where the field hospital had been set up at Tebessa. Who would have thought those clumsy, bad-smelling critters could hump along at such a breakneck pace? The camels were followed by black-clad Bedouin women, their children, and goats. And then, dishearteningly, by American trucks, tanks and jeeps, all straggling back towards the west.

Before nightfall, Colonel Mellish was passing the word. *Pack up the patients and gear and fall back; all the way back to Algeria, if necessity demanded.* Vennie, five other nurses, Captain Marcus and a dozen corpsmen remained, tending the last of a dribble of gravely wounded casualties arriving, as the rest of the 48th struck tents and joined the retreat. Everyone else had gone, save that small party volunteering to keep doing what they could for the casualties, rather than abandon their duty. Just before sundown, a pair of MPs on motorbikes roared in from the main road, in a burst of oil fumes and a spurt of sand.

"You gotta pull out, now," the first MP commanded, as his companion propped up his goggles and looked around at the tangle of vehicle tracks, trenches, and post-holes where the rest of the hospital had been. "Or be prisoners of war by dawn."

Captain Marcus had waved a hand in the direction of the road. "We don't have transport. At the last minute we had casualties come in. We're all volunteers; we knew the risk we were running. They were supposed to send back to collect us all when they could."

"I'll get you transport, sir," the MP had said, with an air of grim determination. "Just be ready to roll when we get back."

Less than forty minutes later, the two MPs reappeared, accompanied by five two-and-a-half-ton Army cargo trucks, just barely enough room in them for the last of the staff and their patients, loaded in and stacked on stretchers in the back. Vennie was by herself in the last of the five, with two corpsmen.

Somehow, in the middle of the night, they lost their escort – the MPs on motorcycles, and the rest of their small convoy. Vennie suspected it would have been when Corporal Barker slowed the truck to a crawl during a sudden dust storm, in order to keep from going off the road and crashing the truck. Now they were alone in the Tunisian desert. Or perhaps it was Algerian desert. Vennie had not felt so alone, since the moment she stepped off the ramp of the barge that brought her to North Africa, or when she and Ruth and Muriel began assessing patients in the dark of that awful night in Arzew.

No. Vennie lifted up her chin. She was in charge; she was a nurse, for God's sake. She could do something. Look after those patients – most of them still unconscious or semi-conscious in the back of the truck. She was also a country girl and how was this North African desert any different, really, than the country around Deming? She knew desert, on horseback and afoot with bare tracks for roads, she knew the night sky and how to read a compass heading or find Polaris, the Northern Star.

"Here is the road, and the direction," she said calmly to Corporal Barker and Private Myers, as she handed the map and compass to the latter. "Keep this star over your right shoulder, Private Myers and your eye on the road, Corporal."

"Ma'am," that was Corporal Rittenhouse, the other corpsman. "You best come and look at this. We got a bleeder again ..."

Vennie swore silently to herself. This had happened several times already; the constant jolting in the back of the truck. No matter how carefully and slowly Corporal Barker nursed the two-and-a-half along a road which was only graded sand and gravel, the gentle jolting still caused surgical stitches to break and abused flesh to tear open on one of their patients' surgical sites. No – she could not let Captain Marcus' work in the operating room to go to waste, or for one of her patients to bleed out. Not going to happen.

"Let me take a look at this now," she added, to Corporal Barker. "Give me five minutes before we start off again."

She had a surgical kit, a large musette bag with more bandages and a box of morphine syrettes. Corporal Rittenhouse had another; fully packed with more dressings, bandages, and extra bottles of plasma. They had only needed to go sparingly into either bag, but it was now eight hours since departing what was left of the temporary hospital.

"Hold your flashlight on the wound," she directed, calmly. "And let me take a look at the patient."

The stretchers were stacked three-high, in a makeshift fashion in the back of the truck. At least it was covered, covered enough that Vennie could stand upright and reach every one of the twelve stretchers within. Corporal Rittenhouse twitched back the blanket which covered the litter patient nearest to the cab, a soldier who had been peppered by shrapnel from a mine.

"It's not all that bad," Vennie said, judiciously, after a long survey under Corporal Rittenhouse's wavering flashlight. "I'll pack it with fresh dressing. His color doesn't look too bad. Hang a fresh plasma bottle; this one's practically empty, and he needs fluids. When any of the boys are sufficiently conscious to be thirsty, we'll let them have a mouthful or two of water, unless they have had abdominal surgery. Right – tell Corporal Barker we can move now."

"D'you want to sit up front for a while, ma'am?" Corporal Rittenhouse offered, and Vennie shook her head.

"No, I'll stay with the boys for now. We'll trade off the next time we break, or we get to Youks-les-Bains, whichever comes first."

Corporal Rittenhouse nodded. He, like Private Myers and Corporal Barker were so very young; just boys really and all three draftees. Vennie felt like their older and responsible sister. Now she said, investing her voice with every shred of confident authority that she could muster. "We'll be all right, Benny. This is the right road and we've come far enough along it to be ahead of the Afrika Corps for now. And it's at night, so we can't be harassed by their airplanes."

In the dim circle of light within the back of the truck, Corporal Rittenhouse still looked worried. "You're certain, ma'am? What if ..."

"We don't get to Youks-les-Bains by sunrise? Then we should pull off the road and spread out the Red Cross flag, to signify that we're part of a hospital. One step at a time, Benny. We'll be OK. Let's get going and try to make time before sunrise, all right?"

"Yes, ma'am," Corporal Benny Rittenhouse saluted – although he really didn't have to; under the current regulations, nurses were not entitled to that peculiarly military courtesy. Vennie was warmed and at the same time horrified by that gesture. They trusted and respected her. In the most interior of her heart, she was not entirely certain that she was deserving of that trust and respect.

"We'll be OK, Benny," she said again, in her most reassuring nurse-to-patient voice. Corporal Rittenhouse vanished over the tail of the truck, letting the canvas curtain they had fixed over the tailgate fall too. She was alone now, with a dozen unconscious or semi-conscious patients. She found a place at the back of the truck, leaning against the slatted sidewall, as the truck lurched and took again to the road. She had her musette bag at her side, and a rolled-up blanket. Lulled by equal parts exhaustion, and the swaying motion of the truck, she fell into a restless doze.

She awoke in the dark, by the roar of a powerful engine, and such was her state that she thought they were being attacked by an enemy airplane. She flung out her arm as the truck rocked to a stop. She was still half-asleep, dazed by exhaustion.

"El-Tee!" a male voice shouted – Private Myers. Vennie swam up to the surface of rationality, recalling who and where she was. *Lieutenant Venetia Stoneman, US Army Nurse Corps, in the back of a truck with twelve litter patients, evacuating from the forward hospital at Tebessa ... now many hours ago. And she was nominally in charge.* She found her feet, stiff as the arthritis-ridden old woman that she hoped eventually to become, as Private Myers appeared at the truck tail, and helped her scramble down.

It was dawn, a pale-pink and pearl-colored sky in the east, directionless light revealing nothing but a stretch of desert and bare rocky hills, barely veiled by low stands of dark-green scrub brush. Corporal Barker, bleary-eyed, was leaning out from the driver-side door. At least he had pulled to one side of the road. Although not entirely off it. The two corpsmen were also there, standing and talking to a motorcycle MP, the same man who had found them transport, and lost them in a sandstorm, how many hours ago?

"Christ Almighty, I'm glad to have found you guys," the MP announced, upon observing Vennie clambering down from the back of the truck. "Thought you were goners, for sure."

"We're glad to be found, Sergeant," Vennie replied, having recovered enough of her presence of mind from the fog and weariness to recognize stripes and situation-awareness. "Where is it that we have been found?"

"Two miles west from Youks-les-Bains, and the rest of your unit, ma'am." The MP sergeant nodded, much relieved. "Sorry as hell to have lost y'all in the ruckus."

"We'd have been all right," Vennie replied. "Straight on, you say?"

"Yes ma'am," He saluted, too again discomfiting her. Still – courtesy for courtesy.

Letter from Vennie to Peg, dated 4 March 1943 – Near Montesquieu, Algeria

Dear Cuz:

On the move again! Honestly, I think I will be able to write a *Baedeker Guide* to all the scenic spots in Algeria and Tunisia by the time that I am finished here. For a wonder here, the hospital is set up in a pleasant green meadow with wildflowers all around – such a wonderful change from the usual sand, rocks and discouraged goats nibbling on dry tufts of grass and thorny bushes. But never mind the natural attractions, or the historic ones – we have cared for patients almost without a break since arriving and setting up our hospital tents here.

The German Afrika Corps was pushed back through the mountain pass and nearly driven from Tunisia, according to what I hear. Great numbers of Italian and German soldiers have been taken prisoner. We have treated many of those who were wounded. They are under constant guard, the Germans especially. They are sullen and resentful about being defeated and remain extremely scornful of Americans. For myself, the scorn is mutual, although Grandpa Fred and his family were German and immigrated from Bavaria all those years ago. I don't have anything the least in common with these Germans, not even a liking for pickled 'Liberty Cabbage', although several of our German POW patients are tall and fair and look as if they were close kin to the Beckers and the Vinings.

There was a very curious Army captain who came to do sketches of our hospital, or to interrogate the German prisoners. I am not entirely certain which; an Austrian nobleman, with a proper 'von' who served in the French Foreign Legion and fought on the Republican side in the Spanish War. A fanatical anti-Nazi, he walks with a bad limp, from his leg having been riddled with shell fragments in that war. He has had exhibits of his art in galleries in New York and London, and even had one of his surrealistic paintings on the cover of *Time* magazine! He did a brief sketch of me, which I have sent to my parents. I was enormously flattered, as he was terribly fascinating to talk with. There are men who will shoot the most unbelievable 'lines' as our British friends say. Then there are those who are every bit the most fantastical heroes that one might imagine in a movie.

Speaking of other curious characters at the hospital; an Italian prisoner was brought in to have an infected wound examined and dressed, and he spoke perfect American English, astonishing us all by asking for a cigarette and a light! He explained that he had been brought by his parents to New Jersey as a baby and raised as an American. Early in 1939 his family returned to Rome for a long visit to family. They had not secured American citizenship. Since he was of military age, he was drafted into the Italian Army. No one could do anything! He was extraordinarily chipper and cheerful about being a prisoner of war. He claims that all his comrades are glad to be out of the war at last – far, far out of it since they will be sent to camps in the US very soon. The German PWs are sullen and disobliging about being captive. Well, if you don't want to lose a war, don't start one, is what I say, and serves you all right!

We had a visit at the hospital from the new theater commander, who descended on us unannounced as a bolt out of the blue. General Millefield knew of him as an able and fire-eating young junior officer; quite the terror for training and discipline; also for killing Mexican bandits. With a cavalry sabre, supposedly. A very tall, Prussian-stern man, in tall riding boots and boasting a pair of pearl-handled pistols at his waist and a chest simply clashing with medals. *(Seriously, I wonder if they clank in tune? No, I didn't ask.)* He came for the apparent purpose of lecturing one of our patients; a young soldier, shot in the chest several times while waving a white flag trying to surrender to German soldiers about to overrun his unit's position in the Kasserine Pass. General P. gave him a stern and impassioned lecture on how soldiers in his army did not surrender under any circumstances, told him he should be ashamed of himself and stalked out of the ward with hardly a word to anyone else. We didn't dare voice any reproof of him for upsetting all our patients, as it would have been worth the career of any medical officer to have said anything at all. Captain Marcus commented rather pithily that we should pray to our Lord to protect and keep the General – keep him far, far away from us!

Even Colonel Mellish wouldn't have dared speak a chiding word to the General. He has been promoted out of command of the hospital in the wake of a substantial reorganization and sent back to the United States to command a medical training school, now that he has had the experience of operations here. We had a lovely party at the hospital for Colonel Mellish before he departed. Now we wait on further events. Hoping to hear from you soon,

Vennie

Letter from Peg to Vennie, dated 20 May, 1943, Postmarked Brisbane, Queensland

Dear Vennie:

Such adventures you have had all through North Africa! Where do you suppose that you will be next? Although I don't suppose you can say – loose lips sinking ships and all. Since I am quite fond of you, Cuz, please don't say anything about where you will go next. Just this very week we suffered through a horrible example of this. The wretched Japs torpedoed a hospital ship, just out of harbor! A hospital ship, clearly marked, with lights and Red Cross markings, torpedoed at sea off Brisbane and sunk with almost all hands, although mercifully they were not carrying patients, as they were heading to New Guinea to bring the wounded home. I cannot imagine anything more bestial and hateful that this deliberate act.

Well, I can, after hearing some of the stories that the men tell, most always in hushed voices and not where they think I might overhear. There was only one nurse among the rescued survivors, poor woman, and she was most awfully injured. Please stay safe, Cuz, Tom still wants to marry you when he grows up. You would not recognize my little man. He turned four years old last month and looks at least a year older than that. Next year he will start school as a day boy, a program for which he is quite impatient as his adoring Gramps has already taught him to read very well, and he has memorized the multiplication tables up to the 8s. And he finally caught a fish big enough for us all to have a meal from. *(Edith did it with a stuffing of whole meal bread and onions. It was good, and we all made it out to Tom as if it were the very best fish ever eaten since time began!)* It has been arranged for him to attend the boy's school around the corner from where we live; the Church of England Grammar School in Oaklands Parade, or as everyone fondly calls it for short "Churchie."

Olivia has just turned a year old, and she is adorable; chubby and mop-haired, with noticeable dimples. She looks like Shirley Temple, and I would keep her hair in corkscrew curls, but that is just too much trouble. She already hates riding in the pram, and stumps along sturdily on her baby legs when we walk up to Mowbray Park to look at the boats, Story Bridge the tall buildings on the far side of the river and say hullo to the war memorial statue, which Tom is utterly convinced is a statue of Tommy.

For Olivia's birthday party Edith searched around and traded eggs for flour and sugar and baked her the most elaborate frosted cake. We had a party for her at the house and invited all the little girls who live along Heath Street ... and some American soldiers who were hanging over the gate, looking longingly at the house when it came to teatime! They were so embarrassed when they discovered they had been invited to a baby girl's birthday party, but recovered magnificently, and one did very clever magic tricks for the children with a handkerchief which he knotted and told them to pretend was a white bunny with long ears, which amused them all. Edith spoils my baby girl – of course, she misses Mavis, but is also quite philosophical. *"They will perch on the edge of the nest and try their wings, you know!"* she has said many a time. Mavis went off to enlist in the Australian Women's Army Service and has been in training at a location unspecified. From her letters to her family, we deduce that she will likely serve in a searchlight battery, which likely will keep her somewhere near a city. The AWAS girls will not serve outside of Australia, which Edith and Stanley are privately most happy about. Whatever happens, Mavis will be safe. Horrors, what if this war goes on long enough that Olivia will feel obliged to serve! What if it continues until Tom will have to volunteer, too?

I try not to think such awful defeatist thoughts, Vennie. But Tommy and I had wanted more children, even more than Great-Uncle and Great-Aunt Richter. Eleven was the number we agreed on; enough for a cricket side, Tommy was adamant. We would have to make up for all those boys who were lost and never fathered a family, and now I'm worrying that Tommy will never come back, and I don't want to have the rest of the nine children with anyone but him. Now I am almost two years older since I last kissed my husband – and how long does one have the strength and health to bear children anyway? You're a nurse and know these things. Write to me soon, dear Vennie.

Love, Your Cousin Peg

Chapter 11 – Coming In On a Wing and a Prayer

Letter from Vennie to Peg, dated 6 July, 1943, Postmarked Bowman Field, Louisville, Kentucky

Dear Peg: surprise! I am back in the US for a while, but not for long. I was recommended for a special course by Colonel Mellish, a course to qualify me as a nurse to supervise patients traveling by air from the front for treatment at established hospitals in secure areas. Everyone was so impressed with how I managed nearly alone for simply hours with a truck full of post-op patients when we suddenly had to relocate our field hospital. Because of merging and realigning some units, a handful of us can briefly be spared from the war effort at the front, so I am spending a lovely month in the mountains of Kentucky, half in the classroom and half in practical exercises – exercises which I know from experience will simply be nothing like the real thing. *(I don't say anything of this to the other students, many of them girls just newly commissioned as Army nurses. I don't want to frighten them, you see.)* I cannot tell you anything much about the course, or what happened in North Africa, or what I think will happen next with the 'Second Front.' Loose lips do sink ships! I suppose that I will just have to rattle on about silly things in this letter!

Like summer in the green, green mountains of Kentucky! Oh, my dear Peg, you cannot believe how lush and green everything looks to me, after becoming accustomed to drab OD green and rocky desert, and skimpy palm trees, like up-ended feather dusters! And stately white houses with columns across the front, just like in *Gone With The Wind*! I cannot get enough of the blooming wildflowers and how green everything is.

Did I say enough how green everything is! And to walk into a restaurant and order a glass of fresh milk. Or a drug store and have a milkshake! Do you have any notion of how glorious fresh milk tastes? Or scrambled eggs, after months and months of powdered eggs. Didn't you mention that Edith wanted to keep hens for their eggs? Your mother-in-law is simply a brilliant woman. I would keep Tommy, just for his mother.

It's very strange, coming back to my own country, after a year, sometimes feeling as if I am looking at it through the eyes of a foreigner. Do you know the most curious thing is that I find myself startled at seeing older people, well above the age of forty or so, and old people with grey hair and people who do not look terribly physically fit! For most of the last year and more, I have been constantly in the company of men of military age and a few women of the same; unless they are foreigners, of course, but those so encountered are rare and only encountered away from the hospital or camp. The older commanders and surgeons among us have grey hair but are generally fit and athletic. I am also honestly startled to see so many civilians – oh, the whole world is <u>not</u> wearing a uniform! *(Although to be honest – a large portion of it is, these days!)*

I finally got to see the movie *Casablanca*, about which there was an awful lot of talk because it came out just after we landed in North Africa! Have you seen it in Australia yet? I suppose the ending came out all very fine and noble but the bits of landscape that I could see really didn't look <u>anything</u> like Oran or Arzew, or North Africa generally. But the actress playing Ilsa is so lovely, I was positively green with envying everything about her: her clothes, her hats, her eyes and cheekbones, perfect hair, and lipstick! Honestly, though; <u>what</u> did she ever see in Rick? Humphrey Bogart just is not my 'cup of tea.' The man is as homely as a mud fence and grumpy as a bear just out from hibernation. I suppose that everything is pretty, and glorious and perfect-ending in Hollywood.

Nice enough for an escape of a couple of hours. For myself, I'd rather see Fred Astaire dancing with Ginger Rogers in a fluffy dress and absolutely nothing – <u>nothing</u> about the war anywhere in the plot, although I suppose that I could endure a plea to purchase War Bonds before and after.

How are Olivia and Not-so-Small Tom getting on? Tom can already read? I shall have to send him some more serious books for him, if that is the case, while I am in a place where I can buy for him. What does he like? Fishing, if I remember from your previous letters. If I can find a storybook about a boy who loves fishing, I will send them! Is it too early for him to read *The Adventures of Huckleberry Finn?* Do you have any photographs of them that you can spare to send me? I loved the account of Olivia's birthday party, and the stray soldier who did

magic tricks for her and her friends, with a bunny knotted out
of handkerchiefs. That is so precious! I want to hear those small
domestic bits, and the cute things that your children do and say.
It's a way for me to remember what this is all about – to keep
those dear children of yours in my heart and memory. Perhaps I
will have my own someday but until then, I will live for cheerful
news from you and yours.

Your cousin – Vennie

*Letter from Peg to Vennie, dated 14 October 1943,
Postmarked Brisbane, Queensland, Australia. Returned
unopened and marked –* **Returned to sender, from APO
NY** *Addressee 1ᴸᵗ V. Stoneman, USA Nurse Corps Missing in
Action 3 Nov '43*

Dear Vennie:

I was so happy to hear that you managed to visit Uncle
Charlie and your mother and all after successfully completing
your special nursing course. I don't suppose that you can tell
me anything more about it, so I will not even ask. I presume
that since the front has moved to Sicily and the Italian
mainland that you are there, as before. I hope that you are as
safe as can be, under the circumstances. This bloody war has
been going on for four years now; honestly, dear Cuz, I can just
barely remember peace, or what seemed something like peace
at the time. Food unrationed, plenty of beef (!) and plenty of
petrol, and the only uniforms that one saw commonly, unless

one visited Fort Sam Houston were those on policemen and bus drivers! What was it like then, not to hear an air raid siren without your heart in your throat, or having to know where the closest air raid shelter was, or carry a gas mask, or even be afraid to turn on the radio of a morning or open the newspaper?

I'll write about more cheerful news, about Tom and Olivia. Tom will begin school in January, and Edith and I have been sorting out what he will need to have by way of proper school clothes. Fortunately, she and Stanley have friends whose sons are at "Churchie" in various grades, or forms as they call them here. They have made outgrown school coats and trousers available to us, so all that we need to do was to save coupons for white shirts and for shoes and socks. Tom is terribly excited about going to school. He is quite a gregarious little boy, and completely fearless. Any books that you have sent to us for his Christmas prezzy will be gratefully received and devoured ... probably even before Christmas dinner is served.

Did you realize that our mid-summer in Australia comes during November? Never a chance of a white Christmas here, even less of a chance than there was in the Texas Hill Country. Edith and I are scrimping and saving our food coupons, as she says that we should have a real plum pudding, and if we must sacrifice the oldest of her chickens to the cause of Christmas dinner ... well, I am in favor of trading eggs with one of her friends who has geese. It seems quite against the spirit of Christmas to eat one of our chickens, especially since the children have named them all. According to Mr. Charles

Dickens, it was goose that was the centerpiece of a rare old English Christmas dinner anyway! I really cannot contemplate the horror of telling Tom and Olivia that we have just eaten Bette, Vivian, Greta, or Hedy! It would ruin Christmas entirely, since the children are so fond of our hens; their tears would practically flood the house, even though it is on tall pilings! I'll try and talk Edith out of this; perhaps we can procure an enormous Spam loaf and carve it into the shape of a chicken or a goose.

On the ranch, we all knew that some yearlings would be slaughtered for beef. Daddy often gave them names like "Sir Loin" or "Lord Hamburger" or "Baron Roast", just to keep it all firmly in our minds what they were intended to be. It's just not the same with Edith's pet chickens, I suspect.

Anyway, I have been reading in my wedding-present cookbook, which has practically no milage on it, as Mr. Song was the cook at Longcot and brooked no interference in his way of doing things. Edith is the same, regarding her kitchen. It's an exercise in nostalgia for that time which seems nearly out of memory. Whole roasts of beef, pork, chicken and unlimited quantities of butter, sugar, white flour, cream, eggs. It's an exercise in hunger nostalgia.

The thing is that Australia could and would provide all these good things in quantities which would make a horn of plenty look niggardly ... it's just that most of these good things must go off to supply England. There's a poster which makes much of this; our food production must go marching dutifully off to England. Just as Australian soldiers must do ... because obligation to Empire and all that. Honestly, every time I sit down to a skimpy meal of rationed foodstuffs and think of that poster, my blood fairly boils. Americans fought a revolution over all that; sometimes I wonder if Australians have the nerve to do the same. But not during this war – which everyone and everything reminds me that we 'are all in this together.'

Well, some of us are in it more than others.

Your devoted Cuz

Peg

* * *

"We're going down," said Sgt. Reyes, the enlisted crew chief. "Everybody buckle in, it's gonna be rough." He sounded unnaturally calm. Vennie turned to the nurse who sat next to her and raised her voice to be heard over the roaring of four mighty engines.

"You know, I had a bad feeling about this flight. Two weeks of bad weather between Catania and Bari. I think God was trying to send a message!"

"I wish He had used Western Union!" 2Lt. Ginger Lloyd shouted back.

A dozen nurses and the same of corpsmen occupied the metal and webbing folding seats on either side of the C-54 transport plane; assigned to augment the forward hospitals on the Italian mainland, for the fighting had turned bitter and protracted – made even more bitter by winter coming on.

So much for sunny Italy, Vennie thought, in disgust, and not for the first time. Malaria in the summer and torrential winds in the fall. She could hardly wait to see what hard winter would bring. Probably ice storms and blizzards. Bloody ... Vennie bit back a word that would have made her mother wash out her mouth with soap. Even North Africa hadn't been as cold and miserable as Italy was proving to be. She and Virginia "Ginger" Lloyd, and a pair of corpsmen, Corporal Eliopoulos and Private Feldman would accompany ambulatory and litter patients on the flight back to a more substantial hospital in Palermo and then on to Tunisia. A broken compass, infamously bad weather, and strong winds had blown the un-pressurized transport plane way off course. Even if there had been windows to see out of, there was nothing much but cloud to see.

Vennie, as senior nurse had even gone forward to the flight deck and looked over the shoulders of pilot and co-pilot; nothing but murky grey mist which they couldn't go above, because the C-54 wasn't pressurized, and lack of oxygen would slowly incapacitate and kill them all. Even at this altitude, the cold might very well have a go. She and Ginger, Corporal Eliopoulos and Private Feldman wore heavy insulated flight suits as part of their routine issue. Everyone else wore layer upon layer of warm woolen underwear, sweaters, mufflers, gloves and every heavy overgarment that the Army had to issue them for the flight north to Bari and the Italian front.

And then they lost radio contact. Which necessitated much swearing on the part of the radio operator, Tech Sgt. Moffit.

That was when Vennie had begun to worry, overhearing what Stan Moffit was saying, with increasing urgency into the radio set. It was something of a comfort to hear, over the roar of engines, the grinding vibration that meant the landing gear was going down. That raised her hopes; perhaps Captain Markham, the pilot, had found a patch of level ground, even a runway. He was a Texas man, a tall and drawling reservist from San Angelo, a lawyer in civil life with a taste for the wide blue yonder, whom she had met fifteen minutes before take-off.

"We're down!" Sgt. Reyes shouted from the rear, as the airplane bounced on something hard – hopefully solid and unobstructed ground. "Hang on!"

The wheels hit again, and rolled smoothly, but only for a few yards.

'We're going too fast,' Vennie thought. After many a flight, she knew the feeling of a good landing, the smooth roll and gradual deceleration. She could feel the aircraft getting ahead of the wheels, knew that Captain Markham had the flaps down, throttled the engines back, sensed that the C-54 was not on a clear and level runway. A particularly violent bounce threw her against the shoulder straps of her seat harness. With an animal-like scream of protesting metal against metal, the aircraft slewed violently to one side, then rocked to the other. Momentum sent her forward, into Ginger's shoulder. One final deafening crunch: the fuselage tipped up and dropped down with shattering violence. Something large flew past Vennie like a thrown ragdoll, landing face-first on the metal floor; the body of Sgt. Reyes, whose booted foot caught Ginger Lloyd full in the face.

They were down, and still. The sudden quiet – a quiet only broken by the ticking sound of metal suddenly cooling – seemed as deafening as the racket had been. With trembling hands, Vennie undid the harness catch and stood up. The floor under her feet tilted at an unnatural angle. The pallets of cargo in back had broken loose from where they had been secured. A metal-strapped crate trapped the legs of the corpsman, Private Rennie, in the nearer seat. Ginger Lloyd's nose gushed blood. Her left eye was already turning the color of an overripe plum. Two other passengers had already banged the hatch open; cold air and pale sunlight filtered into the interior, catching motes of dust sifting down like a kind of sparkling confetti.

"Anyone got a Kleenex?" Ginger Lloyd asked, in a somewhat clogged voice. All around them, the other passengers moved shakily from their seats, Lt. Mary Shipman and Lt. Gladys Powell already attending to Sgt. Reyes, and three corpsmen shoving aside the crate to free Private Rennie.

Captain Markham and TSgt. Moffit emerged from the cockpit, Captain Markham beaming with relief, until he saw Sgt. Reyes, prone on the floor, blood oozing from a long scrape across his face, and more from his head. He was unconscious, unlike the unfortunate Private Rennie.

"They say it's a good enough landing if you walk away from it! Everyone OK back here? Oh, Christ, Ray! You OK, man?"

"Concussion, I'd say," replied Mary Shipman, equably. "I think he'll live. Just knocked silly for a bit. He didn't buckle down."

"He was making certain of the cargo, before we hit," Vennie said. She thought highly of Mary, who was a bit older than the others; like Ruth back in the 48th, she had been a hospital nurse working in an emergency room for a good six or seven years. She fumbled in the pockets of her padded suit and came up with a clean handkerchief for Ginger. Her musette bag of first-aid gear, which she was never without – not since the landing in North Africa a year since – was stashed under her seat. Vennie opened it, retrieved a package of dressing for Ginger, before moving across to Private Rennie, who was so pale that his freckles stood out like blotches on his face. The boy's right shin hung at an unnatural angle, blood already saturating his trouser legs. A corner of the packing case had struck hard enough to snap bone and crush flesh to a pulp.

"Compound fracture, here," Vennie added, deliberately calm. "Any idea where we are?"

"Albania," Captain Markham replied. "From our last heading. The winds kept shoving us dead east, instead of north. Don't know how far inland we are."

"Albania," Vennie sat back on her heels, regarding Private Rennie's mangled shin, revealed after cutting away his blood-soaked trouser leg. She opened her musette bag and found the box of morphine syrettes and a packet of sulfa powder. "It's occupied by the Germans, isn't it?"

"Sort of," Captain Markham replied. "They've got some active partisan groups. Any of you medical people know what language they speak in Albania …"

"No idea," Vennie replied. "Albanian, I expect. Maybe Greek. OK, Stephen," she added, as she expertly slid the syrette needle into Private Rennie's bared arm. "This'll take the edge off when we set your leg. Right? You'll be doing the Lindy at club dances in no time at all, we promise."

"Yes, ma'am," Private Rennie already appeared somewhat less pale. Vennie prided herself on knowing the first names of all the nurses and corpsmen she worked with. In a strange way, they were her sisters and brothers, not of blood, but of calling.

"My parents are from Naplion," Corporal Eliopoulos spoke up. "In the Peloponnese. Southern Greece. An' we spoke Greek at home, all the time. I can make it clear to anyone that shows up that we're Yanks and OK."

"We should take bets," TSgt. Moffit suggested on a note of macabre optimism, "On who'll get to us first: Krauts, partisans or collaborators."

"In the meantime," Captain Markham assumed command of their crash-stranded party, "We'd better vacate. Stan, break up the radio, now. Everything on this bird got pretty busted up, so I would not remove the possibility of fire catching what's left in the fuel tanks. I don't know what y'all's life ambitions include, but one of mine is not dying screaming in a fire."

"Mine as well," Vennie answered, with an interior shudder. There had been such an agonizing death when the

British hospital ship was bombed and sunk off Anzio ... she had spoken to an American nurse who had survived the sinking and spoke of it with horror. The screaming, especially. *No, best not think on it, now.* "Take as much medical gear as we can, though. We're going to need it."

"Stan, put my money on the partisans," Captain Markham offered cheerfully over his shoulder.

Sgt. Reyes had recovered a degree of consciousness, as he was carried from the airplane on a makeshift litter bashed together from a seat, insisting that he was really perfectly OK and put him down, dammit.

"How many fingers am I holding up?" Vennie demanded sternly, holding up all four fingers, as she knelt beside him, in what appeared to be and probably was a harvested cornfield, all dirt punctuated with regular tufts of dead cornstalks. Sgt. Reyes peered at her hand blearily.

"All eight?" he ventured uncertainly, and Vennie sighed.

"OK – who's the president of the United States?"

"That *pendejo* Roosevelt!" Reyes answered, and Vennie sighed again.

"You're concussed, Sgt. Reyes – we can't let you fall asleep for at least ten hours, and you'll stay on that litter if we have to tie you to it, *entiende, sargento*?"

"*Si, teniente,*" Reyes replied, and closed his eyes, until Vennie shook him by the shoulder.

"Stay awake!" she commanded him. Meanwhile, the others were carrying out by bits and pieces, their personal gear and what small cargo had been in the back of the C-54. Mary Shipman made capable work of dressing, splinting, and binding Private Rennie's compound fracture.

As Captain Markham predicted, small yellow flames were already dancing in a tentative way in a puddle of leaking gasoline. The C-54 had settled to earth in a manner that suggested a bird with a broken back, one wing wrapped around a thicket of dead trees at the farthest margin of the cornfield. Beyond lay nothing much – the bed of a dried-up lake, Vennie thought, or a seasonal river. One of those which only had water in it after a torrential downpour upstream. The sky overhead was a faded blue, which promised a very chilly night, especially for those without shelter. All around them stood white-capped mountains, dark blue and lavender in the distance.

Captain Markham had done an admirable job, she thought; a rough landing on rougher terrain, in mountainous country under sketchy occupation by the Nazis, and with only two injured. He had been blessed with luck in even finding this place; steep mountains rose on every horizon to the east and west, mountains touched at their highest with white snow. A wrecked aircraft, for certain – but the factories were turning them out, two-a-penny, if she could believe what was in the newsreels. It might take half a week to make an airplane, but to grow and train the crew to fly it was the work of at least twenty years for each man and possibly more.

The small hill of reclaimed cargo and personal effects sat at a small distance from the aircraft. TSgt. Moffit scrambled through the hatch with an expression on his face which mingled regret with satisfaction.

"All done, Captain," he said. "And the cargo is mostly cleared out. What do we do now?" It was a salient question. No one had any notion of what to do now except that Sgt. Reyes and Private Rennie must be cared for.

"Look for help," Captain Markham was on a bit of a spot – really, what could they do, save bundle up everything they could carry, walk east to the Adriatic, and hope not to run into any Germans on the way. But at that very moment, men appeared on every side, seemingly out of nowhere.

Vennie had grown up in near-desert country, hunting with her brothers and uncles, herding cattle who had the damndest way of hiding in out-of-the way draws and declivities in the hills. She was not nearly as startled as some of the others were, at how the Albanian countryside seemed to have grown men like dragon's teeth, between one moment and the next.

These were men in battered country clothing, with vaguely exotic fezzes on their heads, or fringed sashes around their waists. They had a grubby, unshaven appearance, and more meaningful to Vennie – a lean and wolfish look, as if they had already gone hungry for many weeks and months. The weapons were not being leveled on them all. Vennie counted that as a good thing. These men were not seeing them all as a threat, merely a party of strangers, of whom they were rightfully wary. It didn't escape notice that these men noticed the huddled group of nurses and murmured between themselves. Not with any lascivious threat; merely curiosity and a degree of puzzlement.

"Steve – Corporal Eliopoulos – I think you should try out your Greek now," Vennie murmured, with a significant look at the obliging Corporal Eliopoulos, who did indeed look like a heroic Greek warrior in the classical tradition, albeit in translation as an American Army soldier, lean and dark, with an eagle-like profile, one of those men who was rather gawky in youth, but who would be magnetic and magnificent in middle and old age. Steve Eliopoulos nodded from where he had been stacking up baggage and supplies from the broken airplane. He stood, dusting off his hands on his trouser seat and held them up, spread wide to show that he was not armed or threatening.

Vennie did not hear what he said, as he approached the man who seemed to be the leader, only that it was spoken in conciliatory tones, and that it appeared to have a promising effect. The men brandishing guns took on an appearance of relaxing vigilance. The very youngest among them, a youth of about fifteen in appearance, was put forward.

The boy was about the sort described in novels as 'callow'. but as he began to talk to Corporal Eliopoulos, he seemed to discover confidence and even a bit of authority. The two of them conversed with increasing exuberance and familiarity. Vennie thought that they even began to look as if they were kin, of sorts. Finally, Corporal Eliopoulos nodded, and the young boy began talking, animatedly, with the one whom Vennie judged to be the leader of the local militia.

"What did he say?" Vennie and Captain Markham chorused, as Corporal Eliopoulos rejoined the cluster of airmen, nurses and enlisted corpsmen clustered around the two wounded and their stack of reclaimed luggage and supplies. The wrecked C-54 began to sullenly burn at some distance.

"We're OK. They're partisans, in the Resistance brigade against the Italians. The kid I was talking to, his mom is a Greek from Thessaloniki. They will help us. They hold all the villages hereabouts, but the Italians and Germans are in the cities. It's complicated," Corporal Eliopoulos shrugged. "Everyone against everyone, but these guys say they will help us. They'll send a message to *Tzoni o Anglos*. That's Johnny the Englishman. He's one of those sneaky spy-liaison types, one with a radio, or some way to contact his bosses in England, from what they sort of didn't say. They seem to think that he can arrange for us to be picked up, somehow."

"In light of no better offers received," Captain Markham picked up one of the medium-sized boxes from the stack of goods removed from the C-54, and shouldered it, capably. "And as an alternative to being a prisoner of war, I'd accept their kind offer of shelter and assistance. I'm not cut out to be a foot-soldier for any longer than absolutely necessary. If you would be so kind, Corp – extend to these good gentlemen our thanks for their hospitality and aid. And take us to ... wherever."

"We ought to make most of our medical and food supplies over to them," Vennie suggested. "In gratitude for their kindness, of course. Let them know that, Steve."

"They could take it outright, cut all of our throats and dump our bodies in the nearest ditch," Captain Markham murmured to Vennie, as Corporal Eliopoulos relayed that message to the boy who understood Greek. "They look the sort of brigands who would, without a second thought. I suppose the saving grace is that we are on the same side against the Jerries and the Ities. We'll take our allies where we can find them or where they find us. One thing, Lt. Stoneman; I don't think we should shed our uniforms, under any circumstance. I don't know how the war is run in this part of the world, but if we are in uniform, we are protected by the Geneva Convention, for whatever thin comfort that might be worth. In civilian clothes, we run the risk of being shot as spies out of hand."

"Good to know," Vennie murmured. This thought had never occurred to her. She had never contemplated the possibilities inherent of being stranded in enemy territory. This had happened to other nurses, like Helen Drinkwater – but she had never thought that it would happen to her.

Postcard from Peg to Mr. Charles Stoneman, c/o postmaster Deming New Mexico, dated 10 December 1943, postmarked Brisbane, Queensland.

Dear Uncle Charlie:
My latest letter to Vennie has been returned by the postman, with a notation that she is 'missing in action.' What

has happened? Have you had that awful telegram delivered from the War Department? Please let me know soonest.

Love, Peggy Becker Morehouse

Letter from Peg to Vennie, dated 26 December 1943, Postmarked Brisbane, Queensland, Australia.

Dear Cuz:

I am not quite certain what I will do with this letter, knowing that you are 'missing.' In some careless fashion, has the Army Department merely lost track of you? Or was the ship or airplane in which you were traveling been sunk/shot down, and you are therefore not to be located immediately in any way, shape or form? I sent a postcard to your father, asking for any news; news which I pray every morning and night will be good. I have been so long in the habit of penning long letters to you, my dear cousin and near-sister, so as the old Victorian memoirs have it, I take my pen in hand and set down an account of our holiday revels.

Edith and Stanley went to midnight mass at St. Paul's, which a splendid modern brick church a little distant. Mavis went with them, as she was able to get leave from her post. She looked most splendidly fit and tanned, and very fine in her uniform, and regaled us all with tales of how much fun she was able to have, marching and drilling and playing around with guns and grenades. I pity any feckless Jap soldier *(or any other soldier, period!)* who tried to overpower a girl like Mavis. She would break the poor fellow in half without much trouble at all.

We had a Christmas tree, of course; a very small Norfolk Pine in a tub which Edith keeps in her garden of potted plants on the verandah. Eventually, this tree will be planted in the ground, but for now, it lives a happy little sheltered tree life, and submits agreeably to the indignity of being decked out with glass ornaments and paper garlands once a year. So much happier for the tree, I think, than in that grim Hans Christian Anderson story, about the poor little fir tree, cut down from his place in the forest and put in the parlor for Christmas, and then afterwards cut up and burned as trash. *(Ugh. I don't read those stories of his to Tom and Olivia. I don't want them to have nightmares. Practically everything and everybody in them dies <u>hideously</u>! Whoever said his stories were good for children anyway? Isn't there enough death and tragedy around us, that we must go shopping for more?)*

Tom, Olivia, and Mavis hung out their stockings after supper on Christmas Eve. It's a small thing but touching, Mavis being this tall strapping girl soldier – but still looking to have Santa Claus visit on Christmas Eve, just as your soldiers did last year in the hospital in Arzew, where you and other nurses sewed stockings for them all, to be filled with presents of candy and other small gifts. Edith entrusted to me the presents to put out after the children went to bed, and I did so. We had collected between us rather a nice lot of 'prezzies' but took special care for Tom and Olivia. That nice stray soldier who came to Olivia's birthday party and did magic tricks all those months ago shipped out a bit afterwards, destination unspecified – but before he did, he visited the house and gave me a box, already gift-wrapped. He has a small daughter in his hometown, and Olivia reminded him of her most poignantly. He had his wife buy a stuffed white bunny toy and send it to him, to make a Christmas present for Olivia. We exchanged addresses ... but I do not know if I will hear from him ever. The soldiers, sailors and airmen who come to the St. George's Club are, I think, like ships that pass in the night, after mooring up together and sending messages back and forth. Olivia's soldier is a married man.

Tommy ... is he one of those with whom I moor up for years and then drift apart and never see again? I may very well tear up this letter. But it comforts me to write it, so I will carry on, dear Cuz.

We had other presents for the children; each had a bar of chocolate, from various American friends through the St. George Club. Olivia had her bunny, and Tom had a small wickerwork creel of his own, the better for which to store the fish that he has caught ... with his very own small reel and rod, which are the gift of Stanley. Stanley also made in secret in his workroom a rocking cradle and a high-chair for Olivia's baby-doll, a doll which was her cherished present for her last birthday. Tom had the collections of fairy story books that you had sent, for which I cannot thank you enough. He has sat up at nights with a flashlight under the bedcovers to read them all, from cover to cover several times.

Edith and I also reviewed Edith's trunk of unfashionable clothes from her youth. We cut apart a summer dress of pink Liberty print to make a pretty set of matching dresses for Olivia and Dolly. Edith also contrived in secret to make another dress for me out of another Liberty print garment. She had so many dresses made from good materiel for her social occasions in Malaya, and never wore many of them again once they became unfashionable. Should you ever visit Australia, I am certain that Edith will pull out her old trunk, and size you up with her tape measure and wrist-pincushion and remake a dress for you as well. And the dress that emerges from Edith's treadle sewing machine will be lovely, and the envy of any number of Paris couturiers! And without the use of any ration points, which is why we take the trouble to pick out seams and unravel the stitches attaching trim, et cetera.

We were also reviewing a number of sweaters and cardigans and unraveling them for the yarn; a tedious process, but eventually rewarding, for we have gotten lovely pullover sweaters and cardigans for Olivia and Tom, as well as some sturdy pairs of socks for Mavis. You will already know, Cuz, how hard that issue military boots are on woolen socks!

Enough of our scheme and thanks for gifts – and we did have quite a jolly Christmas supper! Edith did manage to procure a goose for the grand Christmas supper. And the pudding was awesome! I think we are in hock as regards eggs for the next three months or so to the friend who arranged this bounty, but it was so worth it! We made a whole meal bread stuffing with a taste of sausage mince and celery, onions and parsley in it from Edith's bountiful garden. Edith and Stanley invited several friends – including Colonel G. and some other stray Americans, and some dear friends from St. Pauls' – and we had a lovely supper, quite putting aside our worries about friends in this dark time. A 'light to lighten the gentiles' is how the verse from the service goes, I think. I was not in the least religious in the beginning, and I am afraid that I am only attentive to prayers and ritual now because it is a time of crisis. Likely I shall fall away once the crisis is past. Because I am a shallow person –

Love,
Your dear Cuz, Peg

Chapter 12 – Le Chant des Partisans

"They say for us to come with them, quickly," Corporal Eliopoulos relayed to the group of stranded nurses, corpsmen, and aircrew. "The Italians – even the Germans for certain would have seen the airplane going down. They will be looking for it ... and us."

"All the better reason for departing at speed," Captain Markham nodded. "And to haul along what we can carry, aside from Ray and your mangled corpsman, Lt. Stoneman," He added as an aside, and Vennie nodded.

The Albanian partisans were doing a businesslike job of vacating the area, under the direction of an authoritative middle-aged man in a rusty black fez, who sported the most impressive gray mustache that Vennie had ever seen in life – a mustache only equaled in old pictures of the German singing society, or of the brewery workers in San Antonio in the last century. Already half of the armed partisans had shouldered burdens from the pile of supplies and melted back into the winter landscape from which they had emerged. From somewhere there appeared a small cart pulled by two mules, into which Sgt. Reyes and Private Rennie were loaded.

"At least, the jolting will keep your sergeant awake," Mary Shipman confided, in a quick consultation with Vennie and Captain Markham. "Private Rennie is out to sea on a bountiful tide of morphine. He shouldn't feel anything at all – and we padded his poor leg to spare him any further injury. So," she added privately to Vennie, and with a plaintive sigh as they both hitched up their musette bags and personal burdens and fell in line behind the ragged partisans. "It seems like a kind of movie adventure, doesn't it! Down behind enemy lines. I can't recall anything about this possibility being suggested to us when I signed on."

"It's a war," Vennie replied, somewhat bitterly. "In a war, all bets are off. It doesn't matter what the nurse-recruiter or the patriotic posters all said. That we would be shot at in spite of showing the Red Cross emblem, and be on ships that would be bombed or torpedoed? It's a bloody war, Mary, but that shouldn't stop us from doing our part without whining."

"I wasn't whining, Vennie," Mary replied, with mild indignation. "Merely making an observation about working conditions. How long shall we have to walk, do you think?"

"Me, I was thinking of a stiff drink and a good long sleep," Captain Markham added. "Didn't think that it would be in Albania, instead of Italy. But I'll take what I can get, as long as it is this side of a grave. It's a good landing if you can walk away from it."

As they spoke, the last of the pile of supplies were being dispersed among the Albanian partisans. Two of the younger men among them were busy with rough brooms in sweeping away any trace of footsteps.

"I don't know," Vennie answered. She was heartened at seeing how efficiently any trace of how many had been on the wrecked C-54 were being erased, as well as how much of what they had brought with them were being carried along by the partisan rescue party. The fire in the wreck of the airplane was well-along. With luck, whoever among the occupying authority came to investigate would assume that all the crew had bailed out long before before the crash.

What they carried with them was wealth indeed, to an impoverished and occupied country. The medical supplies – plasma, drugs, morphine, bandages, and dressings; all that would be of inestimable worth. They hadn't much in the way of food, though, unless there had been some among the supplies. They had all expected to land in liberated Italy. As far as Vennie knew, none of the other nurses and corpsmen carried three days-worth of canned C-rations, as she and the other medical personnel landing in North Africa had done. She did now. So had Ginger and Corporal Eliopoulos, on her advice.

It wasn't supposed to happen like this! She raged inwardly and fought down that rage as she walked, with Mary and the other nurses, and Captain Markham, trailing after the donkey cart. *No, it was not – they were supposed to fly! This was horrible! What was she supposed to do now?*

It appeared that ... well, nothing much, other than pay attention. After a long afternoon walk through the winter-burned Albanian countryside under the authority of the man whom Vennie had already nicknamed "Mr. Mustache," and skirting the margins of a slate-grey lake and climbing constantly, they arrived at a small sprawling village of whitewashed stone houses roofed with slate or tile. A single unpaved street ran through the village, climbing up the hillside on which it was built, off of which were appended half a dozen muddy lanes, all of which testified to the presence of many goats, horses, and cattle, and chickens clucking happily among the weed-grown margins. Vennie was accustomed to this kind of rural scene – she had grown up on a ranch, after all, a ranch with jagged mountains and swift-running streams within a short walk of the main house. She suspected that those of the stranded party who had come from more urban backgrounds would be utterly boggled. The jagged mountain peaks all around were capped with snow; it would be cold tonight.

"What is this place called?" Vennie asked of Corporal Eliopoulos, as they trudged up the weary heights towards a tall blunt tower crowned with a cross, instead of the crescent that Vennie had vaguely expected.

"Sheper," Corporal Eliopoulos replied. "Sheper. They're Orthodox here, near as I can make out. We're a little bit north of Macedonia. Extremely northern Greek, I think."

"As Oklahoma is extremely northern Texas," Vennie commented. Captain Markham, slogging along next to them under the burden of a box from the cargo, chuckled heartily.

They came to an abrupt curve in the road, a curve carefully carved out of the steep hillside and buttressed with stone blocks. The walls and roofs of the village rose above them. They had come to the church, a plain fortress-like place of stone and slate tiles. Here they paused, for their guides to this place had also paused; all those wolfish, scruffy-bearded men. Mr. Mustache and the Greek-speaking boy also stood there, somewhat elevated with his new importance as a translator.

"They have places for us to stay," Corporal Eliopoulos reported, after a brief three-way consultation. "The men in several houses. We will be led there and treated as honored guests. The two injured, to the house of Madame Marsela, a respectable widow. She is the mother of Kapiten Konstantin, the leader of the partisans in these parts," Corporal Eliopoulos nodded toward Mr. Mustache. "She has a large house and has agreed to shelter the women in our party. He will send word to *Tzoni o Anglos* – to Johnny the Englishman, who has a radio to speak to his commanders in England. But it will be a few days until he comes to Sheper although knowing of our need, he may come sooner than that. It all depends," Corporal Eliopoulos added, with a shrug. "That is what they say to me, sir."

"All right, people," Captain Markham replied. "I don't like that we are all being separated but I suppose that it is for the best. They know the territory and we do not. And it's getting late in the day. We need a place to rest, while everyone figures out what to do next and to tend to our wounded guys."

"We'll see to them," Vennie replied, with mild trepidation. "It's getting late in the day, and cold, too – can they show us all where we are to stay?"

Corporal Eliopoulos nodded, and resumed the three-way consultation with the boy who spoke Greek and Kapiten Konstantin.

"Are you certain that we can trust these people?" Mary Shipman murmured. Vennie leaned against the back of the cart.

"No, not entirely," she replied, honestly. "We're strangers in their country in wartime. But they hate the Nazis and the Italians, as far as we know, and we're useful strangers, since we are also fighting the Nazis and the Italians. And we have medical supplies; not much, really, but probably more than what they might have." Realistically, Vennie thought to herself; all they <u>had</u> was trust, trust in the rough-looking men of Sheper and the unknown Englishman whose real name probably wasn't John.

"They'll take Ray and Stephen to Madame Marsala's house," Corporal Eliopoulos announced, after another consultation with the Greek boy – whose name was Nico, it emerged – and Kapiten Kostandin. Vennie assumed meant what it sounded like in English. How generous and able that rescue might prove to be was a question yet to be answered. Vennie thought privately that Kapiten Kostandin looked like pictures of her Grandfather Freddy Stoneman; a slight and whip-lean man in the few old pictures of him in the album at home, a man as tough as boiled leather, as one might have to be, to have been a trail boss leading cattle to Kansas, and before that, a soldier in the Frontier Battalion during the War Between the States. He had also gone out to California seeking gold, when he was a very young man, even younger than Corporal Eliopoulos, and done a number of things there, according to family legend, including riding for the Pony Express, panning for gold in a California river, and helping Judge Roy Bean escape from a hanging sentence. *(This all was dismissed by the family as a legend, although Granny Sophie had always insisted it was true. Since she was half his age when they married just before the turn of the century, she couldn't possibly have known anything more than what she was told by Grandpa Stoneman, or Steinmetz as he had been known in life, before his son legally changed the family name.)*

Kapiten Kostandin gestured to the driver of the cart, and Vennie and the handful of nurses trailed after him, up the winding street, stumbling a bit here and there over cobbles. They came eventually to a tall square tower of a stone building, built back into the hillside. A wide double gate opened to the street, wide enough to accommodate the mule cart with the wounded men in it.

"Interesting," Mary Shipman observed. "It's like the lower level of a castle keep with the stables for horses and livestock."

"Bit smelly in hot weather, though," Vennie replied, as she looked around. Private Rennie, still blissfully unconscious, was being carried towards the stone staircase at the back of the long dim room. "Reminds me of my cousin's family place, though not as old as this. There was a basement built into the hill, open on one side. It was always cool in the hottest summer. The upper floors were nice, though. The view from the parlor window was amazing."

Sgt. Reyes insisted on walking, once helped from the cart, although he still winced at every move and reacted to strong light and sudden movement as if he had the mother of all hangovers. The straggle of nurses and their patients, and the two partisans who carried Private Rennie reached the top of the stairs, where a woman of certain age, clad in a splendid black costume awaited them at the top of the stairs: the redoubtable Madame Marsala. Corporal Eliopoulos, Niko the Greek boy, and Kapiten Kostandin accompanied them also.

Madame Marsala was taller than her son, with iron-grey hair combed back severely under an elaborate white kerchief trimmed with gold coins and braid. She would have been plain in youth, Vennie thought, but of a forceful character, nevertheless. She wore a black dress down to her ankles, with a short apron over it, and a waistcoat lavishly trimmed with more gold coins and bullion-braid. It amused Vennie to see that her son deferred to her, almost hesitantly. It was curious, Vennie decided; when you didn't understand the language, you needed to watch most intently. One gained a sense of what was going on, even without understanding the exact words. The attitude, the tone of voice, even the very gestures ... all revealed clues to what was going on, and the relationship between people.

Madame Marsala was a partisan herself, of the most fervent kind – that became clear almost at once. She directed the two wounded to be carried to another room within the house, and then regarded Vennie, Mary, and the five other nurses with what might be taken as an expression of welcome and approval on any less-formidable face.

"The madame welcomes you to her house, her table and her bread and salt," Corporal Eliopoulos reported. "She will consider you as kin and daughters. She understands that you all," and Corporal Eliopoulos sent a puzzled look aside to Vennie, "Are a sort of sworn virgin."

"You'd hope!" Mary Shipman muttered. Vennie whispered for her to hush. She had a vague notion of having read about women in Albania, taking an oath of chastity for reasons of assuming male privileges such as wearing trousers, carrying weapons and a degree of social freedom in associations.

"Tell her that we are a kind of sworn sisterhood," Vennie replied. "We are all trained nurses. We have taken an oath of service and put on trousers to better care for our brothers in arms ... our brothers in arms against the Nazis. Tell her that we are grateful for her kindness and hospitality, knowing of the dangers to her house and family that might come to her and to Sheper by aiding us."

This being relayed to the formidable Madame Marsala, who radiated approval, to the secret relief of Vennie, and Corporal Eliopoulos, who relayed the reply from Kapiten Kostandin.

"There is nothing to fear. The Partisans hold the countryside and Sheper. The eyes of a hundred thousand Partisans keep watch on the Germans and the Italians. They do not wipe their ..." Corporal Eliopoulos coughed gently to cover the elided word, as he was young and in spite of being in the Army had imbibed the notion that there were some words not to be said to women, even nurses. "Or ... um..." and here Vennie suspected that Corporal Eliopoulos was skipping over a very much cruder description, "... cuddle with their girlfriends without a dozen eyes of our Partisans watching and making notes. You have nothing to fear."

"We are grateful, indeed," Vennie replied, although she did hope that none of the watchful Partisan eyes would be turned upon them in such a manner. Really, this was as discomforting as some of the tales that Granny Sophie had told of her young days; the sense of always being watched by censorious eyes, ready to take notes and condemn unhesitatingly.

"I have to go now," Corporal Eliopoulos added, apologetically. "The guys are all being taken to where we will stay. But Kapiten Konstantin says that Johnny the Englishman will come as soon as he is notified."

"How long might that take?" Vennie asked, and when relayed, Kapitan Konstantin shrugged, spreading his hands wide.

"He does not know," Corporal Eliopoulos relayed, although it was hardly necessary.

It turned out to be five days; five days which Vennie found rather restful, after a night or two of waking up constantly, expecting that Nazi soldiers were going to break down the doors of Madame Marsala's house and arrest them all and send them to who-knows-what kind of prison camp. But no; they were safe here, almost safer than they might have been in any nurses' quarters when they had been in training. The seven nurses all put aside such fears, all but the youngest of them, Betty Standish, who confessed to having visions of being dragged off and put into a harem, to be ravished repeatedly and enjoyably by an amorous Turk.

"You've read too many trashy novels," Vennie told her, sternly. They were all sitting in the open gallery on the top floor of Madame Marsala's house, an open gallery which afforded a view over half of the village, and the peaks across the shallow valley, the peaks now covered in white to half their craggy heights. "This is Albania. Not Algiers or Turkey. Steve Eliopoulos says that the Greeks and Christians in the Balkans hate the Turks like poison."

"Well, damn," Betty replied pertly, "Another fantasy gone to all heck!"

"We are in a harem, of sorts," Mary pointed out. "Or a convent. Look, there's Steve and Kapiten Konstantin ... and who's the man with them?"

Vennie, Betty and Mary looked down from the gallery, which had been warmed by the afternoon sun, and so was not too uncomfortably chill. This, the top story of Madame Marsala's house was the refuge of women, or so Vennie had gathered. To meet and consult with the men; it was the accepted thing to go down to the main floor, to a hall-like room with an ornate coffered wood ceiling, and a long padded low divan around three sides. An ornate Persian carpet dominated the open space between the divans; a regular pattern of geometric flowers woven on a rust-red background into the center, and a border of dark-gold leaves on dark blue all around. This was the house's main reception room, and mostly frequented by Kapiten Kostandin and the other men. This separation amused Vennie, considerably. It was almost Victorian, having that private female refuge above stairs.

The seven nurses had been welcomed and treated very well, although it meant that they were sleeping two and three in bedsteads in the largest of the upper-floor rooms, all cuddled under rough woolen blankets and sheepskins, since Madame Marsala's house was unheated save for fireplaces in the larger rooms and it was now mid-winter. The additional bodies in bed meant more warmth, on those nights when a howling gale sent icy fingers through the rough shutters and radiated icy-cold through stone walls. The furnishings upstairs were a curious mixture of plain, rough-hewn country make with now and again some delicate and ornate bit of Biedermeier; obviously much prized, and several very elegant, framed mirrors, trimmed with a lot of gilt and strings of crystals. There was an ancient wind-up gramophone with a collection of thick records so old that most of them were recorded on one side only, mostly of badly scratched versions of Viennese waltzes and classical piano pieces so degraded by age and damage that the tunes were often a matter of guess.

There was a single shelf of books, most in German or Greek. From the pictures in the illustrated editions, Vennie surmised that most were the kind of novels that accumulated in Mrs. Adele Millefield's boudoir; romance novels from the turn of the century by lady novelists with three names. There were two in English, which the women fell upon with delight: a copy of Kipling's *Jungle Book* stories and Gene Stratton Porter's *A Girl of the Limberlost*. By which means those two books had come to roost in the shelves of the grandest house in a tiny village in Albania, Vennie and the other women could not think of a rational reason – but they were grateful, all the same. The only other books in their possession was Mary's copy of *Gone With the Wind*, and an Army manual from the flight nurse school course, which Vennie had kept in her kit against possible future instruction.

The seven women, when not tending to the two injured men diverted themselves with knitting while one of them read aloud from the three books of diverting fiction for hours on end and assisting Madame Marsala and two elderly female servants with light housework – sweeping and dusting, mostly. Madame Marsala possessed an inexhaustible supply of heavy woolen homespun yarn with smelled faintly of sheep and whatever compound it had been dyed with. They turned to knitting with it in the gallery on sunny days, when midday and afternoon sunshine poured through the windows. Away across the valley below Sheper and the next range of mountains, hawks wheeled and spun in updrafts. Against all expectation, it was a surprisingly restful routine, Vennie thought. In the middle of war's alarms, German occupation of foreign lands, and onerous duties, it was almost a holiday, to sit knitting socks, mufflers,

Balaclava helmets and pullovers, whilst sitting on a sun-warmed balcony, listening to one of the other girls reading from a novel.

The meals of various dishes of mutton, chicken and ... wild game, perhaps – served with rice or spaghetti, and coarse brown bread were all very good, although in spare helpings and sometimes curiously spiced. There was a war on, after all.

"I wonder if that is not Johnny the Englishman?" she ventured. "I expect that we should go downstairs and meet him. From what Steve said, he is the means of letting our families know that we are not lost entirely, and of arranging us to be evacuated by sea, should we reach the coast by whatever means."

This being agreed upon, Vennie, Mary and Betty went down to the main parlor, or salon in the house, after having spread the word among the other nurses. Presently, Corporal Eliopoulos, Niko and Kapiten Konstantin appeared, along with the stranger – who at first glance appeared as roughly dressed and indifferently barbered as any of the other partisans and dressed in much the same utilitarian dark trousers and heavy woolen pullover sweater. But the stranger's face was rounded and softer looking in appearance. He appeared to have auburn hair, in contrast to the rest of Kapiten Konstantin's partisans and Albanian men in Sheper, who generally were dark and aquiline in feature. The beard stubble coming out on this man's face was sandy-reddish, and he had light eyes.

"Good god, so it's true!" he exclaimed in perfect British English as soon as he set eyes on Vennie and the other nurses, clustered apprehensively in the divan reception room on the second floor. "American women stranded here! I didn't know what to believe at first when I received the message! How'd 'you do, ma'am! John from the Ministry of Ungentlemanly Warfare. I'm here to facilitate your ... expatriation from this unfortunately awkward situation."

"Venetia Stoneman, First Lieutenant US Army Nurse Corps," Vennie replied, nonplussed. A perfect British accent coming from this scruffy tramp; that was a completely unsettling thing, akin to having the nearest ragged, apparently drink-sodden beggar suddenly begin declaiming Shakespeare in a perfectly sober voice. The mysterious Johnny did have a pleasant and resonant voice. He sounded as if he could launch into a Shakespearean soliloquy with very little encouragement. "Pleased to make your acquaintance. I made a list of the medical personnel with our party. We were told that you could send a message, and your superior officer might be able to notify our commander and our families that we are safe. They must be worried terribly," Vennie added, for she thought again with dread of how her father and mothers' faces must have been drained of all blood and hope at receiving a telegram from the War Department. There were too many other families around Deming who had received such telegrams.

"I think that this message may relieve the minds of all your families enormously," Johnny replied, as he accepted the penciled list with an expression of relief. "Look, I'll have my radio op send it at once. We're eight hours from England, you know. It may take some time for the boffins to work their magic, but we'll see every one of you safely out of here. My word on it..." he added. For a brief moment, he looked terribly strained, as of their presence was a complication unforeseen, and he didn't wish to make them all feel they were an additional burden to whatever he had come to Albania to facilitate.

Of course, Johnny the Englishman was in Albania, with a radio operator, no less, to serve some clandestine purpose in the Allied cause. Likely nefarious, violent, and very, very secret. Vennie could only think that they all ought to be grateful for having a conduit into the Ministry of Ungentlemanly Warfare – whatever that meant in the real table of military commands.

Now he asked, in all earnestness, "Look, Ma Marsala and Captain Konstantin are treating you all well? He's a good bloke, and Ma Marsala is a pip. They're in the *Balli Kombëtar* wing of the Albanian resistance, not that bloody Bolshi mob under Hoxha. Right bastards all, but at least the Balli lot aren't planning domination over all, mountain and plain. They only want to free their bit from being bossed around by foreigners, so they've made allies of whomever in convenience ... including scum like us," Johnny the Englishman added with a wry smile.

"Madame Marsala has been a most considerate hostess," Vennie added, and the other nurses all chorused agreement. Vennie added, apologetically, "One of our party has suffered a compound fracture of the leg in the crash. Private Rennie cannot travel until his wound is healed sufficiently. Lieutenant Shipman and I have already discussed this. We'll stay with him here until he's fit to be moved. Madame Marsala is agreeable; of course, he <u>must</u> stay until he is able to travel. Corporal Eliopoulos has already volunteered to remain with us until that time. It may be at least a month, maybe two."

"Oh, first-rate," Johnny the Englishman replied, although he didn't look all that relieved. Vennie intuited his thoughts: *two parties to be evacuated by sea from Albania, not the total of them in one fell swoop and the second after many weeks delay* – and the matter of keeping them safe in Madame Marsala's house! Johnny the Englishman's chore was doubled, and their presence created a major distraction from whatever his main purpose had been, in being sent clandestinely to Albania with a radio set and an operator.

Vennie could hardly imagine what that purpose might be, other than to make life a low-key misery for the German occupying forces, although some grand and spectacular act of sabotage against them was a distinct possibility.

"I'll have the message send out directly," Johnny the Englishman promised again, adding, "It will take at least three or four days to get it through and make arrangements for a rendezvous on the coast. Until then ..."

"We will continue to enjoy the generous hospitality of our hosts," Vennie replied. Johnny the Englishman grinned, "And ensure that our wounded make a good recovery."

"Splendid," Johnny returned, and Kapiten Kostandin made a gesture to his mother that indicated the interview with the women was done, and now he had important matters to discuss with the men. Vennie, Mary and Betty withdrew from the grand chamber and returned to the upstairs, although they visited that small chamber designated as a sickroom, where Private Rennie and Sgt. Reyes were being tended as carefully as if they were in the finest hospital back in the States.

In the end, it took a week for Johnny the Englishman to facilitate passage for the larger party of the group which had survived the forced landing. He appeared again at the end of that time, again in Madame Marsala's parlor, where all the party of stranded Americans save the bed-ridden Private Rennie had been warned to assemble by Niko and Corporal Eliopoulos.

"It's sorted," Johnny the Englishman announced. "First the good news: there'll be a pick-up off a certain beach near Luköve. They'll come every night at midnight for three nights, starting in ten days. That's time enough to get there... It'll be a bit over sixty miles, even taking short-cuts through the hills."

"You'll have to make ten miles in a day's walk," Vennie murmured, recalling some of the elderly relatives and their stories of pioneering days and long-trail cattle drives to Kansas, and those days of training marches on the Salisbury Plain, when she first deployed overseas.

The mysterious Johnny nodded, in acknowledgement. "Less or more than that, since it all depends on how rough the terrain."

"And the bad news?" Captain Markham had raised a skeptical eyebrow. Yes, there was always bad news, some malignant fly in an otherwise satisfactory ointment, especially with regard to military on the front line, or even military somewhat far in the other direction – the wrong direction. Johnny the Englishman shrugged, apologetically.

"Well ... er ... you see, you lot may have to walk most of the way. Motor transport is a bit dicey, y'see. Attract too much attention, traveling on the main roads anyway, attention from the wrong sort. Jerries and Ities – the Occupation, you know. Your party will be handed on, from group to group, but the best and surest way for them is to conduct you by footpaths. Sorry about all that walking, but it's the best way. Our partisan chaps will see that you will stay every night in shelter of sorts, so there is that."

"On foot!" Captain Markham glowered, heavily. "For Chrissake, man, I joined the Air Corps because I would rather fly than be foot-slogging infantry!"

"You'll have to be, if you want to go back to your bloody Air Corps," Johnny the Englishman replied, evenly. Vennie stifled a small giggle at the sight of the wrathful expressions on the faces of the transport aircrew. Although it meant that the five nurses would have to walk as well. Eventually, she and Mary, Corporal Eliopoulos and the recovered Private Rennie would also have to walk. Vennie vividly recalled those long marches with packs over green country roads, on the Salisbury Plain. That was in those training days before being deployed to North Africa. She was certain that she was fit for it herself. Mary and Corporal Eliopoulos would be fit also, but the wounded Private Rennie? The compound fracture had begun to knit, the abused and crushed tissue over it was barely beginning to heal, without the reddened, puffy flesh and seeping wounds which would indicate infection. The nurses were pleased with his recovery so far. So was Private Rennie, who was barely 18 and from a sternly devout Adventist and pacifist although patriotic family. *Cross that bridge when they came to it*, Vennie told herself. Rennie wouldn't be fit to walk, not the less across half of Albania for at least another month or two.

Vennie crossed her hands and schooled her expression to calm. "How soon do they need to leave?" she asked, quietly. *Yes, calm fortitude in the face of any event was one of her talents.*

"First thing tomorrow," Johnny the Englishman replied, evenly, and there was a rustle of excitement and dismay across the room. "Starting at dawn. The trails are pretty rough, and dangerous over the hills in the dark. I'll accompany you for the first leg or two, just to see that everything's in train. You shouldn't have to carry full packs, though. We'll see you to shelter and a good meal every night."

"Thanks for that consideration," Captain Markham replied dryly, and if he were one of her brothers, Vennie would have kicked his ankle under the table. She settled for glaring at a superior officer with her most disapproving expression on her face. This was no time to be borderline-rude to someone facilitating their escape, especially one who was risking his own freedom, life, and other possible mission in doing so. In accordance with Captain Markham's own advice, they were all wearing American uniforms, their identity plain and clear. Johnny the Englishman wasn't – and if captured by the Nazis, he would be risking a bullet-pocked wall and a firing squad at dawn and that would be the very best possible outcome in that event.

Chapter 13 – Don't Sit Under the Apple Tree

Letter from Vennie to Peg, dated March 17, 1944, postmarked APO, written from Foggia, Italy

Dear Peg: I should imagine that you are as surprised as anything to hear from me, after so many months of silence in this quarter! I have been having an adventure ... in Albania, of all places. Doesn't this sound like the title of a Nancy Drew book – *The Adventure in Albania!?* I had letters from Dad and Mom, and everyone in the family waiting, when I got back to Italy! Did anyone write to tell you what had happened? I am certain that you must have worried awfully, but really, it was nothing much ... well, it was <u>something</u>, but not near to the degree as bad as the captivity of my friend Helen from nursing school, or your poor Tommy in the hands of the beastly Japs.

What happened was this; I was on a routine transport flight from Catania in Sicily to Bari, with six other nurses and a dozen corpsmen. The flight was meant to bring in some supplies and relief personnel to the forward hospital there. And from Bari, we were expected to bring back a full load of stretcher and ambulatory patients from the field hospital just behind the front to a well-equipped hospital in the rear – it's my job now, as a specialty air-evacuation nurse, you see; to care for these cases during the flight, which sometimes gets rather dicey, since many of the boys have never been on an airplane before, and besides, are quite often very ill and confused. But instead, the most horrific bad winter weather and a seriously faulty compass forced the AC directly east, until we ran low on fuel and the pilot had to make a forced landing in Albania. Between mountain ranges, on the only almost-flat land for simply miles! It was our good fortune that only two of our number were injured in the landing, and only one badly enough to require a long stint of recovery. And that's where I have been for the last three months – a guest of the Resistance in Albania! It was also our tremendously good fortune to be collected up by a partisan group almost at once and given shelter in a small town that I cannot name for reasons of war security. It seems that in Albania, at least, the German Occupation is not terribly through. It was also arranged, through means that I cannot mention, for the larger number of our stranded party, to be guided to the coast, retrieved by an ally, and conveyed to safety – again, I cannot say anything about this. It was arranged through the same means, for several of us to remain behind at a safe refuge in the Albanian mountains, caring for the one among our party who was severely injured in the forced landing. As soon as that person could travel, we followed the same means of evacuation back to Allied-held territory. And that is it and all that I might say, save that we all nearly wore out the soles of our shoes, for our transport was by shanks' mare most of the way, although there was a leg where we did have horses for transport.

As for my stay in Albania, it was a curiously enjoyable experience, Peg – a leisure of sitting in a sun-warmed balcony, knitting! And only one patient to care for. I came to love the mountains of Albania. Perhaps when the war is over, I might go back there, or to some other place which sports craggy stone-grey ranges of mountains, lightly dusted with snow. But I am back to my usual duties as of this writing, accompanying regular flights of wounded soldiers back from the front to established hospitals in the rear.

Another Christmas has passed – how the time flies! Did you have a wonderful time with Edith and Stanley and their friends? I looked at the last letter that I had from you oh so many months past, and you wrote that Little Tommy was to start school very shortly after the Christmas holidays! Oh, my – he is nearly a grown-up boy now! By the time that you receive this, he will have already been several months in school. Please let me know how he is getting along.

Oh, Peg – I have so missed you, and hearing about all your boring life in Australia, the simple domestic doings and amusing things that your children have said and done. They must be so many things, since Tom is a big boy of almost six, and Olivia is coming up on her second birthday! Send me pictures of them, if you can, and it does not cost terribly much. I want to hear from you and apologize from the bottom of my heart for the circumstance that might have led you to think that I was most permanently 'missing'!

All my love, from your very-much-alive Cuz
Vennie

The first C-54 set down at the field near Castel Volturno, as threatening towers of dark grey cloud blotted out more and more of pale blue spring sky. It was mid-morning and for springtime in Italy, a blustery and windy day. The pilot coasted to a gentle stop, close to where the ground crew waited to empty the cargo, refuel the C-54 and fit out the inside for the return journey with litter and ambulatory patients from the transit hospital. Most always, this could be done in minutes. But with a veil of rain already beginning to fall across the end of the runway, loading patients in driving rain was not medically advisable. Being thoroughly wetted and then subjected to cold at altitude would be too much, even for patients who had been vetted and approved to travel. Waiting while the storm blew over wouldn't harm anyone, and the radio operator had already messaged the transit hospital regarding the delay. Vennie waited for the crew chief to give the all-clear, for her and the assisting medic, Corporal DeSanto, to unbuckle their safety harnesses and get up from the seat.

"We're gonna wait for the storm to clear before we load and take off," the enlisted crew chief said. "It's gonna be pouring buckets in about five minutes. Y'all got time for late breakfast."

"Good," Vennie nodded in perfect agreement.

At her side, Ginger Lloyd remarked, "I will never, ever become bored with successful landings!"

It was the first time they had flown together since the inadvertent diversion to Albania.

"Neither do I," Vennie assured her. "As long as the number of successful take-offs equal the number of successful landings, I am a happy nurse. Then there are those parachute infantry guys who jump out of perfectly useful airplanes - on purpose? They even have a special insignia for being jump-qualified!"

"Maniacs, the lot of them," Ginger replied, as she and Vennie climbed down the short ladder to the prefab metal matting which formed the airfield hard stand. They stood for a moment, enjoying the fresh air. There was nothing more to be heard, over the roaring engines of another C-54 coasting into the hard stand area. Now and again, between fumes of aviation fuel and engine exhaust, gusts of wind tantalized with the scent of newly turned damp earth, crushed green grass and rain. In the silence that fell as soon as the propeller blades of the second aircraft stopped turning, Ginger added, "I expect that in the event of an offensive involving masses of parachute infantry, we will have a lot of patients with broken ankles and legs. Splints and traction, hallowed be thy name."

Vennie solemnly crossed herself. "And plaster casts, amen."

Ginger giggled. A brief moment of levity between worry, and responsibility. Within an hour, ambulances and trucks would begin delivering their patients to be transported to the main hospital, back in Tunisia. Now the pilot and co-pilot emerged from the C-54, and stood with the crew chief, relishing the spring air. Ginger, who had no scruples about exercising her charm on males of every degree, twinkled a smile at them all and asked,

"Where does a girl get shown a good meal around here, Lieutenant?"

Lieutenant Mathison, the pilot, made a gallant half-bow and drawled, "A good meal is purely out of the question, ma'am – but an adequate meal might be had at the chow hall. I understand that the chief cook here is a former restaurateur." Lt. Mathison was from the deep South, with an accent that sounded to Vennie like warm molasses and a gallant manner which lived up to every paeon to that particular breed of southern gentleman in *Gone With the Wind*.

And not half bad as a transport pilot, either. Vennie had flown with him on seven or eight evacuation missions in the last month, and every time, the number of successful takeoffs had equaled the number of successful landings, and the period between them smooth and uneventful, at least aerodynamically uneventful. Vennie appreciated that, as did her temporary patients, especially those who had never set foot in an airplane before.

"I guess we'll just have to settle for the chow hall," Ginger made a brief moue of disappointment, erased utterly next by her brilliant smile, as a jeep appeared from around the corner of the nearest stack of tarpaulin-covered supplies.

"Your carriage awaits, madam, and madam," Lt. Mathison made a courtly gesture as the driver slowed to a halt. "We have about an hour and a half, according to the control tower and the weather observer. Would you care to join us at our table? The attentive staff will make every effort to make your visit to the

Chez Tente de Salle à Manger Militaire a memorable one. We suggest the lobster, or perhaps the chicken a la king."

"In that I hope I'm not vomiting up my socks, four hours later," Vennie replied, and Lt. Mathison grinned.

"Chef Pierre's mess hall does not offer *Homard Americaine du Botulism,*" he replied. "Only the finest of vittles for our brave men ... and women," he added gallantly, and assisted Ginger and Vennie into the back of the jeep. "I <u>was</u> joking about the lobster, though. We might just have to settle for s ... that is, stuff on a shingle."

"It'll be a hot good meal, anyway," Ginger replied. "And with even fresh scrambled eggs!"

Vennie laughed, as the jeep lurched away, running along the dispersal area of the airfield, towards the cluster of dark green Army tents and pursued by splatters of rain. She was thinking how easy it was now that the nurses had practical trouser uniforms. It would have been impossible to scramble into a jeep, or up and down the short ladder to the C-54's hold in the narrow uniform skirt which had been provided to Army nurses when she first volunteered.

"Something funny?" Ginger ventured. The breeze of the jeep's passage ruffled their hair, and Vennie held on to her flight cap.

"Gin, I think you have the lieutenant as your devoted admirer! I was just thinking how we had to cut and sew our own overalls to size, when I first shipped overseas," Vennie explained. "And boots! I couldn't find boots small enough, at first. Although by the time we had to walk around a mountain in Albania, I had a decent pair of boots..."

"I about wore the soles of mine down to tissue paper on that walk," Ginger agreed. "We were so lucky to have been rescued by the partisans. Madame Marsala and Johnny the Englishman; I hope they will be OK. I hate to think that the Nazis would do something awful to them because of us – especially him. He'd be shot as a spy for sure."

"I don't think he's in Albania now," Vennie replied. "He came to see our group just before we left Sheper. His commander was pulling him out of the field, as he was sick as a dog. Malaria, he told me. Jaundice, I would have said, too. He had that yellowish look and I told him so. We talked for a bit ... about home, and what we did before the war and what we were going to do afterwards. He told me his real first name; Tony. I asked him what he did before the war. I rather thought he was regular proper British Army; career service, doing those sneaky espionage things, but no." Vennie chuckled, and Ginger raised an interrogative eyebrow. "He was an actor; can you believe that? An actor, of all things. I never would have thought. And he said he'll go back to that the minute that the war is over. I wonder if we'll ever see him in the movies? I have a distant connection who made it big in the silents as a cowboy star, but Great-Uncle Tom hasn't made a movie in simply ages. I think he sits in his ranch house in California and counts his share of investment profits and the winnings from his horses."

"Takes all sorts to make a war," Ginger agreed. "If Tony from the Department of Ungentlemanly Warfare does make it big in the movies, we can ask for his autograph, because we knew him when. What are you going to do after it's all over, Vennie?"

"I'm not sure," Vennie replied, her voice laden with pessimism. "I try not to think that far ahead. The war isn't near over. We haven't gotten to Rome yet, and if there are landings in France, I should think it will be every bit as hard-fought as Italy. Didn't they call Italy the soft underbelly of Europe when this offensive began? Tough old gut, if you ask me. What do you want to do, Gin? When the war is over?"

"My options are open," Ginger declared airily, as the jeep drew to a halt. "Maybe I'll get married. We certainly have a choice of men, Vennie – they're everywhere!"

The jeep made a half-circle in the wide area in front of the largest tent and came to a halt in a small splatter of mud. There had been more rain in the early morning, and the prospect of more from the oncoming storm. The trampled-down places were already marshes. Someone in charge had the foresight to lay down more of the pierced metal planking that formed the parking ramp for airplanes in front of the mess tent Lt. Mathison came around from the passenger side of the jeep and helped Ginger and Vennie down from the back. Ginger flashed him a particularly warm smile, as he offered her his arm.

Ah, thought Vennie – *another swain, caught in her web of affections*. Ginger was bubby and charming. She had the knack of attracting men and thereafter keeping them attentively revolving at a distance, and Lt. Mathison wasn't married, or at least, didn't wear a wedding ring and mention a wife back Stateside, although likely he had girlfriends at every airfield where he landed. Vennie hopelessly envied Ginger's skill with men, since it was one which was a mystery to her. As near as Vennie could see, it involved looking at and speaking to the chosen swain of the moment as if he were the most clever, brave and admirable male around, but there must have been more to it than that. Vennie's natural habit was to speak and act with them as if they were her brothers, which worked exceptionally well when it came to working with men. As for keeping an attentive herd of possible husbands on the mild romantic simmer, Vennie had no clue at all.

A late breakfast or early lunch in the Army mess tent didn't offer any further enlightenment. They dined on scrambled eggs – blissfully fresh eggs, not powdered, with fried Spam slices, bacon and a choice of biscuits, pancakes, toast, or biscuits – which were a little cold, having been made hours ago. It was true that the very best military chow was offered at Army Air Corps fields. Outside, the rain drummed down, vibrating the heavy canvas roof. A seam in the far corner leaked a narrow dribble of water into a bucket set underneath.

Lt. Mathison urged Ginger to try biscuits with creamed beef, as they went down the serving line with their trays.

"I pass," Vennie answered when she was asked if she wanted any. "It looks too much like vomit."

Ginger blanched slightly, Lt. Mathison laughed, and the mess tent troop serving them gave Vennie a dirty look. They helped themselves to coffee; hot, strong, and freshly brewed from the large urns at the end of the line. The military, like nursing, ran on copious supplies of coffee, just as aircraft ran on av-gas. Generous quantities of each were considered necessary fuel.

Trays loaded, they found empty places at the end of a long table. Since it was already mid-morning, there were only a few others in the long, dimly lit tent. Once seated, and tucking into a belated and generous breakfast, she and Ginger compared unusual in-flight emergencies on previous flights or those which they had only heard about through the medical service grapevine, and skulled out strategies for coping with any new medical contingencies. Because, anything could be on offer, as the Army medical services had embraced such new technologies. It was Vennie's duty to uphold this, with every bit of training and skill that she possessed.

It was, Vennie thought in her most private moments, akin to a holy calling: a calling to preserve lives, to alleviate suffering, to begin the healing of those who had been wounded in a great crusade, a crusade against the cruel and brutal Fascist regime which somehow had overtaken those lands in Europe which had always been held up to her as the pinnacle of culture and achievement. Vennie didn't quite comprehend how all that had happened. Italy was the Renaissance, a ferment of art and culture, Germany was where Grandpa Fred's family had come from, all those decades ago. All the elders had talked about, when they recalled the Germany that they or their parents and grandparents had come from, was pride in the music, the artists and the scientific advancements that had come from German universities. Meanwhile, Lt. Mathison and his copilot talked aviation 'shop' together, and only now and again exchanged mildly flirtatious remarks with Ginger.

"What are you thinking, Vennie?" That was Ginger, breaking into that thread of thought, and Vennie considered for a moment before she replied.

"Nothing much. Just remembering what Dad and everyone said about Grandpop Fred. He was born in Bavaria. Came to Texas with his family when he was seven or eight years old, and never looked back. Grandpop Fred was a hundred and ten percent American; he followed the Gold Rush to California when he was barely in his teens and rode for the Pony Express ... and then he went into herding cattle, up the trail from Texas to Kansas. I wonder what he might have thought of Hitler and his henchmen. Nothing good, I expect."

"I expect that he came from another Germany entirely," Ginger replied, with an air of wisdom. "My mom's family came from ... I don't know, Czechoslovakia, I think. Dad's family is Welsh; he came from coal-mining folk, and he couldn't say enough about how grateful he was, getting away from all of that – his grandfather told stories about going down the mines..." Ginger shuddered. "Ugh. It was all there was for them, you see. Until they immigrated. Grandpa told my Dad he could be anything he wanted, as long as he wasn't going down the mine, and made him stay in school. Was it the same with your folks, Vennie?"

"Something like it," Vennie looked off into the distance. "Grandpa Fred was a bit of a rolling stone, until he settled down on a ranch of his own and married Granny Sophie and had ten children, a couple of them adopted. Look, there's our jeep. Back to the salt mines, we go."

The driver laid on the horn for emphasis, and Vennie looked down at her tray. Yep, breakfast was over. The rainstorm had blown over, and now it was time to get back to work, prepping their helpless passengers of whatever condition for the hours-long flight.

"Had enough, ladies?" Captain Mathison appeared to remember that he and his co-pilot had company at breakfast. "Was everything as good as promised, at *Chez Tente de Salle à Manger Militaire?*"

Ginger and Vennie chorused their agreement; yes, late breakfast in the Army Air Corps mess tent was every bit as good as advertised.

On their hasty return to the hardstand area, Vennie and Ginger separated, each to an aircraft. A long convoy of ambulances and quarter-ton trucks snaked around the perimeter road. The first couple of ambulances were already parked on the hard by the transport aircraft, and there was an officer with a clipboard in hand leaning on the hood of another jeep.

"Not before time," Ginger remarked approvingly, after a glance at her wristwatch. "All right then – see you on the ground."

"Righty-ho," Vennie nodded. Corporal DeSanto was already waiting by the ladder of the first C-54. He waved to Vennie and gestured toward the officer with the clipboard – Captain – no, now Major Marcus, who had climbed down the rope netting from the *Orbita* with her, on the day that the Americans landed in North Africa, two years before.

"Stoneman!" he greeted her with unabashed pleasure. "From infantry to Air Corps! Congratulations are due!"

"The food's better," Vennie grinned with equal pleasure. "What have you got for me today, then?"

"Thirty-two," Major Marcus handed her the clipboard. "Sixteen litter patients, eighteen ambulatory; One of the litter patients is a psych – he's been sedated heavily, so you shouldn't expect any difficulty with him."

"All in a day's work," Vennie agreed with immense satisfaction.

Letter from Peg to Vennie, dated June 2, 1944, postmarked post-marked Brisbane, Queensland Australia

Dearest Cuz:

So glad to receive your latest, and yes, I will send snaps of Tom *(who doesn't want to be called Tommy any more, since that is babyish and he is a big grown-up man of parts who is going to school, and is a Churchie and a St. Magnus boy and whatever it all is that his school honors!)* and Olivia, who is now a grown-up girl of two and some, who distains baby things with all her heart and soul, although she does lisp rather when she talks. With Tom going to school, Olivia wants more than anything to do the same. Edith says that she is old enough to have books without pictures in them read to her at bedtime. I think that Edith misses her girl, Mavis, more than ever. Mavis is gone from the household, now that she is serving in the Australian Women's Army Service. We talked on her last leave at home. She is champing at the bit to volunteer for duty at the front, which is in presently in New Guinea. Edith and Stanley are against this, of course; frantically opposed, since they have already lost Tommy to war, in a manner of speaking, and cannot countenance losing Mavis.

I have a grass-widow sort of life, Cuz. It is three years since I had a marriage, with that last glimpse of Tommy, out the window of Ada's car, as she drove away from Longcot. I don't even know if he is still alive, and more than a year since I have heard anything at all. Captivity in the hands of the Japs is a brutal, vile thing, or so we are told in brief snippets. Survival is not assured, although I pray for it, every hour of every day, but I am still alone – in bed at night, and everywhere else. The children are not so clingingly attached, and I am restless and unsatisfied.

You are the only one in the world who may read my meanderings and totally understand, without condemnation. I have been tempted, out of sheer loneliness. Is it so awful to want companionship? To go out to a movie and a romantic supper, to be admired, loved, forget the war, and all the catastrophes that it has brought to us? To just have fun, to dance and laugh and to forget it all for a while?

If it is that Tommy is gone, well and truly gone, never to return, what am I to do with myself, once that I have come to terms with that? I don't know, I simply don't know. You're the clever one, the one with a mission – can you give me a tiny clue?

Your dearest Cuz,

Peg

He began appearing regularly around noon, on the days that Peg volunteered at the St. George Club in Ann Street, sometime in late 1943, or maybe it was early 1944; an American Navy officer of the middling-junior sort; Peg was still a little bit fogged at interpreting rank insignia. To her mind, it was all a nefarious plot to baffle civilians.

"Hi," he said, the first time that Peg recollected encountering him. "Mrs. Morehouse. The lady at the front desk said that was your name. And that you're American. What a coincidence! So'm I. Roger Field. I'm from California. What crime were you convicted of which merited transportation to Australia?"

Upon Peg's expression of horror, he added hurriedly, "Look if you don't want to say, I'm OK with that. I work in … well, never mind all that. Discretion is our watchword."

He made the most juvenile gesture of zipping his lips and throwing the invisible key over his shoulder, at which Peg had to stifle a laugh. Otherwise, he appeared devastatingly edible: thirtyish, dark, and charmingly. He had a gold wedding band on his left hand, which was somewhat reassuring. Married men were not given to flirt as heavily as the unmarried men.

"I was not transported unwillingly," Peg returned, in her starchiest tones, intended to quell any romantic overtures before such could be launched. "I married an Englishman; he's a prisoner of the Japs in Malaya now, and I'm waiting out the war here in Brisbane with his parents. How lovely to meet you … Lieutenant …?"

"Lieutenant Commander," he replied, looking slightly embarrassed, which Peg found to be curiously endearing. "Sorry about the transportation crack. It was uncalled-for. As for it … the rank. The job. I'm on staff. In the intelligence department. Linguist, since I speak Japanese. My parents were missionaries in Kyoto, and I grew up there. Japanese nurse."

"Say no more," Peg replied, remembering Tom's heartbreak over Miss Hui, his Chinese amah. That was all that passed on the first meeting that she remembered. All the previous encounters, which Roger later detailed with humor and at length – of which Peg had no memory at all – were similarly cursory.

All those encounters took place in the Club; a place for servicemen of every nation to have a bit of familiar home life, a nice meal, a cup of strong milky tea or coffee and a sweet, a dance on an evening when the Club hosted them, a quiet place to write letters, listen to the gramophone, play a sedate game of pool in the games room. Peg did notice, eventually, that the American enlisted naval personnel who frequented the Club usually sidled to the other end of the room when Roger appeared. Sometimes he was accompanied by a devastatingly handsome younger officer – a junior lieutenant named Pierson, or something that sounded reasonably like that. Peg was often cynically amused by the energy with which Lt. Pierson cut a flirtatious swath through the young and susceptible including the ever-susceptible Judy Brooke. But Roger let it drop early on that he was devoted to his wife and that they had a small daughter, almost the same age as Olivia. This made a companionable bond. He regaled her with stories of his childhood in Japan, and of his mother's friends among the colony of expatriates there.

"First time I saw you, I wondered if you weren't kin to my mothers' best friend. A Russian lady; like you, very slender, tall and fair-haired."

Peg disabused him of this notion, almost the first time he brought it up, but he teasingly began to call her 'Princess Aurora' – as his mothers' friend had been a prima ballerina in her youth and danced the role of the princess in *'Sleeping Beauty'* before the Czar and the royal family.

Without thinking very much about it, Peg considered Roger as a friend, especially the day that she and Edith, with Olivia in her pram, were shopping in the slightly faded yet still ornate late-century splendors of McWhirters in the Fortitude Valley. It was coming up to Olivia's second birthday, and they were on the top floor, in the toy section, perusing the sparse selection available in the line of stuffed animals. The stuffed rabbit from America had not the same fond power for little Olivia that Teddy had had for her older brother.

"Tommy had a stuffed monkey from that German company who made the most charming toys for children, and he couldn't be parted from it. I wonder whatever happened to Munks..." Edith mused, as Peg maneuvered the pram between the solid wood tables and glass-sided cases. It couldn't be helped, as artfully as the sales staff in the toy section of McWhirters' had arranged what they had, that the toy options were few, mostly Australian-made; not anything like what would have been in a department store back in the States, even during a war.

"Tom still adores Teddy," Peg replied. "He carried Teddy himself all the way from Singapore and he so wants to give Teddy to Olivia, but she won't have it. Poor Tom; he can't think why Olivia wouldn't take on the responsibility of Teddy! He believes that Teddy has special powers."

"Incompatible animal temperament," Edith replied. "But children are peculiar in their fancies. Best accommodate them..."

"Aurora," a diffident cough interrupted these observations, and both Edith and Peg looked up, startled. "Hullo. I suppose that I shouldn't be surprised at all. Since Brisbane is not that large a city..." Roger Field regarded them from across a table of wooden railway cars and trucks and the wooden tracks that they ran on. Peg replied, pleasure mixed with a little apprehension.

"It's a small town, cunningly disguised as a city! Roger, I'm not surprised at all! I expect that you are shopping for a gift for Alison. We're looking for something for Olivia's birthday present. Roger – this is my mother-in-law, Mrs. Frobisher. And you know Olivia, of course, or you know of her. Edith, this is Roger Field. He's a friend of mine, from the St. George..."

Peg's voice trailed off. She didn't know what Edith would think of Roger, or what Roger might think, faced with the incontrovertible evidence that Peg did indeed have two children and a formidable mother-in-law, and not just be telling stories to keep men in general at arm's length. But Edith merely smiled warmly and exchanged a firm and almost masculine handshake with Roger.

"Hullo! 'Straordinarily pleased to meet one of Peg's American friends from the Club! Peg says that your daughter is almost the same age as our little 'Livvy! We're also looking for a birthday present animal familiar."

"I suppose I should take advantage of having an expert opinion," Roger replied. "Hullo, young lady." He stooped down, until he was almost at eye-level with Olivia. "I'm shopping too, for a present for my little girl, who's the same age as you. I'd welcome your advice, on what she might prefer."

Olivia, overcome with bashfulness, covered her face and giggled, but Peg knew that she liked Roger. She could always tell when her children liked certain adults but was repelled or frightened by others.

"If we don't find something here," Edith said, "then we can always go to TC Beirne, or Overells Toy Town, and then come back for tea later. But Stanley always says that if you can't find it at McWhirters', then you probably don't really need it anyway."

With an eye towards what would be attractive to an intelligent and willful toddler, Peg, Edith and Roger reviewed what was on offer, attended by a hovering McWhirter saleslady, who was about the same age as Edith.

"What do you think, Missy Sunshine?" Roger inquired softly, as he proffered several selections to several selections to Olivia: a small yellow stuffed duck with bright shoe-button black eyes, several versions of Teddies, a koala, a monkey and a pretty and woolly sheep with a silk ribbon and a tiny bell around its' neck. "There's a duck for you, some bears, and all ... which do you like best?"

Olivia grabbed at the duck – a tiny thing, in comparison with the other animals. She loved the ducks in Mowbray Park, and was entranced with a family of little yellow balls of down waddling in a wavering line after their mother, going down to the marshy riverside.

"Guckie!" she shouted, triumphantly. She refused to yield it up again, not even for the hovering saleslady to ring up the sale and wrap it as a gift.

"Well, that's one down," Roger acknowledged with amusement. "What do you suggest for my Alison? Something straight from Australia?"

"The lamb," Edith decided. "After all, what is Australia known for, but sheep! That would be a perfect gift to your little daughter ..."

"Just don't tell her that lambs grow unto mutton and we eat a lot of it here," Peg pointed out and Roger laughed.

"Just as you and your sister didn't want to get too fond of the calves," he added, as Edith looked between them with a suddenly keen expression. But her mother-in-law kept silent.

Chapter 14 – You'll Never Know

"Peggy, dear – is Commander Field a particular friend of yours?" Edith ventured, as they waited at the tram stop. Peg didn't quite know how to reply because Roger <u>was</u> a particular friend. Not in quite the same way that Tommy was, as her husband ... but Roger was very like Tommy, in some ways. And she relished his company in so many ways, none of them in the least romantic.

"I think he is, or he would be," Peg replied carefully. "But we are both married. There has been nothing, no unsuitable behavior going on between us. Just that he is comfortable to be with. I miss Tommy dreadfully, and Roger misses his wife in the same way. It's just restful, being lonely together. I think that he and Tommy would get along just fine, and that I would really like Roger's wife. He talks about her. She seems very nice."

"And I am certain it is," Edith agreed, although there was a note of skepticism on her voice. "I spent so many months and years apart from Tommy's father. Having men friends was gratifying. Having a nice escort for dances and walks in the park and things. But there is the danger of ... well, people talking."

"We've never done anything more than talk at the St. George Club," Peg said, with indignation. "And we dance together sometimes when there is a dance, or step out for coffee, sometimes. There are always other people around when we're together. This is the first time we've ever met, outside of the Club."

"I'm certain there is nothing between you, dear," Edith insisted. "But still – there is a hazard, in becoming too close..."

"We're only friends," Peg replied. "And Roger and I are both faithful in our marriages. I would never be unfaithful to Tommy, no matter how likable that Roger is."

"Well, still, dear – do be careful," Edith sounded mollified, as the blunt-ended electric tram rattled up the road. "You and Roger might be playing with fire."

"I don't intend on getting burned," Peg bent her head over the pram, and lifted out her daughter – Olivia with her "Guckie" still clenched tight in her infant fist.

"See that it stays that way, dear," Edith said.

Letter from Peg to Vennie, dated June 10,1944, postmarked 54 Heath Street, E. Brisbane, Queensland Australia

Dear Cuz: the second front opened at last! The pages of the *Courier-Mail* were full of news of the Italian front, and the fighting in New Guinea for weeks on end, and now nothing but the news of France! Have you been able to see anything of Rome at all? It was liberated by the Allies some days ago, but almost every story about it was crowded off the front page by the landings in Normandy. And General Eisenhower is the hero of the hour. I don't imagine that you have had much to do with this, considering that the fighting in Italy goes on and on, as do the campaigns in New Guinea. The great General McA has vowed to return to the Philippines at some point. A friend in a position to know assures me that yes, it will be in the works eventually, and he would know. As far as is known, the American soldiers and civilians held prisoner there are still prisoners, every bit as much as those of my friends among the British and Australians captured in Malaya. Everyone assumes that the war will go on for another few years, but such are the whispered rumors about conditions under occupation by the vile Japs ... will there be any survivors among them when liberation finally arrives? There was item just the other day in the *Courier-Mail*; there were still unnamed prisoners held, for whom there has never been an accounting! There was also a most awful story last year, of a captured airman about to be beheaded with a sword, which was thought by the Japs to be of such significance that a photograph of that horrible deed was made – as if it was something which they should be proud! It is now three years and a bit since I kissed Tommy and he sent me away with Ada and our little son, and in all that time I have never had a letter from him in response to those that I wrote. Since Malaya fell, I have only heard once that he had survived to become a captive. I live on hope, hope that becomes as thin and transparent as mosquito-netting around my bed at night.

I have dreamed of Tommy three times this week. I dream of embracing him in our bed, of brushing his hair back from his forehead, and kissing him, long and slow and languorous, and of what would happen after those kisses. They are so real, these dreams – and they make me so happy!

And then, I wake, and the bed and my arms are empty, and I am alone. What should I do, Cuz, when the war ends – if it ever does – and Tommy never returns? Sorry to be so depressing. Tell me something cheerful if you can and the censor allows.

Your fond Cuz, Peg

Of course, Edith had been right to serve a mild warning: that in her affectionate friendship with Roger, Peg toyed unwittingly with fire.

"Roger has asked if I would like to go with him to a dance at the Grand Central on Saturday," she ventured on a Thursday afternoon over a meagre tea of cucumber, cheese-spread and whole-meal bread sandwiches. "It's to celebrate the landings in Normandy and the 4th of July, our American Independence Day. I've been so awfully depressed of late, and Roger thought that a good supper at their officer mess and then going out dancing would cheer me up."

"Quite right, dear," Edith replied, comfortably. "A good few turns around the dance floor – and those fearfully energetic dances that are the current craze! That should cheer you up no end!"

"Or at least dislocate your back," Stanley pointed out, genuinely curious. "Are those dances the ones that all those black fellows do in America? Seems to me that some of those dancers ought to qualify for the Olympic team. Gymnastics, they call it. You know, with the rings and the vaulting-horse and all."

"I wouldn't go quite that far," Peg giggled. Some of the dancers she had seen at Club-sponsored dances did venture some athletically astonishing moves. "Still," she added almost wistfully. "I am looking forward to it' there will be the most astonishing band playing for the dance. And," she rightfully interpreted Edith's mild expression of concern. "The dance will go on into the wee hours. Judy Brooke and I are going together, and I promise that we'll be welded together as chaperones. She's going to go with Roger's pal, Lt. Pierson. Roger and Lt. Pierson arranged to bunk in together at their billet in the Central and let us have Roger's room for us to sleep in after the dance. So ... that's sorted. We don't want to be coming back home in the wee hours, all alone in the dark of the morning."

"Quite rightly," Edith agreed. "More tea, dear? No, coming back through downtown in the early morning... most unwise. Nothing good happens at two in the morning, especially not in Ann Street, with all those military chaps fossicking about and likely under the influence of strong drink. The salt of the earth, my dear – but what they get up to when the wine is red..."

"And other stuff is on tap and freely flowing," Peg agreed. No, she and Judy Brooke would go to the dance together, spend the remainder of the night after the dance chastely in a hotel room at the Grand Central. Judy had, over the last two and a half years been engaged at least half a dozen times, to different men that she had met at St. George's, to Edith and Peg's vast and exasperated amusement. Edith speculated that Judy was trying for a kind of romantic grand slam, of being serially engaged to a man representing every single nation and military service who passed through Brisbane. *"She's the original girl in that musical,"* Peg replied to this, *"The one who just can't say 'no'!"*

On that Saturday, Peg packed a suitcase with her prettiest and most full-skirted dress – confected from one of Edith's old gowns, some small necessities and a nightgown, kissed Tom and Olivia, and walked down to the nearest tram stop, wondering vaguely where Judy Brooke was. They had agreed to travel into the city together, since they also had volunteered for the afternoon shift at St. George's, which would be most busy on a Saturday, with all the soldiers, airmen and sailors having weekend passes.

It was a lovely, mild day. Peg waved at the ice-delivery man and his horse, clumping moodily down the road, heavy tires crunching the gravel underfoot, buoyed up by a feeling of mild excitement. She loved dancing, the music of a big brassy band, moving with an expert partner, even a mild thrill from being noticed, relishing the envious admiration of other dancers. Roger was a good partner; she knew that, from decorous dances at the Club. What fun lay in store for the evening! Supper in the American naval officer's mess in the Grand Central, and then the dance party to follow. It was almost like the carefree, flirtatious days before she met and married Tommy!

The thought of Tommy darkened her mood somewhat; she had dreamed vividly of him again, the night before. With some effort, she shoved that memory aside, that and the memory of letters she had written in the early days to him. Some of those letters had been returned, others had vanished into the ether, and she eventually stopped sending them at all. *Why waste the postage?*

The bloody interfering Japanese had required all letters to prisoners of war to be twenty-five words or less, written in block letters, and only personal information to be conveyed. *Twenty-five words! What could she write to Tommy and only use twenty-five words?* She did write to him, now and again, but she put away the completed letters in an old Huntley & Palmers biscuit tin printed in a design of ornamental wood marquetry, a tin which she had found in the back of the wardrobe in the nursery room. She supposed that when the war was over, and Tommy returned, that she might give them all to him to read. Or if he didn't ... she shuddered away from that thought. *No; be like Edith, resolute in not considering the unthinkable.*

Peg thought instead of the dance, and of Roger's cheerful and undemanding company, settling her chin on the edge of her small suitcase in her lap, as the tram rumbled along. From what she read in the newspaper, the war was going – if not overwhelmingly well and victoriously – than in a manner to suggest a degree of hope that it might be over before small Tom and Olivia were of an age to be conscripted to fight in it. The filthy, unimaginably cruel Japanese invaders were gradually being beaten back, all along the fronts in New Guinea and India, on Guadalcanal Island and in the southern Pacific. There was hope now, where all before had been defeat and despair, written over with a brave face and a magnificently stiffened upper lip. And Roger was part of that mighty effort because of his job in intelligence as a speaker of Japanese, knowing of developments which he couldn't really speak of to her or anyone out of his command, because of wartime secrecy. He was confidant of eventual victory. Peg was in herself certain that Roger knew things, important things, which would never be published in the newspapers.

She had been skeptical of newspapers, recalling how the *Straits Times* posted cheerful story after story, in the last days before Singapore fell apart, fell to the Japanese. Since the front in Malaya had fallen apart, she had come to put more faith in the intuition of sensible observers like Ada Dawlish, or Stanley Frobisher, in sifting nuggets of insight from the dross of gossip and personal experience. Even Cousin Vennie, far away in Italy; certain things came through in her occasional letters. For the last few months, she had included Roger Field in that collection of cool heads and calm insight into war news.

The St. George Services Club was set up in a nondescript building on the corner of Ann and Creek streets, directly opposite the tall and vaguely Romanesque red-brick steeple of St. Andrews, the Presbyterian church. Peg carried her suitcase and handbag into the little office to one side of the main entrance, nodding to the volunteer who presided over the reception desk. They knew each other by sight.

"Hullo, Mrs. Morehouse! Have you seen Miss Brooke? She was supposed to be managing the games area..."

"I haven't seen her," Peg replied, now mildly concerned. "We are to chaperone each other at a dance tonight. I thought I would see her on the tram. Maybe she'll be along later."

"Young gels these days," the older woman shook her head, in studied despair. "Flirting with soldiers and them come and gone in the blink of an eye. No good will come of it, I tell you."

"They're fighting a war for us," Peg reminded her. "The least that we can do is to treat them as we would our own brothers and sons." The memories of air raid alarms, even here in Brisbane, and the ever-present danger of Japanese submarines lurking just offshore, were all a matter of recent concern.

"Dearie me, I know that," the other woman replied. "Still, I wish that those Yank chappies weren't so very brash, and all. It gives the girls such unsuitable notions!"

"Oh, I think the girls would have had unsuitable notions regardless," Peg suppressed a smile, recalling how very exotic Tommy had seemed, when compared to her other girlhood flirtations. "It's the charm of the exotic contrast – someone new and hugely different. It was rather like that when I met my husband."

"I suppose that it was," the other woman agreed. "I'd nearly forgotten that you're an American as well..."

The main door opened admitting a couple of American sailors; obviously on their first encounter with the Services Club. Peg flashed them a smile, and put away the suitcase and her handbag, still wondering where Judy had gotten to on this day. She relieved the impatient volunteer in the games section and helped her reset the chess sets and reassemble an abandoned Monopoly game which had left paper bills, tokens and tiny little red and green houses scattered far and wide. In the constant shuffle of uniformed visitors on a busy Saturday afternoon, she quite forgot to be worried about Judy Brooke and wherever she had gotten to, right up until just after six, when she closed the door of the little office to slip on her dress and petticoats, comb out and pin up her hair, and use a little of her lipstick to touch her lips with brilliant carmine. Roger waited at the desk when she emerged.

"Are you ready to go to the ball, Princess Aurora?" he asked, with a mischievous grin, and Peg relished the expression of honest admiration on his face; Roger cut so dashing a figure in his dark Navy uniform and gold-braided cuffs.

"I am, indeed," she replied, and made her skirt sway, and the full petticoat under it crackled a little. For this evening, she had also put on her last unladdered pair of silk stockings – a gift from Edith's pre-war stock of once-fashionable clothes. "But my expected lady in waiting is nowhere to be found!"

"Ah, that," Roger took her arm, collecting her suitcase in the other hand. "She's out in the car with Randall – Lieutenant

Pierson. He … umm, they got married this morning at the registry office. I was a witness, so I know it's true."

"Oh, good heavens!" Peg stood stock-still on the sidewalk. "Now that's a surprise! How could she? Do her parents know?"

"I doubt it," Roger replied with a sigh. "It was all done in a hurry; Randall has orders for … never mind. Away from Brisbane, anyway and within the week. She's of legal age, so I expect that it will stand."

"That's appalling!" Peg exclaimed, "How can they really be certain? Certain enough to marry!" Too late, she considered that she and Tommy had married within weeks. *But,* she told herself, as a uniformed driver opened the passenger door for her and for Roger and took the suitcase; *Tommy was known to the family, a distant kin-connection, and of course, the family. Hers was a hurried wedding but at least, Tommy was a known quantity to them all, and it was done with all proper ceremony, in a church and with all the family present.* If Lieutenant Pierson was known at all to the Brooke family, it was as a passing acquaintance. If they were now legally married, then Judy and her brief engagements with practically any handsome and attractive serviceman had taken it all to a new degree. *How many men had she been engaged to in the last three years?* Peg had honestly lost track. Judy's engagements were rather like the Stanley Street tram schedule; there would be another one along, presently.

"Congratulate me!" Judy demanded, overcome with giggles, as Peg slid into the back of the Navy staff car. There was just enough space for her, next to Judy, flushed with excitement. Judy, Peg noted, was wearing her best Sunday ensemble, with a small knot of flowers pinned to her shoulder. Roger took the passenger seat, next to the driver, and the car lurched away from the curb in front of the club.

"I do!" Peg replied, hoping that she sounded sincere "I wish the two of you the best, and all the happiness in the world!"

She refrained from saying whatever else was on her mind; that this was sudden, unplanned, and that Judy was an impulsive and flirtatious child. *They married in haste, and I expect that one or both might have cause to repent, eventually,* was what she was thinking, as the driver drew the car up to the front of the Grand Central. She and Judy were handed out, with all courtly ceremony.

"The dance doesn't start until later," Roger said. He murmured a few words to the lingering driver and the attendant at the door. Peg's suitcase vanished into the immense and hospitable pile of the Central Grand. "Supper first, I think."

"Champagne to celebrate our wedding!" Judy exclaimed, glowing with happiness as if she were lit from the inside. It may have been Peg's wistful imagination; Judy triumphantly brandishing her wedding ring as she took Randall Pierson's arm. "Champagne for everyone! You will see to it, Ran – and Roger?"

"On the house, Mrs. Pierson," Roger answered, as he tucked Peg's hand into his elbow and let the way into what had been the main dining room but was now the officer's mess. It was still an impressive sight; acres of starched white tablecloths, glittering chandeliers casting a warm golden light on heavy silverware placed with military precision at each place. It reminded Peg painfully of how she and Tommy had dined on their honeymoon, in that pink confection in a grove of palm trees on Waikiki Beach, where plumeria and jasmine perfumed the very air, the splendors of that lovely old hotel in Manila, or how her father's old friend, Commander Nimitz had taken them to the officer's mess there. Even the Tanglin Club held on to a semblance of lavish service after the war began. There were even flowers at every table, just as there had been before the war. So many memories.

It was still early in the evening; about half the tables were occupied, mostly by other men. Most of them, from the casual way they nodded or waved to Roger and Ran, appeared to be friends or at least acquaintances. Not a few of those other men regarded Peg and Judy with a touch of envy.

"They don't dine like this on Guadalcanal or in New Guinea, Ran," Roger pointed out with cheerful cynicism as a hovering mess attendant showed them towards a table. Lieutenant Pierson laughed, ruefully.

"When we do," he replied, "We'll know without a doubt that we have won the war." He held out a chair for Judy, as Roger did for Peg, and asked the attendant for champagne. "To celebrate an occasion," he added grandly.

When the champagne arrived, Peg took a glass – golden and fizzing with tiny bubbling threads. Randall and Judy got progressively more elevated, as their meals arrived; a salad of fresh green lettuce, a clear broth with tiny noodles in it, and a main course of succulent rare roast beef, with stuffed mushrooms and rissole potatoes lightly sprinkled with parsley.

"Good?" Roger asked quietly, as Peg mashed the last couple of forkfuls of potato in the small lingering puddle of juice and fat from her cut of the roast. She did not want to miss a single drop.

"It's splendid," Peg replied, "It's the most luscious bit of beef since ... I don't know; since I left Texas, I expect. My family has a ranch there. For a hundred years now. I can't tell you how much I have missed ... oh, the lot of it. Steaks. Good mesquite-smoked brisket sliced crosswise. Broil with a bit of hollandaise, grand Texas barbeque." She added, wistfully, "For Christmas, my great-uncle Dolph always had a whole beef roasted on a spit; a picnic supper for all the ranch hands and their families. Outside if the weather was good, in the barn if it rained."

"Mercy me! A whole roast beef?" Judy's eyes rounded in astonishment. "I can't even imagine the ration points that would have required!"

Both the men laughed, but affectionately. So did Peg, with a twist at her heart for how swiftly the norm of rationing, of stringent limits on all those satisfying and tasty elements of meals had become something rare and almost unimaginable – save to a privileged few, or those willing to deal in the black market. It was repeated over and over in newspapers and magazines, on the radio and cinema newsreels; rationing of things like milk, butter and cream, eggs, meat, sugar, and good bread made for a healthier population. Peg couldn't see it. Healthier they might be – and Peg had her doubts on this – but it didn't make the preparation and consumption of meals and anything but a grim culinary duty.

They had ice cream for dessert, shared another couple of bottles of champagne with nearby well-wishers, all friends of Lieutenant Pierson before going to the dance. Peg could hear the band, long before she and Roger, Ran and Judy approached the ballroom; they were playing *String of Pearls*. The band sounded hot, swinging every bit as well as Glen Miller's band in the movies. Now she felt herself bounce a little. Without a word, Roger led her to the dance floor to join a dozen couples already there. Within seconds they found the familiar beat. She had so missed this, dancing with Tommy. Roger was exuberant, uninhibited; she supposed it was something to do with being American, rather than the oh-so-restrained English manner.

She danced with Roger, with Randall Pierson while Roger partnered Judy, then with a series of other men, as the number of enthusiastic American men eager to cut a rug far outnumbered those girls given to the daring manner encouraged by the wilder American dance bands and the popularity of the Lindy Hop. When the band declared an interval, and lay down their instruments, she and Roger returned to the table with Judy and Randall, all laughing and breathless with exertion.

"I haven't had so much fun since ... well, I can't remember!" Peg exclaimed, laughing.

"Neither can I, your highness, Princess Aurora," Roger had shed his uniform jacket and loosened his tie a bit, for the heat in the ballroom with so many energetic bodies in it and the pace of dancing was almost tropical. With his hair flopping that way over his forehead, Peg thought he looked a whole decade younger. Randall Pierson brandished another champagne bottle and splashed the golden stuff carelessly into their glasses.

"Drink up, y'all!" he exclaimed. "Ju and I don't get married every day, so it's our night to celebrate!"

"Why not?" Roger agreed and ordered another bottle for a round of toasts. Then the dancing began again, and Peg gave herself over to the sheer enjoyment of it, mildly elevated on the champagne that she had drunk. Not so much as Judy and Randall had, but still more than she had seen in simply months of life in staid old Australia. She felt on top of the world, but when she and Roger returned to the table, they found that Judy and Randall Pierson were gone. They weren't dancing – Judy's light wrap and little handbag were gone, as was Randall's uniform cover.

"I don't want this evening to end," Peg sighed. "But I suppose that it must. One more dance, then – and then..."

"Time to hit the sack," Roger agreed. "I'll show you to my room. I guess that Judy is already there. Hope we don't interrupt her and Ran." Peg wondered if he were stifling a yawn, or if it were just the effect of too much champagne.

"They can always take it to a hotel!" she giggled, and Roger laughed again.

"We <u>are</u> in a hotel, Princess Aurora!"

The last dance was a slow waltz version of *Good Night Ladies*. She floated dreamily across the uncrowded dance floor in Roger's arms. An excellent way to finish off the evening. She was certain that she would sleep very soundly and thought with regret of traveling alone back to Edith and Stanley's house in the morning, through quiet Sunday streets, the silence broken only by the distant chime of church bells. She didn't want the evening to end, and yet it did as all lovely evening must. The last notes from the band fell away, and the last few couples left on the dance floor scattered; some also yawning, some still reluctant. She gathered up her own handbag from the table. The lights had gone up, erasing all the nostalgic romance of the dance, a dance on the edge of a war. All that remained now was for the staff to clear away the detritus, gather up the glassware and scattered empty bottles, shift the tablecloths. The last stragglers from the band were already casing up their instruments. Glamor was erased in harsh electric light, and the knowledge of a harsher morning yet to come.

She leaned on Roger's arm, pointedly ignoring the carefully blank expression on the face of the elevator attendant, an older man in an old-fashioned hotel bellman's uniform.

"Tired, Aurora?" Roger asked, and Peg replied, smothering a yawn before it could express.

"Exhausted – but oh, it was such fun. Thank you so much for inviting me, and arranging with Lt. Pierson ..."

"Our pleasure," Roger said, as the elevator bell chimed faintly, and the attendant opened the doors for them. "If you or Judy need anything at all, Randall's room is along this way, and mine is four doors farther down."

They walked along the corridor, the carpet runner along the middle muffling their footsteps. At the seventh door along, Roger tapped lightly on the door panel.

"Ran, it's me. I'll be along in a minute, leave the door unlatched for me."

From behind the door came the sound of male laughter, and Judy's replying giggle. "Oh, do go away, Roger! We're having our honeymoon!" The snick of the bolt clicking home sounded very loudly in the silent corridor.

"Oh, dear," Peg said, now suddenly and completely sober. *So much for their careful plans.* "I suppose that you could call for a taxi to take me..."

"It's one in the morning," Roger replied. "You'd never get one, not at this hour, not with all the pubs calling time and emptying out all those drunk GI's on the street. Look, Aurora ..." he frowned, obviously thinking hard. "Original plan slightly revised. My room; you take the bed, there's a nice, overstuffed chair for me. I'll be perfectly comfortable. We can even hang up a divider across the room to preserve the proprieties."

"Like Clarke Gable and Claudette Colbert and the wall of Jericho in *It Happened One Night*," Peg agreed with a giggle. *No, it would be embarrassing only if anyone found out.* "We should have expected that Judy and Randall would want to spend their first night together..."

"We drank too damn much champagne to consider the obvious," Roger agreed, taking out a key for his door. "I'll make sure the blackout curtain is drawn before I turn on the light. I had your suitcase sent up..."

"I remember," Peg replied, as Roger swung the door open. An arrow of light from the corridor briefly illuminated a wedge of room, a rug and the corner of a large wardrobe; quite a pleasant room, as Peg could see. Roger closed the door, and she could hear him moving quietly and surefooted. Of course, he would know his own room in the dark, especially if he had been billeted here for more than a year.

"'s OK," he said, and switched on a small desk light. Now she could see it better; a comfortable room, with the air of having been lived in by a man of wide-ranging interests and hotel-housekeeping: books on the shelf over the small desk, on which were scattered some portfolios and files, but the bed was made, and any extraneous clothing items tidied away in the wardrobe. "The ... umm facility is down the hall. Ladies first, of course."

"Thank you, Roger," Peg said, with all her heart. "You're a real prince, you know? I'm exhausted from all the dancing..."

"Understood, Aurora," Roger replied, and at the moment that Roger stepped past her – she thought he meant to turn on the other light – he paused to put his arms around her and drop a small comradely kiss on her forehead, and that simple gesture was so enormously comforting. Her arms went around him, almost of their own volition and they were lost in that one aching moment. Longing and loneliness, too much champagne … and that tiny flame of desire touched the laid fuel and became a bonfire.

It was so nice to be held in a man's strong arms and breath in the scent of a healthy man's aftershave and honest perspiration, to feel his body against hers, and to give over to pure animal desire. Peg was marginally aware of her dress falling from her shoulders, the petticoat as a puddle of tulle at her feet, and then they were on the bed together, Roger on her and then in her, breathing endearments into her hair as he thrust away, her legs wrapped around his hips. No, she wanted this, needed this, couldn't live without this; Tommy was far away, perhaps dead – but she needed life, and if not love, the consideration of affection, the reaffirmation of life and not the stale lingering death of absence without any word.

Sometime in the morning hours – as sunlight seeped into the room, Peg woke. At some point in those insane early morning hours in Roger's room, he had tucked the light blanket and sheet around her shoulders. Now they lay a little apart on the comfortable bed in his quarters. She looked on him, asleep and found the sight to be a strangely satisfactory one. He was comely in his naked body; not very tanned below his face or above his hands, not as Tommy had been, working out in the groves of rubber trees at Longcot. Roger's skin was pale, almost alabaster; the thread of dark hair along and across his chest traced ink-dark lines. *A lovely, aesthetic sight*, Peg thought, considering it now in the milky light of morning, seeping around the edge of the blackout shade.

What had happened here, and what should she think of it, of herself for having yielded to temptation? Well, at least Roger was a friend, a very dear friend, all considered. She ought to leave, though. Soon. Pretend that nothing of the sort had ever, ever happened. She made a move to slide between those light covers and off the bed, and then Roger stirred. His eyes opened.

"Hey, Aurora ... not a dream, then. Am I forgiven for certain liberties?"

"Always, my prince," Peg replied, and instead of slithering off the bed, she kissed him. She didn't intend to do anything more than that – but his arms went around her again ... and it was so absolutely nice ... almost more than dancing together, their bodies moving in cadence... afterwards, Peg lay gasping from the satisfaction which this elicited.

It was so comfortingly normal to lay in the embrace of strong male arms, as the stronger rising sun seeped through the margins around the blackout shade. They lay back on the bed together, their arms loosely linked. Presently, Roger said,

"My dear Princess Aurora … you know that we are playing with fire. You wanted this now, I wanted it last night. We shouldn't ever do it again."

"No, we shouldn't," Peg agreed, thinking of how Roger used the same comparison as Edith had – that the two of them played with fire. "It's … a hazard to the friendship that we have. I like it too much … rely on it too much."

"Agreed," Roger sat up, and Peg considered what they ought to do next. *Perhaps forget that the last eight hours had never happened.*

In any case, she should get dressed now, and leave Roger's room before anyone else saw her.

"I'll see you down to the tram stop," Roger said at last.

Peg shook her head. "No – I think it would be best, that we shouldn't be seen together by anyone."

It did hurt, just a little, that Roger nodded agreement.

Chapter 15 – A Lovely Day Tomorrow

Letter from Vennie to Peg, dated October 20,1944, postmarked APO NY

Dear Cuz:

I am in several minds, regarding how to best advise you regarding the matter mentioned in your last letter, about you and your friend R. I have no intention of sitting in judgement in any case. It's not my place, and not that I think myself anything like your superior in morality; the disruptions of this awful war have scrambled so many lives and marriages. Being thrown together for that one night was a pure accident. Neither of you meant anything to happen out of it. *(Fortunate that <u>nothing</u> else resulted which might give rise to embarrassing revelations nine months down the line, and that Aunt Rose paid her usual visit to you within days).* I do so understand how things might happen when all notions of proper conduct have been upended, turned inside out, and people fear that something fatal might happen at any moment. It's only normal for people to seek comfort of any sort – including the impulsive carnal sort. I think it very sensible that the two of you have agreed to remain strictly platonic friends after this brief lapse.

I took counsel on this with the chaplain attached to the unit, without mentioning any specifics. This is a moral quandary, Cuz, and not my specialty. It <u>is</u> the accustomed practice of our unit Padre, though; we met by chance one morning over coffee in the mess tent, and I put your situation to him. He is RC, terribly humane and sensible, which is why I broached the matter with him in the first place. It is his considered judgement that you <u>never</u> confess about your brief affair to Tommy, ever. Padre Paul reasoned that you would be relieving your conscience at having committed a sin at the expense of another's happiness and confidence. You would make it all right in your own mind at the cost of Tommy's mental well-being and human trust. That, according to Padre P. is an even greater sin. He says that your penance is to keep it to yourself, forever and ever, amen, and to go forth, remaining aware of potential temptation and resolving not to sin in this way ever again.

So that is the judgement of a religious professional, Cuz. I agree; never mention this to Tommy when you are reunited. He doesn't need to know, and it would hurt him dreadfully. That is all that I will ever say or write on this matter. Put it away, and never speak or write of it again. Burn this letter if you will, and I will similarly dispose of the letter in which this matter was first raised.

As for me and what I am doing ... the landings in Southern France have proved largely successful. I am now employed in evacuating our wounded from France, just as I was from the front in Italy. I can't say much more about this, for operational secrecy.

Between the landings in Normandy, as hard-fought as they were, and the liberation of Toulon and Marseilles, France is almost freed from German occupation. The French citizens fulsomely welcome us as liberators, and assure us, solo and in chorus, that they were all in the Resistance. A fair number of them were, as wholesale and murderous reprisals against whole villages by the Germans can attest as they withdraw precipitously. There are also a lot of pretty young women with newly shaved heads, say those of us who have been out and among the new-freed French. There appears to have been a lot of mattress-collaboration for which these poor sluts are now being punished. I wonder if a lot of this fury is a kind of displacement; Padre P. speculates along this line of thought, since it is his line of profession. While there were and are many French who bravely resisted the Germans, against terrible odds and risking the direst of penalties, there were many who collaborated with varying degrees of enthusiasm. Now that liberation is at hand, they are making a show of expiating their craven shame and prove their own tardy valor by turning on each other.

In the next month, Peg, I will have some leave due to me, and I intend to spend it in Paris! We are now operating from an airfield comfortably close to that city, in the newly liberated zone. It is totally possible for those of us in the American forces to spend recreation time in Paris. Can you imagine? One of our surgeons is from Louisiana and had French as his first language. He and my friend Ginger and several of us from the unit are planning to take our leave together. Paris! Can you imagine how much I am looking forward to this? I have gathered that Paris is a little bit shabby now, with the Occupation only just ended, but how I am looking forward to it all. Major Ledet *(it's pronounced Lee-day, if you wondered)* and Ginger and the rest of our party are planning so many expeditions! I want to see the Louvre, the palace of Versailles and the grand church of Notre Dame, and find any booksellers still in business along the West Bank. Major Ledet wants to find the house in the 15th Arrondissiment which his great-great grandfather supposedly owned. Ginger wants to see what she can see of the great fashion houses, for hats and pretty dresses and all, and Captain Allison wants to explore the suppliers of gourmet cookware on behalf of his mother, who loves to cook in the French style. She bought some copper saucepans at E. Dilleherin near Les Halles, on her honeymoon in Paris decades ago, and has wanted more from them ever since.

We all four have put in the paperwork and arranged to stay at a nice little rooming house near Le Meurice, and as soon as we might cadge a ride there on a supply truck, we will be on our way.

Hopefully, by the time you receive this letter, I will be seeing Paris –

All my love to you and the children and my most sincere prayers for Tommy

Vennie

On her second day in Paris – the City of Light! – Vennie conceded glumly that perhaps early December was not seeing

Paris at it's very best. The trees in the Bois de Boulogne, the smaller city parks, the Champ de Mars, the gardens at Versailles and all along the city avenues were bare, the famous Louvre Museum was empty of all the splendid paintings and relics that had once been there, the sky was mostly grey and dripped rain on a discouragingly regular basis. Four hard years of German occupation had emptied shops, markets, cafes, and ateliers of most of the goods and edibles which had made Paris the cynosure of the world when it came to fashion, food and general culture. But still – Paris!

Vennie had read about all those famous places since she was able to read words of more than a single syllable. If the trees were bare, and the shops, museums, and ateliers all but empty, the monuments and buildings were still there and every bit as awe-inspiring as they had been in her imagination, even if the paintings in the Louvre were still hidden away safe in the countryside. It was almost Christmas. France and the Low Countries were nearly free, or within reach of being freed from German occupation. Paris was full of military trucks, and soldiers; American, French, British and some in uniforms that she couldn't identify. Maybe by spring, the Allies would finally hang out their washing on the Siegfried line...

"Oh, Christ, Vennie – another grey stone monument!" Ginger Lloyd groaned. Their jeep was halted in a broad plaza in front of the magnificent, if slightly time-mutilated twin towers and façade of Note Dame de Paris, the grand and ancient cathedral of Paris. "Don't you ever get tired of moldy old stone buildings, Vennie?"

"Not this one," Vennie replied. "It's Notre Dame the most famous church in all of Paris. I want to see the inside, even if they haven't put back the rose windows. They're famous in themselves, you know."

"Another church," Bill Allison remarked, with a particularly dour expression. "After Sacred Heart..."

"Sacre-Coeur," Major Ledet corrected, automatically.

"We've also been to St. Denis," Bill Allison continued, "Where the kings of France are planted for all time until Judgement Day. And St. Chapelle, Napoleon's Tomb, and all those blasted museums with nothing in them because they were taken away to hide from the Nazis. Just agree with me; admire the outside for five minutes, and then let's move on to another objective. I'm a Presbyterian. All this Catholic idolatry gives me hives."

"I want to see the inside," Vennie repeated stubbornly. "This might be the only chance in my life that I will have to see Paris and I want to make the most of it, even if there is nothing much inside."

"Oh, very well," Major Ledet agreed, and set the jeep in gear. "We'll come back for you at four o-clock, right at this place. Will that suit you, Lieutenant?"

"Perfectly," Vennie replied, and let Bill Allison hand her down from the jeep, as she and Ginger wore their formal skirt uniforms, and it was so awkward, having to be so lady-like in the middle of a war zone, scrambling up and down from jeeps and trucks and airplanes in a narrow skirt and stockings that must be kept from being snagged and laddered. Or at least doing that scrambling in what had been a war zone, not too many weeks previously.

Vennie settled the strap of her handbag on her shoulder, straightened the cap on her head at the proper angle – and yes, she knew the crude name for that narrow and easily-folded flight cap. There was but a small scattering of people in the wide paved square before the storied towers and intaglio-carved façade of Notre Dame on this drear and grey afternoon. She marched into that chill and stone-damp smelling space ... and then halted, marveling at the solid weight of the stone, the regular pillars along a triple gallery which went marching along the vista of a magnificent nave, the airy vaults overhead ... she went to the font just inside the entryway and dipped her fingers into it and made the gesture of crossing herself for courtesy. This was the custom, as she knew very well. So many of the ranch workers were devout and Catholic, many nurses she had trained or served with as well, and Padre Paul was a good and responsible shepherd. There was a rack of candles nearby, most of them flaring smokily in the intermittent icy draft from the doors. She fished a few francs out of her purse, put them in the donation box and lit a fresh candle from the jar of wooden spills next to it, silently saying a brief prayer before she walked farther into the soaring interior.

And it was every bit as glorious as she had imagined – monumental pillars and galleries, pale daylight sifting in between them, as if they were stone trees in a mighty and regularly coppiced forest. Vennie breathed in the scent of ancient incense, of age and history and stone. Padre Paul had visited St. Pauls' in Rome, shortly after the day of liberation, and spoke most movingly of how the immense space dwarfed mere humans in the presence of the ineffable divine. This was how he must have felt, dwarfed by the power of belief in the savior of all mankind, a divine first made flesh and blood in Palestine two millennia ago ... and then that belief memorialized by those passionate believers, making their faith manifest in stone, glass and paint.

Halfway up that grand nave, Vennie stepped into one of the ranks of pews, which were relatively scratch things, to her way of thinking. Bare, flimsy, relatively insubstantial, in comparison to the mighty forest of stone, rising all about her. There was an American soldier sitting in one of them, in the rank ahead of where she chose to sit and contemplate the divine and appreciate the artistic labor which had built this place, centuries before. Vennie sat, moving quietly as she had learned as a nurse. This was a private moment for her, as it was for that lone soldier. A sacred place, and a private place, all in one. She quietly drank in the peace and history; there was nothing like this in Deming, where the church of her childhood was a simple frame building – like a child building with sticks, a private den in the weeds, next to this.

She sat and thought about all of that; of her time in Madame Marsala's house in Albania, and of Johnny the Englishman, who was really Tony the actor. Of the soldiers that she tended in those interminable flights, of how many more there would be, once the war in Europe was done. The focus of the war would move against Japan, once Nazi Germany was ground into dust, and into dust they would be. Vennie was already certain of that. But, oh – the human cost of that, paid in the blood of soldiers, blood that puddled on the floor of hospitals like that one in Arzew, on the night that she and her handful of fellow nurses came forward to serve.

Vennie didn't want to think of that – how much more in blood, how many more dying soldiers? She wrenched her mind from that, and standing up, looked over the shoulder of the American in the pew-row ahead. Now she noted, in mild surprise, that he had a notebook in hand propped on his knee. He was making a sketch in charcoal pencil, a view of the apse and high altar, with the watery sunshine sifting in.

"I like that," she said, unprompted. It was a bit presumptive of her, because he was enlisted, with a zebra-array of stripes on his sleeve and she – according to Army regs – was officer-class. But the soldier looked over his shoulder and smiled, without any constraint. He had a very nice smile, Vennie thought, straight white teeth and narrow, sensitive lips. A burly man with dark hair slightly too long for Army regs, about thirty years in age, and wearing heavy-rimmed glasses which lent him a somewhat professorial air.

"Thanks. I'm a shit artist, in comparison to the greats. But I get by. Master Sergeant Burt Vexler. You, Ell- Tee?"

"Venetia Stoneman; my friends all call me Vennie. I'm on leave with some pals from my unit. Are you also on leave, Sergeant Vexler?"

"Burt. Just call me Burt," he replied. "I'm on the job, actually. Research job. It's one of those odd sorts of Army specialties."

"In Notre Dame?" Vennie raised a slightly skeptical eyebrow. "Don't tell me you work for our version of the Ministry of Ungentlemanly Warfare."

He chuckled, richly amused. "No, not one of those sneaky intelligence types. I was recruited to a special unit. We track down looted art, stolen by the Nazis, secure it safely and ensure that those items are returned to the proper owners. Those bastards had the stickiest fingers you can imagine. Nothing too hot or too heavy, as our English cohort put it. They boosted truckloads of art, paintings, sculpture, historic relics. Anything you can imagine and shipped it off to the Reich. They say that Hitler was a frustrated artist. You know, everyone might have been better off if he had been accepted at art school. But that's by-the-by. Were you a nurse before the war, Vennie?"

"Yes, I was," she came around the end of the pews and sat next to him. It was easier talking that way. "I liked it, very much. I was a private duty nurse for a lovely old invalid lady. A friend of mine from nursing school joined the Army Nurse Corps. She told me several times that a war was coming, and I ought to join, too. When my invalid lady died, I thought that my friend might be right. I could read the newspapers, you know. How did you come to be in the Army – the draft, I suppose."

"Not quite," Burt grinned. He set aside his glasses, folding them carefully and fitting them into his uniform tunic pocket. Now Vennie saw that his eyes were a light blue; oddly enough, of that shade that the old folks in Deming always said denoted a stone-cold killer. "I also was talked into it by a friend – my old college advisor. I was teaching art history at this terribly refined old ivy-covered college. My eyesight is bad enough that I was rated unfit by the draft board. I'd be the most ham-fisted and near-sighted infantryman that any army in history has ever seen. But my advisor was terribly persuasive, and I wanted to contribute to the war effort in some way, over and above just carrying a weapon. So here I am enjoying yet another visit, to Paris at Army expense, instead of Pop's trust fund."

"Were you here before?" Vennie asked, frankly envious. Only the very wealthiest of the Richter and Becker cousins had traveled much beyond their home ranches, much less repeatedly to Europe. "Even before the war?"

"Several times," Burt coughed, almost apologetically. "That first visit, I was only six. My mother's honeymoon with her fourth and final husband. She insisted on bringing me. My stepfather was a peach – he's the one that she stuck with, finally."

"Your holiday suppers with all the family must have been interesting," Vennie remarked, without any malice. She was fascinated, almost in spite of herself, and Burt grinned again.

"Oh, yeah. Dear Ma-Ma hasn't a malicious bone in her body – and a very nice body still, for a sixty-year old. She was in the Floradora Girls chorus line in her younger days. I think all her former husbands and my father are still partly in love with her. For my own self, I fell in love with Paris early on, and never recovered. The maid in charge of Ma-Ma and Charles' rooms would bring me fresh-baked croissants and take me out to walk in the Bois for hours. I think Charles must have bribed her to do baby-sitting duty while they snogged away the afternoon. I was a self-centered little bugger and didn't care. Marie-Claude took me everywhere, to see everything that was suitable for a little kid to see. I think that I loved Paris from that moment. It was so very different from Chestnut Hill. That's where I grew up. Just outside Boston."

"Boston? My grandmother was from there! She said once that she couldn't get away fast enough," Vennie replied. "Now, when *I* was six years old, my Dad took me out to help with rounding up cattle. I learned about all this," and she gestured at the heights of the arched roof, "from my grandmother's books. She was a Vining. They were fearfully old money, back in the day, but she came out West and married a rancher with a place in New Mexico. Until I joined the Army, I'd never been farther from home than Galveston."

"A ranch; I'm envious," Burt replied. In turn he sounded as if he was also fascinated. "In the movies, they have singing cowboys and sagebrush and all that. I don't suppose that was real; movies and storytelling for dramatic effect – but enormous fun for a kid. Where have you been since then?"

"North Africa. Italy. Now France and Albania, too, but that last was by accident," Vennie admitted, and Burt grinned again.

"Italy for myself, until we landed in France. Say, were you one of the nurses stranded there by a plane crash, and had to walk out? I read about that in the *Stars and Stripes*. Good for you, Vennie."

"We didn't have to walk all the way," Vennie chuckled, rather smugly. "They found horses for us to ride, on one leg. The expressions on the faces of our escorts when I took to the saddle and trotted the horse around the pasture and made him take a jump at a gallop; we all laughed about that for days."

"I guess they had expected you all to be city folk," Burt sounded admiring.

"We simple country girls do have unexpected talents," Vennie replied. She looked at Burt and considered him to be deliciously attractive. She liked him, more than she had ever liked any of the other men she had encountered in three years, and wanted very much to know him better, discover everything about him. He was kind, funny, toweringly intelligent and at least as much attracted to her. He had the promise of a future beyond the Army, and beyond medicine. He was, as Peg said after meeting Tommy for the first time – a potential possible.

Peg had always had a woman's intuition for that sort of thing. "Also, I can find a vein, suture up a surgical wound and start a plasma drip practically blindfolded. And," she added, "I can make a darned fine batch of peanut brittle, too."

"Peanut brittle?" Master Sergeant Vexler stood up, tucking his sketchbook under his arm. "Ma'am, I do declare that I am mightily impressed. Would you like a tour of this cathedral, from an expert? I'm not, but my friend who is meeting me is."

"I am all yours," Vennie replied, in as demure a manner as she could command.

There was a footstep in the aisle behind them; a tall elderly Frenchman wrapped in a shabby overcoat which once must have been fashionable. Now it was patched, the edges of hems practically worn threadbare, and the garment hung on his old bones like something meant for a larger man, but the elderly gentleman had a fine silk scarf wrapped around his throat and tucked into the neck of the overcoat, and he carried a handsome ebony cane with a polished silver head.

"Burton, mon cher fils!" The elderly gentleman rushed forward and embraced Burt with exuberant affection, kissing the younger man, French-fashion, on each cheek, to Vennie's vast amusement. *"Bienvenue à notre pauvre meurtri Paris!* – Welcome, welcome indeed, to our poor bruised Paris!"

"It's good to be back, Professor Leclerc," Burt replied, returning the embrace. "Couldn't have been any sooner, I'm afraid. Too many Germans in the way."

"*Sale Boche!* – the filthy Huns!" Professor Leclerc looked as if he wanted to spit on the floor, and only being within sacred precincts held him in restraint. "Our little Burton a soldier! What a war, eh?" He spoke English very well, but with a noted accent. The professor turned his regard on Vennie, who had been watching the fond reunion. "The Army must have made you forget your good manners, *cher* Burton! You have not introduced me to your martial lady-friend!"

"Lieutenant Venetia Stoneman, although I do have plans," Burt replied, and the elderly professor bowed slightly, and took the hand which Vennie proffered, and kissed it with great reverence. "This is my old friend, practically the oldest that I have, the honored and revered Professor Henri Leclerc, of the Sorbonne. We met when I was ... I dunno, about ten?"

"*Enchante!*" the professor exclaimed. Vennie was immediately charmed. No one had ever kissed her hand before, like in one of those movies set in olden times.

"Sergeant Vexler has promised that I should have a tour of the cathedral," Vennie confessed. "A tour conducted by an expert. I always wanted to see Notre Dame, and this is my first chance, ever!"

"Ah, your first visit to our poor bruised Paris!" the Professor exclaimed. "And you have an interest in history?"

"I do," Vennie replied. "All the time that I was in Tunisia and Algeria, and then in Italy, we were neck-deep in historical ruins and remains, but no one around could tell me very much about the places we were in. Since our people were being shot at and bombed ... well, interest in actual history became rather a back number."

"Never mind, my dear," the Professor took her arm, and Burt took the other. "Now, I will give you the student-tour of our marvelous and venerable cathedral. You do know, of course, that much of it was reconstructed in the mid-19th century by Eugene Violette-le-Duc. The Revolutionaries made it a temple, and later into a warehouse. But the use of rib vaults and exterior buttresses for largely glass walls was revolutionary..."

Burt looked sideways down at her and grinned again, as the Professor burbled on. "You'll be sorry you ever asked," he murmured, those pale blue eyes vastly amused, and Vennie thought that her heart was melting, like butter over a warm fire. So clever, so handsome, and quite thoroughly decent. No one since she had been fifteen and had a crush on the handsome son of a neighboring rancher back home in Deming, had made her feel so breathless and dizzy as Burt did at that moment.

Vennie replied, in the same quiet voice, "No, I won't. You promised me a tour by an expert. I have five hours, until my friends come back for me, out by the steps to the main door."

"Tight ... but I expect that Professor Leclerc can squeeze a whole semester-worth of lectures into five hours or less."

"Brevity is the soul of wit," Vennie replied. It pleased her enormously that Burt chuckled over a bit of humor which she had heard somewhere else.

It was a completely satisfactory afternoon, an afternoon where Vennie hung on to Burt's arm, drinking in all that Professor Leclerc said, of this or that venerable feature. At the end of it, Vennie thought that she knew Notre Dame de Paris as well as if she had ever known the ranch, or the simple frame Episcopal church in Deming, which had been built – according to family legend – after funds were raised in a charity poker game. All the while, she knew that Burt was looking at her with the same slightly dazed interest.

At the end of that afternoon, she stood in the shelter of the great center archway, out of the bitter wind which swept across the open stone-paved square, watching Professor Leclerc stump away, jauntily swinging his cane and regretting that the afternoon was nearly over. She could just see the jeep, turning the corner from the *Rue de la Cité* into the *Parvis Notre Dame*. At her side, Burt cleared his throat and said,

"Well then ... did you enjoy the guided tour?'

"Enormously," Vennie replied. "It was ... fantastic. Thank you so much. For everything." She hesitated, and then took a plunge. "We have two weeks leave in Paris, until the 20th ... Will I see you again? I'd like to, very much."

"I'd like that, too," Burt answered, quite simply. "I've got a briefing and a bit of work to do tomorrow, but I'm free in the evening. The Professor invited me to Sunday supper at his place – across the way from here, on the other island. *Quai de Bourbon*. I'll come and get you ... the Pension Algerie in the Rue Saint-Honoré, you said? I'm pretty certain I can find it." He hesitated a moment, while he made a note in his sketchbook and then added. "You know, there's not many public places we can go together."

"I know," Vennie agreed, not for the first time regretting the customary segregation of officer from enlisted. It made things complicated, and sometimes ridiculous. "I'll give you my unit and postal address. We can swap letters. No one can recite the Uniform Code of Military Justice at us for writing letters."

"Damn straight," Burt wrote his own address on a blank page of the notebook, tore it out and gave it to Vennie. "Here's mine. Are those your friends?" he added as the jeep rocked to a halt."

"Yes, they are," Vennie tucked the scrap into her handbag, suddenly feeling completely breathless. "I'll see you tomorrow then, shall I?"

"Depend on it."

It had the sound of a solemn promise. And it was.

Burt arrived the next afternoon, at the front door of the Pension Algerie, while another man waited at the wheel of the jeep. Ginger, Bill Allison and Major Ledet all looked him over, critically: Vennie had told them all about the tour of the cathedral, and the handsome, scholarly sergeant she had met. They kept their amusement and curiosity under tight control; Vennie thought later that she must have babbled like an absolute fool.

"Bring her back by midnight, Sergeant," Major Ledet ordered with a straight face, and Bill Allison scowled like the most imposing of protective big brothers, "Or I'll see that your jeep turns into a pumpkin.

Ginger whispered, "Oh, isn't he a dish! I can see why you got all weak-kneed and giggly when you came back from your big cathedral yesterday. Vennie, sweetie, does he have any handsome friends?"

"I'll ask," Vennie hissed over her shoulder, as Burt helped her into the passenger seat.

The jeep driver wore American uniform, with the shoulder flash of the Free French. He smiled at Vennie, and Burt performed a shouted introduction as they whirled away down the Rue Saint-Honoré, as Vennie held on to her seat with one hand and her cap with the other. "This is Professor Leclerc's nephew, Andre Mattheiu. He's with the Free French. Andy, this is my friend, Vennie Stoneman."

"Allo!" Andre grinned; a very much younger version of the Professor, but there was little time or inclination for conversation in the noisy jeep, and the ice-cold air, whipping past. It was all much more pleasant in the Professor's apartment, even after a hike up three flights of dark stairs; Burt took her hand in his to guide her.

"No elevator," he whispered. "But the view is amazing!"

So was the Professor's place; high-ceilinged and to be frank, rather cold in all rooms but the kitchen, but the tall old windows in most rooms framed a view of the marvelous rooftops of Paris and the apse end of Notre Dame, across the channel of the Seine which divided the two islands, moored like overlarge barges in the middle of the river. Professor Leclerc greeted them with the courtly fondness of an old-fashioned relative, and introduced them to his sister, Madame Mattheiu, who appeared hastily wiping her hands on her apron.

"Alas, it is too cold now and there is no coal for the central boiler for more than a few hours in a day, so we will eat in the kitchen, like peasants," the Professor announced cheerily. "A small roasted chicken, which young Andre provided, through means which I don't want to contemplate. But a glass of good cognac from a bottle that that I have been saving ... each day when I wake up, I feel like a boy on Christmas morning, when I remember that Paris is free again, those filthy Huns are gone, you have returned, and Mathilde's boy is safe with us, again."

The drawing room was, indeed, too cold to shed their overcoats, but the setting winter sun slanted golden into the west-facing window, making the room feel at least a little warmer. The Professor fussed over pouring five small glasses of cognac as golden as the sunshine, and briskly shooing a sleeping cat from one of the chairs.

"To victory," he raised his own glass, and Burt, Vennie, Andre and Madame Mattheiu echoed. "And to our valiant generals; de Gaulle, General Eisenhower, General Montgomery, and to our brave soldiers!"

Vennie blushed a little, when he added a toast to "Our brave and beautiful ally, Mademoiselle Stoneman!"

"Thank you," she stammered, "But I'm not so brave, really – I just do my job. I think that those who stayed in France and resisted the German are the brave ones."

"Ah, my dear," Professor Leclerc replied. "I also just did my job in my classroom, as best as I could. I did listen to BBC broadcasts; the extent of my resisting the Occupation! Kept my head down and endured, although at the end, in those last weeks when liberation was near, I did help at a barricade. An old French tradition, you know, manning a street barricade. As for the Resistance, I was never a part of that."

"You're the only Frenchman I've met so far who will admit it," Vennie pointed out, with dry asperity.

Professor Leclerc chuckled. "Wasn't it your English playwright, Shakespeare, who said that at heart, every man thinks meanly of himself for not having been a soldier? Well, I was a soldier once, but then I was young and without responsibility. These last years: I had my students, my sister to think of, my library, and my beloved Lady of Paris ... but do not think of me as a craven, my dear Mademoiselle. I did not collaborate with the filthy Boche; of course, they never pointed a weapon at me and demanded it, or tempted me with blandishments, but there were times... Mademoiselle, you said that you lived for all of your childhood in a small town in America?"

"Yes ... my sister and I went to school in a small town, although we lived on the ranch, in the main."

"But in small towns ... and perhaps in larger ones," Professor Leclerc set down his cognac glass and regarded her with Socratic detachment. "It is a fact unavoidable that everyone living there will know almost everything about everyone else, *n'est-ce pas* – and more importantly, will note ... oddities. Things like unaccustomed visitors. Unknown strangers being present. A change in a long-unchanged routine, an established habit. Strange and curious happenings ..."

"Yes. One would tend to notice something irregular," Vennie replied, recollecting the old family story of how a man dressed as a woman had tried to rob the station restaurant in Deming, and was foiled because Granny Sophie had noticed that the woman had a male Adam's apple and very large feet.

"Ah, you see then. It was like that for many of us over the last four years," Professor Leclerc replied. "We saw and noted things. Things like my neighbor across the stairway seemed to be buying much more in the market or in the boulangerie than what was allowed for her household. She was hiding her Jewish friend and her friend's young daughter in her apartment, as it turned out. I saw all of this and suspected something of the sort, but I ... I turned my head aside and pretended that I saw nothing. Heard nothing. Did not inform the police, although I entertained suspicions; suspicions that the filthy Huns demanded that good patriotic Frenchmen act upon, sweetening the order with many blandishments. And many did, to our shame. I do not know what happened to the woman and her daughter," Professor Leclerc added. "I believe they were gone –

perhaps into the Vichy zone, maybe somewhere else in safety. My neighbor was arrested and taken away early this year, so I did not ever have a chance to ask. Nor will I if she returns. Perhaps there was something I could have, should have done. Something simple, although to my knowledge she was a Communist – of that I cannot approve. Another incident," Professor Leclerc topped up his cognac and swirled the golden liquid in the tiny glass in his hand. "I had reason and permission to travel to Lyon. About a year ago. It seems an age, now. To settle the estate of my cousin; nothing to do with the war, my cousin hadn't been outside of his house in ten years. I had to travel by train. A miserable journey," he added. "At every stop and sometimes between, clod-hopping Hun soldiers and their secret police worked through the cars, demanding that everyone show their papers. Mine were in perfect order, of course. I had no worries, unlike some of the others in the same car."

"There was something … something odd about them?" Vennie suggested, and the Professor nodded, seeming to be pleased with the reply of a promising pupil.

"Indeed," he replied. "Two young men, tall and appearing healthy; I would say American. Canadian, maybe. There is a manner and appearance which cannot be mistaken, to those who have the wit to see. An older woman accompanied them. She was with the Red Cross, as I overheard her in conversation. There was also a boy, a French boy as escort. The two young men, they had good teeth," he added, almost irreverently.

"Strong white teeth, from good food. And French clothes and satisfactory papers, but they seemed all wrong to everyone in the railway carriage but the clod-hopping Huns. Too tall, too strong, too healthy. There is a look to free men that stands out, you see, Mademoiselle. They were Allied airmen, I believe – being smuggled to safety by the Resistance."

"What happened, then?" Vennie asked, hardly daring to breathe. She remembered vividly the adventure in Albania, of how Johnny the Englishman and her own American fellows had stood out physically, in comparison to the Albanian partisans.

"Well, the filthy Huns came into the carriage," Professor Leclerc replied, with smug satisfaction. "They came in, and the effect was electric. At once, every other passenger began ... making a fuss. Talking loudly. Reaching up into the rack for their baggage. Going out into the corridor, in the way of those clumsy, heavy-booted Huns. None of us had ever met before, none of us were Resistance. We knew nothing about the two young men, or what was going on – but we knew absolutely that they were strangers to France and the filthy Huns shouldn't look at them or take more than a cursory glance at their papers. That," Professor Leclerc announced, triumphantly, "Is how the greater part of us resisted, in our own small way, if we had not the courage or the opportunity to become full-fledged members of the Resistance. We looked away, pretending that we did not see what we suspected might be going on. We made a fuss in a railway car, and ignored strange goings-in the next apartment, the next street. We looked away, and kept our mouths shut when we could have informed for a reward, you see. That was our resistance, Mademoiselle; looking away from what we suspected was going on, and keeping our mouths firmly shut."

"Most likely appreciated," Vennie replied. "Alas, I don't believe that anyone would give you a medal for it."

"I agree on that point," Professor Leclerc replied. "It took no great courage..."

"Only human decency," Vennie assured him. "A greatly underrated quality and one that doesn't receive public rewards nearly enough."

They ate supper in the kitchen, where it was warm, and lit by old-fashioned gaslights, although there was an enormous silver candelabra in the center of the table. It reminded Vennie of meals in the old Stoneman ranch headquarters house, before electricity was run out to the place, and it had been entirely lit by kerosene lamps. The Professor's apartment, at a squint had many of the same old-fashioned features as the Stoneman main house; tall French doors in every wall, the monumental ice box, and the shelves of crockery and china on the kitchen dresser shelves. Vennie felt quite at home on that account. It had been so very many months of a life spent living in spartan military quarters, of temporary billets, tents and airplane hangars, of meals served on metal trays; those months in Albania in the house of Madame Marsala being the sole exception.

Professor Leclerc sat at the table head, while his sister bustled back and forth between table and stove. She dipped up bowls of onion soup from a tureen on the back of the stove, topped each bowl with a small slice of toasted bread and a hint of melted cheese, for the first course. The soup was magnificent and warming; Vennie had not tasted anything so good in months. When the soup was done, the Professor carved the chicken; a rather small and scrawny one, served with baked Jerusalem artichokes, but it was also absolutely delicious, and the wine which accompanied the meal tasted like sunshine. Professor Leclerc kept apologizing over and over, for the relative paucity of the meal, until Burt said,

"Madame Matthieu's cooking is as good as it ever was and a hundred times better than anything in an Army chow hall, or from a C-rat can. There won't be any complaints from us, I promise."

The conversation sparkled. Between the Professor, Burt, and Andre, how could it not? Stories, reminiscences, speculation on how much longer the war would last, what all three would do when it ended. Vennie talked about her work, about her childhood on the ranch. And when the last crumb of pear tart was done, and they had finished the last of the coffee, Burt and the professor went out on the balcony off the drawing room to smoke. Vennie meant to stay behind and help Madame Matthieu sort out the dishes, but that indomitable lady shooed her out of the kitchen.

Following the sound of voices, Vennie went to the now-dark drawing room. Pulling the blackout curtain aside, she stepped out on the balcony.

"Oh!" she exclaimed, taken aback at the night-time view all over again. A few thin clouds scudded across an ink-dark sky sprinkled thick with stars. The stars seemed larger and more luminous, since the moon was new, and Paris still mostly blacked out in wartime. Starlight silvered the steeple and stone ribs of flying buttresses on Notre Dame, rising at some little distance above the huddle of rooftops, frost-rime glittering like a hem of diamonds on trees and roof-edges, outlined the ripples in the river, flowing past a bare stone-throw from where they stood on the narrow balcony. It was a vision in black, gleaming silver and starlight, a vision from a fairy tale.

"Beautiful, isn't it?" That was Burt, a taller shape than the Professor, with his Army overcoat pulled around him.

"It is, and cold!" Vennie replied with a shiver – there was a little wandering breeze outside.

"Come here, then," Burt opened the front of his overcoat, and she stepped inside that shelter, leaning against him, resting her head against the harsh wool serge of his tunic, closing her arms around his waist, as he wrapped his own arms and the front of the overcoat around her. It was perfect. She leaned her head against his chest, feeling the regular thud of his heartbeat against her ear. Safe, warm, and together. When the Professor had finished his pipe and gone inside, Burt kissed her, and she kissed him, and it was even more perfect than before.

Chapter 16 – Wonder When My Baby's Coming Home

Letter from Vennie to Peg, Dated 20 December 1944, postmarked APO, New York. (Somewhere in France)

Dear Cuz: I had the most wonderful time in Paris, on leave there with my friends. We were supposed to celebrate Christmas there, since at the time it looked as of all were quiet at the front, but on Monday last, Major Ledet came to us and said that all leaves were cancelled and that everyone – and there were so many Americans, etc in Paris for the same purpose – had to return to their units <u>at once</u> if not sooner. It was quite a mad scramble, to get back to {location redacted by censor} on a moments' notice. Paris was like a massive anthill that had been kicked over. The Germans launched a massive, armored counter-offensive, in the middle of winter, pushing their main forces west through the Argonne Forest. No one seems to have expected this. Many units are cut off and surrounded. Alas, the war is on again, full tilt. Major Ledet says that the feeling that he gets is this will be one last hurrah by the Nazis. As soon as the weather clears, and our planes are flying regularly, it's all over but the formal surrender for them. The pilots that I know all say that they haven't seen hide nor hair of a German fighter in simply weeks.

So much for the discouraging news; now for the good. I met a wonderful guy in Paris, and we spent as much time as we could together. This wasn't much, since he is an enlisted man and had to work most days, and there was hardly any place that we could go to be together. He is terribly brainy, quite handsome, even more handsome than Tommy, I must admit to bragging, and so very intelligent! My own perfect Mr. Darcy. His name is Burton Vexler, he comes from a town near Boston, and taught art history before going into the Army. We swapped addresses almost the first day that we met. He has a kind of staff job, which he and I cannot say very much about. He is not in any danger of being sent to the front lines, even in an emergency like this, as he is almost as blind as a bat without glasses – but oh, we are serious, serious enough that he bought me a ring to prove his intentions and to cement an understanding. There is nothing like a definite date being set – we just have an understanding that we will most definitely marry at some time in the future. Don't share this with anyone, as I have not said anything in letters Home, or to any of my friends. Our secret. Did you ever think it possible that I might fall totally, hopelessly, happily in love?

Yours,

Vennie

"Mumma," confessed Tom on one afternoon in January, when Peg came to walk him home from school. "Do you think that Papa will ever come back?" A Churchie lad now, solemn in the grey school uniform blazer and shorts which he was on the verge of growing out of, yet once again. He looked up at her earnestly, from under the brim of his school hat, as he swung his satchel in one hand with the other in the grip of his little sister.

Startled out of all countenance, Peg stopped walking. The question hit as if it had been a physical blow, for all that she had been wondering it in her own mind, especially when she tossed and turned in bed in those sweaty Brisbane nights when the suffocating heat and flash-bang of a thunderstorm blowing in startled her awake and kept her from sleeping. It had been three years and a month since she had seen Tommy alive; that was more than half of Tom's young life and all of Olivia's. Little Olivia, now near to three years old, stumped along sturdily on her short little legs, one hand in each of theirs. Stubborn, Olivia only submitted to being carried in the pram when she was very, very tired. In spite of the enervating heat and humidity of a January in Brisbane, Olivia insisted on walking with her mother to meet her brother outside school, her small face pink and damp with perspiration, as the gray-clad boys of all sizes and ages scattered at the end of the school day.

"I am certain that your Papa will come back to us," Peg replied, aware that she did indeed have doubts about this. "Because he loves us. He <u>will</u> come back."

"Preston Major's papa hasn't come back," Tom, continued, in a detached and scholarly fashion which reminded Peg of her Cousin Vennie, who had the knack of cold-blooded practicality. "He loved Preston Major as much as Papa loves us. But Preston

Major's mama has applied to have him declared dead so that she can marry an American soldier."

"Eddie Prestons' papa was on the *Perth* and torpedoed in the Sunda Straits three years ago," Peg replied, "And he has never, ever been listed on any list of prisoners by the Japs or anyone else. The Navy is certain that he is missing, presumed dead. The situation with your papa is entirely different. He was alive at Longcot and on dry land when I last saw him, and he was posted on a prisoner list, six months later. We have ever so much better reason for hope than Mrs. Preston. It's not at all the same, Tom." They walked on for a little way, Olivia between them. Peg disliked the winter and early spring weather in Brisbane; gaspingly humid, hot, and altogether awful. Not even summers in the Hill Country at the Becker ranch had been quite that uncomfortable. And next month, it would be even worse. February swelter. At least that would be over with after another few weeks, but when would this war ever be? The Australians were clearing northern New Guinea of the beastly Japanese, inch by bloody inch, and the Americans had begun landing in the Philippines. The great General MacArthur was about to move on from Brisbane, or so the rumors which Stanley heard from his friends hinted.

"Mumma," Tom mused thoughtfully. He wasn't ready to let go of the subject; again, like Vennie, who worried at such matters like a small dog with a bone. "Do you think that I will even recognize Papa when he returns?"

"You can't really remember what he looks like?" Peg asked, with a touch of sorrow at heart. "You were only the age of Livvie when you saw him last, so I don't think you should worry about that. There are plenty of pictures of him in Edith's albums and there is our wedding picture."

"I can't really remember," Tom tightened the grip on his school satchel. "I honestly try, Mumma, but I can't really remember Malaya much at all. Just short little scenes like in a movie. Birds in the trees, squawking at night. Amah singing to me in Chinese. Chandeep Singh showing me his knife and saying that if I were his grandson in blood, I would be a Sikh and have one like it. You and Papa dancing to the gramophone and laughing – that was a nice one. I think that Papa held me up at a window once, to see a tiger walking along the tall hedge by the kampong. I know what Papa looked like," Tom confided. "But I can't really bring to mind <u>what</u> he was <u>like.</u> Like a real person, and not all bits and pieces of memories. And Mumma – I'm not entirely certain if what I think I remember is real, or if it is just something that I was told about so often that I believe it is a real memory."

"Oh, your memory of the tiger along the hedge is real," Peg assured her son. "You were two years old; I think. It was late at night. Your father and I had come back from the club in Ipoh, and you were fussing because the chickens that roosted in the hedge were fussy. I think the tiger had frightened them to bits. Miss Hui brought you into our bedroom so that I could nurse you and sing you to sleep again, and your father was standing at the window with the 'chik' drawn back, and he exclaimed, '*My god, Peg, it's a tiger! Look at that magnificent beast!*' I carried you over to the window, and he took you from me, and held you up at the window, and told you all about tigers. It really was magnificent; a huge, yellow and black-striped beast, with white chin-whiskers, stalking along the casuarina hedge, as if he owned the place. We watched for quite a while, and then the tiger walked away into the jungle. It was a bit before you could go to sleep, though," Peg added. "Your papa spun a lot of tales to you about how the tiger was Sher Khan, and ready to leap up through the window, thinking that you were Mowgli. Really, I could have beaten him over the head with my hairbrush. It was as if he wanted you to have nightmares from then on."

"I don't remember that bit," Tom confessed. "Honestly, Mumma, would Papa really do that?"

"He had a completely bizarre sense of humor," Peg replied, with a catch in her voice; all the things that she remembered of Tommy would only be a series of scraps, most of them at second-hand in the memory of his son. And Olivia would have no memory at all of her father.

They walked around the corner of Oaklands Parade into Heath Street, towards Edith and Stanley's sprawling bungalow and Peg begged the fates and the Almighty that Tommy <u>would</u> come back, when the war was done. For the good of her children in having a real father, and not just insubstantial memories and black and white snaps in a photo album, if anything of him at all. She waved towards the shaded veranda of the Brooke house, where Judy Brooke Pierson languished on a deck chair, heavily pregnant. It seemed that the brief honeymoon in the Grand Central after the 4th of July dance with her lieutenant had been most productive. Peg would, on the pain of death, never mention to anyone how the flighty Judy's insistence on spending the night with her husband had sent her inadvertently into Roger's arms, but her inchoate resentment of Judy was a simmering anger. Both Roger and Judy's husband had been gone from Brisbane for months. Roger had left a brief note for her at the St. George Club – *Farewell, Aurora*, he wrote. *This is my home address; my wife and I would welcome any brief communication from you when the war is over.*

Peg had torn up the note, and dropped the tiny scraps into the dunny, and resolved to follow her cousin's advice. Forget <u>that</u> night had ever happened at all. Difficult indeed, when Judy presented the proof that it had indeed happened, every day that they encountered her, or her mother, wittering about dear Judy and her American husband.

Letter from Vennie to Peg, dated 10 May 1945, postmarked APO NY (Somewhere in France)

Dear Peg:

It's over, here in the ETO. Germany has surrendered to the Allied armies, Hitler is dead, Berlin is in flames and ruined. We all listened to the radio here at {location redacted by censor} and heaved a great sigh of relief. It's over. I want to write that, again and again. It's over, over here. The immediate flood of our soldiers needing immediate care will, diminish to a trickle within weeks, although there will be many who will be in hospital for months, or years, or even for the remainder of their lives. Probably within a few months, our field hospitals here in France will only be treating men needing prophylactic treatment after having loved not wisely but too well. There were ecstatic celebrations in London, and I presume in Paris, too. We listened to the radio, to President Roosevelt's broadcast announcement, and our commanders brought out beer and champagne in the mess tent for all – for the nurses, doctors and corpsmen, and those among patients in transit who were well enough to partake as well. Today I borrowed Major Ledet's bicycle, and went for a long ride myself, out in the country a little way from where we are established, after receiving a letter from Burt.

We're in a beautiful part of rural France: there is a quaint old stone village with an ancient church, a tiny chateau of blue stone with a weathered copper roof that looks like a dollhouse or a fairy-tale castle in miniature, with an avenue planted on either side in tall, pollarded trees between the chateau and the church. Everything fresh and new and green, as if the war were just a bad dream and now it is a bright morning. In the time that we have been here, I loved to look on that view of the old church, and the road towards it, straight as an arrow, and the steeple framed perfectly between the trees. If Burt ever visits this place, I will ask him to sketch this scene for me.

I wanted to sit in a quiet place and read his letter unobserved. I am teased dreadfully by my friends. They say, with considerable mirth, that the unconquerable Fortress Vennie has fallen at last, now that I am in love with an enlisted man! He is in Germany now, with the occupying forces, searching for and documenting all kinds of treasure troves looted by the Nazis. You would have seen the newsreels about the prison camps and death factories for Jew and other enemies of the Reich, as have I. Burt says that he has seen several of these camps, and the reality of them is even viler than the newsreels and those pictures in the newspaper can convey. Bales of human hair, enormous bins of babies' and children's shoes, lampshades and book covers made from tattooed human skin, and heaps and heaps of bodies, little more than bones with a bit of skin stretched over them, so many that they had to be buried in mass graves, the surviving prisoners little more than walking skeletons – so many unimaginable horrors! The smell was the absolute worst. Even hardened combat troopers tell me that it was the worst that they had ever endured. Burt says that more than a few of his fellows were violently sick upon seeing what the SS jailors had left of their handiwork in some of the work camps. Even that our General Patton, old Blood and Guts, about vomited up his socks almost, upon having toured one of the worst camps. Imagine! The extermination camps were the worst of all. The most appalling thing is that the vilest, most sickening accusations made against the Nazis by the most dementedly imaginative Allied propagandist didn't even begin to come close to what was really being done. What a horror! And that yours and mine's ancestors came from Germany, too! What would they have thought of it all, but that they had the sense to leave, all these many years ago – so long ago that we have long thought of ourselves as nothing but %100 pure American! I'm even glad I never had to grow up speaking that beastly language. *(Although it might have come in handy, now and again.)*

This is merely a brief pause, and a rest before we turn to the remaining business, the war with Japan. Another desperate and bloody business, we expect. But for now, I'm sitting on a little marble bench in a French churchyard, with Burt's letter crinkling in my jacket pocket, and writing to you. A moment to catch my breath, enjoy the glory of the day, and not to think about the coming burden.

All my love to you and the children, and my continuing prayers for Tommy.

Vennie

In mid-summer, when the jacaranda trees began coming out in bud – with the promise of a wealth of lavender blossoms throughout most of the neighborhood – and the weather had turned pleasant once again, Peg came into the veranda for a late breakfast, after seeing Tom off to school. Now, being in the middle of his second year at Churchie, he declined to be walked there, insisting that this was for babies. Although he was not averse to meeting her at the corner of Oaklands Parade and Heath Street, for the short walk from there to home. Peg often felt that she and Tom had their nicest and best talks during that brief walk. That and the stroll down to Mowbray Park. Tom had regretfully admitted only a day or so ago that perhaps the statue of the Light Horseman in the War Memorial wasn't a statue of his Papa after all.

It's a part and parcel of growing up, my dear, Edith had consoled her, when Peg told her of this momentous revelation. *Of letting go of babyish things. When he is a man grown, don't tease him about this, in front of his own children, or his wife.*

Now Peg wondered if and when she should tell Livvie that the Light Horseman statue wasn't her Papa, after all. She settled at her place at the table, admiring yet again the aspect of Edith's garden, with the red and barred black-and-white hens scratching busily about in that quarter of it allotted to them. It was the eggs from those hens which permitted a tasty breakfast, with their eggs added to the meagre sausage mince and whole-meal toast which the ration books allotted.

"There's been the most extraordinary story in the paper," Stanley said, folding and passing the first section of it towards her. "It seems that you Americans have gone and dropped this singular bomb on a Jap city. Place is demolished."

"We've been blitzing Jap cities wholesale for months," Peg replied, helping herself to a tiny portion of butter on her dry whole-meal toast and a larger spoonful of honey – traded from a neighbor who had taken up beekeeping in exchange for eggs. "Not surprised, really, and more power to the US Air Corps!"

"Ah, but you see," Stanley folded away his reading glasses, and applied himself to sliced mango and orange, dabbled with a splash of honey. "It was a single bomb. From a single airplane and destroyed almost all of the city. An atom-splitting bomb. A huge technological development. I can't quite follow the science of it; not that far gone into the scientific aspects: Beyond my simple understanding. May as well want to teach a chimpanzee to understand French, and that's my grasp of it all. But it's ... an interesting development in the war, don't you think?"

"It is," Peg agreed, more to have Stanley pay more attention to his breakfast so that she could eat hers in peace. "Efficient of us, I must say. Would that they could do this to every single one of their wretched cities. Anything to force them into surrendering."

"They say that an invasion of the Jap mainland will be bloody," Stanley regarded his dish of fruit without any fear or favor. "But after reading so many stories in the *Courier* – I just don't think they will be brought to surrender easily."

Three days later, another one of those city-obliterating single bombs was dropped on another Japanese city.

"If the Americans keep to this schedule," Stanley observed, after perusing the newspaper stories, "And have enough of those atom-bombs, there won't be a single city in Japan left.

Which will be a pity, I think. I visited Kyoto, once in '02 or '03, I think. Beautiful place. I hate to think of it all blasted to smithereens. Daresay the Japs don't really want to see that, as well."

"They should have thought of that before starting the whole bloody war!" Edith said, with vehemence and Peg agreed.

"Our ranch manager used to tell the young hands, '*Screw around with the bull and get the horns.*' I'd say that the Japs are getting what they richly deserve. I'd rather see every one of their cities in rubble from air raids than a single one more of our own soldiers injured or dead." Peg thought of Vennie's prediction; an Allied invasion of the Japan home islands would be a desperate and bloody business. Defeating the Japanese on New Guinea, the Solomon Islands, and reclaiming the Philippines had been a long cruel slog. Peg hated to think that all that was only the prelude to invading the Japanese home islands. Rumors and tension abounded over the next week. Was another Japanese city to be obliterated, or would they accept the inevitable and put up the white flag? A trickle of stories in the *Courier-Mail*, and on the radio hinted at hope. The Japanese Emperor Hirohito had ordered his military to surrender.

"Almost too good to be true," Edith said. "I hardly dare look at the paper, lest it all turn out to have been a dream or an elaborate pretense."

"I don't think that it is," Peg replied. "Did you see the story about military nurses and officers being sent to Malaya to care for our freed POWs? Surely, they wouldn't be planning to load whole ships in Sydney harbor with relief supplies for them, if the Japs hadn't really surrendered at all!"

The tension in the Heath Street household ratcheted up to an unbelievable degree, as the last week in August crept by, without a word about Tommy. On the day that the Japanese government formally surrendered on board an American ship anchored in Tokyo Bay, another story in the *Courier-Mail* reported that the promised aid to freed POWs and internees had reached Singapore, and that those ex-captives would be returned by the speediest and most expeditious means possible.

"Air evacuation, I expect," Peg said. "That's what my cousin does. She's been a specialty nurse, overseeing medical evacuation flights for some two years now. Faster than hospital ships, I expect."

The household poured over the pages of every newspaper, even the ones from Sydney and Melbourne, which Stanley procured through a news agent. They were searching for every scrap of news, and closely examining every picture of freed Australian and British POWs in Singapore and Malaya.

On the afternoon of the seventh of September, Peg returned to the house with Livvie and Tom, the latter excited beyond all words that the war was now over and his father would be coming home.

"When, Mumma?" Tom asked, earnestly, for about the hundredth time, as they walked up the path across the lawn towards the house.

"I don't know," Peg repeated. Her patience was in shreds. All these weeks, and no word about Tommy and Reg Dawlish, about Arthur Nicholl, Miss Hui and Chandeep Singh and all the folk at Longcot. News had seeped into the newspaper pages about how brutal the occupation had been in Malaya, on Batavia and Sumatra, on New Guinea and a hundred other smaller islands. Why, there had even been reports of starving Japanese soldiers killing and cannibalizing captured Indian soldiers, which Peg would not have believed, but for the demonstrated and proven example of German brutality and the systematic extermination of Jews, Gypsies and Slavs in Occupied Europe. Nothing in his horrible and brutal war was entirely beyond belief.

Edith and Stanley were waiting on the verandah for her. Peg's heart sank as she regarded their faces.

"This came for you just now," Stanley said, and Peg looked at the little envelope that telegrams came in. It lay on the verandah table. Peg regarded it with a feeling of overpowering dread. Telegrams did not commonly bring good news, not these days. Bad news – of death, most commonly – arrived in the truncated words and mechanically printed words of a telegram.

"We didn't open it," Edith said, and her face was deathly pale. "It was addressed to you."

"Who is it from?" Peg moistened her lips, lips suddenly dry. She felt a queer kind of faint buzzing in her ears.

"I don't know," Stanley replied, his age-worn face full of honest dread and concern. Stanley had been a wonderful stepfather to Tommy, the most loving grandfather-not-of blood to Tom and Olivia. "It was addressed to you. That's why we didn't open it."

And if it was the worst news, Peg sensed; *he and Edith wanted to put off the fatal moment for a little bit longer.* What a wonderful sense of propriety was this! As long as the telegram was not read, a man still remained alive in the minds of his kinfolk.

"Tom," Peg struggled with her sense of propriety and duty. If the telegram, lying on the table like a species of poisonous snake, related bad news, she did not want to read it in front of the children. If it contained bad news, she was afraid of what she might do; break out howling in grief, and that would scar the children in the most horrific fashion. "Go take Livvie to the nursery. I'll be all right," she added as Tom took his small sister's hand. "Go ... read her a story. If it's news of your father, I'll come and tell you directly."

"Yes, Mumma," he answered. Such an obedient, good boy, Peg thought, as he and Livvie vanished into the house.

That was the moment. Peg nerved herself to pick up the telegram, and the silver letter-opener which Edith silently handed to her, both she and Stanley watching her with the utmost attention. She slit the envelope and unfolded the contents, read the few truncated words within.

ALIVE STOP. HOME SOON STOP. LOVE ALL TOMMY STOP.

Peg felt the buzzing in her ears rise to a horrific roar, blotting out all the sense of the day. The verandah whirled around several times and the floor of it finally rose up and struck her a horrific blow to her hip and shoulder.

When she came back to her proper mind, Stanley was mopping her face with an ice-cold cloth. She lay on the floor of the verandah, with Edith crouched next to her, weeping and rocking to and fro with the crumpled telegram in her hand, exclaiming,

"Alive – my dear god, alive! Our prayers are answered... my dear god, alive!"

The wave of relief which swept over Peg left her as dizzy at the faint had done, dizzy and light-headed with relief. Tommy – alive and promising to be home, soon. She presumed that meant to Brisbane.

"I'm all right, Stan," she said, and levered herself off the floor on one elbow. "I must go and tell the children."

Letter from Peg to Vennie, Dated 15 September 1945, postmarked Brisbane, Queensland.

Dear Vennie:

The telegram came last week; at first, we were afraid to open it, but it was from Tommy saying that he was alive and coming home to Brisbane soon. Just today we received a letter from him with a little more information. He was in the main camp for military POWs at Selarang Barracks, after being captured up-country with the Volunteers late in January 1942. In mid-1944 he was transferred from there to a labor camp at Blakang Mati, an island just opposite Singapore where there had been another large British Army establishment. He did not say very much in the letter, save that he had been quite sick in the last days, through malaria, dengue fever, tropical ulcers and semi-starvation. He is in hospital even now, although soon to be flown to Australia with other newly freed prisoners.

Reg Dawlish is dead. He was killed early on, in the fighting for Malaya. Tommy did not say anything more on that, so I fear that he died in quite dreadful circumstances. They were old schoolmates and terribly close friends, long before Reg married Ada or Tommy married me. We went to so many occasions at the Club in Ipoh. When I close my eyes, I can imagine him laughing with me and flirting with Ada, even though they were long married. Dear old Chandeep Singh is – or was alive when Tommy last saw him in 1941: he and the Indian or Chinese or native Malay Volunteers were told to take off their uniforms, tear up their paybooks and go home. This was the night before the others were all taken captive. I hope that he still is alive, along with all the other Volunteers from Ipoh.

Tommy heard from another freed prisoner who was interned in Shanghai that Ada Dawlish's brother Arthur died in Changi of chronic illness late in 1943. He was neither a young or well man, not fit for the rigors of escape or internment, and I think that he knew that. I will always be grateful to Arthur for insisting that Ada and I with Tommy leave Singapore when we did. Hearing what internees and POWs have had to endure, I don't think that I would have survived at all. The first time that some beastly Jap threatened Tom, I would have gone all berserker on him, and there would have been the end of me. I don't know if I should write to Ada in England just yet. She may not have been informed of Reg's death and I don't want to be the one to break it to her and her daughters.

Tommy also wrote that Miss Hui and Arthur's butler Ang regularly smuggled messages, medicine, and food to Arthur until a half a dozen ships were sabotaged and either damaged or sunk one night in Keppel Harbor. The Japs rounded up and shot many Chinese in reprisal for this. Miss Hui and Ang stopped visiting around that time; Tommy is certain that they were among those arrested and executed.

The Allies are making every possible effort to rescue and return internees and freed POWs with all speed – have you heard from your friend, Helen Drinkwater? Is she all right?

Hurrying to finish this letter. In a few days, we will go to meet Tommy at the military hospital in Greenslopes where our repatriated soldiers are being treated. I am not at all certain what we will say to him, or how this will go.

All my love from Peg

Chapter 17 – There'll Be Bluebirds

Peg looked at herself in the mirror over the dressing table, wondering apprehensively if she looked any different. Older. Apprehensive. Her face was certainly not as girlish and rounded as it had been when she and Tommy married. Grey hair – oh, certainly no, and not for decades, and would it show among her fair blonde mane anyway? On reconsideration, she decided that she had some years to go before that eventuality. She combed her hair out on her shoulders, thinking that she should try and put it up in the elaborate rolls that she wore in those early days of marriage when she dressed for a dance, or some special event, rather than scraped back into a plain every-day bun on the back of her head.

In an hour or so, she would be reunited with Tommy after four years. How much had happened to them since that hurried parting at Longcot! Would they even seem to be anything like the people they had been, before war wrenched them apart?

A light tap on the bedroom door, and Edith asked, "Dear, are you nearly ready? Stanley is bringing the car around, and the children are ready."

"In a moment," Peg replied. She powdered her face, touched her lips with the nubbin of bright red lipstick, saved for such special occasions, and took up her handbag. She made certain that she had a clean handkerchief in it and made one last survey of herself in the mirror. She wore her best outfit for this; a dark blue woolen suit cut down and remade from one of Edith's pre-war outfits. It brought out the color of her eyes. She hoped that Tommy would notice.

Edith waited for her on the verandah, with Tom and Olivia – Tommy in his school uniform, and Olivia in the Liberty print dress which she had not yet managed to outgrow. In the space of a year, Olivia had grown taller, shooting upwards like a spindly weed and shedding the baby-toddler plumpness, so the dress still managed to fit, although Edith might have to let the hem out once again. The child had also defiantly rejected brief pigtails for her hair, hacking them off with Edith's sewing scissors some months past. Now she sported a short bob, those straight fair locks looking like duckling feathers. Having sensed, in the way of small children, the apprehensive mood of those adults around her, she clutched 'Guckie' in one hand, adamantly refusing to leave it behind.

Stanley had his little Austin around in front – he beeped the horn, and Tom took Peg's hand,

"Let's go see Father," he announced, resolute and cheerful. Peg could have kissed him. He was the only one among them not apparently wracked with dread. All three of the adults had read the stories of horrible mistreatment of Australian POWs in Malaya and Borneo, stories of murderous brutality so horrible that Peg had flatly forbade that they be shared with the children, so Stanley had burned several issues of newspapers containing such before Tom could see them. Out in the street, Stanley opened the doors of the sedan for them all, dropping a husbandly kiss on Edith's cheek – courtly, old-fashioned consideration. Peg thought with grateful affection; he was a good representation of a breed of a certain old-fashioned sort of gentleman, not loud, brash, assertive. How fortunate that Tom had a grandfather like Stanley to look towards and set an example, in the absence of his father.

Stanley drove to Greenslopes in considerate silence. This was an enormous hospital complex to serve military patients, constructed just after the war began, on what had been rolling green pastureland south of Brisbane, where far-flung suburbs raveled out to open and rolling country spotted with stands of gum trees. There were no trees, or at least, no well-grown ones, on the grounds of Greenslopes. It was all too new and raw. Only the ranges of ward buildings with their long balconies open to the air and patches of lawn in between, and personnel in military and VAD uniforms going to and fro with an air of importance. They already knew what ward that Tommy was supposed to be in, among a draft of patients newly arrived from Malaya, Batavia, and Borneo, and in very bad condition, just able to endure the journey by air from Singapore.

"I'll stay here with the kiddies," Stanley said. "They won't let children into the ward. Meet you here, then; will we, love?"

It came to Peg that Stanley also had absorbed something of the nervous attitude that she and Edith had felt.

"Yes. We'll meet you if we are allowed to bring Tommy outside." Edith replied, and she and Peg walked into the ward. "Surely they will allow this, dear – as long as he is not deathly ill."

"I should imagine so," Peg replied, although she wasn't nearly as certain as she sounded. "If he is fit to see visitors..."

She and Edith lingered hesitantly at the door to the long ward to which they had been directed: a long room, painted in creamy white and pale green, scoured clean, with sunshine pouring in through tall windows all along one wall. The ward was lined on either side with tall metal beds, on which were draped white mosquito nets, now pulled back for the day. A faint odor of sickness mingled with carbolic hung in the air. Every bed that Peg could see was occupied by patients, all men, all thin to the point of near skeletal-emaciation. None that she could see looked anything like her husband, although the man in the second bed on the left turned his head on the pillow and gazed fixedly at them both, making a feeble attempt at rising from the bed.

"Ma'am, can I help you?" Peg started as a young VAD trainee spoke to her. She was still searching the faces of the patients in that ward for Tommy.

"Yes..." Edith spoke for her. "We're here for Corporal Thomas Morehouse; Malaya Volunteers, seconded to the British Army. He's been a prisoner in Singapore for the last four years. I'm his mother, and this is Mrs. Morehouse – his wife. We were told he would be here, in this ward, and that we could visit him."

"Of course," the VAD beamed all over her pleasant and rounded young face. She looked about eighteen. "Tommy! Of course, he is such a charmer, asking after his family from the minute they wheeled him in! He said that his mum lived in Brisbane and she would be around since wild horses couldn't keep her away," the girl lowered her voice. "But he really isn't strong, so try not to tire him out too much, this first day, dinky-di?"

"All right," Peg agreed, her eyes still roving over the ward. No one in it resembled Tommy in the least.

"I'll show him to you," the girl agreed. "Follow me, but if he is asleep, let him alone for a bit. They all really had a filthy time at the hands of those Japs. I expect they are the lucky ones, though. I overheard one of the doctors say that he reckons that most of those chaps have had ten or fifteen years cut off their lives, just through having been prisoners, even if they recover their health in the next few weeks ..." she walked ahead of them into the ward, and stopped at the second bed on the left, where the patient was still struggling to sit up in bed. "Hey, Tommy – it's your Mum and missus come to pay a visit... oh, let me!"

The VAD rushed to fetch a pair of pillows from a stand between the beds, and capably hoisted Tommy – for it was Tommy – to a sitting position, while stuffing the pillows behind him so that he could sit and meet their eyes.

Peg felt like bursting into tears once again ... that or fainting. Throwing up was not a tactful option. The man in the bed before her smiled crookedly at her, with Tommy's hazel eyes, and Tommy's smile, so familiar in that gaunt and unfamiliar face burned brown from the tropic sun.

"Guess I really look like perfect shite, Peggy. Been too damn long for the both of us, but I knew you in a heartbeat, if that would be any comfort."

"Oh, Tommy!" Peg leaned over the bed, her arms going around her husband and the tears came unbidden and unwelcome. But nonetheless, they came, and Tommy's arms went around her, until she sniffed and tried to stifle the tears. "My god, Tommy, I'm crying all over you. I'm so sorry... sorry for everything. I should have stayed in Singapore, I'm sorry. I could have done something!"

"Dear old thing, I won't melt," Tommy whispered into her ear. "And here wasn't a damn thing you might have done, if you had stayed with the old firm. It was the one thought that I had as a comfort, all during this hell just past; being certain that you and the kiddy-winks were safe with Mum and Stanley." He let go of her shoulders and sank back onto the pillows, still smiling. His eyes went beyond her to Edith, who was dabbing at her eyes with a handkerchief; Edith who was normally the epitome of stiff-upper-lip reserve. "H'lo Mum. I've bet Patsy here that you'd be charging into the ward immediately after breakfast. You're late and it cost me a bob!"

"Oh, you go on!" Edith sobbed and likewise embraced Tommy, while Patsy the VAD protested, in vain that she wouldn't take a penny. "We had to feed the children..."

"Little Tommy!" Tommy exclaimed. "And the baby..." he looked extremely rattled. "A girl, someone told me, but they never said..."

"I named her Olivia," Peg replied. "We brought them with us today. They're outside with Stanley, waiting to see you."

"That's settled then," Tommy threw back the light bedcovers and began swinging his feet to the floor, where a pair of hospital slippers awaited them. "I want to go to them, now this very instant. Hasn't it been long enough?"

Patsy the VAD protested, "But Matron ordered ..."

Tommy said something extremely rude about what Matron could do with herself, and Patsy yielded, rather grudgingly.

"I'll fetch a wheelchair, but if you overdo and run a temperature in consequence, and Matron and Doctor blame me ... You wouldn't want me to get into trouble, would you, Tommy?"

"I would not, Patsy-my-nightingale angel. Fetch out the bloody wheelchair, if you simply must!"

Peg thought to herself how the old Tommy charm hadn't been beaten out of him entirely. In a moment, Patsy returned, pushing a wheelchair in front of her, and trailed by what Peg and Edith assumed must be a doctor, for the man wore a white coat and had a stethoscope looped around his neck, and didn't seem to disapprove at all.

"Finest thing, fresh air," he said, after introducing himself as Doctor Reynolds. "Corporal Morehouse, mind you don't overdo it on your first day with us – half an hour, no more. The better you follow sound medical advice, the sooner you're shed of this place, understand?"

"Perfectly," Tommy submitted to having a blanket tucked over his knees, only grousing under his breath. Peg took his hand into his, though, as Patsy the VAD pushed with the energy of youth, and the doctor took Edith's arm and followed. Peg could hear Edith and Doctor Reynolds conversing in low voices. It sounded as if Edith were asking questions, and the doctor being reassuring, but all she could hear were the tone of voice, not actually what was being said in the exchange.

The hospital itself was so recently constructed that the regular spaces between the ranges of buildings had barely begun to be planted. There were few trees and none of any size at all affording relief from the bright sun overhead. Stanley had found a corner of shade in the lee of a taller building, standing soldier-straight with Olivia and Tom's hands in his. Olivia clutched Guckie to her chest, as Patsy pushed the wheelchair closer to the group, her eyes wide with uncertainty. Tom stood very straight, looking out levelly and without apprehension from under the brim of his school uniform cap. Patsy the VAD murmured, and tactfully effaced herself, showing a great deal more sensitivity than Peg would have expected from a girl barely out of school. "Half an hour, the doctor said. I'll be back then."

Peg cleared her throat. "Tom ... Livvie. This is your father."

For a long moment, Tommy and the children just looked at each other in silence.

"H'lo, young Tommy," Tommy ventured. To Peg's ear, he sounded unaccustomedly uncertain. "D'you remember me, then? I'm your father... how d'you do, this fine lovely day? Do you remember me, at all?"

"Very well, thank you, Father," Tom replied, equally formal. "I do, I think. But I prefer to be Tom. The older boys at school will laugh at me for being a baby, if they think everyone calls me Tommy."

"You have a point, young gentleman," Tommy replied, and Peg knew from the tone of his voice that he was caught halfway between laughing and perhaps weeping, unmanly. "All right, Tom it is. You look well, lad. A Churchie boy, I see. Very nice."

"I am, so," Tom returned and shook hands very formally with his father. "Second Form. You don't, Father. Look well, that is. You were beastly treated by the Japs, I expect."

"Not so bad, Tom," his father answered, and Peg knew, instinctively, that Tommy was downplaying it, for the sake of the children. "I'm still alive, you see. More than a lot of the chaps can say. And this is your sister. Hello, little Miss Olivia Morehouse. I'm your father, y'see. Although you don't know me..."

Stanley urged the shrinking Olivia forward, but she clutched Guckie desperately, and went to hide her face in Stanley's trouser leg. Stanley exchanged a sympathetic look with Peg. *Don't force it,* that look seemed to say. A sentiment with which Peg wholly agreed. This family reunion was going to be difficult, all the way around, although in the movies it would have all been ecstatic and relatively painless. But that was movies, where the heroine danced off effortlessly in the arms of her hero, and nothing bad could ever happen, whereas in hers' and Tommy's real-world life, everything bad had already happened, several times over. She had gone to bed with Roger – well, only once – while Tommy had been brutalized for nearly four years as a prisoner of war. His children barely or didn't recognize him at all, and she herself was not entirely certain of how she would handle this. It would almost like being introduced again. As if they were strangers, again in Granny Jane's sunny parlor in San Antonio. The parlor where they first had met.

Only now there was so much history between them, and four years of pain and separation. Was there a means of getting beyond all that? Peg didn't know. Oddly, she wished that Vennie might have been at her elbow to advise her, instead of the very young VAD Patsy, and the hovering Doctor Reynolds. Vennie had been dealing authoritatively with soldiers, wounded, sick, and almost-dying soldiers for years.

She would have known what to say, and how to cope with Tommy and his truckload of pain.

Letter from Peg to Vennie, Dated 20 September 1945, postmarked Brisbane, Queensland.

Dear Cuz:

Tommy has finally been released from Greenslopes and permitted to come home with us once he recovered from a round of malaria. The doctors suspected at first that he had also contracted tuberculosis in captivity, but eventually determined that he had not, thank God. He was also demobbed from Army service, but had absolutely nothing in the way of clothing, save single threadbare and much-mended uniform shirt and trousers. Very fortunately, he was supplied with a set of civilian clothing, but little else. Several days after he was released and Stanley drove him home, Edith and I went with him on the tram to McWhirter's in Fortitude Valley, for he needed so many other small things – socks, and shaving kit. Olivia came with us, too. You will be glad to hear that she has warmed to her father, after initially being quite wary of him as a stranger. He began reading to her, every evening just before bedtime, and making up adventures for her little stuffed 'Guckie'. 'Guckie' has had the most marvelous, fantastical secret identity as a spy behind enemy lines, you will be surprised to hear. She smuggled secret messages from the French Resistance to Winston Churchill, among other daring feats.

Tommy has had an easier time rebuilding fatherly relations with Tom, who at least does remember him, and they have so many interests and qualities in common. Boy-like, Tom has a great amount of respectful worship for a certain breed of adult male; gentlemen like Stanley, and certain of the younger teachers at Churchie. His amah, Miss Hui told him on the evening that we departed from Singapore that Tom was the son of a brave soldier, and that he must always behave in a way that brought honor to his family. That talk stuck with Tom. She was so sensible in relaying simple life-enabling truths to a small and frightened boy. I shouldn't be surprised that when Tom is grown to adulthood, that we shall find that Miss Hui played a large part in forming his character. Brave and stoic Miss Hui! I pray every night that she survived this ghastly war and the occupation of Singapore! I should like to hear that she has returned to Longcot...

Mavis has also returned on long leave, until she will be formally discharged from Service. The war is over, now there is no more need for so many soldiers and volunteers. I think that she is a little disappointed at having to think of something else to do with herself. She is considering taking some secretarial and bookkeeping courses which are offered to demobbed servicemen and women and looking for employment. She says most emphatically that she has no toleration for vomit and an endless series of bedpans *(so nursing is out!),* and none at all for enduring the company of numbskull children, so that eliminates teaching. I think that she is a little bit at a loss. Her friend Judy Brooke, who married an American Marine officer went off with her baby some weeks ago on a bride transport to the States. The government organized a special transport for all those women who had married Americans. There was a great hullabaloo in the newspaper about their departure. Honestly, Cuz, I sometimes think that sudden peace is just as unsettling as sudden war.

As for Tommy and I, I think that we are most of the way back into the comfortable marital habits that we had formally. We sleep together in the same bed, wherein Tommy has mildly exercised something of his old marital command, a thing which I have missed excessively since we parted, but since he has been so dreadfully ill and worn down, not to any greatly energetic extent. We kiss, and cuddle and talk a bit, in the old companionable way – and then sometimes something happens, and he seems to withdraw and turn away. *(Letter left unfinished for several days.)*

Peg woke at sunrise, wakened by the early-morning fussing of the chickens in their coop. She had fallen asleep on the daybed in the room that Edith and Stanley used as a library-cum-workroom, where Edith's sewing machine sat in one corner, together with her dressmaker's dummy. She had been too distraught, woken in the middle of the night by Tommy shouting in a jumble of Malay and Japanese, his hands wrapped around her throat.

The noise of that, her violent struggle and strangled cries had roused Mavis, Edith and Stanley – mercifully not the children. Peg was grateful for that. As soon as he was fully awake, Tommy was sobbing out broken apologies. Peg didn't know which was more horrifying; that Tommy had tried to strangle her, or that he was weeping. A man weeping was even more distressing than a woman, because she was accustomed to female tears. It was almost the expected thing – but for a man … no, quite awful, that deep, wrenching sorrow.

Stanley led him out to the verandah, and Edith took her and Mavis into the kitchen, lit one of the burners on the stove and fixed cocoa for them all. She splashed several measures of whiskey in all of their mugs and sent the yawning Mavis to carry two of them out to Stanley and Tommy. Once they were alone, Edith sipped from hers and ventured,

"Dear, do you have any notion of what brought all that on?"

"I don't know," Peg confessed. She felt her throat carefully, with the fingers of the one hand not wrapped around the comforting warmth of the cocoa mug. She was certain there would be bruises there. "He must have been having the most appalling dream. Didn't you see how he was, after we saw those people outside McWhirter's yesterday. Oriental. I suppose they could have been Japs. I think that Tommy assumed that they were. Didn't you see how Tommy was so quiet and cold after that?"

"Not really," Edith replied. "Your daughter was too busy telling me about Guckie's wartime adventures. Really, such an imagination! I've often thought that my son should have written books for children, instead of planting rubber trees."

"He was horribly shaken," Peg took an experimental sip from her cocoa. "I believe that it was something to do with his friend, Reg Dawlish. Our nearest neighbor in Ipoh, and they were in the volunteers together. But Reg was killed, I think early on, when they were first taken prisoner. Tommy shouted out Reg's name, and then '*you yellow bastards!*' That's when he put his hands on my neck and started to choke me. Edie, darling, I don't quite know what I should do, now!"

"Finish your cocoa," Edith said, bracingly. "And go for a lie-down in the office, when you are done, if you don't really want to go back to your bed. Stanley is talking to him, now. Stanley is excellent at this sort of thing. I have often thought that he is one of those who should have taken up a career, administering the talking cure. Of all of us, I think he has the best idea of what Tommy endured."

"Stanley?" Peg stared at her, round-eyed with disbelief, in the glaring light of the kitchen gas lamp. "How should he?"

That the gentle, erudite Stanley, with his workshop, his fishing rods, and his facility with doing crossword puzzles in ink – have a notion of what Tommy had lived through, for three and a half ghastly years as a prisoner of war? It boggled the mind. Edith sighed.

"I don't suppose there's any reason for you to know of that; it's something that Stanley put behind him, years ago. He hasn't talked of it in ages, to the point where it's almost an academic exercise to him. But he was a prisoner of the Turks for something like two years. He was taken at Kut in Mesopotamia, during the last war. By the time that we met ... it was something that he had moved beyond. I think that the experience was how he came to be such a father-confessor to those young men in Ipoh when we met. Didn't I say once that he should have been a sort of Mr. Chips? Leave it to Stanley, dear. He is the very best person there is for my son to talk to. Talk to me for a while if you should like. I think I will have the worst time, getting to sleep again, after all this excitement. But I did put a healthy dollop of whiskey in the cocoa. I wonder if I should talk to Mrs. Burton about herbal teas? Lavender and chamomile are said to be sovereign remedies for nightmares. Not valerian, though – she says that tends to make them rather worse..."

Peg listened to Edith talk, wondering if Edith wasn't rendering her own variety of talking cure. Now she felt sleepy herself ... and wondered exactly how big was that dollop of whiskey with which Edith had amended her own cocoa? Eventually, she went to the study and lay down on the daybed. When the chickens woke her at dawn, she discovered that someone had covered her with a light blanket and tucked a small pillow under her head.

She set it aside, in the early dawn grey, and wandered in her bare feet out to the verandah. Her husband sat there on the first stair down to the garden, smoking a cigarette, barefoot and in the pajama shorts in which he had gone to restless sleep the night before. She regarded the white scars on his wrists and legs, the ones on his back; the white scars which had mostly healed, the livid red and pinkish of newer injuries. Beyond Edith's garden, a faint mist rose from Norman Creek, twining around the trees like the wisps of drifting bridal veil. The chickens cheeped querulously in their pen. It was barely light.

She sat down on the step next to Tommy, and he silently passed the cigarette to her. She nodded a grateful thanks and passed it back.

"I gave it up, thanks."

"You OK?" he dragged deeply on the cigarette and looked out at the garden. "I'm so sorry, Peg. So sorry. It was ..."

"Something that you couldn't help," Peg replied. They looked together for a long moment at the garden, at the sleepy chickens beginning to root for insects among the sparse grass in their pen. "Right, then. This is about Reg, isn't it? What really happened to him? I expect that you told Stanley all about it, now tell me. You owe me, Tommy. Reg and Ada were my friends, too. He's dead, and you were there. What happened?"

"It was my fault." Tommy dragged deeply on the cigarette. It burned down to the last nub, and he dropped it on the step below and crushed it with his bare foot, a foot so deeply callused that he could do that without feeling any discomfort at all. "You remember how Reg and I were always making foolish jokes with each other, making each other laugh?"

"I do," Peg confessed, thinking back on all the times that Reg and Tommy batted witticisms back and forth, like adept tennis players for the amusement of each other and those listening. Sometimes she had thought it even better than watching a movie or a play. Even better, for it was not a script, but genuine and spontaneous wit. She took up Tommy's hand in hers. "You should tell me, I'm your wife. You told all to Stanley; I assume. You should have the guts to tell me. Reg was my friend as well, as was Ada."

"Right, then," Tommy sighed, and kissed the back of her hand, still enclosed in his. "But never tell Ada – the whole thing was ugly, and I ... I just don't ever want her to think of how it ended that way. It was early in January; I think a month after you and Ada left for Singapore. Aftermath of the fight for Trolak at the Slim River. Luckily, we had warning of what was to come, the day before. The commander of the unit we were attached to … he slipped us the word, told us to scatter, every man for himself. We told all the native Volunteers to take off their uniforms, burn their paybooks, go home and forget they ever had anything to do with us. Good chaps; most of them did. Even dear old Chandip Singh, although he took a hell of a lot of persuading. Good thing that we did. We heard afterwards that the Japs slaughtered the native Malay and Chinese volunteers in job lots in Singapore after the surrender. The Indian chaps, too. God damn those bloody Japs to hell everlasting, Peg. Those poor chaps trusted us, and we ran away or surrendered and let them be executed in scores." Tommy looked as if he wanted another cigarette. He fished one out from his pajama pocket, put it in his mouth and clicked the lighter, fruitlessly. His hand was shaking too badly to light it properly.

"Let me," Peg took it from him and touched the flame to the end of the fresh cigarette. They sat, while the sky lightened, pearl and touched with peach towards the east. Tommy smoked as though it were the last cigarette on earth, looking out into the mist-shrouded trees around Norman Creek. "What happened then, Tommy?"

"They caught up to us in the end – we were trapped, no way out, either way we could run, there were Japs in the way. They came to take us all prisoner, then." Tommy laughed, mirthlessly. "Reg and I, a couple of other Volunteers and half a company of Argyll and Sutherland Highlanders and their junior officers. All that was left, as the senior officers had already surrendered or buggered off in another direction. Can't blame them, really. Anyway," he took a deep drag from his cigarette and let the smoke trickle out from his nostrils. "We were lined up, a bunch of shouting Japs with their bayonets, and some other Japs with a movie camera on a stand. Newsreel chaps, by the look of them. Oh, they were going to make raree-show of it all. God, I hate them so, Peg. I suppose I'll be forgiven for that, eventually. The Jap guards bludgeoned us all into a line at bayonet point, and then … this officer of theirs emerged from a staff car…" Tommy chuckled mirthlessly again. "Roly-poly fat little bugger all dressed up like a panto version of Tojo, glasses, buck-teeth and all, with a dress sword that he looked about to trip over every time he moved. This fat little bugger steps down from the running board, damn-near trips over his own sword, and steps with a splash into a mud-puddle, right up to his ankles. Did a nice job, that mud spoiling the polish on those boots … and he was furious! It's a matter of losing face for those bastards, y'see. He was about to look like a fool in front of us, and his own troops and those newsreel wallahs. And I… I was standing next to Reg in the line, and I nudged him with my elbow and said, *'Look there, it's the Oriental Tweedle-Dee himself! D'you suppose that Tweedle-Dum will be along any minute?'* And Reg laughed – couldn't help it. He laughed out loud and everyone heard him. The fat Jap officer <u>was</u> the very image of Tweedle-Dee. And then…"

Tommy dragged deeply on the cigarette for a long moment, so long that finally Peg hinted gently, "Then what happened, Tommy. If you told Stanley about all this, then you can tell me. I've a right to know."

Tommy had already smoked that cigarette down to another nub. He lit another, this time his hand wasn't shaking. Peg thought that might be a good indication.

"He looked as if he was going to burst, his fat face swelling up rounder and rounder; redder and redder, just like a bullfrog about to burst. He screamed out something in that filthy language, pointing at Reg and three of their soldiers ..." Tommy's hand with the cigarette began to shake again, and Peg's heart sank. Tommy took a long draw from it and confessed in a rush. "They sank their bayonets into Reg, like he was a training dummy. One-two-three, just like that. And again, scientifically, as if it were an exercise. I don't think Reg made a sound. And I was standing next to him. His blood splashed on me, and on the Sutherland Highlander standing on the other side. We were just standing there, shocked with the suddenness of it all. And then – that fat-faced officer..." Tommy drew again on the cigarette, which now was almost to another nub again. "He took out that sword ... my god, the yellow bastard could barely handle it without sticking it into something unintended – and he posed with it over his head and took a long downward swipe – and took off Reg's head. I'm certain that the Jap newsreel chappies got every moment. One swoop. I'm sure that a Tower headsman would have been proud."

"I see," Peg replied, deeply shaken. She knew that Reg was dead – Ada had been certain about this upon leaving Singapore on the Eastern Star. But in such a ghastly manner ... no, that was a detail that Ada and her daughters must never know of. At least, not now, when the war still so new and raw in memory. Perhaps later, when fury had cooled to a degree where it could be handled with bare unshielded hands. Perhaps then, Ada could be told the details. But not now. She took Tommy's hands in her own.

"It was not your fault," she assured him, pouring all sincerity and assurance into her voice. "It certainly was not your fault, not entirely. Reg laughed and that was on him, for between the two of you, you should have known already what they were like. It was brave of you to crack wise in their very face ... but silly of Reg to laugh out loud. Didn't we already know that those treacherous bastards were like, then? No sense of humor at all."

"No, not a scrap of it," It seemed to Peg that Tommy seemed a little lightened in mood. He crushed the second cigarette butt under his foot. "So, where are we going now, sweet Peg of my heart?"

"We should go home to Longcot," Peg replied, without any further thought. "It's our home, and your business."

"Indeed," and Tommy smiled at her – the sweet and uncomplicated smile that had first won her heart in Granny Jane's parlor. "We should, that. And I'll be damned if anyone should chase me out of it, again. Ever."

(continuing letter of November 20th) My husband is plagued by the most awful nightmares. This worries both Edith and I: sleep which ravels up the knitted sleeve of care and sleep that should be restful, and restore his health, and yet he sometimes thrashes violently in the bed, and talks in his sleep – evidently relieving quite brutal events. I woke up yesterday in the early morning, his hands squeezing my neck, and shouting at someone in Malay. It was fortunate that he was still very worn down by illness and I am quite fit and strong from working in the garden and riding a bicycle simply everywhere ... but still. I was terribly frightened, and so was he. He has since slept in an armchair beside the bed on those nights when he is most troubled.

Stanley says only that we should expect this kind of thing. It appears that he was a prisoner of the Turks when he was out in Mesopotamia as a soldier in the last war. Tommy and Stanley sat out on the verandah, talking together for many hours, until the sun was well up. We had a long talk ourselves, afterwards over what is the cause of those nightmares. It seems that our friend, Reg Dawlish, was bayonetted and beheaded by Jap soldiers almost the minute that Tommy's group surrendered to them in Malaya, in January 1942. It was quite sudden, and out of the blue, almost. Tommy is still quite awfully shaken by this horrid event.

We must return to Longcot. We have agreed upon that, since it is the only means that Tommy has of earning a living, and it is his family property. We shall remain with Edith and

Stanley through Christmas and look for an inexpensive passage for the two of us and Olivia on any cargo or passenger ship return to Singapore from Brisbane. We agreed let Tom remain and continue school with them. I don't much care for the separation from my boy, but it seems to be the customary thing. We simply must reclaim Longcot; it is ours and Tommy is adamantly resolved on this. We were chased away once, and this will not happen a second time. Tom is happy at Churchie and extremely fond of his grandparents, and I absolutely couldn't bear to send him all the way to England for schooling there! At least in Brisbane he is only a short week or so away from us, instead of all the way in England.

Enough of my woes; I was so glad to hear that you and your handsome and erudite soldier will soon be married! I am most desolated that I cannot return to the States to be your bridesmaid, as we promised so long ago. We simply cannot afford it, as we will have to get loans for our return and to cover those costs in starting up the rubber-harvesting enterprise again. We are certain that the war and occupation have left Longcot in ruins.

I suppose that you will do the deed in the old church in Deming – send me pictures, please!

Your dear Cuz Peg

PS – we have received a letter from Chandeep Singh! Most of our folk at Longcot are well, although with fortunes much battered and diminished by the Jap occupation. The house still stands, although somewhat derelict, and our people there are well, and ready to resume limited operations as regards harvesting rubber. Mr. Song the cook, and our amah Miss Hui both survived! She has returned to Longcot, after many narrow escapes and much tribulation! I can hardly wait to show her snaps of Tom, in his school uniform, and tell her of how brave he was in those weeks and months after leaving Singapore. And introduce her to little Olivia, and her brave Guckie! *(Although I don't think that Guckie could have been any more courageous or wilier than our dear Miss Hui.)*

Wedding Announcement – January 1946

Mr. Charles and Mrs. Cornelia Stoneman, of the Stoneman Ranch and St. Luke's Episcopal Church, of Deming, announce the recent marriage of their daughter, Miss Venetia Irene Stoneman to Mr. Burton Vexler. Miss Stoneman is a 1939 graduate of the Sealy School of Nursing, in Galveston, Texas, and has lately served as a nurse in the US Army Nurse Corps, throughout the late conflict in North Africa and in the European Theater. Mr. Vexler is the son of Lillie May Bronstein Vexler Pearlman Martin and Albert H. Vexler, of Cambridge, Massachusetts. He was educated privately, and graduated with high honors from Princeton, class of 1935. He has recently been returned to the States after honorable service in the US Army in France and the Occupied Zone of Germany. Miss (1st Lieutenant) Stoneman and Mr. (MSgt) Vexler were married in Paris in December, before a company of friends. As both bride and groom have been discharged from military service, they plan to stop in Deming for a short visit later this month, on their way to California, where Mr. Vexler will take up a teaching position on staff at Occidental College in Los Angeles. Mr. and Mrs. Stoneman are planning a reception at St. Luke's parish hall for family, friends and well-wishers. Invitations to all are forthcoming.

Becker – Stoneman Family Tree

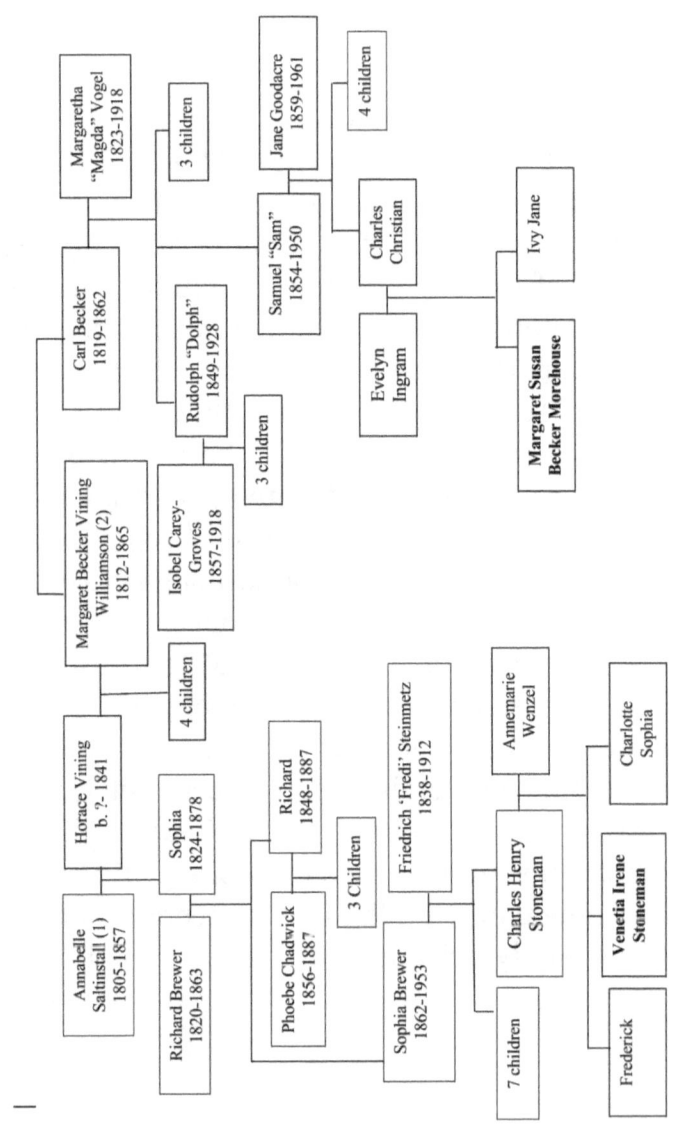

Celia Hayes

Historical Notes

It was a bit of a leap for me to go forward, from the 19th century setting of my previous historical novels, although I grew up more or less marinated in WWII history. I was born a bare nine years after it was all over, to parents who had been teenagers during it, grandparents who remembered the home front vividly, a great-aunt who had been one of the first-recruited WAACs, and neighbors, friends and teachers who were veterans of the war in various theaters and services. It was an easy leap into a world and a mind-set with which I was already quite familiar, and many of the books which I depended on for specific incidents were already on my bookshelves.

For much of Vennie Stoneman's wartime experiences, I drew on a history of Army nursing in that war by Evelyn M. Monahan and Rosemary Neidel-Greenlee: *And If I Perish*. Vennie's experiences in the Torch landings, at the Arzew hospital *(including the Christmas celebrations there in 1942)* are taken from that volume, blow-by-blow including some conversations which are practically verbatim.

The forced landing of a C-54 in Albania, which necessitated the escape and extraction of crew and those military medical personnel who were passengers, including seven nurses, from nominally-occupied territory – actually happened, and was facilitated by Albanian resistance organizations, assisted by the British OSS agents in country. Although the actor Sir Anthony Quayle was in Albania during that period as an OSS agent, I can't find that he had anything to do with facilitating the escape and extraction of the American medical party and the aircrew. I have always been amused and impressed by the fact that an actor who played the part of an agent in occupied territory bent on sabotage, subversion and misdirection in the movies had actually done that life-threatening tour of duty. I can only think that it must have been a completely schizoid experience for him to play a part before the camera which he had previously done in real life and in life-and-death earnest. This brief turn on the fictional stage is my compliment to him – and to those other actors who have also moved from real life to a part played before the cameras. I extend my heartfelt respect to such. There are a few. Not quite as many as there were, post WWII – but a few.

The reports that I can locate do not pinpoint exactly where in Albania that C-54 went down, or in what town the aircrew and medical personnel were sheltered, or from where they were evacuated along the coast: I extrapolated from the few details given and selected a possible site from maps, and Sheper because it looked like a small, scenic, and out of the way little town.

Peg Morehouse's life in Malaya and her escape with Little Tommy and the unborn baby Olivia are also drawn from life. The memoir *Journey by Candlelight* by Anne Kennaway was especially rich in detail about life in the Malay States on a prosperous rubber-growing plantation in the late 1930s. This author also touched on the general ambiance in Singapore during the lightening-fast Japanese advance through the Malay States, and the Dutch holdings in present-day Indonesia. I have drawn on that historical record for details in this novel.

Charles Allen's collection of interviews of old Malaya hands *Tales From the South China Seas* was also a rich source of personalities, experiences and small details. Both these books were recommended by members of the Malayan Volunteers Group on Facebook. A deep dive through their various posts, links and archives turned up all kinds of fascinating materiel, including details on various evacuation ships before Singapore surrendered, and escape in various small boats afterwards, and scans of the handwritten pages of the diary of Shirley Joice. Shirley Joice's diary provided those details of Peg and Ada's abrupt journey from Ipoh to Kuala Lumpur.

The escape from Singapore harbor of the *Empire Star* is drawn from accounts by those who escaped at the last moment of that fortunate ship, a ship later sunk through enemy action in the Atlantic in October 1942. It is true that the Australian nurses – who otherwise had no place to travel on that grossly overcrowded cargo vessel – were down in the holds usually used to ship chilled beef, and singing pop songs, and *Waltzing Matilda*, during the long ordeal by fire on that first day. Speaking of pop songs; all the chapter headings are the titles of contemporary pop songs.

It was rumored at the time that some of the Australian troops on the *Empire Star* had deserted their posts and forced their way aboard. I can find no evidence in records available to me one way or the other, at this late date. Considering the brutal conditions in which Australian POWs were held in the hands of the Japanese after their conquest of Malaya – conditions every bit as brutal and life-limiting as those experienced by Americans held captive in the Philippines – one can only conclude that those Australians who chose to act proactively and in defiance of orders from above spared themselves a great deal of grief by extracting themselves from the ultimately no-win situation in which their superior command had placed them. The Bataan Death March was not a one-off atrocity when it came to Allied prisoners of Japan.

The Colonel G. mentioned in Peg's letters was the semi-legendary Colonel Paul Irwin "Pappy" Gunn, formerly a naval aviator, pioneer in commercial aviation in the Philippines and a wartime innovator of no mean engineering skills. The artistic and venturesome anti-Nazi Austrian mentioned in one of Vennie's letters from North Africa was Rudolph Von Ripper – painter, adventurer and OSS intelligence officer – about whom a whole 'nother book could have been written.

The 'Battle of Brisbane' mentioned in Peg's letters also happened, for pretty much the reasons given in her letter. American enlisted soldiers were relatively well-paid, well-supplied, and sharply uniformed, in comparison with their fellows in the British and Australian forces. *"Overpaid, over-sexed, and over here!"* was a common wartime lament – to which the common American riposte was, *"Aww, you're just sore because you're underpaid, undersexed and under Eisenhower!*" (or MacArthur, depending on the theater.)

The incident in the French train related by Professor Leclerc in Chapter 15 is based on a real incident but experienced by one of the surviving crewmen of a B-17 shot down over France after the 'Black Thursday' raid of October 1943. My mother's older brother, Sgt. James Menaul was killed on that day, but six others of that crew of ten survived. In the early 1990s, I traced down and interviewed one of them, James Festa, of New York, who was picked up and smuggled out of Occupied France by a Resistance escape line. He was one of two evaders, traveling by train with a pair of Resistance operators – an older woman with Red Cross papers and a teenaged boy. When the German authorities came through the coach, inspecting papers, every other passenger in that coach spontaneously began distracting them – although only the two Resistance escorts knew for certain of their true status as escaping Allied airmen.

In the interests of fidelity to history and racial attitudes of the 1940s with regard to the Japanese and to a lesser extent, the Germans, the current social climate requires me to add the following caveat; yes, the general attitudes of American and Australians towards the Japanese were by current standards, viciously and unrepentantly racist. However, this book is, as nearly as I can make it, written with an eye to fidelity to the historical record. I will not cut and tailor my fictional cloth in accordance with current fashion. 'Presentism', wherein the accepted fashionable attitudes and conventional opinions of the current day are retrofitted, however unsuited and historically unlikely, onto those characters living in past decades and centuries, is a grim transgression against the art of bringing a past era into life, warts and all. Writing a so-called historical novel merely by placing 21st century characters in different costumes and strange technological shortcomings is a disservice to the past, and a hampering to complete understanding. It's the past – they did things differently, back then.

As for wartime feelings, Americans, Britons, Australians, Chinese and other participants, even the 'inadvertent by reason of geography' had no reason to think well of the Japanese who made bloody, brutal, and imperial war upon them and plenty of excellent reasons to think ill. A brief list of those reasons begins with the war in China, including the 'rape of Nanking' and similar atrocities, the attack on Pearl Harbor while diplomatic negotiations were underway, the opening of aggressive hostilities throughout the Pacific theater of operations, extreme brutalities inflicted on those with the misfortune of living in Japanese occupied countries, and the horrific treatment of interned civilians and captured military by the Japanese. The most charitable comment which one can make on this all is that at least they were ecumenical in administering barbaric treatment to all those unlucky to experience the Greater East Asia Co-Prosperity Sphere at first hand. Americans are, or at least used to be, conversant with the Bataan Death march, but that was just one of the gruesome atrocities against Allied POWs during the war front in the Pacific. Even ghastlier than the Bataan forced march of POWs was the Sandakan Death March, a series of forced marches which took place towards the end of the war on Borneo. Internees and POWs were forced by the retreating Japanese Army to abandon a massive camp at Sandakan airfield and retreat 160 miles through the jungle with them. Of 2,500 British and Australian POWs at the start of those marches, only six men survived by escaping during the confusion. Ritual cannibalism, medical experimentation on living prisoners, mass forced prostitution of women, the deliberate sinking of the *AHS Centaur* by a Japanese submarine off the coast of Brisbane, massacres of medical personnel and patients at the Queen Alexandra Hospital in Singapore, mass executions of native military there and in Hong Kong, the execution of civilian and military personnel on Bangka Island, the executions of American POWs at Palawan towards the end of the war when all seemed to be lost for the Japanese, the horrific treatment and the death rates of impressed civilian laborers and POWs on the Burma-Siam railway, the wanton destruction of Manila... All of these and even uglier accounts of Japanese brutality were publicized in the last months and weeks of the war, just as the reality of German concentration and extermination camps emerged earlier in 1945. Knowledge of these horrors was why contemporary opinion approved with mild reservations the atomic bombing of Hiroshima and Nagasaki, even if many were startled by the suddenness of the events, baffled by the science, and apprehensive regarding the implications of atomic weapons.

A further element had to do with knowing how fanatical Japanese resistance had been in New Guinea, on Guadalcanal, on Tarawa, Iwo Jima, and Okinawa. An invasion of the Japanese home islands could only be much, much worse. And yet, planning for such an invasion went forward. Part of that planning involved a massive order of 1.5 million Purple Heart medals, in expectation of a huge number of American casualties. That backlog of medals was not drawn down sufficiently for another order until 2008; this after the end of WWII, Korea, Vietnam, Grenada and two wars in Gulf and the many pinprick casualties from random terrorism over the following seven decades. Knowing that the cost in blood and human lives would be almost unbearably high for a ground invasion of Japan, among the invading troops, the defending Japanese and the hapless Japanese civilians, the choice for atomic bombing was a necessary albeit cruel calculation. Japanese cities were being pounded unmercifully by American bombing, with destruction and death by many conventional bombs equal to a single atomic bomb ... I'm on the side of those historians who believe that turning segments of Nagasaki and Hiroshima into radioactive glass saved lives. A cruel calculation, but one which saved the lives of Allied soldiers who would otherwise have died in an invasion, the lives of Japanese civilians who would have been thrown into the maelstrom and saved the lives of prisoners and internees all across the Japan-occupied territories who were about two weeks from being killed by starvation or hours and minutes of being murdered outright.

Imagine, if you will; how it would have gone if President Truman had let the invasion of Japan go ahead – with all the casualties; the massive deaths of soldiers, civilians, prisoners, and internees ... and then finding out that all that torment could have been avoided by dropping two bombs on Japanese cities *(cities already being systematically destroyed by conventional bombing)*. No, the use of the atomic bombs on Hiroshima and Nagasaki was, as many of these historical choices come down to – the least worst choice of the lot. This is why practically everyone who would have had a real stake in this choice – their lives, the lives of those whom they loved and who would now survive because of it – heaved a sigh of relief at the outcome of a mushroom-shaped cloud over Hiroshima and Nagasaki. A perilous choice and one with regrets attached. Because of that decision, they and the ones whom they loved – would live.

The most amazing thing about writing historical fiction – is that most times, what really happened – is even more incredible and dramatic than anything which I could possibly create out of thin air.

Celia Hayes
San Antonio, 2021